Crises on The Cumbraes

The Unlikely Adventures
Of a
Retired Accountant

Edwin Deas

Crises on The Cumbraes: The Unlikely Adventures of a Retired Accountant

Edwin Deas

Cover design by James Christ & Ross Holtz

Editing by Bronwyn Jenkins-Deas & Dr Helen Ralston French

First printing in 2015

Published with CreateSpace Independent Publishing Platform (2015); Update 1

ISBN-10: 1511926821

ISBN-13: 978-1511926829

This book is dedicated to

Bronwyn Jenkins-Deas

for believing.

Chapter 1

Doctors Calum Davies and Nerys Jones-Davies were seated on the patio of their Irvine, California home. The early December evening was warm and pleasant, nothing strange there. Their idyllic peace had, however, gradually evaporated as their discussion became heated. Alas, nothing strange there either.

'Ca.......lum, you are driving me nuts. Why did you ever choose to retire when you had no plans for what to do afterwards?'

'You know I was never much of a planner,' was the unhelpful response.

'Well, perhaps it is now the time to start. You cannot sit about the house doing nothing. What do your accountant friends do in retirement?'

'They tend not to retire because they don't know what to do in retirement. After an exciting career among the debits and credits, it is difficult to find something else as stimulating.'

Nerys rolled her eyes. She was never quite sure, even after ten years of marriage, when Calum was being serious and when he was seriously just trying to be funny. She knew that his careers in the professional accountancy office and in the university in Scotland, then Canada, and now in California had been richly rewarding. He had earned his retirement but he had not planned for it.

A palace revolt at the California University, Temecula Campus had brought the retirement on. Calum had always loyally supported the long standing president through thick and thin. When he was finally ousted by a rabid pack of disquieted faculty, his replacement naturally wanted to clean house and that meant retirement for the old president's loyal supporters. Calum at first was angry with the feeling of being rejected simply because he had shown loyalty. His teaching reputation was first class and the limited amount of research he did was quite well respected but that mattered for nought. Loyalty to the right person who became the wrong person had done him in.

However, once he got over the hurt he had become quite excited by the prospect of leaving the university grind and back-stabbing and moving to a new phase of his life. In fact, he almost immediately decided that finding another academic position was not a priority.

If not working, what was the rest of his life going to look like? After all, he was just over sixty years of age and in good health despite his mildly hedonistic life-style. And, that was the problem. Initially, the euphoria of simply not having to manfully try to instill the vagaries of Accounting 101 into the reluctant minds of student freshmen more inclined toward sport, drinking, and the opposite sex had been enough. It was fine to spend mornings reading online financial papers from around the world and afternoons sipping chilled white wine on the patio. But that had worn off and a creeping boredom had set in; and with it a faster creeping tetchiness which was starting to put a strain on the Davies marriage.

That did not sit well with Nerys. She was a busy lecturer and, on top, an active researcher in international politics. Approaching fifty years of age, she did not yet have tenure and so was on the research and publish treadmill. Calum had never bothered with tenure. In his field, where the typical accountant had one foot on campus and the other off campus potentially in the professional accounting office, job security that really was what tenure was all about was unimportant. For Nerys, however, pursuit of tenure meant long hours on campus and more work at home. She needed a supportive husband, even if he did not prepare the evening meal, to give her the space to do her thing. She did not need a high-maintenance wreck who was desperate to go out and do something with her the minute she appeared because he had not done anything all day.

'Why don't you take on some part-time accounting work?'

'I wouldn't want the hassle of starting up a company again. I did that a hundred years ago. It was easier then. Government seemed to know its place then. Now it pokes its nose into everything accountants do. That is why I snuck into higher education in the first place. Government does not have any say there. Just the commie faculty and they are not quite as bad as government.'

'No. I meant volunteer your accounting services to a worthwhile organization. Give something back as they say.'

'That might be possible if it weren't for the other volunteers. You know I can't stand volunteers. All self-righteous and jolly hockey sticks.'

'I have no idea what jolly hockey sticks means. Is that something you picked up in Canada?'

'Good Lord no! The way they play hockey there, there is nothing jolly about it. More like a legalized form of committing grievous bodily harm while skating around brandishing cudgels. Nothing jolly in that! I think the term comes from the Old Country and means excessive enthusiasm for something that ought not to elicit enthusiasm in the first place. You know I am very suspicious about enthusiasm. Accountants are trained to be sceptics who reluctantly accept the inevitable, but don't get enthusiastic about it.'

Sensing the time for a change in subject and knowing that preparation of dinner was no closer to being commenced, Nerys got up and suggested the ultimate compromise—a drink. That was often the compromise that caused peace to break out in the Davies household.

'Good idea,' said Calum. 'But, it will have to be red. I drank all the white this afternoon.'

'You know I prefer white. Why did you drink it all when you can, and frequently do, drink anything in the cabinet?'

'Well, the fridge is closer to the patio than the cabinet and the white was in the fridge. Why don't we go out and you can have a nice bottle of white all to yourself?'

If Nerys Jones-Davies PhD had been the kind who stamps her foot to make an important point or to signal the onslaught of spousal battery, she would have stamped her foot at this point. Instead, she calmly yet firmly stated, 'No. I cannot spare the time to go out. I have to read a journal and start to write an article immediately after I prepare dinner. But before I do that we are going to conclude this discussion of your hopelessness.'

'I am not hopeless. In fact, I am full of hope. It is just the purpose that is unclear at this point in time.'

'Look, if you won't volunteer for something, get a hobby. Take up golf. Accountants should be pretty good at keeping score.'

'I have always viewed golf as a huge waste of one's time. I have always been too busy to spend hours chasing a little white ball in the undergrowth.'

'You have plenty of time on your hands now.'

'I may not be doing anything but my time is still precious.'

'Aagh. Pour me a glass of red. Or a scotch. Or a glass of red and a scotch.'

And so, that was how the good doctors settled down to an evening of substantial imbibing. No dinner was ever prepared. No journal was ever read far less an article written. But, in the end a far-reaching suggestion was made and a story was begun.

As the evening wore on, Calum slumped lower and lower in his chair and started to reminisce about Millport. He had a habit of doing that. Millport was on the island of Great Cumbrae in the Firth of Clyde, Scotland. Millport was his spiritual home. As a child brought up in Edinburgh, his family had vacationed in Millport for most of his early years. And, after that he had been hooked. He kept returning even though the journeys got longer than from Edinburgh, first from the west coast of Canada, and then from California. Every year or two was the routine. That made for at least fifty visits and he had never tired of it. Upon his divorce in Canada and his move to California, Nerys had been found, courted, introduced to Millport, then married—in that very deliberate order. Had she not fallen in love with the little town on the ten miles around island, there probably would have been no marriage. But fall in love she did. Their visits were often short in duration, one had been just for a weekend when more time was spent in the air than on the island; but just enough time to get a spiritual fix Calum had insisted. And, Nerys had inclined to agree.

'You know Cal; it might be a good idea for you to take off to Millport for a while. Just chill out. I will join you later in the year once classes are finished.'

'Mmm. Might be OK. But I only like going there with you. What would I do on my own? It would end up just being like here.'

'No. It is your spiritual home and where you are most likely to have an adventure that will change your life and set you up for a productive retirement.'

'Mmm.'

'Ah but wait a minute. You are an accountant aren't you? Accountants don't have adventures. We need to rethink this.'

Calum leapt out of his chair, defying an aging body and a considerable volume of drinks consumed. Standing up to his full six feet height, he waved a hand in the air in objection much like an impassioned advocate in the High Court.

'Just you wait a minute. I resent that. There is no reason why an accountant can't have an adventure. And, Millport is just the place for one. I am going to go there just as soon as I can make the arrangements.'

Nerys smiled and said, 'There you are now. I knew you could come up with an idea for retirement if you tried hard enough. I will come over in the summer when there is an outside chance of a little sunshine and hear all about your adventure.'

Chapter 2

Calum Davies was feeling good. He had spent just over a week making arrangements for his removal to Millport and now they were complete. He now thought about those arrangements that were about to unfold.

A place to stay had been solved with something of a brainwave. Over the years he had stayed in most of the hotels, bed and breakfasts, and self-catering establishments on the island. However, this most important visit of all warranted a very special place to stay. The town of Millport consisted largely of two-storey buildings containing very small apartments and large stand-alone stone houses built by the tobacco and sugar barons of Glasgow in the nineteenth century as their summer get-aways. The latter had each been mostly split into four units over the years but a unit generally consisted of two or three bedrooms and offered much more space than the typical single bedroom apartment.

One such sub-divided house in the West Bay, called Barclay House, included the very unit where the Davies family had vacationed each year in Calum's childhood. While he had not stayed there since, he had lately got to know the current owner. An IT baron from Glasgow (a much more rewarding arm of baronage today than tobacco or sugar) now had a get-away in Millport to go with his real summer home in the Algarve. It had taken a fair bit of persuasion on Calum's part for the owner to lease out his lower left share of Barclay House and it had been at a lease-rate that had left the accountant wincing. But paying over the odds was acceptable on this occasion given the importance of the trip.

An open-ended flight ticket had been purchased too. Who knew how long he would be over there? A lot would depend on the nature of the adventure and how often Nerys could get across to visit. As he nursed a glass of red wine in his favourite armchair, Calum thought just how lucky he was to have such a supportive wife, she was really the one behind the whole venture. And, if getting out of her way helped her with her work, then it was the least he could do. It was a fine idea indeed.

Later, as he contemplated the need to get up to refill his glass, he decided that if he had to get out of the armchair anyway, he might as well wander over to his desk and see what was happening in the world of the Internet.

After reading the financial papers from capitals on several continents, Calum resolved that he was not going to let the depressing themes spoil his good mood. What did he care about economic downturns, credit ceilings, and banking shenanigans? He was going to Millport. Millport had a single bank that only opened two days a week and an ATM machine that frequently ran out of money on public holidays. Linked to global financial tension however, it was not!

He turned to sports sites to catch up on the latest. He had now spent more than half his life in North America but his interests still lay in Scottish football, rugby, and speedway, to be followed by English versions of the same, to be followed by versions of the same sports in any other country in the world. After that very long list came hockey, the only sport he had picked up any interest in across the pond; and not making the list at all came the American staples of baseball, their football, and basketball. The Internet allowed him to follow his favourites as if he were still based in Scotland as long as he did not forget the eight hour time difference. Getting up at three in the morning to follow the texted minute-by-minute as-it-happened report on a game was a favourite pastime.

An article caught his eye on the plight of Scottish football; not from the perspective that the national team had not qualified for the World Cup in decades and only one team made much impression in European competitions but from the business perspective. Scottish football was essentially bankrupt and the higher the level of club, the worse it got. The Elite League consisted of ten teams but most people around the world would tell you that there were only two teams in Scotland, both based in Glasgow—the Protestant White City Ibrox, better known as WCI, and the Catholic Glasgow Erin. The religious divide, so pervasive in Scotland for centuries, had distilled itself into supporting either WCI or Glasgow Erin. Each had more supporters than all of the other teams combined. In most cities, including the capital Edinburgh, the population was split between the two Glasgow giants. Then a small minority would defy tradition and support the local team. Even Edinburgh with the next largest teams in the League—Protestant Edinburgh Waverley and Catholic Leith Albion—had always functioned within this great divide. The two big teams had always tended to just get richer and more successful, the rest of the teams just about survived. That was until now. The Scottish Elite Football League was now in real crisis.

Calum homed in on an opinion piece from someone he knew very well. Neil Christian had been his hero while growing up following Edinburgh Waverley. Neil had broken into the Waverley side as a sixteen year old and had enjoyed a career of over ten years that was blessed with team and personal success. That was a great time to be associated with football in Edinburgh. Always a no-compromise player and an outspoken commentator on the game, Neil had eventually suffered an ignominious transfer to lowly Ayr FC where he had been expected to simply play out his days. However, not only did he become a leading part of a Cinderella period for Ayr, the club eventually cashed him in through a money-spinning transfer to Leeds in the English First Division where Neil continued to shine. Eventually, he made his way back to Scotland in his mid-thirties and even had another spell with Edinburgh Waverley. By then, however, the club's fortunes were on the slide and he was no longer able to weave his magic although he remained a firm fan favourite. Calum had left for Canada before Neil's return so his memories were firmly rooted in a winning team and Neil Christian scoring goals from all angles and distances.

In the late 1980s, Neil immigrated to Canada too and that is where Calum first met him in person. Calum was volunteer coaching in youth soccer (before he became cynical about volunteering for anything) and Christian was a star guest at a special training camp. As they both lived in Victoria, British Columbia, they developed something of a friendship based in part on what both would like to do to promote the game in a country where it still ranked behind hockey and football (the Canadian kind, not even to be confused with the American kind) and in part on their enjoyment of reminiscing on the past at Edinburgh Waverley. Neil, usually fortified by several fine malts, was never slow to praise the Scottish football of the 1960s and to bemoan where it had slid to today. His article would be worth reading.

"As football thrives around the entire world, it truly is the number one global sport; I despair of where it now sits in my native Scotland. If we did not invent the game, along with most other things worth having in life, we Scots were at least at the very forefront of its development in the late 19th century. For a small nation, we were always able to do well at the local, national, and international levels and that was because the game was essentially a humble game

for humble folks. It did not take much money to run a club and most players were recruited locally. I know that personally growing up in Edinburgh; my only ambition was to play for Edinburgh Waverley, not another team in Scotland, certainly not Leith Albion, because they were the enemy. They were Catholic. And that was the first cause of Scotland's eventual fall from grace.

Scotland is historically split into Protestant and Catholic just as much as Ireland ever was. And where it shows to the greatest extent is in its football. It is not obvious at all in any other sport like rugby or cricket. But football is a grass roots sport, and religious division comes directly from the grass roots. In Glasgow, the great divide comes between Protestant WCI and Catholic Glasgow Erin. Most people forget there were three other teams in Glasgow. They did not matter because they had no religious affiliation. In Edinburgh, religion divided Edinburgh Waverley and Leith Albion although there were probably more WCI and Glasgow Erin supporters than there were supporters of the local teams. In all other towns, the big two Glasgow teams creamed off the majority of support leaving the minority to follow their local team.

In spite of this unhealthy but permanent support structure, teams did manage to battle the "Big Two" and the Scottish League was known as being quite competitive most of the time. I enjoyed some great seasons with Edinburgh Waverley. We won the First Division as it was called then, the Scottish Cup, the Scottish League Cup, the UK Cup, and came close in the European Cup. And in that time, we beat out the "Big Two" occasionally, Leith Albion frequently as well as English giants like Manchester and Spurs. We even beat Barcelona once at the Nou Camp. Those were heady days indeed! I never got rich but I made a comfortable living. Then the rot associated with the money set in and Scottish football found it could not carry a second burden.

For some reason, almost overnight football became big business. It was no longer a humble sport played by humble folks. Players got freedom of contract and were able to increase their earnings twenty-fold, sometimes more. Television had woken up to the fact that people wanted to watch games all day for seven days a week and so pumped millions into the big leagues like England, Germany, Spain and Italy. (However, precious little ever came to the lowly Scottish League, even from the inaptly named British Broadcasting Corporation.) And lastly and most importantly of all, the nouveau riche around the world, whether they had earned their billions honestly or otherwise, decided that football was a good place to park their loot. However, again Scotland appeared to be able only to attract the shady businessmen and those who were not quite as wealthy as their press releases first suggested.

So where is my little country now? The Elite League consists of ten teams. Eight are in some form of receivership where their continued existence is solely at the pleasure of a British or foreign bank and their loans could be called tomorrow. The two Catholic teams, owned by successful and philanthropic Catholics, are relatively stable. They don't have the money to be very competitive outside Scotland but they are not in receivership either. Why should that be? Have Catholics better business acumen than their Protestant counterparts? Is there some sort of divine intervention for the sake of the beautiful game? I really don't know. But that leads us to the giants on the other side of the great divide. I am terribly saddened to say that dear old Edinburgh Waverley is bankrupt and in the process of being wound up. It is quite likely that it won't exist at all by the end of this season—not a season in which they didn't win anything, not a season in which they get relegated to the lower division, but a season in which they cease to actually exist after 140 years. How sad can that be? Their failing was that they tried to compete with big boys by paying ridiculous wages and looked to fund them through a newly minted Russian millionaire. Alas, his funding dried up quicker than the puddles on the turf at the Waverley Stadium after an Edinburgh rain shower.

I leave WCI to last. They are perhaps one of the six biggest clubs in the world with a huge following in many counties beyond Scotland, albeit constructed on time-honoured religious bigotry. In the last three years, they have been rescued from bankruptcy each year by a new found millionaire who has only lasted a season. One went to jail, one was banned from running any business, and the other just ran out of money. In that time the fortunes of the team have plummeted and it is no longer able to compete in Scotland never mind in Europe where it still believes its rightful home to be in this new global era. Now a new saviour has emerged who is an unknown American with no previous connection to any sport far less football and has made his reputed fortune in environmental research. Now that to me seems to be a little odd. Normally, I would associate any kind of research with spending money, not making it, but Mr. Joel Wannamaker is alleged to be rolling in it and committed to making WCI great again. I suspect he is not a Catholic. We shall see, but the very future of Scottish football not just that of WCI may be dependent upon him.

Enough of my little weeps at the Old Country. Canada is where I now live and Canadian soccer is where I place my commitment for the future. I just hope it is has the common sense to continue to organize the sport according to its means and not be tempted to go the way of Europe. It could end up like Scotland."

I should have stuck with the financial papers thought Calum; they made more cheery reading than that. Imagine the beautiful game on its knees in Scotland. Edinburgh Waverley is going out of business and Mr. Wannamaker is the last hope for WCI. He wondered where he had heard that name before.

Chapter 3

Nerys Jones-Davies had insisted on driving Calum to LAX on the day of the departure for the great adventure. In spite of it being a busy day for her on campus, it was not clear if her insistence was down to love or just to make sure that he actually took off. Whichever, she was with him all the way to the check-in and ensured that both he and his luggage were booked directly to Glasgow.

Calum looked at Nerys and saw an extremely attractive woman look up at him; on her tip-toes she still fell six inches shorter than he. Tearful but happy sobs accompanied their last embrace as he set off to security and she to rescue her car for the drive back to the California University, Temecula Campus.

Calum was one of the very first on board and settled into his seat immediately. First Class no less. Nerys had insisted. This was no ordinary journey. Back in his professional days, First Class had been the only way to go, but an academic career seldom supported such luxury and it was quite a while since he had been greeted by a friendly flight attendant with a glass of champagne. Not accustomed to travelling much on his own these days, he wondered who might be destined to sit in the seat beside him.

Well into his third champagne and with the door of the plane about to be ceremoniously closed, it looked like he might be seated on his own when a tall slim woman of around his own age, with flowing red hair and enwrapped in furs, with much more carry-on luggage than was normally permitted, suddenly exploded into the cabin and plunged down next to him.

'Holy Shit, I did not think I was going to make that,' came the first uttering.

'Neither did I,' replied Calum.

Once settled in to her seat with the minimum effort on her part and the maximum effort on the part of not one but two flight attendants, the plane began its take-off taxi. Declining a glass of champagne, which Calum graciously offered to take instead, in favour of a large vodka tonic, his fellow passenger leant toward Calum and turned on a radiant smile. Calum was already impressed by everything about her demeanour including her approach to alcohol and the smile was just the icing on the cake.

'I'm Calum Davies. It's nice to meet you.'

'Mr. Davies, it's nice to meet you too,' came the response with a magnificently bejewelled hand offered to confirm it.

Calum attempted a customary humorous response, the kind that caused Nerys to roll her eyes, by saying, 'Well, actually it is Dr. Davies but let's keep that between us because I am a doctor of education not medicine and I am always afraid that I will be called upon to deliver a baby every time I fly.'

There was no roll of her eyes but just the light hint of a flutter.

'I'm Margaret Wannamaker. Most folks call me Maggie.'

There followed what might have seemed an endless silence with two people staring at each other wondering what was going to happen next until Calum would have jumped from his seat were he not restrained by his seatbelt.

'The actress! Of course, I should have recognized you. I am a great fan of your movies,' Calum blurted out while trying desperately to remember the name of one in case he was called upon to say more.

'How sweet. I am not sure just how many doctors of education I have in my fan club.'

'I am an accountant too,' he said with some sense of importance and hope that it counted for double recognition.

As the flight progressed pleasantly, aided admittedly by First Class food and drinks, small talk eventually subsided and our travellers napped for a while. Calum was quite excited to be sharing the flight with a celebrity and had even remembered the name of her last movie. Upon noticing that she was awakening from her slumbers too, he was keen to continue conversation.

'Ah Maggie,' for he had been invited to call her such, 'you are awake. I was just thinking how much I enjoyed your part in Forever Insecure. You really did deserve the Academy Award for that. It seemed like such a challenging role.'

'Thank you. A lot of people thought that. When you get to my age, it is difficult to get good roles. That was one for sure. It was just my misfortune that Meryl Streep chose to make another movie again and beat me out at the end. She really is more retired than active but is still a wonderful actress.'

'Indeed,' Calum replied, thinking that sounds a bit like him—more retired than active, but still wonderful. 'But I am sure it is only a matter of time before you win the Oscar. Are you headed to Scotland to make another movie?'

'Would that I were, my dear Calum. Would that I were. No I have been ordered to Scotland by my husband to join him in his insane venture into soccer, which they call football over there for some reason.'

'Of course. Joel Wannamaker must be your husband,' Calum exclaimed showing a sharpness of name association that he was not normally known for.

'Oh you know about this stuff do you? I did not think Americans would know anything about WIC.'

'Actually it is WCI. About a hundred years ago, I was born in Scotland and I have retained a keen interest and fondness for the game of football, if not for that particular team. I read that your husband has rescued them with a timely investment.'

'I don't know what he is thinking about. His interest is in making money, lots of it. As I understand it, these soccer teams don't make money. They just bleed it.'

'That is about right. He will not get rich, or should I say richer, from owning a Scottish football team.'

'He says it is all about tax and currency advantages. At that point my eyes glass over and I say whatever you like dear. You make the money. It's yours to use as you see fit.'

'Is he religious by any chance?'

'Funny you should ask that. I wouldn't say he is religious. I think he is some kind of lapsed Presbyterian. However, he has been getting ticked off with Catholics for the last couple of years. He calls the Vatican the biggest money-laundering racket in the world. Although what that has to do with soccer I would not know.'

'You would be surprised,' came the cheerful response. 'You are in for a treat. You might even be able to make a movie out of it.'

As the plane touched down in Glasgow, Calum regretted that the flight had passed so quickly. Normally he found transatlantic flights interminable but with such an enchanting partner it was just his luck that this one had galloped by. Farewells were said with flamboyant hugs even. He did not suppose that he would run across Margaret Wannamaker again even among Scotland's small five million population. But you never know, do you?

Meanwhile, Nerys had successfully negotiated her way out of LAX, no mean feat in itself, and by way of Highways 105, 605, 91, and 15 to her campus in Temecula. Temecula was a fast growing new city, built around the wine and recreation industries that had now moved into the higher echelons of sophistication with a campus of the California University, itself the fastest growing private university in the State of California. While not yet attaining the academic standing of the University of California and the California State University, the California University, so named it seemed just to annoy its public competitors, had built up a good name in graduation rates and research. It had attracted Nerys along with many younger academics seeking to forge careers outside of the very traditional public university system. But first, there was the matter of tenure.

The tenure system at the California University, while not so brutal and some would say divisive as that of the public universities, was still a tough slog of research and publication, with a little teaching thrown in, under the watchful eyes of fellow faculty. Nerys was close, indeed very close. She felt that one more notable research project written up for a half-decent journal ought to do it. It was with that in mind that she was seated in the office of her dean, Professor Anna Salisbury, to discuss her idea for pursuing research in the ethical and moral disposal of radioactive waste from a political and public policy perspective. She opined that it was a hot topic to focus on then wished she had not used that expression; it was much more in keeping with Calum's style. Rather than concentrate on the established countries like the United States, Canada, UK, France, and Germany where it could be assumed that policy on radioactive waste disposal had already been thought about and sensibly devised, she proposed to study the emerging economic giants—the so-called BRIC countries Brazil, Russia, India, and China—where an ethical and moral foundation for public policy might not be such an obvious assumption. However, that meant more complex and costly research but with definite payback upon successful completion.

Dean Salisbury was enthusiastic about the direction Nerys was proposing and not too despondent about finding the funding. Not well known on campus and certainly news to Nerys, the California University had its own research corporation called the SoCal Environmental Research Corporation, more commonly known as SERC, set up to fund environmental research from various perspectives. While most of its money went to pure scientific research, there was every possibility that it would favourably consider a research proposal on public policy from a political scientist. The Corporation seemed to have considerable funds at its disposal gleaned for various levels of government and from the private sector. In fact it was the partnerships with several large but little-known private research corporations that made it unique in the field and kept it under the radar on campus. Environmental matters were often so controversial and divisive among academics that a little secrecy was justified in order to support the leading edge work it was sponsoring and that would someday allow the California University to sit right up there with the University of California and the California State University.

Before the day was out, a meeting had been arranged with the research grants committee of SERC solely on the basis of a telephone conversation between the dean and her high-ranking contact at the corporation. To say that Nerys was elated would be an understatement. If she could get the funding for an assistant and several visits to BRIC countries, she could produce outstanding results that could have global interest. She had already ascertained that no-one else had yet entered into the field. Time was of the essence.

With Calum gainfully employed in pursuit of an adventure, she could afford to dedicate the next year to her project. After that she should surely be a shoe-in for tenure. With tenure, she could scale back her hectic research schedule and have more time for him. Maybe she would have more time to spend on his precious island.

Chapter 4

A few days later, the research grants committee of the SoCal Environmental Research Corporation met on the 20th floor of a downtown hotel in Los Angeles. The only item on the agenda was to consider a grant application from Dr. Jones-Davies supported by Dean Salisbury.

Nerys was given ample time to outline her research idea and had come well prepared with not only a sound academic rationale for the proposed work but also a very detailed business plan as to how the grant funds would be utilized. The latter had been prepared on the advice of Dean Salisbury who emphasized that they would be dealing with hard-line business people who would want to know just what their money would be used for and what the return on their investment, academic and monetary, was likely to be. This was a slight departure from the normal grant application but Nerys had done her homework and had incorporated some of the analyses and comments she had seen Calum quote over the years.

The committee consisted of seven men in suits. Each asked a perfunctory question which Nerys answered with ease. The chairman asked a couple more questions, it seemed to Nerys to be just fillers, and she could not believe how well it was going. However, that changed to some extent when a previously quiet member, one Cyrus Macadam, proceeded to ask a string of questions about the location of the research, seeking assurance that it was limited to the BRIC countries, and that it would not include North America or Europe. Nerys assumed this was to do with the need for the research to be new and not just replicating earlier efforts and the fact that much work in the latter geographical areas had already been done. She assured the committee that her focus lay on the BRIC countries and would extend no further.

Macadam stated with what seemed like unnecessary emphasis. 'Your funding would be totally dependent on you living up to what you have said.'

Nerys was somewhat taken aback by the ferocity of the condition but was also sharp enough to realize that he was now talking about the grant being more of a reality then a possibility. She simply nodded her head in agreement to the condition.

The committee then asked the two academics to leave while the application was considered. Seated outside, Dean Salisbury smiled knowingly. Nerys could not help but fidget. This was a new experience for her.

Ten minutes later, they were called back in and given the good news that $500,000 was to be granted for the research project. Nerys gasped. This was more than had been requested and even that had been more than she had ever asked for before in her research career. The committee members warmed up and offered smiles and words of congratulations and good luck to the two delighted academics. That is all the committee members except Mr. Macadam. His stern face never changed as his eyes seemed to bore into Nerys'. Oh well, he must simply be what Calum would refer to as a hard-nosed business man with a heart of stone.

That night at midnight, to allow for the time difference, Nerys telephoned Calum. It was the first time they had spoken at any length since his departure. At first, they were both desperate to share their news and overlap of voices made for unintelligible conversation. Then each said for the other to go ahead and a silence ensued. Finally, Calum said for his wife to go ahead with what he sensed was important news from her.

Nerys took the next fifteen minutes to give a blow-by-blow account of the hugely successful grant application and how the funds would allow her to hire an assistant, travel to South America and Asia, and do the most meaningful research she had yet engaged in. The work was sure to lead to publication opportunities and who knew what else including the coveted tenure.

Her enthusiasm was not even diminished by Calum's predictable sarcasm. "Yee Haw, a job for life.'

'That's right, a job for life so that I can keep you in the manner to which you would want to become accustomed. You know I will always be younger than you and there are lots of things I still want to do in my career. This funding will allow me to take a huge step forward.'

Suitably chastened, Calum moved the discussion on to the funding agency. He had never heard of SERC. Neither had Nerys she confessed. She had her dean to thank for making the connection. The accountant's scepticism training kicked into action as Calum enquired as to what strings were attached to such a sizeable sum of money. Forgetting Macadam's strict condition, she professed that there were none she could see. The corporation was just committed to providing the wherewithal for cutting edge research. It showed how committed the California University was to getting into the major league of research universities and that it had cleverly formed SERC to tap into both public and private funds. Calum could only agree but made a mental note to do some research himself into SERC.

Eventually Nerys exhausted her story and encouraged Calum to share what he had been up to on the island of Great Cumbrae and metropolis of Millport. Ignoring the sarcasm, he reported that he had settled in well after an exciting flight across the Atlantic in the company of Ms. Margaret

Wannamaker of Hollywood fame. Being winter, there were very few visitors around on the island but that had allowed him to get to know some of the locals better than he had in previous visits. There was some opportunity to help in the economic planning of the island and he intended to offer his services. In addition, there were other opportunities for him to step out of his comfort zone and get involved in a fledgling museum that was being developed and also to explore things he could do with the Cumbraes Environmental Research Station which was based on the island. He was to have a meeting with the station director later that very day.

'Well well. You have been busy becoming a volunteer. Who woulda thunk it?'

'You can tease all you like. It is different here. It already feels like family. You know I have always thought of this as my spiritual home.'

'And the roving lad has returned?'

'Something like that. I feel at home. Not necessarily to stay all the time. I still want to return to California. But I intend to spend a fair amount of time here. I just have this feeling that something is going to happen that I will get involved in.'

'Cal's big adventure, perhaps?'

He remarked how strange it seemed that each of them was happy, in fact happier than they had seemed for ages, and yet they were physically apart. He hoped that did not bode badly for their relationship. Both agreed that perhaps a break was good and each getting their teeth into something on their own while supported by the other might in fact be very good for their relationship. Nerys was always very good at extracting the positive from what might seem the negative. The sceptic, on this occasion, was happy to concur. With the wonders of modern technology and an ever shrinking globe, they would keep in touch constantly, meet from time-to-time, and support each other in their new endeavours.

Over an hour had passed to the undoubted delight of their mobile service carrier. Nerys was exhausted, yet exhilarated, and needed to get to bed. Calum was refreshed from a wonderfully restful sleep, was now exhilarated too, and was raring to go with another day on his island. Both said their slow but necessary farewells, each reluctant to let the other have the last word.

Chapter 5

Calum was keen to build on the enthusiasm from his transatlantic call and, lifted by the surprise of a bright January sun, he set out from his home immediately after breakfast. He was of course on foot. Although these days many locals and most visitors brought cars to the island, it served to destroy the ambient image of walking or cycling everywhere. After all, the island was only ten miles around.

He headed into town and, as he was rounding Cosy Corner to pass the police station cum house, he came face-to-face with the local officer for the first time. He was a tall thin young man on whom the uniform seemed to hang as if it had been intended for someone else.

'Ah, you will be the Yank.'

'Well, sort of. I prefer to think of myself as a Scottish-Canadian presently a resident of the US of A and a temporary guest of your good island.'

'Scotty Green referred to you as the Yank. Until he revises his description that is what is written down in the visitors' book.'

'I have already had the pleasure of making Mr. Green's acquaintance. I shall be sure to let him know more of my origins the next time I see him so that the record can be set straight.'

Calum had already discovered that nothing happened in Millport without Scotty Green being involved. Before the reorganization of Scottish counties and towns, he would have been provost, a quaint title unique to that land and similar to a mayor. Now all judicial and governmental power resided in London, or Edinburgh or the District of North Ayrshire on the mainland. There was based in Millport a Community Council for the Cumbraes, being Great Cumbrae and Wee Cumbrae, with Scotty Green as its long-standing chair and on paper it had very little power. In reality, it had as much power as Chairman Green could exact from the other power bases and that was a considerable amount. Not that he was a bad man. Far from it, he had the welfare of the two islands in the forefront of everything he said and did. It was just that he was a little crusty and not known to tolerate fools for very long, if at all. On meeting him, Calum had taken a liking to him right away and Green had not rejected him, probably because Calum had professed a great love for the area and a desire to provide help in any way he could. Fearing that might be construed as the offer of a monetary donation, he had given Green a brief personal and recent career history and what he might be able to turn his hand to. Hence the acquisition of the Yank moniker.

Calum was keen to get on the right side of the law and proffered a hand. 'My name is Calum Davies and after visiting Millport all of my life I have come to stay for a while. My wife back in California thinks I am destined for an adventure here.'

'Pleased to meet you. We don't tend to have too many adventures here. That is why I am the only police officer for the two islands. I would prefer to keep it that way if you don't mind. My name is Henri Jardin but once you get to know me you can call me Harry.'

The police officer waited for the anticipated response to his French name that had been delivered in a somewhat odd, mangled, French and West of Scotland accent. He was taken by surprise.

'Surely you must be related to another Henri Jardin. I knew him as a police officer here when I was just a teenager. I never, however, got to call him Harry.'

'That would be my father, now departed. He retired in the 1990s and passed away just two years ago in August. It was always my ambition to be a police officer and to get this posting. And, now I have done it.'

It was obvious that Calum's knowledge of Henri Jardin the First went a long way to breaking the ice with Henri Jardin the Second. For the next hour they sat on the low wall overlooking the ocean in Cosy Corner and reminisced, something Calum was good at, especially when he got the right audience and Constable Jardin was an attentive listener and occasional commenter with a pawky sense of humour.

The father had been quite a character in the '60s and '70s. As well as being the only police officer, he also operated a coal delivery business. In those days, the main form of heating in Millport was coal-fired and it was probably quite a lucrative business to unload the coal delivered by the puffer boat Saxon and deliver it all around the island. Presumably he found a way to get the coal to Wee Cumbrae as well for the mansion house and the lighthouse, the only two abodes on the smaller island. Calum remembered him driving all over the bigger island a tractor which pulled a trailer loaded to the top with coal in burlap sacks. Heaven knows what would have happened if a police emergency call came in while the second job was being taken care of. The son stated with a smile that nothing was ever a real big emergency in Millport therefore both lines of employment could be scheduled appropriately according to need. Coal for the fire generally rated ahead of crime, except maybe a murder and there had not been one of them since 1932. And even then there were doubts about that. The bottle may have simply been in the air and the victim may have simply walked into it. Instead, Ellie Macpherson was accused of killing Hamish Macpherson by hitting him over the head with a bottle. Fortunately, Hamish's drunken aggression was taken into account by the High Court in Edinburgh and Ellie was returned to the island in fewer than two years and lived there for the rest of her life until 1982.

Jardin senior was not content with just two jobs. Calum well remembered coming to Millport for the end of season weekend with some of his friends from Edinburgh. They had fairly recently discovered the joys of drinking in pubs, rather than sneaking beer and wine out of their homes and consuming it under cover of darkness in either a park or alleyway. Pubbing was so much more sophisticated. The trouble was in Scotland you needed to be aged eighteen. The lads were just fifteen. Most landlords tended to turn a blind eye to under-age drinking. After all what else was there for them to do?

Imagine Calum's horror when his little gang swaggered their way into the McGillivray Arms across the Quayside Square from Millport Old Pier to be faced by the bartender, a certain Henri Jardin. Perhaps it was his police training; it certainly had nothing to do with his coal delivery business training, but Jardin immediately announced to all who could hear, 'You lads look underage, you are not local, where are you from?' No more than two of the six voices that could possibly have answered replied at a level barely audible, 'Edinburgh.' Jardin thought for a moment then boomed, 'Ah, foreign tourists. Oh well, your money is as good as ours. What will you be having lads!' Tears were running down Calum's cheeks as he told a story he had not told for decades. And there might even have been a hint of dampness on the cheeks of the current police officer.

Lest he be suspected of not being as hard-working as his father, Jardin junior clarified that those were grand days but now there was so much paperwork to be filled in for Police Scotland based in Tulliallan, Perthshire that it was only possible to hold down one job. 'I know exactly what you mean,' replied the accountant. In any case, there was no coal whatsoever on the island now and the McGillivray Arms had been demolished to make way for vacation apartments. Imagine the likes of that in Scotland!

Leaving the young police officer after he had been granted the ultimate accolade—'you can just call me Harry'—Calum set off for his intended destination, the Cumbraes Environmental Research Station and his meeting with the director. The station was slightly out of town at the opposite end from where Calum resided. That meant he had to walk along the long promenade with its array of charming Victorian shops and apartment buildings. Any postcard or photograph of Millport most likely featured the promenade, from the black and white days when it was so busy with tourists that they had difficulty moving around and nary a car was to be seen to the days of colour when the people were fewer but the vehicles abounded. These days many tourists brought their cars over on the ferry, parked them with great difficulty on the promenade (hence them featuring in the post cards and photographs), then never used them again until they left the island. Millport was still famous for walking and cycling. Why not leave the cars on the mainland thought Calum? Progress takes strange turns at times.

After the promenade came the East Bay. It was not similar in physical terms to the West Bay being more curved into a sheltered cove but it shared the same large houses built by Glasgow's business tycoons. Here, Calum noted, fewer of the houses had actually been sub-divided into four smaller abodes. Therefore, they were pretty grand homes and most had been handed down within families from the days of roaring trade in tobacco and sugar. He could also recall the 1960s when some Scottish actors and entertainers had bought homes here, just before the advent of cheap flights to Spain that caused an exodus to actual summer sunshine and less expensive homes there. There was even a rock band that bought a large house and turned it into recording studios but that had been back in the West Bay, in fact outside of town beyond the West Bay. Calum could see the house and the band in his mind's eye but could remember the name of neither just at the moment.

Eventually he reached the research station. It was another fine red sandstone building from Victorian times with additional buildings added on and what looked like dormitories, presumably for visiting students. The station was well known throughout the UK for its labs and facilities as well as its scientific staff and hosted high school and university students for stays of varying durations. Calum approached the reception desk and announced that he had an appointment with the director.

'Ah, that will be Dr. Randall. She is expecting you. Just go right in the door up there on the left.'

Calum was just getting over the fact that the station director was a woman when he entered a spacious office with a stunning view out over the Clyde. As he offered his hand, he glanced from a pretty face to the name on the desk—Dr. Heather Randall, Director.

'That's funny. I went to high school with a Heather Randall; same name as yours.'

'That was me you nut. Where have you been for the last forty four years?'

Chapter 6

The rest of the morning, a pleasant lunch in the research station cafeteria, and most of the afternoon were spent reminiscing. After all, Dr. Heather Randall and Dr. Calum Davies had a lot to catch up on. Upon graduating from high school in Edinburgh in 1969, they both went their separate ways never to meet up again until now. However during the high school years they had been very close friends. Strangely they had never dated each other but had always remained friends while dating others. For some reason their relationship never got beyond that of just being very good friends which is unusual at that age. The fact that it was able to rekindle after such a long time was also somewhat unusual. But rekindling it was.

Calum went straight from high school to join an accounting firm and began his training in accountancy which would lead ultimately to his designation as a chartered accountant. Heather went the university route from school and eventually completed degrees at the bachelor, masters, and doctoral level in environmental science which at that time was something of a blossoming scientific field. After completing her academic studies, Heather had wanderlust to travel the world and ended up spending periods of time in South Africa, Australia, and California. At each stop she did leading edge work in environmental science and built up a reputation that was recognized with increasingly more important employment positions. Along the way she had a failed marriage, probably due at least in part to never settling in one particular place for long. Almost 10 years ago, she met and married a leading attorney, Nicholas Gorman, who was also a Scot but was then based in Los Angeles. They decided to return to Scotland where he established a law practice in Glasgow and she was appointed to the position of director of the Cumbraes Environmental Research Station in Millport. At first they lived in Glasgow and she commuted but that proved to be a terrific draw on her time and eventually they also purchased a home in Millport that allowed her to be based on the island and her husband travelled. down from Glasgow to join her on the weekends.

Calum noted that Heather talked most enthusiastically about the work being done at the research station. During her time as director, she had been successful in building up the station's reputation among universities and schools throughout the UK. Hundreds of students who had previously never heard of Millport or the Cumbrae islands had been able to come and study at the station and to do hands-on research in biological and environmental fields. In the great majority of cases, this greatly enhanced their educational experience and gave them the practical experience to go with the ultimate certificates or degrees that would assist them in finding work in the environmental field. In fact throughout the United Kingdom and Europe, graduates now holding down important positions in government and educational sectors attributed their success to the time spent doing research at the station. It seemed inevitable that Heather's love of education and love of her scientific field would create the enthusiasm that would make the programmes she led so successful.

Although Calum had been visiting Cumbrae most of his life and had been aware of the research station, he had never really known too much about what happened there and certainly was not aware of the high esteem in which it was held. He was quite thrilled to learn about the station and the fact that its success was in large part due to his old school friend.

Heather in turn listened to Calum's life story with great interest. The fact that he had really had two careers, both in professional accounting and in education, pleased her in addition to the fact that he had also been based for a long time in Scotland, then Canada, and now in California and that was in some ways similar to her own experience. They laughed at the commonalities that they shared even though they had never planned them and in fact had never even talked for forty odd years. In particular, they discovered that they shared a deep affection for Millport and Cumbrae. And, they professed their good fortune that both their spouses had developed similar affections that enabled them to focus so much of their attention on the tiny island.

Talk turned to contemporary issues facing the research station and the island. Heather spoke at length about the major event that was having a significant impact on the work of the station. In the early 1960s, a nuclear power station, one of the first few in the United Kingdom, had been built at Farland, almost directly across from Millport on the mainland. The event at the time created a great deal of controversy. Nuclear power was to a large extent still in its infancy as a form of power generation. In addition the large and imposing structures created blight on a beautiful environment. The view from Millport itself would never be the same again as one's eyes glided across the sparkling water to the mainland and to lush green pastures on rolling hills, only to be suddenly rudely interrupted by the monster that was the power station. There were all sorts of misinformation about the new state of the art power station including the dangers of nuclear power itself and its association with the atomic bombs of World War II, which at that time was still fresh in a lot of people's memories. In addition, there were bizarre predictions that the nuclear power would actually increase the temperature of the ocean thereby allowing Millport to develop further as a vacation destination. Employment opportunities were predicted to be huge and that was always going to be exciting for the young of Millport who generally had to move far away from the island to find work. Lastly there might even have been some wilder forecasts that the nuclear power would give lasting cheap electricity but none of these things materialized and in reality nothing really affected the island very significantly other than the loss of the view.

However, now in the new millennium, several of the UK power stations were being decommissioned including Farland. The greatest difficulty in such an action was what to do with the nuclear waste. In keeping with other developed countries such as United States, Germany, and France, Britain had struggled with the development of public policy to deal with the storage of nuclear waste. For storage was the only option other than some limited ability to recycle the material into further processes; however, that recycling was both difficult and expensive. And, storage had to be long lasting for some of the waste would take millions of years until it was fully decayed. The UK ultimately opted for several strategies including the use and expansion of existing salt mines and the creation of huge tunnels in scarcely populated areas of the country. The major considerations in any form of storage were to minimize if not eliminate possible environmental contamination and to maintain safety relating both to human and animal health and to prevent the theft of waste and its possible reuse in making nuclear weapons.

In the case of Farland, it had been decided to dig a tunnel beneath the uninhabited island of Beagg, one of farthest west of the Outer Hebrides and to ship the waste there. The laborious but high-risk task of gradually shipping the waste had now begun upon completion of the tunnel. The sea at both the Farland end and around Beagg could be very unpredictable and it had been decided to move the waste in small solid steel flasks aboard small container crafts in order to minimize the risk. At the beginning of a week, a fully-loaded craft would leave Farland and by the end of the second week it would have completed its careful voyage to Beagg to allow storage of the flasks in the tunnel. In the event of bad weather, there were several ports along the route that could safely accommodate the small crafts. If a craft left Farland at the beginning of every second week, it would take three years to complete the task.

The work was being undertaken in joint venture by the UK and Scottish governments along with BritPower, the national utility company that owned the Farland Power Station. They had created a very deliberate communication plan for the public that was open and transparent in some aspects but guarded in others. The key was to provide a level of comfort in general, in the knowledge that that not everyone could be fully satisfied. In particular, massed groups of environmentalists had concerns about how Farland would be left at the end, the safety of the sea transportation strategy, and of course the ongoing safety of the Beagg tunnel. In order to give the communication plan some credibility, two agencies that purported to be independent of the main players, had been engaged to oversee all aspects of the power station decommissioning. One was the Cumbraes Environmental Research Station and the other was an American organization with an impressive track record in exactly this type of work called the SoCal Environmental Research Corporation or SERC.

Heather confided that in reality that while her organization had the expertise it simply did not have the resources to do more than provide a cursory watching brief and some sample testing if it was to maintain its other commitments to education and research. Furthermore, she noted that the relationship with SERC was unusual. SERC itself was based in California but SERC UK had a head office in London and there was a special team based in Glasgow headed up by a Cyrus Macadam. Although she and Macadam met frequently, their conversations did not seem to get beyond the theoretical aspects of the decommissioning and she was not party to any real evidence that they were carrying out the quality assurance for which they had been hired. Indeed, although she only saw executive summaries, Heather felt that the monthly reports being presented by SERC to the governments and utility company were superficial at best. They seemed to be telling their masters exactly what they wanted to hear and that information was in turn being fed into the public communiqués that assured everyone that the decommissioning was proceeding exactly as planned. In contrast, she felt that her station had been able to carry out limited but credible testing and thus far was able to confirm the same results but through far greater thoroughness.

Calum immediately remarked on the presence of SERC and Mr. Macadam and how they had entered the life of his researcher wife.

'Funny that you should express reservations about that outfit. Without really knowing much about them at all, I formed exactly the same reservations after their dealings with Nerys. It all happened just too easily. It is convenient to look at them favourably because they are helping her but I am left wondering what is in it for them.'

'Well, they are being well paid for their work on this side of the pond but it is their work that bothers me.'

'Are they scientists or public relations experts or some kind of business feeding off the science?'

'Exactly.'

Calum expressed an interest in helping Heather in whatever way he could. This was not an accounting challenge per se but the forensic nature of the oversight which her station had taken on was not dissimilar to some accounting investigations he had worked on. In fact a while back he had been assisting the Royal Canadian Mounted Police in fraud cases involving large amounts of government funding being paid out and neatly accounted for but the work was never done or was only done to a limited extent that the purpose of the funding in the first place was never met. They agreed the circumstances at Farland were not altogether different.

Heather was not in a position to hire Calum and in fact he did not desire regular employment. However, it was agreed that for the duration of his stay in Millport, he would make himself available to her for consultation and the odd simple investigation if the need transpired.

'It will be like old times,' Calum enthused. 'We used to work well together on my French assignments in Grade 11.'

'That was the Fifth Form then and the similarity escapes me but the opportunity to reconnect with you is really welcome. And if you can help me even a little, I shall be very grateful. I don't need this added stress at my advanced age.'

'What do you mean? You are a few months younger than I and I certainly don't consider myself of advanced age. I am recently very early retired, and simply looking for an adventure!'

Chapter 7

Through the next few weeks the cold clear days of January morphed into the warmer but decidedly wetter days of February. It was debatable whether it actually felt any warmer because one had to be constantly wrapped up against the frequent driving rain which came in from the mainland. However, Calum busied himself with his various interests that he had developed during his short stay.

In particular, he tried to do in-depth research into SERC by tracking its activities both in the USA and Europe. For all that the Internet now provides almost unlimited information on every possible topic; it would appear that SERC had managed to go about its business without an awful lot of information finding its way onto the *"net"*. He could find references to research projects which SERC had funded or had been paid by agencies and government departments to perform but they always seemed to be mentioned at the outset of the research. Seldom could he find any results of such projects. This only served to heighten his suspicion of what actually went on at SERC behind its very limited and guarded public image.

Cyrus Macadam's name came up frequently. He seemed to be a member of the seven person board of directors which also served as the committee that gave out research grants. In addition, he seemed to be the chief operations officer and actually led projects that SERC itself was undertaking. He also seemed to be in charge of European operations based in London.

Calum unearthed minutes from a SERC board meeting where a motion had been passed to enter into a contract with Joel Wannamaker for the latter to provide interim financing for a project in the amount of $10 million. Two things struck Calum—firstly, the board expressed pleasure in again transacting with Mr. Wannamaker, suggesting there was a standing business relationship, and secondly, $10 million was not exactly petty cash. Where did Wannamaker get that sort of money even if it was only intended as bridge financing?

Calum continued to establish a good relationship with Scotty Green. The latter was a weather-beaten, somewhat-stooped, curmudgeon of indeterminate age but could reminisce about events between the two world wars. They met almost every other day for a coffee or beer or occasionally for dinner and talked about all the things that Scotty was trying to do to improve life on the island. They explored opportunities for Calum to provide some assistance. Scotty was in agreement that Calum should take over the cataloguing of the great many museum items that were currently in storage with a view to developing exhibit themes that would bring more of the exhibits into the public view by way of rotating displays. The museum had been Scotty's dream for almost fifty years and during that time he had been collecting exhibits from most of island's inhabitants as well as families that had left for all parts of the world who now wanted to return their little parts of history to their rightful home. However, seldom had any more than a very few actually been catalogued and put on display so the plan adopted by the two enthusiasts was to push this along with Calum taking the lead. He settled into a routine of spending two or three mornings a week digging through the exhibits and cataloguing them from the information contained in the exhibits or by researching the Internet or simply by asking Scotty who seemed to know everything and everybody that had resided on the island for the last hundred years and more. Progress was interesting if very slow.

One day, Calum was standing on the promenade chatting to his new found policeman friend Henri "Harry" Jardin and learning about the French connection with the island constabulary. Harry's grandfather was French and had settled in Scotland after World War I. He married a Scottish woman and they moved to Millport to start a business as the local coal merchant. That was how both the coal business and the police business came to be taken on by their son, Harry senior, and the latter business continued by Harry junior. Just as he was parting from the police officer after a long chat, Harry always seemed to have time for long chats, Calum was approached by Scotty Green and invited to meet a special guest who was currently visiting the island. Scotty was very circumspect and would give no more information but insisted Calum would enjoy the company. Arrangements were made for them to meet in the bar of the Royal George Hotel that evening.

When Calum entered the bar later, the person seated next to Scotty seemed familiar but no name jumped to his mind. The face was older than what he remembered and there was a severe lack of hair compared to what he associated with the person but still he could not place him. Scotty solved that problem with a grand announcement, 'Calum Davies, meet Evan Davis.' Of course Evan Davis, legendary rock star and founder of Dubus, probably the most successful Scottish rock band of all time that started in the '60s and lasted through various reunions until the '90s. Calum recalled that the band and Evan, in particular, had been very keen on; you guessed it, Millport and Great Cumbrae. At the height of their earning power when their records charted and tours of Europe and North America were frequent, they had invested heavily in a large house just outside the town and had converted it into their recording studios. That house was Westview, now owned by Scotty Green.

Once Calum got comfortable being in the presence of rock royalty, the threesome had great conversation. It helped that Scotty suggested they might be related because their names were so similar.

'Well, if that is the case, I must be the one that missed out on the musical talent in the family. I can't sing a note,' lamented Calum.

'I have been accused of that too,' came the response from Evan.

In truth, he had enjoyed a long and interesting career. Dubus had recorded almost half their catalogue at the Westview studio but it marked a time when the members were no longer just childhood friends drawn to play music together but had become hardened and at times disillusioned rock veterans. The albums seemed to take longer and longer to complete and each of the members had their own bad habits involving legal and illegal products that often created delays. Consequently, many weeks were spent on the island living at the Miller's Stone Hotel and working at Westview. The boys, although none was as committed to life on the island as Evan, did at least value the privacy that the locals afforded them. They were generally treated as just ordinary folks and many a reporter travelled up from London to seek them out but could get no help from anyone as to where the band could be found. In return, once in a while Dubus would play an impromptu concert in one of the bars to try out new material. Some of the local worthies were not slow to indicate what was likely to be a hit and what was not upon hearing a new song.

Evan was a fair bit heavier than in his hey-day, and the long curly locks had been replaced by a shaven head. A lived-in face had emerged with age from the boyish good-looks that had been featured in every teen magazine and music paper in the UK and America. However, he still had a twinkle in his eye and clearly cherished the life of Dubus and its headquarters on Cumbrae.

'I don't think we would have lasted as long as we did if we had been based in London or even Edinburgh. The big cities just ate up young musicians as life got faster and faster. We were different. We could always chill out. Mind you, that was very much my view. Some of the others, particularly Brian Rodgers, used to complain about being bored stiff and would jump on the ferry from time to time to sample the delights in Glasgow. Me, I could have stayed here full time when we were not on the road.'

Calum mentioned that he had continued to come to Cumbrae during the time when the band owned Westview but he had never run into them. He had only ever seen them in concert in Edinburgh and Glasgow.

'That's because we were the island's best kept secret and we like it that way. Scotty was instrumental in keeping us under wraps. And, good old Monsieur Jardin did what very few policemen were prepared to do—he turned his eye the other way when we got up to mischief!'

Eventually the band broke up and each member sought out solo careers or formed new bands. Apart from a very occasional visit from one of the others to do a short piece of recording, only Evan continued to use Westview for most of his recording. However, that came to an end when some of new sidemen who were heavily into drugs created problems that even Harry could not cover up. Then Harry retired and it was time to end the musical association with Millport. Evan, with minimal interest from the original members of Dubus, sold Westview to Scotty with the latter's intention of converting it into a small hotel. Evan moved to America to be based in New York, then Los Angeles, and now Nashville. But every couple of years he made a pilgrimage to Millport and stayed at Westview.

'That sounds like an awfully familiar song,' said Calum.

'Yes. The place gets into your blood. I still love it.'

Scotty mentioned that the studio was now gone. In fact it was now the dining room of the hotel. But room number six with stunning views of Wee Cumbrae, Arran, and Bute was always available to Mr. Davis.

On one occasion, it was New Year's Eve and the dining room had been vacated by the guests now either headed on to parties around the town or having retired to bed depending on whether they were Scottish or not. Evan was visiting and as midnight was sounding he sang to an audience of two, being Scotty and his chef. He debuted some new introspective songs about earlier days on the island and recorded them on a small tape recorder as he picked on a twelve-string guitar and sang. Those wonderful jingle-jangle songs never made it to release, they were not considered commercial enough. Only two copies of the midnight concert ever existed, one was in Nashville and the other in Westview.

'One is still my favourite song after all this time.'

'That could be a fine exhibit in the new museum if Evan is willing,' Calum said hopefully to Scotty.

'Maybe, let me think about it.'

The conversation was interrupted by the barman.

'Have you people no homes to go to? We are long past closing time. I don't want to get into trouble with the police.'

'That would never happen,' all three said simultaneously. But they did agree to leave and planned a dinner at Westview before Evan had to return to Nashville.

Once back at Barclay House and before collapsing into bed, Calum sent a long email to his wife about his latest adventure. She was probably too young to remember Dubus but who would have thought that this little island could produce so many interesting characters.

Chapter 8

Dr. Nerys Jones-Davies sat in her office with her newly hired research assistant, the impossibly young and impossibly handsome Troy Cameron. Calum had referred to him as her toy-boy but he was in fact an all-but-dissertation completed PhD student with a strong record already established in research. And, all that had been done by the age of twenty-five.

Considerable progress had been made in preparation for the visits to China and India. A good deal of the public policy on nuclear waste disposal of those two countries had been found on the Internet. Clearly both countries were making great efforts, at least on paper, to adopt morally and ethically responsible standards for dealing with the problem even though nuclear power stations were a relatively recent innovation for them. Nuclear weapons were another matter. Disposal of redundant weapons could not be managed by simply firing them over the border to the next remotely hostile country. Their disposal required similar considerations as power station waste. And, both countries had built up quite a stockpile of weapons as they transitioned into superpowers and became junior members of the self-appointed world police force.

The next step was to verify that the policies and laws that had been adopted were in fact being followed. For that, it would be necessary to go to China and India to meet with government and agency officials in Beijing and Delhi respectively and, if possible, to visit actual sites where safe disposal of waste could be seen first-hand. The latter was always going to be the more difficult task to pull off. Government types will always afford foreigners a courtesy meeting in the capital but are usually reluctant to let foreigners stray into the field. The researchers had already made overtures using endorsements from Dean Salisbury and, thanks to her, the new president of the California University; the same new president who had forced Calum into retirement on her arrival. They now had to consider if there was value in enlisting the help of the US State Department and perhaps even SERC.

'SERC is a wild card. It is really difficult to get a handle on what its reputation is like in these countries. It might help us or it might kill the requests stone–dead,' Nerys opined, sounding very worldly in comparison to her young colleague but in reality feeling well out of her own comfort zone.

'Did your husband come up with anything on SERC? You told me he was trying to research them.'

'He said the more he looked, the less he found. They seem to have done a good job of building up an impressive face-value reputation without much on any results to back it up.'

'On the other hand, perhaps if we ask for their help it will put us in good standing if we need more research funds.'

'Aren't you the seasoned researcher and political animal? You might be right however. If only we knew just a bit more about them.'

'Perhaps you can ask your husband to do more digging at his end. SERC seems to have quite a prominent profile in Scotland?'

'I fear he may be too busy making the acquaintance of Hollywood actresses and old school flames, but I can try.'

As Troy showed confusion on his face and clearly wanted to hear more, Nerys thought about herself and her close relationship with her toy-boy scientist. Changed days indeed. Adventures all round. She resolved to phone Calum that night, just to hear his voice for one thing.

The old school-flame had been described by Calum in slightly different terms as a dear old platonic friend from high school days. He was now concluding a very pleasant dinner with her and her husband at their charming home in a divided-into-four house in East Bay, close to Heather's place of work. From the bay window, if you craned your neck, you could see Barclay House, Calum's abode in the West Bay. For some reason, that realisation caused Calum to resolve to acquire a pair of binoculars.

Nicholas Gorman was an archetypal successful lawyer, somewhere in his early seventies, corpulent of girth, and supporting a coiffured mane of silver hair, longer than normal but without a strand out of place. In their short time together, Nicholas had demonstrated to Calum his affability, good hosting skills, and love of good food, fine wine, and finer cigars. And, he liked to talk. It was interesting to see Heather, who had impressed Calum as a very confident and knowledgeable professional play decidedly second fiddle to her spouse. And, their physical comparison could not be greater for Heather was petite, fit, and did not look a lot different from her high school days in Calum's view. Her pretty face always looked inquisitive and interested.

'I find this whole story of you two being school friends just a hoot.'

'It is kind of. There was no-one more surprised than I when I walked into Heather's office. I have been to the island at least five times in her time here but never come across her or you for that matter.'

'And, she tells me you never went out on a date. What were you thinking about man?'

'I know. I know. There always have to be regrets in life. The—if only I had done something—moments. I think I probably held her in too high regard to inflict me on her.'

They all laughed and the station director showed decided signs of a blush. Trying to change the subject, she asked what Nicholas was working on since she last saw him.

'Funny you should ask that. You are going to see more of me in the next little while. I have work to do in Millport. Interesting case. Involves big names. At least my partners are impressed. It could lead to more work.'

Nicholas went on to talk about how he had been engaged by Joel Wannamaker, the new owner of the football team WCI. He started to explain more about Wannamaker but Calum assured him that he was long familiar with the team, without love ever having been established, and the individual, although in reality he knew very little about the latter other than what he had read Neil Christian saying about him and the tenuous connections he had found between him and SERC. Wannamaker had engaged Nicholas to purchase for him the largest house on the market in Millport, an undivided monolith just half a dozen houses removed from the one they were currently sitting in. But, the complication set in after that because Wannamaker wanted to exclude his wife Margaret from ownership. This would involve the creation of a secret trust of some kind that Nicholas had to dream up. If that were successful, Wannamaker wanted more of their assets separated from his wife and placed where he had sole ownership effectively. Apparently from Wannamaker's perspective, the marriage was not over however. It would continue in the meantime because the appearance of an idyllic couple suited both for public relations purposes. But, the marital assets were not to grow; instead they were to transition his way if that could be done secretly and effectively. The first challenge after the house would be the ownership of WCI, then their joint property around the world including several homes in California.

'Surely, they are both rich in their own right and have the ability to separately earn decent money. Why the subterfuge?' asked the accountant.

'The Wannamaker couple is rich, very rich, but most of it comes from Margaret's family and her acting career. My client feels he could not function on his own so he needs to tilt the pile a little his way.'

'Is that legal, dear husband? You need to watch that you don't get into something shady.'

'Thank you, my dear, for your free advice. Anything I design for Mr. Wannamaker will fit snugly within the parameters of the law and will stand up to scrutiny on both sides of the Atlantic.'

'But it will not be in the interests of Margaret Wannamaker, will it?' Calum regretted immediately saying what was a little naive and showed his leanings toward the wife.

'How true. But she is not my client. He is. You know how it works Calum. I am sure you have been in similar situations. After all, an accountant is just a lawyer that knows numbers better than words.'

Calum tried hard not to bristle but as his eyes uncomfortably met Heather's, she jumped in to his defence.

'That was not funny Nicholas. Lawyers and accountants are both supposed to be professionals bound by codes of ethics. I do not like the sound of your engagement with Wannamaker. Please be very careful. I don't suppose Mrs. Wannamaker will take this lying down.'

Nicholas resisted the obvious opportunity to say that by the sound of it there was not too much of that going on right now—hence the marriage gently sliding on to the rocks. Instead, in an utterly patronizing voice, he replied, 'Well said my dear—for a scientist. We professionals all do better when we stick to what we were trained to do. Now, how about another brandy Calum, for the road? I have to get back to Glasgow first thing in the morning.'

Calum, somewhat to his own surprise declined, professing he had a long walk to West Bay and did not want to fall in the harbour on the way. Heather saw him to the door while Nicholas waved and remained seated in his armchair. She whispered to him, 'I would like to talk more about this. I don't like the sound of it. Did you know Joel Wannamaker has some sort of relationship with SERC? Cyrus Macadam mentioned it to me one day. Then he looked like he regretted it immediately.'

'I was aware of it. I came across it when I was researching him in connection with his football team and again when I was researching SERC for Nerys.'

'Let's get together soon.'

'We will make it my place. You haven't been there. I will get in some fish suppers and a bottle of vintage Irn Bru.'

'You were always a flash spender and chick-magnet in high school.'

As Calum wandered around the waterfront toward West Bay he tried to work out what the evening had revealed. It had been a wonderful meal amid good conversation with gracious hosts. He had taken a liking to Nicholas Gorman. That was until the conversation got onto the Wannamaker scam, or trust as it was referred to. He had not revealed that he had met Maggie and that perhaps his concern on her behalf was because he had been quite smitten by her during their too short flight across the Atlantic. It may have also been due to a growing dislike of everything to do with Joel Wannamaker. And the fact that WCI was remotely involved had to bring out a lifelong prejudice that Calum could not deny. More was going to come out of what had been talked about tonight.

The fact that Heather shared his concern brought a smile to Calum. He would have to remember to temper his excitement when talking about this night to Nerys. She had seemed to be missing him a great deal from their last telephone conversation. He would phone her tomorrow because it was much more personal than an email.

Chapter 9

The Dancing Midge Café on the promenade traditionally closed over the winter months when the tourist trade virtually disappeared. It would normally open in late March or early April depending upon the weather. This year, however, late February had brought unseasonably warm and dry weather and the owners had decided to open up early.

On the first morning of their new season, Calum was seated in the café along with several locals. He was enjoying a croissant and espresso, not typical west of Scotland fare and exactly why the café was so popular. He had picked up a copy of the Daily Record that was lying around and was surprised to find it was today's edition. In time honoured fashion, he started at the back on the sports pages and worked his way forward. He had almost finished his breakfast and the paper when a story caught his eye on page 3.

It was reported that a spokesperson for the utility company BritPower, based in Beagg, had expressed concern that the number of solid steel flasks containing the radioactive waste from Farland stored in the tunnel was lower than the paperwork suggested it should be. The Daily Record had picked up the story and sought comment from the utility company person in charge of loading and shipping the flasks at the Farland end. He had, however, referred the matter to the SoCal Environmental Research Corporation and its spokesperson Cyrus Macadam had moved quickly to dispel any rumours.

"It is just in all probability a case of paperwork mix up at Farland. The correct number of flasks left Farland and arrived in Beagg. We know that because no craft has gone missing and no craft has reported the loss of any flasks. In fact, the weather so far has

been most cooperative. There is nothing to worry about. We will ensure that the paperwork is corrected."

A very simple answer thought Calum but is it correct? In spite of the danger associated with the cargo, the shipping of a set number of flasks on each craft and a set number of crafts were relatively simple business transactions and no paperwork error should have occurred. However, paperwork errors often happen for no good reason. It should be possible to confirm the error by estimating the waste still to be moved, adding it to what was in Beagg and comparing it to the original total estimate. That was probably what SERC had done although the story did not say so. It just quoted Macadam. The story concluded with a vague suggestion that all was well but wondered if the various environmental groups would be as satisfied.

Calum walked around to the research station in the hope of discussing the story with Heather Randall. However, he discovered that she was away on business in London so he left a detailed message referring to the Daily Record story and asked her to call him. He suggested that a low key verification of the SERC assurance should be possible by simply visiting the Farland shipping centre and studying their record keeping. That might be something that the research station could be reasonably expected to do and he was willing to make the trip.

Later, he went on the Internet and checked other newspapers, television, and radio. Almost nobody was carrying the story and those that were had basically copied it from the Daily Record. Calum wondered if he was in danger of making something out of nothing or was the SERC reputation such that their reassurance was enough. It certainly underscored the power that they seemed to wield in their oversight role.

That evening Calum was looking forward to dinner at Westview with Scotty Green and Evan Davis. The latter was returning to America in the morning and it would be the last opportunity on this visit to get to know the rock icon and his interesting association with the island. It was doubtful that there would be many if any other guests so they would likely have the dining room to themselves.

Indeed, there was only one table occupied when Calum walked in. However, in addition to the men there was a woman with flaming red hair seated with her back to him. All eyes turned toward Calum.

'Surprise! Bet you didn't expect me to be part of your little men's rock and roll club. How are you Dr. Davies?'

It was Margaret Wannamaker, large as life, who jumped up to give Calum a big hug and bigger kiss.

Once they were all settled down and drinks had been served, Evan explained the surprise guest.

'Maggie and I go way back in LA. When she was just a slip of a lass, she had ambitions in the singing field. I was still leading the Country Rhodes Band and we were getting a bit stale so we thought about bringing in an Emmylou Harris-type to sing harmony vocals with me.'

'I soon found the music scene was not for me.'

'As sweet as she was and still is, Maggie was just not cut out for the honky-tonks. I told her she would make a better actress. Boy, did I get that right!'

'So Evan quietly slipped me out of the band as quickly as he had slipped me in and instead we slipped into bed for a while.'

'And a very good time was had by all I seem to recall.'

'That proved to be the problem. All was not always just the two of us.'

'Well it was the rock and roll era and it couldn't just be all drugs and rock and roll so the sex had to come into it too.'

Any worries Calum had about this past relationship coming back to haunt tonight's dinner quickly dissipated. It was obvious that Evan and Maggie had gone on to become good friends and just that. She explained her arrival in Millport.

'You remember Calum that I was telling you my goofball husband had bought himself a soccer team. Now he feels he needs to handle the stress of not losing his shirt on the team so he wants a little retreat on this quaint island.'

'I had heard that he was buying in the East Bay but I would not exactly describe it as a little retreat.'

Scotty laughed and agreed. 'After this place and the Royal George Hotel, it is probably the largest complete house on the island. Just a little retreat to you Hollywood-types however.'

'We have just about completed the legal work and we will be taking occupancy in the next few weeks.'

Evan stated, 'Well, if you think that qualifies you for membership of our little club, you are going to have to put a proposal to the members.'

'Approved,' said Calum.

'Approved,' said Scotty.

A long and pleasant night of fine dining and equally fine drinking ensued. Evan regaled them with never before reported stories about Dubus and other recording artists getting up to all sorts of high jinks in the quiet seclusion of Millport. The locals seemed to take most of them to their hearts and in turn the rock stars became very comfortable in the isolated environment. Many artists felt they had done some of their best work in the Westview studios because they were away from the pressures and distractions of London or Los Angeles.

It might have been that Millport would have become a haven for the rich and famous because of its association with the rock royalty but that never happened, probably because the islanders chose to treat them as welcome but secret guests. Very often, an album was almost completed before the music press became aware that a band was even recording at Westview.

The only time the island blew its cover was in 1969 when Dubus put on an all-weekend music festival featuring big names in addition to the hosts. That was supposed to be a pastoral postscript to the mega-gatherings of Monterey and Woodstock but it almost got out of hand. Thousands of Brits descended upon the little island and with accommodation of any kind totally exhausted, the ferries had to be stopped thereby preventing any more people making the crossing. It was estimated that almost 50,000 fans made it. It was estimated that almost 150,000 claimed to have made it. The local shopkeepers quickly sold out of everything they had to sell and Dubus had to pay for emergency supplies to be shipped in. The band never made any money on what was intended to be their grand musical statement and thank you to the islanders for their hospitality, in fact they lost a good deal of money. But it was still talked about today in musical circles and in Millport. Not a single arrest was made by Constable Jardin or the other police officers flown in by helicopter as the festival grew and grew. Some folks even believed the fixed smiles on the policemen's faces had been induced by illegal substances but that was the stuff of legend.

'You know I never made that festival even though I was here in Millport so often in the '60s. I was away on an accountancy training course, my very first if I recall correctly. If only the festival had been publicized in advance, I would have skipped the course,' bemoaned Calum.

'If it had been publicized, the island would have sunk. The numbers were amazing without any advanced advertising. Fraser's Bar sold every last drop of alcohol it had by the Saturday night including emptying bottles that had sat half-finished on the gantry for twenty years or more,' Scotty remembered. 'I am not sure if we really believed it was an act of thank you from Dubus. But we forgave you over the years.'

As the night wore on, Calum noticed that Maggie was dropping out of the conversation.

'Tired, are you?'

'Just a tad. I also have lots of things on my mind.'

'Need a sympathetic ear to hear them?'

'As a matter of fact, that would be just ideal. Are you around tomorrow?'

'At your service. Do you cycle? A little jaunt around the island while we chat and an ice cream at the Ritz Café at the end of it does wonders for things on one's mind.'

The smile confirmed acceptance and they made arrangements to meet the next day at the bike rental shop.

As Calum wandered back to Barclay House he noticed a message on his mobile. Heather Randall was trying to get in touch from London. She had heard about the story and had reached a sceptical conclusion just as he had. She agreed that it might be a good idea for him to visit Farland on behalf of the research station. It was well within their contractual mandate and the inquiry could rightfully be undertaken by an accountant rather than a scientist. She would be in touch tomorrow to settle arrangements.

Chapter 10

When Maggie Wannamaker showed up next morning she was definitely showing signs of wear. Her Hollywood beauty was still there but too many drinks the previous night had taken their toll. Calum could not remember her being anything near drunk when he took his leave of her and the others had already retired for the night. He could only assume that she had continued to imbibe on her own. She obviously was troubled by something heavy. Yet as they cycled at a leisurely pace around the quiet perimeter road of Great Cumbrae, she seemed reluctant to open up about what was troubling her.

Calum tried to cheer her by regaling her with tales of his childhood memories of the island. What seemed like amusing incidents to him had little effect on her. He tried to get her to share some Hollywood tales but they were delivered half-heartedly. It was only when they had almost reached the north end of the island that she suddenly pulled up.

'Can we stop here?'

'Perfect. It just so happens that beyond those bushes is one of a number of hidden coves with their own little private beaches. Let's go sit there.'

'You seem to know everything about this place.'

'Well I have been coming here all my life. I know most of the secrets but not all of them. Scotty Green does seem to know them all, however. Did you notice last night that he knew more than Evan and I combined?'

They left their bikes by the side of the road and battled through the overgrown bushes with Calum bravely taking the lead. On emerging, Maggie was stunned by the beauty of the little private beached cove. She immediately flopped down on the sand and started to cry.

'My favourite beach is not supposed to have that effect on you. Why don't you tell me what's bothering you?'

After a long spell of simply looking out to sea, she turned to him and unloaded.

'When I met you on the plane I was complaining about coming to this cold miserable country to see a soccer team. The only thing that was keeping me going was the thought of seeing Joel. I now realize I had that all wrong.'

'How so?'

'Well, first I have grown to love your cold miserable country and especially your little island. But, I also realize that I am growing to loathe every day with Joel. Whatever there was between us seems to matter nothing now. All he seems bothered about is getting his finances into better shape. And I say his finances because that is all he talks about now—him and his finances. I don't think I even trust him anymore. He didn't bring me here because he wanted us to be together. He brought me here to get me away from our business and legal advisors in California, to control me, and……'

She dissolved into further tears that prevented her saying anything more. Calum held her and let her sob until soothing words and a hand running through her red hair calmed her down.

'I am not sure that he does not want to get rid of me. We have never ever talked of divorce. We have never even discussed if we have a problem in our marriage. He just seems to have gone totally off me. Now it is all about his business.'

Calum struggled for the right words.

'I am sorry to hear that. You deserve better. Is there someone you both know that could act as a kind of mediator to at least let get the two of you talking about your marriage?'

'Not here, there isn't.'

'How about just getting on a plane back to California? That would at least create some space and time. He is surely not going to dedicate his whole life to WCI. He will come home at least at the end of the season in May.'

'I don't trust him to just leave him alone here. The things he is talking about needing money for mean we will have to dip pretty heavily into our investments and even my trust funds that my parents gave me. I have always thought about those funds as ours but now I get the sense that he sees them as his and I just need to sign some papers.'

'You definitely need your financial advisor to step in.'

'He is Joel's golf partner back home. I don't know that I even trust him.'

Just as Calum was feeling out of his depth and unable to come up with any words of wisdom he sensed that they had got closer and closer and were now holding each other very tightly.

'Thank you for being a friend Calum. I feel very lonely here apart from when I am with you.'

'I will help in any way I can,' he replied without knowing what that meant.

They were now lying tightly together and nothing was more was said for a few minutes. Then Maggie ran a hand down Calum's face and smiled at him with eyes glistening from tears.

'Can I stay with you for a couple of days? The big house is not yet ready and I am supposed to be staying at Westview until he comes down on the weekend. Scotty is sweet but the hotel is empty now that Evan is off today. It feels too much like a haunted house. Can I?'

Calum tensed. He was tempted to say yes. But that was not going to be fair to Nerys, whether she learned about it or not. He did not know what he was going to say but words came out anyway.

'Of course you can. No problem. However, do you want to risk Joel finding out at this delicate stage?'

She appeared not to notice the hesitation on Calum's part and instead launched into reservations about the big house.

'I don't even know if buying this house is the right thing to do. He says that we will have to put it into a special Scottish trust to avoid double taxation. He will have to be the sole trustee because he will be here for more than six months in a year. I will not qualify because I will not be here long enough. Yet it is my money that we are going to have to use.'

'That does not sound exactly right.'

'Well that's what he and his fat Scottish attorney Gorman tell me. They seem to be in cahoots. Joel knows nothing about English law and I know even less. We seem to be in the hands of Nicholas Gorman.'

'Actually it is Scots Law and it is different from English Law and American Law for that matter.'

'That does not make me any more confident that our finances are secure.'

'How does Joel make his money?'

'He puts money into environmental projects and gets a return once the projects are sponsored by governments and agencies. He is kind of like a special bank for environmental projects and we live off the spread in the loans he makes. It is all a bit weird because as far I can tell he cares shit about the environment. But where he makes most of his money is through SERC. He is a silent partner in SERC which is sort of owned by a university back home. He puts money into SERC and they raise enormous funds around the world. Then he gets more than his money back. SERC seems real busy, even here in Scotland, but he complains that he is not making enough out of it. That's why we need to tap into our investments and my trust funds.

Calum's gut ached with what he was hearing and what he knew from the conversation with Nicholas Gorman. What should he do? If he warned Maggie what Nicholas was hatching on behalf of Joel, what would that do to Heather? She didn't like the course of action Nicholas was charting but he was after all her husband and she would feel obligated to stand behind him. And, where would that leave Calum as the one who spilled the beans? Yet, he so much wanted to help Maggie.

He thought back to Nicholas's rationalization of his plans saying that Joel was his client and the one he owed loyalty to, not Maggie. Yet Calum was no longer in business. He did not have a client. He owed loyalty to no-one. He just wanted to do the right thing. But siding with one woman potentially hurt the other and vice versa. Fuck! Eight weeks ago neither was in his life. Now they were pulling him to pieces.

Maggie shook him from his almost comatose state.

'I was wrong to ask you to take me in. That would lead to trouble for me and most likely trouble for you too. Will you just be my friend and advise me as much as you can?'

Calum's sense of relief made his legs shaky as they made their way back to the road and their bicycles. The circumnavigation of the island was completed with very little conversation. However, having returned the bikes to the rental shop and retired to the Ritz Café for the promised ice cream, they sat with heads close together and hands touching. They could both feel a growing attraction for the other; born out of the tension that each was feeling toward Joel Wannamaker. Suddenly, Maggie blurted out, 'Thank you,' took Calum's face in her hands and gave him a deep lingering kiss. Unable to resist, Calum responded with no thought for the witnesses, few as they were, around the café. It would be around Millport in no time—'Did you hear about the Yank and yon actress melting their ice creams in the Ritz?'

Maggie decided she needed to go back to Westview to rest up. Calum was more than a little relieved to get her out of the café and to walk her back. Nothing much was said on the way. It was obvious Maggie was going through emotional ups and downs beyond her control. As she silently entered the hotel without saying goodbye, Calum glanced toward the dining room window and saw Scotty staring at him with all-knowing-eyes. Christ he thought, he knows and it only happened twenty minutes ago. Other than a quick wave, Calum was quite content to turn about and set off back to Barclay House.

It had only passed noon but Calum had made up his mind to call Nerys. That meant she was awakened at 4 am.

'What's up? What has happened?'

'Nothing, love. I just wanted to hear your voice.'

'It is not usually at its best at four in the morning.'

'It still sounds pretty good to me.'

Calum knew he had just lurched into the call without thinking and now he was unsure what to be talking about. He told her about the latest Farland news and that he would be going over to the mainland to check it out. That caused her some concern because she knew that SERC was there in the background and SERC had extracted a promise from her not to do research in Scotland. Did that extend to her husband? They talked about it for quite some time and decided he should proceed carefully. There was no reason to ruffle feathers for no good reason.

He also told her about the previous night with Evan and Scotty; he left out Maggie. She noted that he seemed to be in his element reliving his formative years in the company of the rock and roll star. He agreed and said that if he ever thought about writing a book he now had a wealth of material that had never been published before.

She brought him up to date on the plans to travel to China and India. She had been successful in getting meetings and visits set up in both countries and she planned to travel with Troy Cameron in four weeks' time. Calum could not help but wince at that news. And yet, he started to think about what he had been up to over the last few days and wondered how Nerys would be with that. Nerys realized she was talking and he was not listening.

'Are you OK with that?'

'Huh? Of course I am. I support your plans wholeheartedly.'

'You don't have a problem with Troy accompanying me?'

'Are you asking if I trust you? If you are, of course I do. Just as I know you trust me in this little hotspot of Millport.'

It was probably just as well that they moved on to other topics as Nerys brought him up to date on California and local matters. One of Calum's old colleagues who had chosen to throw in his lot in with the new university president after distancing himself for the old one had been let go by the new president. Calum stated that he did not miss that kind of crap one little bit. He realized there was more to life than the unhealthy campus environment. He was always inclined to quote Henry Kissinger's comment about the futility of educational politics but he could never remember the exact words. They would come back to him some time.

Finally, later in the day a call was placed to Heather in London and they discussed at length the impending visit by Calum to Farland Power Station. She had made arrangements with the senior utility company employee whose responsibility it was to supervise the loading and shipping of the solid steel flasks containing the radioactive waste. Heather had always got on well with him and he seemed quite willing to give time to a visit from Calum.

He thought seriously about telling Heather what was happening to Maggie Wannamaker but in the end he kept quiet for fear that it would put her in an untenable position. They resolved to have that fish and chip dinner soon after he got back to the island from Farland.

Chapter 11

Calum learned later from Scotty Green that Maggie Wannamaker had remained at Westview for a couple of days before she headed back presumably to Glasgow. During that time she never left her room, even taking all her meals there. Mind you she did not do justice to any of the meals and never touched a drop of alcohol.

'I hope you were not involved in her appearing downright unhappy, Calum. That does not fit with the happy island image we are trying to instill here.'

'No. I don't think I made her unhappy. In fact I tried to cheer her up but I don't think I did very well at that either.'

'Did that take place in the Ritz then?'

'No. That was just something that happened. I think she was feeling very emotional and I happened to be there. I suspect what is bothering her resides at home.'

'Well I hope it does not cause them to change their minds about buying the big house,' came the reply from the uncrowned King of the Cumbraes with thoughts of economic development forever uppermost in his mind.

The rest of their coffee time in the Garrison House Café was spent chatting about the progress being made on the museum project and the prospect of a new exhibition to be launched in time for the holiday season in July. One of the great advantages for the museum was being located in the Garrison House. With an historic past as the principal private house on the island, it had later been transferred to public use. Then disaster struck. A devastating fire in the early years of the new century all but destroyed the signature building. It was touch and go as to whether it would be restored or the remaining shell simply pulled down. Eventually it was saved through the tremendous fund raising efforts of the Cumbraes Council, led by Scotty, and a non-profit organization set up for that specific purpose. Several governmental grants were procured and over a two year period the fine old building was restored to its past glory. In fact, many people believed the semi-open plan design of the ground floor greatly improved the original layout. The restoration project was recognized through several awards and the Garrison House returned as the jewel in the Millport crown. The museum now enjoyed not only its own dedicated, if a little small, space for storage and display but also the ability to mount exhibitions in the large open plan area. Calum and Scotty looked forward with relish to making full use of all the space available.

In preparation for his visit to Farland, Calum went on several bracing walks around Great Cumbrae while he put his mind to what he was going to say and do. The chap he was going to meet was apparently cooperative and he had to find a way of establishing a relationship, like he was a colleague and not an inspector, or worse still an auditor. He had had plenty of that in his younger days. He remembered causing abject fear in the junior accounting clerks upon the announcement that the auditors had arrived. At first he quite enjoyed the power of the position but it soon wore off him. Alas, it did not for some of colleagues who enjoyed the notoriety of the auditor for their whole careers. The island was a great place on which to walk and think and Calum seemed to have a lot to think about. Only three months ago his only thought was deciding at which point he would stop reading on the Internet and start drinking wine each day. Now, he was feeling healthier and fitter and his mind was being challenged in several different ways.

The Farland Power Station was about ten miles south of Largs which was where the Cumbrae ferry was based. Calum's determination to do without a car was no problem on the island but presented a bit of a challenge when going to the mainland. He figured bus to the island terminal, ferry to Largs, and bus from Largs to Ayr which seemed to pass close by to the power station would work. There was nothing else at Farland other than the power station so the workers must have driven there from their homes in other towns or caught the bus. Buses ran every three hours so that would allow him ample time to do his thing before repeating the journey in reverse.

It was with a little bit of excitement and a welcome sense of purpose that he set out on his assignment. Heather would be back the next day and he was hoping that he would have good news or at least some news for her. The journey went exactly as planned and he was deposited at a bus stop in the middle of nowhere but with the imposing structures of the power station looming ominously about a mile down a special road constructed solely for access.

As he walked up to the gates, he could not get over the sense of silence and emptiness. All that remained of what was probably a noisy thriving operation at its peak were the empty shells of buildings and two curious concrete semi-globes which presumably housed the reactors. God they look like a pair of boobs he thought as a guard stepped out of the hut and gave a none-too-friendly greeting.

'Aye. Can I help you?'

'Good Morning. Am I your first visitor of the day?'

'You are the first visitor of the year. I take it you are Davies?'

'That I am. Dr. Davies here to see Mr. Wilson.'

'I'll take you up to Wilson's office.'

After unlocking the gate, ushering Calum through it, then locking it again, the guard walked him about the complex. There were precious few workers around and the place had the feel of a ghost town. Rounding the corner of a building they came upon an enclosure with a high fence that contained the obvious solid steel flasks. Narrow rail tracks ran through the enclosure and out down to a wharf about a hundred yards away at the edge of the ocean.

'This must be where the waste is packed up,' said Calum just to make conversation.

'Hmm.'

'Do you have anything to do with that?'

'No chance. I just guard the gate, walk the fence twice a day and go home. I don't know what those buggers are up to and don't want to know.'

The guard deposited Calum in an outer office and said, 'Jenny here will look after you.'

'Are you Mr. Davies?'

'Yes. I am here to see Mr. Wilson.'

'He's no' here.'

'Do you know when he will be back, Jenny?'

'He never telt' me.'

'Should I just take a seat and wait for him? Is there any way you can contact him?'

'No.'

'I'll just sit down then.'

'Suit yersel',' came the response coated in equal measures of apathy and hostility.

Calum sat for almost half an hour that felt like two hours. He could not help noticing that Jenny seemed to have very little work to do and every few minutes would glance at the front door then the other door in the office which presumably led through to Wilson's office.

'Are you sure there is no way you can contact Mr. Wilson?'

'Aye.'

Just when Calum was trying to decide what to do next the front door burst open and a tall blond man strode through the office, opened the other door and disappeared into the adjoining office without a word to either the staff person or the visitor.

'Mr. Wilson I presume,' was met with no response from Jenny. However, strangely enough raised voices could be heard behind the inner door. Then the door slowly re-opened and a small man walked pointedly toward and through the outer door, stopping only to say to Jenny that he was going out.

'Mr. Wilson perhaps?'

No response came from .Jenny but a voice from within growled, 'Send him in,' and she sheepishly simply pointed to the inner door.

Calum was met by the tall stranger sitting casually on top of the desk. He was dressed quite formally in a business suit, shirt and tie. But, there was something menacing about his look. This was a not a gentleman you would want to get on the wrong side of. He had the appearance of a Chicago mobster.

'You must be Mr. Interfering Davies,' was the greeting delivered in a North American accent.

'Actually Dr. Interfering Davies and you would not be Mr. Wilson?'

'I am Cyrus Macadam from the SoCal Environmental Research Corporation.'

'My appointment was with Mr. Wilson.'

'He is far too busy to waste his time on your interfering. Why are you even wasting my time when SERC has already dealt with that matter dragged up by the Daily Record?'

'I am here on behalf of the Cumbraes Environmental Research Station.'

'Has the station got time to waste duplicating the efforts of SERC?'

'It is not a matter of duplication. The two organizations are basically partners in quality and safety assurance. We just need to be sure that everything is OK. Any statement, even a rumour, from the Beagg end that flasks containing radioactive waste might be missing is serious and needs to be treated seriously.'

'Thanks for the lecture. What is it that you intended to do here?'

'My intention was to have Mr. Wilson describe the procedures for filling and loading the flasks on to the container crafts and then to do some spot checking of the paperwork associated with the shipping. It amounts to a pretty standard audit approach. It would give the station comfort which could then be relayed to the governments and utility company. Hopefully, I would be able to back up what you were quoted as saying in the Record.'

'So you are an auditor now?'

'I was and I still know the procedures.'

Macadam got up and moved around the desk to sit in the big leather chair thereby signalling if it was not already obvious who was in charge of this conversation.

'Here is what I am prepared to do and then I want you to get your ass out of here. I will describe the procedures to you but checking of any paperwork is off limits.'

'What do you have against me taking a look at the paperwork?'

'The alternative to what I offered is calling security right now and have you slung out of here in two minutes flat.'

The two stared at each other for what felt like a long time then Calum nodded. Macadam motioned for him to sit down and then over the next fifteen minutes he described pretty routine procedures for the filling of each solid steel flask with hollow metal rods that held ceramic pellets containing the spent plutonium, the completion of the accompanying paperwork, storage of the flask within the secure compound, then transfer of both flask and paperwork to a container craft.

'So you see, unless a craft is lost at sea, and that has not happened, it is well nigh impossible for flasks to go missing. The so-called discrepancy was simply in the paperwork. Human error. One of Wilson's guys screwed up. He has been fired. End of story.'

Calum could not find any fault with the procedures as they had been described to him. They were straight forward and obvious. He also knew that a lack of match between physical evidence, i.e. flasks, and paperwork could very often be down to paperwork error. He tried to prolong the conversation.

'Sounds OK. And, you are definitely satisfied that no actual flasks are unaccounted for? I don't suppose you want missing flasks any more than more than we do.'

'What the fuck are you trying to insinuate?'

'Calm down. I am not trying to insinuate anything.'

'Then, unless you have any sensible questions, this meeting is over.'

Before Calum had a chance to say anything more Macadam shouted to Jenny to call the guard to escort Mr. Davies off the premises.

As they stood by the opened outer door waiting for the guard, Macadam extended a hand to Calum.

'I hope we can count on continued cooperation from the research station as a result of your visit. Cooperation with SERC is important to show the public that the project is proceeding just as it should be. I hope we can count on your cooperation too. Talk to your wife. She is a good example of someone cooperating!'

Chapter 12

Calum found himself back at the bus stop. The problem was his truncated visit had not gone as planned over three hours and now he had the best part of two hours to wait for the returning bus. There seemed to be no alternative to waiting other than going back to Cyrus Macadam and asking him for a lift into Largs. And, that was no alternative.

What an objectionable guy. He had basically destroyed Calum's whole plan of approach with unbridled aggression. And where did he get off bringing Nerys into it? Was that some sort of threat or just a cheap shot? Either way, he did not like it.

After about an hour with the light fading fast, a car pulled up just beyond where Calum was standing. There had been precious little traffic in the time he had been waiting. The driver had wound down his window and obviously intended that Calum approach the car. It was likely that the driver needed directions and maybe even possible that he intended to offer him a lift.

As Calum stooped to address the driver, the door was suddenly swung open violently, smacking him in the face and knocking him to the ground. Two other doors immediately opened and three men in dark clothing got out quickly. All Calum could remember after that was them setting about him and taking turns to punch and kick him. He must have lost consciousness quickly after the first wave of blows.

Sometime later, he had no idea how long he been out, he began to come around. However the massive traumas to his body rendered him incapable of getting up so he was forced to just lie by the edge of the road where he had been knocked down. Fortunately, he was probably in little danger of being actually run over by a vehicle but he was dependent upon someone both seeing him and being prepared to stop. After three vehicles simply sped by, he despaired of ever being helped. He tried to roll over in order to make himself more visible but the pain precluded any movement at all.

As the trauma, assisted by the chill of the now full darkness of the evening, caused his body temperature to plummet, he was on the verge of losing consciousness again when the bus finally arrived and stopped to allow a passenger to dismount. The passenger, who proved to be the power station guard arriving for the next shift, immediately spotted the prostrate body and alerted the driver before he had time to take off.

The driver and guard, assisted by the only other two passengers, did what they could to make Calum comfortable while they awaited the police and ambulance from Largs, having been summoned by mobile phone. Several layers of coats and jackets were piled on top of him to try to stop his temperature loss. After what seemed like an age, it was probably only twenty minutes, the emergency services arrived and prepared to transfer him to hospital. Given his state of shock, minimal enquiries were made at the scene as to what had happened and the patient was only able to mutter "mugged" before drifting out again.

When Calum awoke later that night he found he was in the Brooksby Hospital. A doctor informed him that while he had suffered a severe beating, amazingly nothing was broken. However, he had suffered numerous cuts which had since been stitched up and multiple contusions for which unfortunately there was no real remedy other than time needed to heal of their own accord. The pain, which was considerable and likely to remain so for at least seventy-two hours, could be managed with fairly strong medication. That accounted for Calum's dreamy state. The doctor informed him of his wish to keep Calum in hospital under observation for the first twenty-four hours. If there was no relapse or adverse reaction to the medication, he could look forward to being released late tomorrow afternoon. With that, the doctor permitted a young police constable to come into the room to obtain a statement.

Calum's recall was quite good, all things considered, and he could now remember the car stopping, he did not recall any conversation taking place, and he had some memory of the beating from the three men before he had obviously passed out. He remembered a dark blue, possibly Japanese car and three individuals each dressed in dark clothing, possibly jeans and hoodies. He also relayed how he came to be at the bus stop and the nature of his visit to Farland Power Station. When asked if he had any idea why he been attacked, he recalled to himself the unsatisfactory nature of his meeting with Macadam but was not prepared to suggest that the attack was connected with it. With no reason forthcoming, the police officer professed that they were at a loss too because there did not seem to be a motive of robbery. Calum's wallet and mobile phone were still in his pockets although the latter had been damaged. As he was unable to add any more to the statement, the interview concluded and the police officer gave a standard undertaking that enquiries would continue but in the absence of witnesses the likelihood of arrests was not strong. There had been no similar attacks reported in the area. Perhaps Calum was just in the wrong place at the wrong time. With that, the officer left after making sure he knew where Calum would be going after he was released. He stated that he would pass on some information to his good friend Constable Jardin in Millport.

Calum spent a restless night punctuated with spells of medically induced deep sleep and periods where he suddenly awoke in a cold sweat in full belief that he was currently receiving a beating. However, more medication and some soft foods and liquids during the day caused him to improve sufficiently that when the same doctor did his rounds in the afternoon, he was confirmed for release on condition he went straight back to the island and took it easy for a few days. When asked if there was someone to keep an eye on him, he was sharp enough to lie in the affirmative lest it be made a condition of his release.

Before leaving the hospital, Calum borrowed the mobile phone of a friendly nurse in order to text Heather Randall. He had just remembered that tonight was their dinner date for fish and chips and Irn Bru at his place. The thought of such a repast made him feel instantly queasy, even if his mouth had been able to accept the grease and fizz. He messaged—*"need to cancel our date; will call in at your place to explain."*

Public health cuts precluded a lift to the ferry terminal so Calum was required to travel by taxi. Then he had to wait for a ferry which was still on the less frequent winter schedule. Consequently, by the time he alighted from the island bus just outside Heather's house it was well into the evening.

'Oh my God. What happened to you?'

'Don't worry. They told me my good looks will be unaffected. Let me in and I will tell you what happened.'

Later seated and drinking ginger ale through a straw, having declined an awfully tempting scotch, he told the story from start to finish. She was visibly shaken and immediately connected the attack with the meeting.

'Obviously, Macadam did not think his boorish behaviour was enough to scare you off. He must have arranged in advance to have those thugs attack you afterward.'

'I know it is easy to reach that conclusion but I don't think there is any way to prove it without witnesses. As the police said conveniently—wrong place at the wrong time.'

'Where do we go from here? I feel so responsible.'

'I think we need to focus on what can get out of the meeting with Macadam, such as it was. Obviously, he has a lot of power over Wilson. He was able to dismiss him thereby preventing me from meeting with him. On the other hand, Wilson looked quite content to be out of it. They must be in cahoots. So much for SERC's independence and objectivity!'

'But how can we prove that? It would be a pretty serious charge to take to the Scottish or UK government. There could be legal ramifications for the research station.'

'Agreed. In any case, other than interpreting the rudeness and refusal to fully cooperate as some sort of indication of guilt, I did not succeed in proving anything against SERC. The procedures being followed by the power station staff were pretty much as I would have expected. Perhaps, it really was just a paperwork error. Apparently, someone was fired over it.'

'Do you think we should just continue to keep an eye on things and chalk the attack up to being an unfortunate coincidence?'

'That is what I am thinking. I would dearly love to make somebody pay royally for my aching body but I don't see it happening.'

Heather insisted that Calum stay the night at her place, In less than fifteen minutes, he was tucked up in a warm bed in one of the spare rooms with the eminent scientist exhibiting hitherto undemonstrated nursing skills.

As she turned out the light, she resolved that she would handle Nicholas's impending arrival tomorrow when it happened.

Chapter 13

Gradually Calum emerged from a deep sleep. His mind became alert, somewhat, but his eyes were still shut. He tried to place where he was. The whole Farland incident played back in his mind up to the point of the attack and thereafter from his time in a hospital. Largs it was. Then he had gone to Heather Randall's. He must still be at her place.

Calum now fully awake wanted to know how he looked and was it as bad as he felt. He was told that those two probably coincided exactly. He needed rest and Heather was insisting that he remain where he was for a couple of days. She would have to go to work but she would always be just ten minutes away if he needed anything.

'What will your husband make of you playing nurse?'

'I was preparing for that but I just got good news and bad news in a text from him a few minutes ago. He was supposed to be coming down from Glasgow this morning. The good news is he is not coming down now until Monday. The bad news is he is bringing down the Wannamakers with him. They take possession of their house on Monday.'

'You did not really answer my question.'

'Nicholas knows me to be a caring person first and foremost. That I would take in an injured friend, especially where I had a hand in leading to his injuries, would neither surprise nor upset him,' she said with a definite air of virtue and her fingers crossed tightly.

Thus, Calum began his recuperation. With a reduced intake of painkillers, he was beginning to feel better. He spent most of that day in bed gazing out of the window at the stunning view of Wee

Cumbrae and Arran behind it. The sky was blue and the sun shone brightly disguising a cold Scottish day.

When Heather looked in to see how he was, he asked to borrow her iPhone as his own was beyond use and would have to be replaced. He typed a long message to Nerys which contained an edited version of all the events as he remembered them. His growing feeling of *"mizpah"* toward her had caused him to resolve to be fully open about how Heather had taken him in and was continuing to nurse him back to health. He felt good about the message but knew that it was likely that Heather would see the reply; at least the beginning of it, for it would come through on her iPhone. Oh well, let the chips fall where they may.

It was quite late when Calum next saw Heather. She had stayed later than usual for a meeting of the Cumbraes Council taking place at the research station to discuss joint initiatives for the upcoming holiday season. Heather had not intended to say anything about Calum's misfortune or his present location but Constable Jardin had the news from the mainland and soon imparted it all to those present. She felt obligated to provide an update to the police officer's report. As a result, Calum could expect visits tomorrow from at least Constable Jardin and Scotty Green if not others. She reported that initial reaction to her taking him in had been received with relief and thanks amid mutterings of "good idea". The gossip would probably emerge later on throughout an island notorious for widespread comment on things that happened and even things that only might have happened.

Calum expressed his concern that maybe he should try to get back to his own place in order to preserve Heather's reputation but she would hear none of it and insisted he stay the two more days until Sunday.

'OK You are very kind.'

'Wasn't I always?'

'That you were. Did you by chance happen to get a reply from my wife to the message I sent on your phone?'

'Oh my God, with all the excitement I clean forgot.'

She produced the phone after much fumbling in a large bag and handed it to him with a pious look on her face.

With some trepidation, he opened up the message and read a long response from Nerys. With a mixture of concern for his plight and thankfulness for the care he was receiving, she was asking whether she should fly over if she could get a substitute to teach her classes. And, she was asking for her deepest thanks to be passed on to Heather with the hope that they would meet soon.

'Did you read this?'

'No! Well just the first two lines. You can't help do that because they show up when you get alerted to the arrival of the message. She seems nice.'

'Read it all,' he said handing her phone.

'Wow. You have a pretty amazing wife.'

'Indeed I do.'

Next day Calum was able to get up and move around without too much difficulty. He used Heather's desktop computer to email Nerys. He gave her more details of what had happened and even some predictions on what might happen next, but in truth the future was decidedly unclear to him. He assured her that his recovery was well under way and that there was no necessity for her to upset her students' learning schedule by taking time off to come over to Millport. He would look forward to her coming during the summer break in classes if she could fit it in with her research travels. In spite of all that had gone down, he felt his email was upbeat and that the decision to come over from California still had been a good one for him. He expected that Nerys was feeling the same in regard to what she was achieving back home. This had certainly been a change of pace for both them but not unwelcome.

Scotty and Harry dropped by together. Both were very keen to hear Calum's take on things first hand to add what they knew from the Largs police and Heather. Calum tried to play down the original purpose in visiting the power station in case it started a new rumour. He characterized it as simply helping out the research station in its liaison with SERC. By omitting the capricious nature of the reception from Cyrus Macadam, he succeeded in heading the two men off the possible conclusion that the attack was connected to the visit. Instead they were left to speculate on what appeared to be a random act.

Scotty was moved to opine, 'Damned hooligans, we need to keep their likes off the island.' Calum smiled to himself—always a consistent message, "Millport comes first".

Harry did not improve the quality of the discussion by noting, 'It is not as if you are an obvious American and as such likely subject to attack.'

'I would hope that no American would be subject to an attack just for being an American. Well I should qualify that. There is one or two who might be at risk. And, there is another couple that I might wish an attack on.' They all laughed.

Chat turned to Millport matters and the upcoming holiday season. Calum confirmed his intent to be around for most of the time, at least until fall. He might manage a trip back to California but it would depend on whether his wife could make it over here. They talked about him continuing his museum project with a view to mounting a completely new exhibit over the season. In addition, there would be summer activities like charity cycle rides round the island, sailing regattas, and a big summer fair which all required a lot of local volunteer help. As he was now an honorary local, Calum would be welcomed to get involved and agreed to whilst chuckling when recalling his conversation back in December with Nerys when he pooh-poohed the idea of volunteerism.

Calum returned to Barclay House on the Sunday after thanking Heather profusely. He was pleased to hear her report that she had talked on the phone to Nicholas about her guest and he had been fully in agreement with the arrangement.

'Perhaps our guilty consciences caused us to doubt the likely response of our spouses,' she suggested.

'The trouble is we had no need to have guilty consciences.'

'I will still hold you to the fish suppers and Irn Bru when you feel fully recovered.'

'You bet.'

The following day, Calum got back into a routine. He had spent most of the morning at the museum and was now feeling famished. As a little treat to himself, he decided to lunch at Minstrels, touted as the best restaurant on the island, which had also just reopened after a winter break. He enjoyed a fine lunch at a little table in the corner of the bar at the back of the restaurant, made all the more pleasant by being joined by the owner for a complimentary glass of wine. Calum had made her acquaintance on previous visits when she always seemed to be saying she was on the verge of selling up and he would try to talk her out of it. She always professed that their conversations brought a change in her thinking and new enthusiasm for the not easy task of making a living in a limited market of a very seasonal nature. The latest talk centred on the usual topic of maybe selling up after Calum had, upon request, briefly explained away both the Ritz incident and Farland incident. God he thought, how things get around this island quickly.

'You are becoming a bit of a celebrity.'

'That is the last thing I want to be.'

'Och, you know nothing much ever happens here. And, when it does everybody likes to know about it and gossip about it. Somebody else will soon take over the front page, so to speak, and you will be able to relax.'

Calum made a mental note to check the combined local Largs and Millport newspaper to make sure he was not on the front page. To hope that the Farland incident was nowhere in the paper was probably too much to hope for.

A good lunch and good *craic*, as the Irish called it, were definitely assisting the healing process thought Calum as he passed through the restaurant on his way out. He was not paying attention to a threesome in the corner when he was suddenly hailed.

Nicholas Gorman's voice boomed over the restaurant, 'Hey Davies. Over here. Come and meet two new clients and friends. Let me introduce Joel Wannamaker and his wife Margaret. Joel is the reputed saviour of Scottish football among many other things and Maggie is the pride of Hollywood.'

Calum shook hands with Maggie and said, 'Hello again.' He explained to the others that they had met on the plane coming over. Her response was muted to say the least. He then shook hands with Joel who had risen to meet him eye-to-eye.

'Holy Shit what happened to you? You look like you had an argument with a door. Was it a door you should not have been nosing behind? Or was it an irate husband repaying you for nosing around somewhere else?'

'Pleased to meet you too I am sure.'

An awkward silence followed until Nicholas got into the act, "Do you want to join us Davies? Your nurse will be along in a few minutes. You might need your dressings changed.'

Calum, who was not usually stuck in this position, was at a loss as to how to come back with some witty response to diffuse the situation so he just mumbled about some other time and he had things to do. Without even saying the obvious good to meet you to the Wannamakers, he made a fast exit. He could detect at least two separate laughters as he moved out of earshot.

Calum strode up Cardiff Street. Twenty one paces took him into Fraser's Bar and almost immediately he was seated at the bar caressing a double Glenfiddich. The stress caused by the restaurant encounter brought on a need for several more scotches which, together with even the reduced dosage of painkillers, soon had him feeling no pain, in fact feeling not very much of anything.

Largely ignored by a bartender who was not unaccustomed to the practice of drinking into oblivion, he might have nodded off to sleep as his head rested on his arms which rested on the bar, had it not been for the arrival of a local dressed in oilskin jacket and trousers.

'Pint of the foaming ale if you please Robert.'

'Coming up. Give that guy beside you a nudge before he passes out.'

The newcomer gave Calum a shake and they proceeded to converse within the limitations of Calum's current ability.

'Ah. You are the Yank.'

'Kind of. Calum Davies. I am actually Scottish and more Canadian than American but I answer to anything.'

'As long as you talk funny you are likely to be taken for a Yank around here.'

'What about the English? They talk funny. Do they get taken for Yanks too?'

'The English are the English. And they don't get taken for anything. Other than thinking they are our lords and masters.'

'Ouch. I hit a raw nerve.'

'When you meet as many as I do, you form an opinion. And that opinion is not a very high one.'

'I feel like I have seen you someplace. What's your name anyway?'

'Jimmie Morrison and you seen me at the research station. I look after the station's fleet of boats.'

'That would be it. What do you do with the boats?'

'I mainly take groups of students on field trips. Funny name field trips on the water, no field involved. That is where I am exposed to the snooty little upstarts from England.'

'I see.'

'I also take boats out masel' and collect samples from all around here.'

'Sounds like an interesting job.'

'It is. The best part is that I get to fit in a fair bit of fishing while I am out on my own. Nobody there to check up on me ye ken. Your pal Dr. Randall chooses to turn a blind eye so that makes her my pal too.'

Calum's increasingly foggy cognition concluded that must make them pals as well. He went on to recall his unhappy lifetime relationship with fishing. He was not a keen fisherman, in fact he had only fished a couple of dozen times in his entire life. He had fished the ocean, stream, and lake from the bank and from a boat and in all that time he had never caught a single fish.

'Och, well. We will have to remedy that.'

'Are you going to take me out then?'

'Nae bother. We will wait for the right opportunity.'

'Sounds like another adventure.'

'I widnae go that far. In the meantime, how about I give you a lift home? You look like you could benefit from a little lie down.'

'I only live 200 yards away.'

'That could take you the rest of the day to negotiate.'

And so Calum was ferried home by his new found pal.

Chapter 14

Nerys called Calum for the first time on his new mobile phone. It was a disposable model with a local number which he had surprisingly been able to obtain in Millport. Although the type of phone was normally associated with criminals because the calls could not be traced, it would serve him just fine until he could get a replacement iPhone from his California carrier. He still had his iPad which was fine for emails and text messages too so he was fully covered for communications although his new number was only known to those he had chosen to email with the information. Consequently, he should be spared expensive crank calls or sales calls.

She brought him up to date on things happening on campus. Plans for the visit to China and India were finalized. A fair bit of interest had been generated by the subject matter. The US State Department had not been asked for their help but had found out about it from some unknown source. They were interested in her findings. Her response that they would have to buy the book had not gone down particularly well. They meant they would like advance notice of all findings. And, if need be that could be arranged with the president of the California University so her cooperation was going to happen on a voluntary basis, or not. Nerys expressed concern to Calum that she wondered where it was all going to lead.

'You can assume that the sixteen intelligence agencies purported to exist in the United States do not talk to one another. Ergo, you can expect another fifteen calls.'

'Are you making that up?'

'Partially, but I don't know what is true and what is not?'

'I should have chosen a simpler topic.'

'That would have been easier but probably less rewarding. You might want to think about consulting the university's research department and legal department just so you can be sure you stay on the right side of the regulations. You know what California is for regulations.'

'The research proposal went through Faculty Senate and was approved. That should have been enough.'

'For your average research that is purely academic and of interest to no more than twenty five people world-wide, yes. But you are venturing into the real world with your topic. Radioactive waste and its disposal are of interest to all sorts of branches of governments and the media. I would suggest you get as much backing and advice from the university as you can. If you don't believe me, talk to your dean. She seems fairly worldly.'

Nerys agreed to start with Dean Salisbury.

Calum did not have much news on the Farland front but he suggested she Google the Largs and Millport News for a front page report on his assault which was something he did not want hanging over him but could do nothing to avoid.

After ending the call, he walked up to the Millport Golf Course to meet the Club Captain and Secretary at the request of Scotty Green. This summer, they intended to revive the Marquess of Bute Cup after several years of inactivity. Scotty had extolled Calum's virtues and they wondered if he would be interested in heading up the organization of the event. The intention was to advertise extensively and attract the top amateurs from the west of Scotland and beyond if possible. Being amateur, there would be no prize money but there would be the famous old trophy on loan to the winner along with a replica keeper and gift prizes for various low scores, longest drive, longest putt etc. In addition, as a gimmick, there would be a prize of a Mediterranean cruise to anyone shooting a hole in one. All of this would have to be arranged over the next four months.

'I know next to nothing about golf and don't play myself. But I am happy to help out so count me in.'

The two men were delighted and called for drinks from the clubhouse bar even though it was a full hour before it was due to open. Over large gin and tonics, they shook hands to clinch the arrangement.

'Of course, we can't pay you anything for this. Perhaps we should have said that up front.'

'Oh I think we might just have found a means of compensation,' replied Calum while offering up a toast. 'Now I intend to do something I have never done before in all my years of coming here to the island. I am going to walk the course. I know there are stunning views although most golfers probably do not notice them in the heat of the competition.'

The walk was amazing with steep inclines and declines. Calum reckoned that a mountain goat might be most likely to shoot par on this course. There were incredible views of Wee Cumbrae and Arran to the south; Bute and Kintyre to the west, Cowal and almost all the way to Glasgow to the north, and to the east the mainland, blighted only by that power station. On the course itself, he came upon the two reservoirs that used to supply all the water to the island and sometimes supplied no water at all during a drought necessitating it be shipped in by tanker truck. There was a pipeline from the mainland now leaving the reservoirs as hidden fishing treasures virtually only visible from the golf course.

Calum always felt he did his best thinking and planning while walking. He had used that opportunity to think out problems at work, prepare lectures and presentations, and generally get his head straight when required. Now he was walking almost every day that he spent on Cumbrae and feeling all the better for it. Today he was trying to make sense of the latest episode in Minstrels. Nicholas Gorman was just showing off in front of his moneyed clients when referring to Nurse Heather. At least that was what he assumed given that Heather had indicated his support for her actions. Then again, maybe not. He would have to be careful. Mr. Gorman was not someone he wanted to be at odds with.

The pointed comments of Joel Wannamaker were something else again. They were as close to outright threats as he could have got without calling for a duel at dawn. Keep away from SERC business and keep away from his wife. It was obvious how he knew about the former; he would have been briefed by Cyrus Macadam. The worrying thing was that if his assault had been planned by Macadam, it must have been known and approved of by Wannamaker. And, how did he know about the latter? Was someone on the island keeping him informed about Maggie's movements and had reported on the Ritz incident?

Her behaviour in the restaurant was strange to say the least; she showed none of her trademark warmth and friendliness in his presence. It was as if she wished he were someplace else. Was that the result of a browbeating from Joel or had she just cooled her jets toward him? It was all very confusing and he found it difficult to reach coherent conclusions. His best guesses were Joel and Cyrus were corrupt and had arranged his assault as a warning, try proving that; Maggie had been scared off by Joel, leading to what kind of future between them he wondered; and Nicholas was perhaps a little pissed by Calum's out-of-the-blue friendship with his wife, but was probably relatively harmless. There it was, all neatly analyzed and interpreted. But he did not like the answers he had come up with.

He realized he had been walking for a couple of hours on inhospitable terrain and was quite exhausted. His legs were weary and the strain of the hike had actually caused all the aches sustained in the assault to return. Today he had sworn himself off the remaining painkillers after the drinking episode the other day and so he carried none with him. Partly as a result of a need to rest and partly because he had not spoken to her since the Minstrel incident, he flopped down on the grass and called Heather at her office.

She reported that it had been a strange lunch. Nicholas had noted that he had been pleased to meet Calum and was sorry he could not stay to join them. Maggie had said very little and had shown no particular enthusiasm for meeting Calum, meeting Heather, or taking possession of their new house. And, Joel had been quite gracious toward her but gave very little away of interest. He just wanted to talk about how so pleased he was that his wealth permitted him to do good things for Scotland by owning WCI and the house in Millport. Heather had heard of the image of the Ugly American. In fact, she had encountered a few in her time in California. Joel Wannamaker fell easily into that club.

She understood that the Wannamakers had stayed overnight at the Royal George Hotel and then had left again for Glasgow. Furniture was being delivered from the mainland to the new house over several days without any direct supervision that she was aware of. And, Nicholas had been most satisfied with the transaction and the lunch and left again for Glasgow shortly after conclusion of the latter.

Calum shared with Heather the very cryptic comments that Joel had directed toward him but left out Nicholas's jibe. She was inclined to agree with Calum's interpretation of the warning about nosing around Farland. That was a clear threat and needed to be taken seriously. She did not understand the comment about someone else's wife.

'You haven't been sniffing around Maggie, have you?'

'You make me sound like a bloodhound. No I have not.

Heather obviously must have been the only islander not to have heard about the Ritz incident. He preferred to leave it that way.

Chapter 15

Calum was just completing an enjoyable cycle around the island on the bike he had now hired for the duration of his stay. What made it most pleasant was the fact that at this time of year, before the holiday season began, there were relatively few cars around meaning one could literally cycle along either side of the road or right down the middle if you were a Canadian like Calum and have no fear of an accident.

The early March weather was changeable. Something that could be said of the weather in Scotland during all twelve months of the year but right now a bright morning could be followed by a wet afternoon and a warmish day could be followed by a freezing day with the wind blowing in directly off the Russian steppes. This morning had been calm, bright, and warm and begged to be taken advantage of. As Calum wheeled his bike up the side of Barclay House to park it round back he did not care what the afternoon brought, he had already had a fine day.

His calm serenity was disturbed the second he opened his front door and spied a hand-written note that had been slipped under the door.

"Must see you. Have been trying to reach you on your mobile but it does not sound like it is working. I am at the house for the next two days overseeing furniture arrivals before Joel comes down. Please come by. I am getting desperate. Maggie x"

Calum had not emailed Maggie with his new mobile number. He had reached the conclusion, given all that had happened recently, that it was probably better to create a bit of distance between the two of them. Now he was suddenly faced with this latest cry for help and he instantly knew he would respond. He immediately texted her stating he would call at the house at 2pm.

He was conscious of the information that seemed to be finding its way to Maggie's husband and he did not want to add fuel to the fire by just walking up to the front door of their house and knocking on it. Part of the problem was he did not know how the information was getting to Joel. Was it a local or someone Joel had hired to watch things on the island? Calum had not noticed any obvious strangers around but he was not a trained intelligence agent who would look out for that sort of thing. In fact, he was notoriously unobservant according to his wife, who always said it was quicker fetching something herself than giving him instructions as to where it could be located.

Career spy he might not be, but he had hatched a plan to hide his arrival at the Wannamaker house as he walked from West Bay to East Bay.

He walked past the house in question without even looking over the road and continued along to Heather's home. He thought she would be at the research station but he rang the bell just in case. He might have to take her into his confidence if she had decided to goof off for the afternoon. The bell went unanswered.

He walked around the side of the house to the back garden to implement his plan to cross from back garden to back garden until he arrived at Chez Maggie, all the while being unobserved from the road and hopefully from the back windows of each house. He had noticed that there did not seem to be much sign of life at any of the houses and that was not surprising because most were only occupied on weekends and for a few weeks in mid-summer. Such a pity he thought but today it could be turned to his advantage.

Were he to have been observed, he might have come across as a somewhat comical spy. Getting up and over dividing walls was managed but not with the grace he might have exhibited forty years ago and even before the beating he had recently sustained. And his sprint across each lawn was never going to lead to a call-up for the Commonwealth Games team. But mission was accomplished as he tapped on the window to attract Maggie's attention.

Maggie unlocked and thrust open the back door.

'How did you get there? I have been watching out the front window for ages and did not think you were coming.'

He squeezed by her outstretched arms and strode into the house pulling her firmly in behind him.

'Let's not waste the stealth of the undercover agent by making out on the back lawn and risk being spotted by someone.'

'You sure are funny. And I mean funny peculiar as well as funny ha-ha.'

'That's me.'

'The furniture is supposed to be coming over on the three o'clock ferry so we have just over an hour. Can I get you a drink? I brought some wine with me. We can sit on the sofa in the front room. That arrived yesterday.'

And so they sat, kind of close together, on a plush white leather sofa, sipping not very chilled white wine, and gazing over that stunning view to the south. For a few minutes nothing was said. Both seemed to be processing all that had happened and what was likely to happen next. Eventually, Calum broke the silence.

'Tell me what has been happening. How come Joel was able to throw all that shit at me in the Minstrel? What has he been saying and doing to you?'

Maggie told him she had been confronted by her husband over spending time with lowlifes (his description) like Evan Davis and Calum Davies. How he knew about it she did not know. She had not told him anything until the argument had begun and even then she had pleaded that one was an old friend and one she just met and neither was anything other than a friend. It must have come from someone on the island, but who? The Ritz incident might have become common knowledge but how many people know about the dinner at Westview?

'The only other person I can think of that knew about Westview is Scotty and there is not a chance in Hades that he would have reported it to your husband.'

'It gets worse.'

She told him that after the argument when she was emotionally wrecked, Joel had laid out his plan to restructure their asset base by transferring most of their holdings in California, as well as ownership of the soccer team, to a special trust to be located on the Isle of Man. This strategy had been developed by a new financial advisor in San Francisco, whom Maggie had never heard of far less met, and endorsed by Nicholas Gorman. It was reckoned that the trust would be subject to a fraction of the taxes that the husband and wife currently paid. Maggie's movie earnings would still have to be treated as taxable income as before because it was important to at least throw the IRS a bone to chew on.

'But here is the hooker,' Maggie exclaimed with anguish. 'In order to have the low tax Isle of Man Trust, there must be a master trust in Scotland. And the best that Nicholas can come up with is that Joel must have a 51% holding because he will have residency and I will have 49%. I could never have residency and the 51% because I would get hammered for taxes on both sides of the pond on my movie earnings. It feels like Joel is gaining control of most of our assets and I don't think there is anything I am going to be able to do to prevent it. The papers are drawn up and only await my signature.'

'You need to get independent advice.'

'Huh! Joel already had an attorney in Hollywood, who has worked for me in the past but not him, look over the trust papers and he confirms there are distinct tax advantages to us as a couple. As long as we are a couple. And that is where the big argument came back into it. He feels that this new more solid financial structure will make us stronger as a loving couple. I just have to stop playing around. Why do I feel I am being screwed?'

'Perhaps because you are?'

'It gets even worse. Just in case my promiscuity prevails, he is proposing a post-nuptial agreement whereby if either of us causes the marriage to be ended through infidelity, that person will forfeit 25% of the assets to the other. And of course, in the event of death of one the other gets 100%.'

Just describing the details had clearly exhausted Maggie and she sat slumped on the sofa with her now empty wine glass fallen to the floor. Calum was not much better. He had spent a career working with complicated financial arrangements and agreements but this one blew him away. It was simplicity in itself and seemed on the face of it to lean so heavily toward Joel. But it had been blessed by professional experts, presumably passed the sniff test with the different tax authorities, and only required that they remain a loving couple for it to be of great advantage to them both. So it had a moral foundation too. Yet it stank the place out.

'All I can say is don't sign anything. Get a second opinion. Get a third opinion. I can maybe set you up with somebody independent here but I think you also have to get back to the States and come up with some advice there. Maybe your agents or your studio can help there.'

'I feel so alone. I don't know if I can hold out. I need you,' she said throwing herself on top of him and kissing him hungrily amid floods of tears.

It was hopeless to suggest otherwise in the heat of the passion, so Calum succumbed and they embraced in ever heightening fervour and gymnastic contortions.

That they would have made love was absolutely certain, had they not been abruptly interrupted by the door bell suddenly ringing.

'Fuck. The furniture!'

Standing outside were a large van with name "Elite Furnishings" on the side and three men peering in the window from the side of the street with a fourth standing at the door.

'Quick, get out the way you came in. You will have to crawl across the carpet or they will see you.'

As Calum made his way out the back door, trying to disentangle himself from a distraught Maggie who was half holding him back and half pushing him out, he heard her say, 'I never got a chance to tell you what Joel knew about you being attacked. I will call you. Now get going.'

Calum quickly realized that it would be redundant to follow the path he had taken in reverse to Heather's house so he simply slipped down the far side of the house next to Maggie's, crossed the road, and jumped over the wall on to the beach. Fortunately it was low tide because at times in winter high tide came right up to the wall. He had taken this course of action so that he could return to the main promenade and onward to West Bay without passing directly in front of Maggie's house and running the risk of one of the furniture delivery men remembering him. There seemed to be nobody else around but he could not afford to take that risk.

All went well in his improvisation plan and he soon arrived on the promenade in the main part of the town. Only then did he feel that he started to breathe properly again. These adventures were getting too much for him. He quickly assessed what had gone wrong at Maggie's because one thing was for sure; he did not want to get romantically involved with her. But every time she poured out her problems with her husband to him she seemed to end up falling into his arms as her potential saviour. In addition, she obviously had information that might help in the SERC case. How did he continue to engage her but not get involved with her?

He decided to sit on one of the many benches stretched out along the length of the promenade. Each bench was provided by a family and dedicated to a deceased relative with a love and history of Millport. There must be hundreds of deceased relatives because there were hundreds of benches all over the island.

Calum was sitting letting his head clear in the light breeze coming off the ocean and thinking maybe he would look into sponsoring a bench in the name of his late parents, who after all had been responsible for bringing him here in the first place and starting the life-long love affair.

Suddenly, his mobile rang. "Oh no, not Maggie,' he said out loud. He was relieved to see that the number was a strange one and not her's.

'Is that you Calum?'

'Yes. Who is this?'

'It's Neil Christian old buddy. I picked up your new number from your wife. I got your email about my article on the state of Scottish football and I wanted to talk to you about some follow-up stuff I want to write. When I could not get through to your mobile number I called your home number in California. You are in Scotland?'

'Yes I am. I am in a place called Millport. I don't suppose you have heard of it. Few people from Edinburgh have.'

'I've heard of it. In fact, I went there a couple of times as a child. Nice place. I remember playing football in the West Bay. I was only about twelve but

I got to play in a game between Millport and The Visitors.'

'I don't believe it. This little place seems to have so many secrets that are coming out since I came here a couple of months ago.'

'Nerys said you were looking for an adventure.'

'That's how it started. Now it feels like the adventures are looking for me. The next time I am up in Victoria we must get together. I have some amazing stories to tell from this place.'

'We don't need to wait that long. That's why I am calling you. What are doing on Saturday?'

'Are you in Victoria? I can't come there on Saturday.'

'I am in Glasgow. I was brought over to tape a piece on Scottish Television this week built around the Internet article. I was billed as the doom and gloom predictor of the death of Scottish football and they had that guy, Joel Wannamaker, on as the saviour. The yin and the yang.'

'How did it go?'

'Quite well. Alan Cameron who was the moderator knew me better from the old days than he did the slippery Yank so he tended to side with me and threw me a few soft balls, so to speak.'

'When it is going to be broadcasted?'

'This Sunday. The funny thing was I did not like Mr. Wannamaker one little bit and things got a little heated at times, but after the taping he invited me to White City Stadium on Saturday for a reception before the game, then the best seats for the game against, wait for it, Edinburgh Waverley.'

'Oh no!'

'Oh yes. WCI are only in mid-table but Waverley is bottom of the league. It might be the slaughter of the innocents but I wouldn't miss it for the world. He said I could bring a guest as long as it was nobody connected to Glasgow Erin. Some things never change! Anyway, that is what I am asking. Do you fancy coming with me to the reception and the game?'

Calum hesitated as he felt another adventure coming on.

'Why not? We may not like the guy but we can always drink his alcohol.'

'And, you never know, miracles do happen. Maybe Waverley will take them for six!'

'That I would just love to see.'

'Great, you will be coming into Glasgow Central train station I assume. I will meet you in the bar at noon. We will need a quick one to stiffen our resolve before we go into enemy territory.'

Chapter 16

Calum was seated on the 10:50am train from Largs to Glasgow Central. This was *the* only way to travel. It involved a short walk from the ferry terminal to the station in Largs and once in Glasgow no parking problems and a variety of transportation options. He had always loved travelling by train. Throughout Europe, they were in plentiful supply and fares were quite economically priced. Alas in North America, they had become quite a rarity and fares could cost you your first born.

He picked up a discarded Daily Record. It was by no means his favourite newspaper but it always seemed to be the one that was left behind by an earlier reader. Perhaps it was some sort of gratuitous communication of news among the great unwashed to whom the newspaper generally appealed.

As the train click-clacked along merrily, he focused on a story that just would not go away. Apparently, the member of the Scottish Parliament for North Ayrshire, which included Farland, had raised a question in the chamber about the earlier Daily Record story. He was hearing rumblings from his constituents and from environmental groups that the American contractor SERC had not taken seriously enough the rumour that some solid steel flasks containing radioactive waste were unaccounted for. Their explanation had been too matter of fact. Calum nodded in agreement. Then as he read on, he became nervous.

The MSP was noting that he did not want to cast aspersions toward SERC, he was sure they were quite competent. However, did the Cumbraes Environmental Research Station in Millport not also have a contract to oversee the radioactive waste disposal? As the Scottish government was not only paying their contract but also providing a substantial portion of their operating funding, he was suggesting a formal request should be made to the research station to check into the matter at Farland further. No motion or vote had been taken but the suggestion had been tabled for further discussion. Calum was not sure how the station director would react to that. Scientists and educators generally did not like being ordered about by government at the best of times and would not in this case where the research station was supposed to be independent of both governments and the utility company. On the other hand, if Heather wanted to poke her nose in or have him poke his nose in again, she could argue that it would now be mandated by the highest authority in the land.

Calum strode into the station bar, which was very busy. That was another good thing about train travel. There was a tradition of repairing to the bar while waiting for a train or after arriving on one that simply did not exist in bus terminals or airports. Neil Christian had been looking out for him and waved him over to a table in the corner. They shook hands heartily, slapped each other on the back, and remarked how well each was looking. Neil had ten years on Calum but nobody would have guessed it. He had obviously looked after himself after his long football career even though he enjoyed a tipple just as much as Calum.

Over an hour of several good malt whiskies, they exchanged stories about what they had been up to since they had last met almost three years ago. Neil was quite intrigued by Calum's adventures over the last two months.

'Hollywood stars, childhood sweethearts, nuclear espionage, and punch-ups. You make my life feel very ordinary Calum.'

'It wasn't really planned. Nothing I have done over the last year has been planned. I didn't plan on getting pensioned off and I didn't plan to get involved in all these things in Millport. My big adventure was bit of a joke conjured up by Nerys. Now it is taking on a life of its own.'

'Maybe I will be able to come down to the island before I go back next week. I might be able to get fixed up with someone as well. I have been single for too long.'

'That would be great and I will see what I can do on getting you fixed up. Or else, I am prepared to share.'

They laughed and then turned their attention to the game. They were both looking forward to seeing Edinburgh Waverley for the first time in a long while. But they bemoaned the financial crisis it was embroiled in. Each joked they had always assumed the other was wealthy enough to be able to bail out the famous old club.

'That's been the problem. We are too poor. For far too long the club has been owned by small-time business folks who have not had the necessary disposable funds that a successful club needs these days. Then when they made their pact with the Devil and brought in that Russian bastard that was just the beginning of the end.'

Neil's tenet that had been so strongly espoused in the article had come to the surface and caused his face to take on a florid hue that suggested perhaps he was not as healthy as he first appeared. Or perhaps he just cared too much about his beloved team.

'Let's get going to meet this American asshole who now owns the biggest team in Scotland. I am not sure he even knows what the shape of a football looks like.'

A quick taxi ride deposited them outside the imposing White City Stadium and a greeter showed them into the opulent boardroom which was crowded with the rich and famous of Scotland from high court judges to oil tycoons, all from different walks of life who shared only one thing—their religion and devotion to this team. Drinks were plentiful and the guests were helping themselves to a sumptuous buffet.

'Neil, glad you could make it,' boomed the host coming over to shake hands and then coming to a sudden halt.

'What are you doing here? Aw Neil, surely you could have come up with a better guest than Dr. Interfering Davies?'

Neil was confused and a little embarrassed at the negative reaction to Calum. Calum was interested in the moniker attributed to him and recalled where he had last heard it.

Then Wannamaker became a little conciliatory and whispered to Calum.

'I suppose I will have to put up with you for one day. You are not a Catholic are you by any chance?'

Calum was tempted to confirm he was just to annoy him but settled for an alternative jibe.

'My religion is unimportant to me and to you but I will confirm that I am a staunch Edinburgh Waverley supporter and will take great delight in witnessing along with this legend of our great club beside me the annihilation of your tawdry team this afternoon.'

Wannamaker did not know whether to be offended or to enter into the banter so common among football fans of opposing teams in Scotland so he simply turned on his heels and saw someone across the room that he just had to talk to.

Neil laughed, 'That sorted him out. Now we just need our players to back up your bluff and bluster.'

After enjoying the WCI hospitality and listening to conversations among the invited high-ranking guests that would have made interesting reading on the front page of the Scotsman or Herald given their profanity, bias, discrimination, and in some cases illegality, it was time to take in the game. They truly had the best seats in the stadium in the directors' suite. White City Stadium was rocking. There were 57,000 WCI fans baying like wolves and 3,000 Edinburgh Waverley fans trying to return the vitriol while probably secretly fearing for their lives.

'I was only ever here once in 1968. I was scared stiff. It was like being in a war-zone. You wanted your team to win but you feared that they just might and you would be massacred as a result. We lost 1-0.'

'Yeah and I missed a penalty. Thanks for reminding me.'

'Did you never feel intimidated playing here or at the jungle on the east side of Glasgow?'

'Sure. You could almost cut the hatred with a knife most times. But I will tell you, there was never a better feeling than sticking one on them. As long as the police were in sufficient numbers to keep us safe. We did it a few times here but not often enough. My hat-trick in 1965 here ranks right up there with my all-time favourites.'

The earth shattering roars that greeted the arrival of the teams meant further conversation was impossible so they settled down to watch the spectacle. It turned out to be a good game. WCI attacked mercilessly for first thirty minutes but Waverley stole away to score first. The silence was deafening around the cavernous stadium but two people made a fair bit of noise in the directors' suite. WCI finally scored two goals on either side of the half-time break that their all-out efforts deserved but Waverley conjured up an equalizer out of nothing mid-way through the second half. It looked like the game might end in a draw, which would have been a tremendous result for Waverley given their financial plight and all too evident lack of quality players, but WCI scored a goal which looked yards off-side near the end. The resultant cacophony of sound had not even abated when the Waverley defenders finally succumbed to the realization that they were not meant to win and surrendered another goal which reignited the crowd once again.

4-2. The result was just about what all the pundits had predicted. But for a little while there, Waverley had looked good for a draw only to have it rudely taken away from them. Calum thought the players might change, the coaches might change, but the almost preordained outcome stayed the same.

'The team tried their best to back up my bluff and bluster. How the referee did not give off-side on that third goal I do not know.'

'Aye the referees may change but the decisions still go the way of WCI in this stadium when they have to.'

Their commiserations were interrupted by Wannamaker leaning over several people to shout at them.

'Well Davies, looks like you are a loser again. At least you got to see a good football team win out.'

'How much did you have to tip the referee this time?' He valiantly tried to counter, then decided it was churlish and conceded it had been good to see a live game for the first time in ages.

'And Neil, you must have seen a lot of positives today—big crowd, good team—things are on the up and up for WCI with me at the helm. You should adjust your pessimism.'

Neil and Calum hung around for a very short time and then were glad to be able to make their way out of the stadium. Just as they were leaving, Calum felt a tug on his shoulder and turned to face Wannamaker stooping to say something in his ear.

'You know I have other business interests and your wife, what is her name again, is benefitting directly from them. Then I have you making a nuisance of yourself over here poking your nose into affairs that you know nothing about and have no right to be even bothering about. I want that to stop right now. I would hate your wife's funding to be put in jeopardy. And another thing, keep away from my wife. She is a bit of a nut-job these days and she does not need you confusing her. Understand?'

Chapter 17

Troy Cameron wandered into Nerys's office without knocking and proceeded to anger her, not once but twice, with his familiarity. I have got to do something about the presumptuous Mr. Cameron she thought.

'Nerys. Can I put a call through to you? It came in on my line. The person asked for you but beyond that I have no idea what he is saying. I think he is speaking some kind of English but I can't be sure.'

'Did you get a name?'

'Maybe. Sounded a bit like Muscle something.'

She thought for a moment and then it came to her.

'Dr. Michael Musselwhite. He is probably calling from London. Quick, put him through.'

Nerys had met the legendary environmental scientist and crusader when he spent a semester as a visiting lecturer at the University of California Santa Barbara while she was doing her PhD. He had taken a keen interest in what she was doing toward her dissertation and ultimately agreed to become an additional dissertation advisor. She had never forgotten the value that his standing in academic circles brought to her final paper. He had even returned from England to witness her dissertation defence and a couple of soft ball questions from him that allowed her to spout just how much she knew about her topic had been more than enough to gain her the committee's approval.

They had become quite good friends and every three months or so they would exchange emails on what they were doing and what was happening in their field of common interest. She had not seen him since that dissertation defence day and they seldom talked on the telephone. She wondered why he would be calling.

She also understood why Troy would have such difficulty understanding what he had been saying. In spite of having accumulated earned and honorary degrees in spades and being considered across the globe to be the foremost authority in his field, Mick was a Cockney and proud of it. No amount of education had caused him to change his accent. Nerys recalled the looks of consternation on the faces of her class at UCSB when he first delivered a lecture. But they soon realized the value of what he had to say and learned to attune their hearing to that very special dialect. However, even he admitted subtitles would have been useful at times.

As far as she knew, he was employed by the University of London and did a bit of teaching to the lucky few but he seemed to travel the world advising governments and delivering keynote addresses at prestigious conferences. On top of that, he once let slip that he worked closely with some branch of British intelligence in the fight against environmental terrorism, whatever that was. A very interesting man all round.

'Ello me little cock sparra. 'Ow is life treating you in that cesspit called California?'

'Mick, so nice to hear from you. I was just getting around to thinking it was my turn to email you. I have lots to tell you.'

'I know that, lovey. That's why I am calling. I have been following your waste disposal project on the old "net". Good for you. Goin' where angels fear to tread. But, I 'ave some information that I fink will be useful to you.'

He went on tell her that her that her research project had piqued the interest of the British government which was always concerned as to how the emerging superpowers like the BRIC countries were going to handle the thorny problem of disposal of radioactive waste. Were they going to take the high moral ground and adopt procedures that were ethical and scientifically responsible but at the same time would always be cumbersome and expensive? Or, were they going to cut corners and do a sloppy job now that would just create enormous problems down the road, just as they often did on matters of public policy? Or worse still, were they going to adopt a totally irresponsible approach of offloading the waste to anyone who would take it away, thereby providing opportunity for every rogue country and terrorist organization around the globe? And, there were plenty of those lurking in the background.

One of the jobs that Mick did quietly on the side for the benefit of an intelligence department the name of which he could not reveal or else they would be required to liquidate somebody was to follow goings-on world-wide to locate illicit transactions involving radioactive waste. In most cases, the seller was a country too lazy to deal with the waste properly or in dire needs of cash. The buyer was generally one of the rogue countries or terrorist organizations well known to the civilized world and under almost constant scrutiny by most of the members of the United Nations Security Council, in particular America and Britain. And in most transactions there was a middle man, a shady organization drawn from a small list world-wide which did all the leg work including negotiation, procurement, logistical transfer of the waste, and transfer of funds, all for an exorbitant cut of the proceeds. There were relatively few transactions in any year but there were sufficient to pose a real threat to global security and to make these middle men very rich.

Mick noted that none of this was exactly top secret—security leakers, investigative journalists and the like had proven beyond doubt that such transactions did take place. However, the actual transactions that succeeded and the many that did not because of some sort of intelligence intervention were known only to a very few people. He was one. He was instrumental in discovering a good number himself and a few others who worked on behalf of other Security Council members and did exactly the same job as he found the rest. Together they shared their information for the common good except when the Americans chose to fly solo as they occasionally did or two members fell out about something else and all cooperation was suspended, which happened more often than was reported in the press.

Now Mick got serious.

'I cannot say any more because the line may be secure at my end but I cannot guarantee it is at yours. I can only say I may 'ave discovered some information that may 'ave a bearing on your research ducky. I can't say no more. I can only invite you to come over to The Smoke where I will share what I know wif you including some detailed physical evidence that must remain in this country for security reasons. You will 'ave 'eard that kind of thing from James Bond no doubt. I have, however, been able to obtain clearance for you to view the evidence under my supervision.'

Nerys could hardly contain herself.

'What evidence? How does it affect my research? Which country is involved? All four?'

'Stop! You can't ask and I can't say. Just be assured I am not messin' around wif you. Seriously think about coming over and as soon as you can.'

'You will let me see the evidence?'

'I said so. But there is always a price.'

'What price?'

'My government needs you to agree to share all your findings from your project wif us.'

'You are not the first to ask.'

'I didn't expect we would be. On a good day, your government would share wif us in any case. It's just that not every day is a good day. You are potentially into something pretty heavy here.'

'Jesus Mick. You are scaring the shit out of me. You really think there is a risk to my project?'

'I fink there is a risk to your project and maybe even a personal risk to you, lovey. You need to know about the sharks you are going to swim wif.'

'OK. OK. Let me think about it. Is it alright to discuss things with my dean? I also have a project assistant. I will get back to you in a couple of days.'

'Your dean will probably be OK but don't be talking openly about this including the fact that you are going to London. That is if you decide to come over. I suggest you get back to me in a couple of hours not a couple of days. Just email yes or no. If yes I will be in touch with further details. Got it?'

'Got it.'

The line went dead. Nerys slumped back in her chair. She felt the mother of migraines coming on. Troy wandered in enquiring what that was all about and she could only summon up the strength to yell. 'Out! I will call you in when I need you.'

She sat and stared at her computer screen for a long time. The screensaver showed Calum sitting on a capstan at Millport harbour. Boy could she do with him being here right now. What would he do? He could be a bit belligerent at times. He would not react well to all the pressures she was facing from the outside. It would probably make him all more determined to charge ahead with the project. And, in some ways she had shifted her thinking over the years and tended to adopt the same characteristics as he. *"Damn the torpedoes"* was one of his favourite sayings when political hacks on campus were advising a different course of action. But look what happened to him eventually.

If she were really being honest with herself, she probably wished she had never started the project. She had been naive to think that you could get involved in something so overtly political without real politics coming into it. A political scientist cannot dwell only on theoretical political science. The better the research and the better the findings, the more likely the politics being studied were real. And it did not get any more real than this—trying to engage four ambitious but not overly friendly governments and now being harassed by not one but two supposedly friendly governments. She called Dean Salisbury and asked for a meeting. Without going in to any details, the very tone of Nerys's voice was enough for the meeting to be granted immediately.

Nerys prefaced her description of all the facts by warning her dean, something quite unusual in itself.

'I don't know how to say this any other way. I need you to agree that everything I am going to tell you will be kept in confidence. I know you don't generally go around blabbing about faculty members' research but on this one the bar has to be higher. I ask you not to talk to anyone unless we have agreed they ought to be brought into our confidence. I am leaning on you here, I know it. But I am really nervous. Will you agree to my terms?'

The look on the dean's face suggested that she had never been put in this position before. Sometimes research was to be kept confidential but that meant outside of the academy and still allowed for discussion among the faculty. Collegial dialogue was an essential prerequisite of the academic environment. But, she respected Nerys and the urgency and probable legitimacy of her concern for confidentiality were all too evident.

'You have my word that everything you tell me will be kept between us until and if we agree it should be shared with anybody else. I am probably sacrificing my decanal responsibilities by doing that but I will cut you some slack. Go ahead.'

Nerys took well over an hour to recap everything that had happened basically since she got the funding go-ahead from SERC. That triumph had been followed by success in setting up what looked like real productive meetings in China and India. Then it started to go pear-shaped. She mentioned the controversy that SERC seemed to have got involved in over in Scotland and how Calum had stumbled in to it and had been rudely warned off. And, he had got himself beaten up probably just to emphasize the point. Then the US State Department had basically bullied her into sharing her findings with the threat that they could close the project down if she did not cooperate. Then finally, the respected Dr. Musselwhite, who was not unknown to the dean, had presented her with a two-edged sword—the offer of top secret information that would affect the project in return for agreement to share the findings with the Brits too.

Dean Salisbury had listened patiently to the story without interruption. Once Nerys was finished, she simply exclaimed, 'Holy Crap. You are the meat in one big God-damn sandwich. It was a complicated research project to start with, that is what made it attractive to me and I am sure to SERC. By the way, I am sure you have got the Scotland thing wrong. SERC has a good reputation. The university president has quickly become very proud of the work it does. They have been very supportive of you. You don't want to jeopardize that. Maybe you should be telling Calum to concentrate on his museum project, he can't get into any trouble there surely? But the governments are a different kettle of fish. We need to think this out.'

The discussion that followed went on well into the evening and included moving from the campus to a local bar for drinks and then supper. At the conclusion, it had been agreed that the State Department should be kept at a distance for as long as possible, with Nerys neither definitely agreeing nor disagreeing with their request. Further, she should go to London to try and get as much information as she could again without making a definite agreement to share her findings. If she assessed the information to be crucial to the project and could not get full access to it without meeting the condition, she may have to make some sort of tentative agreement. The research was hers and the findings were hers at the end of day. Nobody else including the University and SERC had any proprietary interest in them legally. However, her employer and her sponsor could still make things difficult for her. The biggest threat, however, probably came from the State Department which likely did not have any legal recourse unless they could prove the research project was a matter of state security. But it did have a lot of political power and tended to get its own way on matters such as this. That way would almost certainly not include a willingness to have the findings shared with their oldest allies, the Brits. That was just the way international relations worked.

It was not a clear plan, it was not a plan that made her comfortable, but the first thing to do was to make arrangements to go to London. Nerys emailed yes to Mick. What would happen next was anybody's guess.

She thought about contacting Calum. They usually talked out a problem facing either one of them just as they would a problem they both faced. But, bearing in mind Dean Salisbury's reservations about what he had come up with in Scotland, she decided to hold off meantime. It would be odd to be in London and so close to Scotland without telling him but perhaps something could be worked out later.

Next morning, she called in Troy who seemed a bit huffy about being dismissed the previous day. She had decided to take him to London to assist with recording of the physical evidence and so she found that first she had to apologize to him in order to get him on board, She had felt that lately he had exhibited a tendency to overstep the mark in both their professional and personal relationships but she need him to make this a quick and efficient visit so she ate some crow. Then she gave him an abridged version of Mick's call and what she and Dean Salisbury had agreed should be done in response.

He seemed excited and well and truly out of his funk when she asked him to be ready to make arrangements for the two of them to fly to London just as soon as she heard back from Mick.

Chapter 18

Calum had been invited to a meeting of the Cumbraes Council by Scotty Green. The main item on the agenda was discussion on the preparation of a development plan for Great Cumbrae. The reality was that the island, and Millport in particular, had to rebrand itself if it were to maintain its paltry market share of the British tourist business, never mind increase it.

Scotty introduced Calum as a frequent visitor to the island, and currently resident for an extended period, who could offer an external professional perspective. His profile matched that of the typical Millport tourist. He had come to the island as a child, formed a life-long love for it, and kept coming back frequently. Those visitors were most welcome but the future of the tourist business depended on attracting new visitors, ideally young couples with young families.

Calum, who had met some, but not all, of the members of the Cumbraes Council individually, prior to the meeting, was given an opportunity to speak. He gave a brief synopsis of his career and its parallel relationship with Millport, stating his willingness to help in any way he could to develop a plan. He did not profess to be totally *au fait* with the vacation trends in the UK but he felt he could bring an off-shore perspective particularly from North America.

There followed some constructive discussion among the members with an apparent consensus that Calum would be a useful addition to the project. Sensing that, Scotty called for a motion to approve inviting Calum to assume a non-paying position as consultant to the council for the purpose of preparing the development plan. A mover and seconder were obtained and Scotty opened up the meeting for any discussion, seeing it only as a formality as members had already had their say at the conclusion of Calum's presentation. He was about to close discussion and call for the vote when Alec Taggart the local gas station proprietor spoke up.

'Mr. Davies talks a fine line in that American twang of his but I have heard that he has been making a bit of a nuisance of himself among some of the business community in the area. I am not sure he will bring much credibilityness (he meant credibility) to our project.'

The outburst caused a pregnant silence. Some members had some idea what he was alluding to, although it probably only involved the Ritz Café. Others had no idea at all and felt quite embarrassed by the pointedness of the comment. And still others noisily shouted Taggart down for his unsubstantiated smear. Nobody seemed to know how to proceed, notably Calum who had seen an innocent act of goodwill come crashing down about him. Eventually, somebody spoke, 'Get on with the vote Scotty. That will settle things. It always does.'

The Cumbraes Council voted 4-2 in favour of the motion without Scotty having to vote.

'Not exactly a ringing endorsement was it?' said Calum to Scotty after the meeting. 'Perhaps it would be best if I just declined the invitation.'

'No. No. Don't do that. I don't know where Alec Taggart was coming from. He is usually way too busy gouging the islanders on petrol prices to get much involved in council affairs. I wonder who has been whispering in his ear.'

'And yanking his chain. Who was the other guy that voted against?'

'Tommy Duncan. You don't need to worry about him. He hasn't a brain in his head. He always just votes the same way as Taggart. He is a farm labourer.

The council is very democratic. Some would say too democratic.'

'Well, I will try to keep a low profile and work behind the scenes through you. Just tell me what you want done.'

Over in California, Dr. Michael Musselwhite had emailed to Nerys instructions for her visit to London. He had said that they should first meet in his office at the University of London. Then, he would take her to the archives department of a government agency close to the University where he would give her access to paper files and Internet information, which was not now readily available online but had been saved there. She would be allowed to take as many notes as she wished but would not be allowed to remove any material from the department, He suggested that three days of the following week would be sufficient and even proposed flights from LAX to Heathrow and a convenient hotel, the Roxburgh. Nerys was impressed with his efficiency and passed the information on to Troy Cameron for action. Then she confirmed with Mick that Troy would be accompanying her.

The following day, Neil Christian called Calum to say that he would not be able to come down to Millport after all. Edinburgh Waverley had been in touch to ask him to meet with the board of directors and the trustee appointed by the court to oversee the club's bankruptcy. He felt that he could not miss that opportunity, given that it would be his last day before going home. The club's relationship with Neil and many other ex-players had been virtually non-existent during the "Russian Era". Maybe now that they were on the brink of extinction, an olive branch was being held out although most likely it was a case of being too little too late.

Calum fully understood Neil's decision. As long as there was a faint heartbeat at the club, it was worth trying to revive it. Calum would have made exactly the same decision were it required of him. He closed by offering his own help in any way possible but could not help thinking he had been doing that a lot recently and most times it got him into trouble. Thoughts of the Russian mafia briefly wandered through his mind. The two resolved to get together sometime soon either when Calum made one his infrequent sojourns north or when Neil felt the need for some sunshine in the south during the dank days that were so common in British Columbia.

That evening, Calum met Dr. Heather Randall for dinner at Fraser's Bar—a plain, nothing fancy meal washed down by a couple of pints of his favourite Belhaven beer in his case and two glasses of an undistinguished chardonnay in hers. It was a warm cosy place on a cold wet night and they both enjoyed the local ambience and their own company. They consciously tried to steer away from some of the troubles they had recently been associated with and spent most of the evening reminiscing about people they could remember from high school. In spite of the fact that both had spent lots of the intervening period away from the UK, Heather seemed to have kept in touch with or know of far more former students than Calum and he enjoyed hearing what they had done with their lives. In turn, he amazed her with his memory of these same people while they were in high school. Between them, they ended up remembering some fondly, reinforcing some long held disparaging opinions of others, and having a good laugh at others.

Just when they were making up their minds whether to leave or have one more for the road, the conversation lurched into matters concerning Farland. Sensing that it would not be a short conversation, Calum presumed to break the tied vote using executive fiat on whether to leave or have another (initial voting was probably fairly predictable).

'Sounds like I better get another round in. Do you want the same again?'

'Alright, we probably need it. I don't think I have ever said I need a drink in my life but since I re-encountered you my values seem to have changed, In fact, I think I will have a brandy please.'

'Good idea. I think I will have one too. Doubles?'

Calum told Heather about the football match in Glasgow. She had not known that such a match was scheduled far less that Calum had attended it with an Edinburgh Waverley legend, whom she had never heard of. Sports were never her strong suit in high school and it appeared that nothing had changed in forty four years. She was, however, most interested in Joel Wannamaker's performance after sitting patiently through a blow-by-blow account of the actual game. She was alarmed to hear of the unsubtle threat to Calum and to Nerys should he persist in interfering with Wannamaker's business interests, i.e. Farland. And, she was again troubled by the reference to Maggie Wannamaker.

'Are you sure there is nothing between you and Maggie? Not that it would have anything to do with me of course.'

'I have a met her only a couple or three times and each time she has poured out her soul to me about her husband basically trying to screw her out of her share of their assets. And the soul pouring has got hot and heavy toward the end each time. Not of my making I assure you.'

'Like in the Ritz Café?'

'Oh, you have heard about that, have you?'

'My admin. assistant, of all people, told me about it. She was kind of proud of you for pulling a Hollywood star. She reckoned I must be the last person on the island to hear about it and recommended that I get out more.'

'That may well be right. And here you are out with me and risking your reputation no end.'

'I can handle it,' she said squeezing his hand.

'I like Maggie but I don't want to have an affair with her. I am at a loss to know where caring and offering a sympathetic ear crosses over to you-know-what. And, I am further at a loss to know how her husband is so well informed. I can't believe she is telling him but you never know. She is obviously under a lot of emotional pressure.'

'I kind of like Maggie too but I think she is trouble for you. If I were to give you some advice, it would be to stay away from her.'

'Thank you Mother,' he replied in his best impersonated John Lennon voice for some reason.

She did not see the joke and probably failed to make the connection to the dearly departed Beatle; instead she gave him a glare.

One more double and one single brandy were procured during the necessary time-out and then they moved on to discuss Farland. Heather expressed her deep concern about Wannamaker's threat regarding any further involvement from Calum because she was feeling that she was being coerced into having the research station do a more open review of the waste inventory situation.

The Member of the Scottish Parliament for North Ayrshire had connected with her directly to discuss his intended motion about the research station getting more involved. From his perspective, it made perfect sense because SERC seemed to have done a superficial job on the rumour. She was in a quandary. She did not want to share with him her doubts about SERC or Calum's intervention and consequent assault. Without that information, she was inclined to acknowledge the MSP's take on the situation and felt that she had no ability to block his upcoming formal request. The question was not whether to approach the power station but how; and should it be done independent of SERC, probably for objectivity reasons, or with SERC, to contain the animosity and fall-out that was probably inevitable once they learned that the research station was going to act on the government's request.

The second dilemma for her was whether to involve Calum or not. He had the training necessary, probably more so than she or any of her staff, but he also had the baggage. His response was immediate.

'If you do this, I don't want you doing it on your own. These SERC people are bad. I would say that you don't go behind SERC's back but you make it a condition of cooperating with them that I am involved too.'

'Do you think that might work?'

'I can't say, but if they turn down my involvement you should decline to cooperate with them. Then, you are simply responding to a request from your government to essentially check up on them. If they refuse you access to the records, you report it back to the MSP.'

'Oh this is such a high-stakes game. Whatever happened to my pure science career?'

'Sometimes we get things thrust on us that we know we have to take on whether we want to or not. I suspect you and I have been thrust together and there is no getting out of this now. It is all my fault. I was just looking for a simple adventure for a recently retired accountant.'

They agreed that they both understood what the next steps should be and Heather said she would connect again with the MSP to indicate the research station's willingness to follow through once the government made the formal request. She would hold off from connecting with Cyrus Macadam until the government vote had been held because it would give her some leverage in trying to keep him from going ballistic.

As they left Frasers, Heather turned to Calum and said, 'I am glad that we met up again and I really appreciate your support on this SERC thing.'

She turned down his offer to walk her home on such an inclement night. She then left for her longer walk to East Bay. He turned toward his shorter walk to West Bay. He had not completely climbed Cardiff Street when his phone indicated a message. What had she forgotten? Maybe to say thanks for a great night. It had been a great night. He read the message.

"Must see you as soon as possible. Things are getting even worse. It can't be at the house. I am certain I am being followed. Text me.   Maggie xx"

Chapter 19

Wednesday 2am GMT

Calum had agonized for the entire day over what to do about Maggie. He was very nervous about another meeting, particularly with the news that she believed she was being followed. On the other hand, he did not want to abandon her either. The limitations of being confined to Cumbrae were also bothering him and he did contemplate suggesting a meeting on the mainland. However, he realized there was only one way off the island on the ferry and if she were being followed, any advantage of leaving for the mainland would likely be lost if the tail was maintained. In the end, as sleep was about to overcome him he texted back the best suggestion he could come up with.

"Meet me at the Glaid Stone which is the highest point of the island and has the advantage that you can see anybody coming from the east or west. Go to the cycle shop by the back street, not the promenade, and hire a bike. The Glaid Stone is only 400 odd feet high but it is a bit of a slog to cycle. Quicker than walking however. Meet me at noon today.   Calum."

She responded immediately. She must have stayed up waiting anxiously for the text. He felt guilty he had delayed acting.

Wednesday 2am GMT and 10am Pacific Standard Time (PST)

Instead of taking off from LAX as scheduled, Nerys and Troy Cameron were going nowhere anytime soon because the airport was badly fogged in.

They retired to the executive lounge that Nerys's frequent flyer status with the airline permitted. This was a new experience for Troy and the delay did not seem all bad to him as he helped himself to breakfast and coffee for the second time that morning. Nerys had a coffee only and drummed her fingers on the chair arm.

At 11am PST, it was announced that the flight was further delayed until 1pm PST. Nerys was now getting concerned. Their scheduled arrival in London had been Thursday 6am GMT which would have given her plenty of time to get to the hotel, get Troy settled in, and then go to her meeting alone with Mick at noon GMT. She felt that Mick would be more open about a subject that he was treating as top secret if she were on her own initially. Troy would be brought in the following day to help gather the details. Now the schedule was getting tight at the London end. Troy busied himself on the Internet using the free Wi-Fi offered by the lounge. He seemed to be mainly playing games.

At noon PST, it was announced that the flight would not be able to leave before 2pm PST at the earliest. At that point they started to avail themselves of the complimentary wine. Actually if Nerys had been travelling with Calum they would have imbibed from 10am PST onwards but she felt that she needed have her wits about her when in the company of Troy.

Wednesday 8am GMT and 4pm PST

Calum woke from a restless night. He had not slept soundly since 2am and he knew he was not going to get any more sleep now. He thought about the upcoming meeting with Maggie. What could have worsened in her situation?

Then he thought about Nerys. It was 4pm her time. He would like to have called her but that time was notoriously bad for her. Most days she had a class to teach until 5pm. Instead he sent her a short email just saying Hi.

At 4pm PST, the United Airlines flight direct to London finally took off six hours late as the fog had eventually burned off leaving the California sun, offset by the omnipresent LA smog layer, to light up the sky for a short period before the early March sunset. They were seated in Business Class and for the next twelve hours there was not much do but to exhaust the small talk, although that had been pretty much exhausted in the lounge, drink the complimentary drinks, pick at the ever worsening quality food once it was served, watch a movie and then try to fall asleep.

They would now arrive at noon GMT on Thursday at exactly the time of the scheduled meeting with Mick. She had texted him to explain the delay and they had rescheduled the meeting for 2pm GST. It would be tight. She would go directly from Heathrow to the University of London and Troy would go directly to the Roxburgh Hotel where they would meet up later. It would work she felt. She was feeling excited and nervous about the purpose of the trip and her mood had lifted now that they had finally taken off. She had also been lifted by the little message from Calum she had read just before she had shut down her iPhone. Funny that he should just come on out of the blue as she left for a trip to the UK that she had still not told him about.

A twelve hour overnight flight is depressing because the cabin is darkened to allow passengers to sleep when very few can. Certainly it is more comfortable in Business Class than in Coach Class but sleep for any length of time usually proves elusive. For those that cannot sleep, there is the prospect of watching endless movies or simply sitting in the darkened cabin with only one's personal light above to rely on like a shining beacon in a darkened wilderness. That artificial environment does however allow some to continue to drink the complimentary beverages, (sorry, they are not complimentary on United Airlines Coach Class), and that is what they did.

Somewhere over mid-Atlantic, Nerys was vaguely, very vaguely, conscious of she and Troy getting closer and closer, into what might be called a little cuddle, and finally into some sort of embrace. Thereafter, they probably both fell asleep in an awkward tangle because Nerys woke up again soon afterward. She disentangled herself, stopped drinking even when offered, and tried to sleep sitting straight up. She must have dropped off again.

Thursday noon GMT

Calum had cycled from Barclay House all the way to the Glaid Stone without stopping or getting off to push as was often the case on the steep rising road. This day he had a deadline to meet and at exactly noon he arrived at the top.

The views from the highest point of the island were famously stunning on a 360 degree sweep, even more so than from the golf course which was not quite so high. However, today the sky had turned jet black and you just knew that rain was on the way. No mention of that on the BBC this morning thought Calum. Typical! In this part of the world, it could develop into a sudden very heavy rain shower and then the clouds would quickly move on and the sun would come out. Or, it could develop into the light misty rain that still soaked one and tended to hang around all day if not for a couple of days. The unpredictable variety of Scottish weather so contrasted with the predictable certainty of California.

Fifteen minutes later, there was still no sign of Maggie. He could see the road wind eastwards back all the way to the town and there was no cyclist visible.

Suddenly a car pulled up at the top having coming up from the west side which had not captured Calum's attention because that was by far the longer cycle ride and not the way Maggie would have chosen. It was a taxi cab. In fact the taxi cab, the only one on the island. Maggie jumped out and waved to the driver as he set off again. Then she ran the few steps up to the Glaid Stone monument itself.

'What on earth! I never expected you to arrive by cab.'

'Hey I am American. I was born in New York and I now live in LA. Cabs are my way of life.'

'But in Millport?'

'Well, I had brainwave. I told you I was sure I was being followed and the house watched by a curly haired guy driving a little blue van. He keeps popping up everywhere. I figured he would able to easily follow me on a bicycle so I hit on ordering the cab. Then I asked the driver to set out to the ferry terminal as if I was headed to the mainland. This is the clever bit now.'

'Do tell'

'Well I gambled that the van would not just simply follow me on to the ferry. I figured he would have to get instructions from whomever is paying him, probably Joel. So I got the cabbie to cut off on the internal road right before the terminal just as the ferry was pulling out and to wait there until the ferry had pulled out. Then he came up with the idea of bringing me up to your Glaid Stone by the west route. I imagine the van came ˋbarrelling round to the terminal and Curly Hair assumed I had given him the slip by getting on the ferry.'

'Brilliant!'

'I was so happy when the cabbie said there is another way up to the Glaid Stone from the west side and here I am.'

Still Thursday noon GMT

The United Airlines flight from Los Angeles touched down at Heathrow almost on time, at least its rescheduled time. Nerys and Troy were bleary eyed, headachy and bodily stiff thereby revealing jet lag, cruel punishment on a body over a twelve hour period, and diminishing drunkenness/emerging hangover in equal measures. They only had carry-on luggage at Nerys's insistence, it was the only way to travel, so were able to head straight for ground transportation without the delay of waiting for checked in luggage to be disgorged from the plane.

Before they leapt into respective cabs, she went over the plan again as much for her own groggy benefit as for her uncertainty generally about Troy. She would go to the University of London to meet with Dr. Michael Musselwhite. He would go to the Roxburgh and check them in. She should be at the hotel by about 4pm and they would get together to debrief her meeting, have dinner, and plan out the rest of their two days in London.

Her cabbie, so typical of the London cadre of taxi drivers, knew all about the many buildings that make up the University of London. He even knew Lanchester House where Mick resided. And he wanted to talk endlessly to make sure he was the first to extend a warm welcome to this American visitor. By the time, they reached the university; she could add an exceedingly dry mouth and the beginnings of a migraine to her list of ailments. But she was fully caught up on the state of play of British politics, indiscretions among the Royal Family, forecast of the weather (it did not look promising), and even the likely result of the cricket test match at Lords between England and the West Indies which was actually not due to be played until July.

Thursday 2pm GMT

Nerys smiled broadly as she encountered her illustrious colleague. He had not changed at all. He must be at least Calum's age but appeared older. His appearance as always could be likened to an unmade bed.

Mick heartily welcomed her and, immediately sensing jet lag, at once arranged for coffee to be served. He then proceeded to talk about his work and how he had uncovered information that he thought she should know about, given the circumstances around her chosen research project.

'That is if you want to carry on with your project. Don't get me wrong, it is a brilliant topic and definitely needs doing. It is just that I am quite fond of you and I wonder if you should put yourself in the old Stewart Granger. I do 'ave to warn you.'

'Stewart Who?'

'Oh sorry, old 'abits. Stewart Granger is danger. You are heading into danger. Some people call it The Lone Ranger but I am old enough to remember Stewart Granger.'

'Mick, stop it. I don't know if I am more afraid of your language or your message. Just lay it all out for me after you order some more coffee. By English standards it is not half bad. Or would that be not half Alan Ladd?'

'Very good my duck.'

Mick gave her a solid grounding on what had been picked by him and his colleagues around the world. There seemed to be a mass of new information that she had not found on the Internet. Suffice it to say, most of it pertained to one or more of the countries she intended to study and that did not really surprise her. Some of the information was scary but, and Mick underscored this,-- it made her research all the more potentially powerful--that was assuming she did not get bumped off along the way. He told her he would also be able to share some speculative, and not yet fully proven, information about her funding agency that would probably surprise her.

'Still want to do it?'

'Are you kidding me? Of course I do. What you have told me just makes want to get on with it right now.'

'That's my girl. I knew you would but I just wanted to warn you.'

'And I will be prepared to share my findings with you. I trust you to use them thoughtfully.' Nerys had immediately agreed the *quid pro quo* because she sensed there to be value in being associated with Mick and the unknown people he had behind him. That was not a sense she felt toward the US State Department.

They then left his office and walked a short way to a faceless building on Smith Street. The plate beside the door said the Department of Environmental Information and Logistics. When Nerys commented that it did not mean much she was told that was quite deliberate. It was just meant to be a dusty repository of old governmental records.

Once inside, Mick had to provide his own security ID and iris and finger prints even though he was obviously well known to the staff. Then he asked for Nerys's passport which the security personnel examined, copied, and then matched with various records on computer. Then they asked her to initiate iris and finger prints. When she mentioned that a colleague would be joining her tomorrow they were not best pleased.

'He should have been here today. We should be doing a match of the two of you before we clear both of you for entry which we obviously can't do if one of you is missing. Can we?'

Nerys feared that she was going to fail to gain admittance but Mick intervened and said he could vouch for both of them and her colleague would be along tomorrow to provide his details. That was good of him because he had never set eyes on Troy Cameron. Clearly, Mick had clout because not too much later they were into the archives and he was showing her the physical records and how to access the top secret computer records using her newly minted Security ID. He pointed out a place for them to work and reiterated that they could take their own notes in long hand or on a laptop but they could not copy anything and most certainly not remove anything. When they left the building they would be physically searched and expected to show what was on the laptop or notebooks. They should not be offended; he was subject to the same rules every time he came in to the archives.

'That should be you set for tomorrow. I will drop in during the afternoon to see how you are getting on.'

'Mick. I can't thank you enough.'

Still Thursday 2pm GMT

The rain had arrived, the light but very wet misty variety. They were sheltering as best they could in the lea of the bothy used to store the curling equipment beside the nearby pond. Every few years, the pond would freeze over sufficiently to support a game. There seemed to Maggie to be no end to Calum's knowledge of the island.

Maggie had poured out her new information which was really just the old information that had got worse. The most important thing was that she had succumbed to the browbeating of Joel and the gentle persuasion of Nicholas Gorman and had signed the documents authorizing the creation of the two trusts. The only thing she had managed in her favour was to get a side agreement that there would be a so-called cooling off period of forty-eight hours during which the details of the trust agreements could be reopened for negotiation. Once the forty-eight hours elapsed, the agreement was binding and the trusts were created.

She said that several professionals had looked the documents over and basically had all offered the same opinion. The twin trusts was a good tax avoidance vehicle for the couple as long as they remained a couple. The vehicle was just on the right side of legal and should stand up to scrutiny by the UK and American tax authorities.

Joel was now doing his best to make up with her having secured her signature. He had come down to the island last night and arranged a specially catered candlelight dinner for two in their new home. She wanted to believe that everything was above board and maybe things were going to be alright between them but she still had nagging doubts. She could not forget how aggressive he had been in getting the documents signed. He had returned to Glasgow first thing this morning.

'I am not sure there is anything more than can be done in less than forty-eight hours. You may have to just rely on the opinions you have already received.'

'I guess so.'

'Any business transaction is largely built on trust between the parties. Only you can know if you truly trust him.'

'I want to.'

'OK. We better be getting you back before he learns that we have met again. That certainly seems to send him off half-cocked.'

'Thanks for being my friend. I am in this now for better or worse but I will never forget you.'

'Me too. Now you take the bike and use it get back home as fast as you can manage. That way you will not catch pneumonia. I am more accustomed to Scotch Mist so I don't mind walking home in it.'

'Can't we both get on the bike? It's all downhill after all.'

So just like Katharine Ross and Paul Newman, who also had raindrops falling on their heads, they doubled up on Calum's bike. He sat on the saddle and she on the crossbar. First they cycled around in circles to get their balance right and then they set off down the hill. The decline meant no pedalling was necessary but judicious use of both brakes was called for. They started to laugh and Maggie swept her soaking red mane of hair out of Calum's face and turned to kiss him.

'No. No. We are going to crash.'

More laughter ensued as the bicycle made-for-two glided around the curves of the downward road heading toward Millport. Just outside the town the road bisected the buildings of a farm and as they approached it Maggie yelled.

'Stop. Stop.'

'I can't.'

'You must.'

Calum took what only action was open to him and turned hard left on to a lesser road leading up to the Lady Margaret Hospital. Thoughts of his favourite motorcycle speedway and those riders' skills in skidding around bends at high speed flashed through his mind. Although they were on a slight incline now, the momentum that had built up coming down the hill carried them almost up to the gate of the tiny cottage hospital.

Together they kind of fell off the bike, as it finally halted, into an untidy heap. Their reactions were a mixture of laughter, exhilaration, and abject terror on Maggie's face.

'Did you see it? The little blue van was parked at that farm.'

'I did not notice it. You hair did not allow me to see very much of anything. Talk about driving blind.'

'What are we going to do now?'

They picked themselves up and walked into the hospital grounds. It was a very small place with very few staff on site. The medical coverage came from the doctors in Millport based at the Garrison House.

Calum exclaimed, 'Now it's my turn to be brilliant. We will call the taxi cab from inside the hospital, have it come to pick you up and take you home. As long as you stay low down in the seat you should not be noticed as it passes the farm. It will look like the cab had business at the hospital.'

'Brilliant! I love how the Brits say that word.'

The receptionist in the hospital was only too glad to let them use the phone. It looked like she was pleased to get her first visitor of the day.

The cab arrived in twenty minutes and the driver, though he looked a little perplexed to be meeting the eccentric American again, was not going to turn down a fare. As the cab took off, Calum waved to the bedraggled Maggie, who despite the thorough Scottish soaking she had suffered, had a big smile on her face.

'I will come to your place at 8 tonight,' she half mouthed and half said as she wound the window down briefly. 'And, I will bring my toothbrush!'

Calum had no opportunity to reply as the cab sped down the side road and turned left toward the farm. Instead he picked up his bike and proceeded to follow it. As he was cycling though the farm yard, a tall curly haired man came out of the barn and made to get into the little blue van parked by the side of the road. Calum stopped and addressed him.

'Mr. Duncan it is, isn't it?'

'What if it is?'

'I have been meaning to talk to you since the Cumbraes Council meeting. I wanted to find out what you had against me helping out with the development plan.'

'Mr. Taggart and Mr. Wanna.........' He turned away and said, 'What if I don't want to talk to you?'

'Maybe you just did. But I can't force you. I will probably see you later.'

Calum remounted his bike and started to pedal off.

'Where have you been anyway in this pissing rain?'

'Just enjoying the beauty of this fine island even when the weather does not want to cooperate. You better report that in to Mr. Taggart and Mr. Wanna.'

Chapter 20

Nerys arrived at the Roxburgh Hotel having walked from the archives location, her head spinning with the information that Mick had already given her. She now knew that she had to contact Calum because some of it would be of direct interest to him.

She mentioned her name to the receptionist and asked for her key. He checked the computer, and then he checked the box where the keys were kept and then he somewhat hesitantly informed her that Mr. Cameron had taken both keys for Room 112.

'You don't mean there is only one room, do you?'

'Yes. That is what Mr. Cameron requested. So we let the other room go half an hour ago. We are surprisingly busy for this time of year. I am afraid the hotel is full. Were Mr. Cameron's arrangements not to your liking?'

'You could say that again. Would you kindly call up to 112 and ask him to meet me in the bar.'

Nerys was already nursing a large gin and tonic, all thoughts of hangovers now superceded by other problems, when Troy wandered in smiling.

'There you are. What in hell are you thinking about cancelling the two rooms and taking just one?'

He stared at her for a while, the brashness of his demeanour rapidly disappearing.

'I thought that we had gotten on so well on the plane that this was the next logical step. You have been giving me all sorts of messages before that even. Have you not?'

Nerys's mind raced through the somewhat ambiguous relationship she had allowed to develop and then the drunken caper on the plane. Here she was, all but fifty years of age, happily married, and in a responsible position in higher education. In spite of his looks and impressive qualifications, Troy was half her age. In an instant, she took a position.

'You have got it so wrong Troy. You are my research assistant. And you will not be my lover. If I misled you into thinking otherwise, I apologize.'

His stunned face was now turning stark white.

'We will not be sharing a room in this hotel or anywhere else. Do you get the message now?'

He dumbly nodded. In the short time since he arrived in the bar, she had plotted out what she had to do next.

'There is going to be a change in plans. As a result of my meeting with Dr. Musselwhite, I will have to do other things so I will not need to stay here anyway. You will start doing the research tomorrow into the files and computer information on your own. I will give you the address and you can walk there. It is not far from here. I will ask Dr. Musselwhite to meet you there at 10am to arrange your security clearance. You will need to take your passport. Does all that make sense to you?'

'I guess so. Where will you be?'

'I have other business to take care of. I will be back the day after tomorrow and will join you in the archives. We can finish off the notes in time for our evening flight back to LA.'

He nodded his understanding without showing a great deal of enthusiasm. That was so unlike him.

'I guess I need to ask you. Given your misinterpretation of our working relationship, do you want to continue to serve as my research assistant?'

Nerys knew this was not a foregone conclusion. She also knew that if he were to choose to take off, her whole visit to London would be messed up.

She continued, 'I am prepared to just forget the misunderstanding. I greatly value your research skills and the effort you have already put into *our* project. I hope you will continue.'

She was counting on his not inconsiderable ego dictating his response and she was correct. He agreed to do the work tomorrow just as she had suggested.

Nerys made a play of shaking hands formally and then made to leave the bar to collect her luggage. Time was of the essence.

Still Thursday 4pm GMT

Calum sent a third text message to Maggie suggesting her planned visit to Barclay House was not the best idea. Just like the first two, it went unanswered. She could be headstrong, almost imperious at times, and he imagined her just ignoring the messages because they went against what she wanted. He tried calling her, something he had never done before because they had agreed earlier that the security of mobile calls could not be guaranteed. The phone rang but there was no answer. He did not leave a message

He thought about cycling round to her house but if anything the rain was heavier. And, he did not want to run the risk of confronting Tommy Duncan again.

He tried to get his mind around her visiting him. He would spend some time with her and then try to persuade her to return home. That was the best solution. But, in this rain? Maybe it was OK to have her stay over. Was he mad? Ever since he had met her, she and her husband had caused him trouble. He was in over his head. But how to get out of this mess? He should talk to her seriously and then insist she goes home. Maybe there would be no harm in one night. One last night. She was an incredible woman.

No clarity whatsoever emerged from his random thoughts. Play it by ear was one of his favourite expressions. In the absence of a game plan, it looked like he would be doing exactly that.

In the intervening four hours, no message had come from Maggie. Calum, he had no doubt driven by a looming sense of guilt, had texted Nerys but she was not answering either. Where the hell was she?

In the run up to 8pm, Calum peered out of the window northward on West Bay Road. That was surely the way Maggie would come. There was no sign of her. Remember how she had arrived at the Glaid Stone, he turned to study southward on West Bay Road just in case. There was no sign of her. How would she come, by cab surely in this weather? But, perhaps on foot?

Eight o'clock came and went without Maggie arriving. The night was now black dark and the rain was sheeting down. It was difficult to see more than twenty yards ahead but he was up and down every few minutes to look left and right, to no avail.

Thursday 9pm GMT

Calum's anxiety was at fever pitch. He felt like he was going to have heart attack as the wait continued. From being dead set against Maggie's visit, to being reluctant enough to text her, he was now somehow desperate for her to show up. What was keeping her? He did not think she was the kind just not to show up when she had decided that was something she wanted to do.

Suddenly the doorbell rang.

The silence he had been sitting in was shattered. He had missed her on his many looks out of the bay window. She was here. Maggie was here. What now? That heart attack seemed imminent.

He slowly walked toward the front door.

The bell rang again.

He hesitated behind the door until the bell rang again, then he slowly opened it and peered out.

Nerys said, 'For fuck's sake let me in. Does it never do anything but rain here?'

'What? What are you doing here?'

'I was in the neighbourhood and I just thought I would look in on you. Are you going let me in or will I just make a puddle in the hallway?'

Nerys came in, stripped, and stepped in to a revitalizing hot shower. All the while, Calum peered right then left out of the bay window.

They settled down together. Nerys had been pleased and surprised to find chilled white wine in the little fridge, something she would not have thought Calum would have bothered about when he was left to his own devices and given the amount of bottles of red wine on the shelf above the fridge.

'You must have known I was coming after all,' she purred.

'Not at all, I am so surprised to see you.'

'Well I have a lot to tell you. Come away from the window and I will tell you all about it.'

She proceeded to tell him the whole story starting with Mick's surprise call to California. Calum remembered Mick as a bit of a character and knew that they had kept in touch. She described how she and Troy Cameron had come over for a very short visit to look at Mick's evidence. That was why she had not told him she was coming. She thought she would have no time to visit Millport on this occasion.

She carefully omitted all of the mistake or misunderstanding with Troy, whichever it was, before going on to describe in detail all of what Mick had told her. Without even waiting for careful examination of the evidence, Troy would start that tomorrow; she knew that she had to find a way of letting Calum know. So she had simply hopped on the five o'clock flight from Gatwick to Glasgow, the seven o'clock train from Paisley Gilmour Street to Largs, the last ferry at 8.15 pm and here she was.

They talked for a good two hours about the information that Nerys had brought. Calum paced the room, alternating between glancing out the window and staring at his wife. Only one car had approached but thankfully it had carried on beyond Barclay House. Later, he thought he had caught sight of it going the other way toward town.

'What can we make of this? It is getting more and more confusing.'

'You need to process it. Perhaps discuss it with Heather Randall. Will I get to meet her tomorrow?'

'I don't even know if she is on the island right now.'

'Let's go to bed. I want to make mad passionate love with my husband. I will give you an adventure.'

'I think I might have had too many of them. But I will accept your invitation.'

The doorbell did not ring again that night.

Chapter 21

Nerys and Calum did not rise early the next morning. They lay in bed watching the rising sun from the east project a sunbeam across the ocean from the mainland to their window. They now felt closer together than they had for quite a while in spite of the trials and temptations that both of them had faced during their separation, or perhaps because of them. They would only have a day before she had to leave but they intended make full use of it.

The rain had finally blown itself out and the morning had arrived crisp and bright. Everything felt fresh as it often does after heavy rain. They considered getting a bicycle for her but in the end opted for walking. While he had had plenty of practice in the last two months, his absence from California had meant that she had not been walking much of late. Cumbrae was just the place to get back into the habit again.

They walked slowly along the promenade as Nerys took in the sights again. All were very familiar yet she felt like she was seeing them for the first time. They fully intended to share with each other all that had happened since he left on that December day from LAX, or at least most of it all, but for now they just strolled silently. They were happy to be together again and happy to be in the place he loved the most and she loved because he loved it.

A leisurely breakfast was taken at the Dancing Midge Café. He was eating continental food as he had developed a taste for it and she was a devouring an artery-busting, full Scottish breakfast while glancing at him and wondering what had brought about the change in him. Calum spied a discarded copy of the Daily Record lying beside him and decided just to leave it there, twice that newspaper had been the bearer of bad news for him. They both consulted their mobiles. He was relieved to see no messages from anyone. She had messages from Troy and Mick. Both seemed to think that Troy's scrutiny of the archives was already going well after the first hour. She could not help but feel a little guilty at being far from where the work was being done. But, she also knew that the information she passed on to Calum was worthwhile and actually getting together with him was even more worthwhile.

Eventually at close to noon, they set off by East Bay to walk completely around the island. It would take at least three hours without setting a demanding pace and that is just what they intended. Almost immediately they had to pass the Wannamaker House. Calum knew this was a calculated risk but there was no sign of life about the place. Somehow, that did not surprise him. He suspected that Maggie had broken their date and taken off for Glasgow yesterday afternoon. If so, that would be a good thing.

Next, he pointed out the home of Heather Randall and her husband. Again, there was no sign of life. That was not so surprising. Nicholas would be in Glasgow. If Heather were on the island, she would be at the research station. Nerys showed keen interest in meeting Heather so as they arrived at the research station they entered on the off chance that she would be free. The receptionist reported that Heather was in Glasgow. At that moment, Heather's administrative assistant passed by and said in a very friendly voice.

'Good morning Dr. Davies, or is it afternoon. How are you today?' Then her eyes and smile pointedly shifted to the other person, clearly wanting to be introduced.

'Hello Mary. This my wife Nerys in on a flying visit from California. I was hoping we might catch Dr. Randall.'

Mary's face momentarily betrayed the processing of a potential collision between Calum's wife, his long-time school friend, and the Hollywood star, then she regained her composure.

'Dr. Randall will be sorry she missed you. She is up in Glasgow meeting Mr. Macadam from SERC about the request we got yesterday from the government to do work at Farland Power Station.'

'Cyrus Macadam?' Nerys asked.

'Yes. Do you know him?'

'That I do. It is a small world is it not?'

'She will be back tomorrow afternoon. Can I make arrangements for you to meet with her then?'

'I am afraid that will not work. I have to leave for London first thing in the morning. We will need to make it another time. I am still hoping to make it back over in the summer.'

Calum said, 'Mary, if you could find some time for me to meet with Dr. Randall in the afternoon, I would appreciate it. I have some things to discuss and I will be interested to hear how things went with Mr. Macadam.'

'How about four o'clock, I know she is free then.'

'That will work fine. We are off to conquer the island. Goodbye for now.'

Nerys and Calum walked slower that they would normally and used the walk to bring each other up to date with the news. The Lion Rock was passed, then the National Watersports Centre where things were quiet this being the off-season apart from some kayakers paddling in the protected area; obviously they were beginners. By the time they reached the ferry terminal for the short crossing to Largs, they had imparted much of the information they had each gathered. The common interest in Cyrus Macadam and SERC was as troubling for one as the other. And the indirect connection to Joel Wannamaker further complicated things. If the information that Mick

Musselwhite had unearthed proved to be accurate, they were both likely going to be affected and it would bring Heather Randall into the equation as well.

Nerys had described in detail the arrangements that she had made to visit China and India, in particular the high ranking politicians and bureaucrats who had agreed to cooperate with her. She could not hide her excitement and pride over how things had progressed so far and Calum too was proud of her. He worried about some of the emerging risks but knew that Nerys was extremely competent and very confident in her own abilities. She had also started to make preliminary arrangements for Russia and finally Brazil. It was obvious that the next year or longer was going to be a busy time for her. He realized that if he were still sitting around in California, it would be hard for him to take her absences and the intensity with which she was throwing herself into the project. But now that he had so many things going here, it would work out fine. They could both concentrate on their projects without feeling guilty about the other.

As they made their way down the west side of the island, having chosen not to cut up to the Glaid Stone as Maggie had done, they continued on the flat road that hugs the coastline all the way round. The intensity of their sharing of information with each other had now diminished as they exhausted the topics. Instead, they started to have periods of silence while they just soaked up the ambience of an early spring day and other periods where they started to talk about the future. Once Nerys had her tenure and had put in the necessary fifteen years with the university, she could consider taking early retirement with a decent pension and the all-important health benefits secured.

'I thought you always said that you had lots more to do in your career. The way you are talking now, you could be done in five years when you are fifty five. Why the change of heart?'

'I have watched you from afar over the last three months. I see there is more to life than just work. I also see there is more than just living in California all the time. You have changed your whole attitude and it looks good on you. Maybe I would like to try some of that too.'

'You mean live here part of the time?'

'You never know. I had a warmer climate in mind but there is a lot of character here in between rain showers. I could get used to it.'

'I like it a lot. I would not want to move here permanently but if we could organize our lives where we were out of the rat race and able to do meaningful things in both California and here, it might be perfect.'

'Sounds like a plan.'

'No, it is far from a plan. But it might be a damned fine idea. We need to work on the plan.'

'OK.'

'And first we need to get you through your project and into tenure. I know that is important to you.'

'I love you. You do know that don't you?'

'I think I do know it. And, the feeling is mutual.'

Eventually they reached Westview and went in to call on Scotty Green. He was delighted to see Calum's better half, as he had come to refer to her when hearing stories from America. He was most disappointed to learn that her visit was not to extend beyond tonight but insisted that they have dinner with him. Nerys was delighted to accept because she did not feel much like cooking and she doubted that Calum had changed his ways that much that meal preparation was on his revised curriculum vitae.

After a swift drink with Scotty, they completed their walk back to Barclay House. As they passed Wee Cumbrae, Nerys admired it in the cloudless sky.

'I would like to visit there one day. It looks just like a smaller less developed version of Great Cumbrae. I bet there are great walks. Have you been there?'

'Once as a child, I went to visit the lighthouse you see there on the right. That was a long time ago. The lighthouse is not even operational now.'

'Do you think you will get over there while you are staying here?'

'No. I can't think of any reason to. I will wait until you are able to spend some time here and then we can explore it together.'

'Does anybody live there?'

'Nobody permanently that I know of. The lighthouse people are all gone. There is a mansion house on the other side that you can't see from here. I think it is owned by Glasgow folks but I read that since they bought they have seldom ever visited.'

They spent the rest of the afternoon just relaxing except when each checked their mobiles. Calum had no messages but Nerys got constant reports from Troy. With each new piece of information about China and India, she talked about how it would affect the research and influence the findings to be published.

That evening they enjoyed a perfect dinner at Westview. Scotty was the consummate host. He flirted shamelessly with Nerys and she just encouraged him. She showed keen interest in his knowledge of the history and people of Millport and that was all the encouragement he needed. It was Calum, even though he was thoroughly enjoying the evening, who had to remind them both that Nerys was planning to catch the first ferry in the morning. Reluctantly, the party broke up just before midnight with firm resolutions made to resume the fun when Nerys came over in the summer.

Calum waved to his wife as she departed in the island taxi cab for the ferry terminal before the sun was even up next morning. He could not help wondering where the last person he had waved to had gone.

Chapter 22

Nerys's fleeting visit to Millport was completed without incident. She arrived at Gatwick just before 11am and was back in the archives department just after noon. She was pleased to see Troy Cameron working diligently away while munching on an early lunch sandwich.

He was relieved to see her back and immediately took her through all the notes he had prepared from the physical files and the top secret Internet references. It was obvious that both China and India had struggled to develop coherent policies for radioactive waste disposal that could be consistently and effectively practised. Numerous failures had been experienced in both countries that had caused the policies to be reviewed and revised. None of these failures had been openly reported because they had led to significant contamination affecting the food chain and directly to human deaths.

Sorting through the reports in chronological order, it was apparent that progress was being made but at high costs and neither country was at a point where they could say they had the problem solved on an ongoing basis. It occurred to Nerys that she may have to expand her research project to feature not only successes but also failures, and the reasons why, if she could determine them. That was going to be more delicate in getting cooperation from local politicians and officials.

'Did you get a sense why both countries still seem to be moving forward on a trial and error basis? Why would they not take the best of what the developed counties have already adopted and perhaps customize it to their own needs? I can't believe the

US policy would not be a good starting point for any country's own.'

'I would have thought that too, but you would be surprised. Dr. Musselwhite gave me access to some American material. Since the President put a halt on the creation of a deep geological repository at Yucca Mountain in Nevada, the United States has had no coherent strategy for the long-term storage of radioactive waste. No strategy. Nada. It is kind of scary to know that storage of the spent plutonium rods is to be managed on site at San Onofre which is not far from where we work and even closer to where you live. You have to wonder about the safety standards.'

'Wow. I was not aware of that.'

'I suspect the vast majority of the American people are not aware either. And San Onofre was just a relatively small power station. What about places like Hanford in Washington State?'

'This is beyond the scope of our project but I suspect that the good Dr. Mick led us by the noses to the American information so that we can create a baseline comparison to the BRIC data.'

'What will we do with the information?'

'I think we have no choice other than to broaden the scope of the project. It would be bad academic form to draw conclusions solely from the Chinese and Indian data without placing them in a developed world context. Did you come across how the Brits are doing?'

'I did not do much on them but what I picked up seemed to suggest they have adopted a stratified strategy using existing mines and new tunnels in remote areas. Maybe, they have less political pressure on them than we do.'

'I suspect they will have different political pressure but no less than we do. I wonder if we can subcontract with my husband to do a baseline analysis of the UK public policy. He already seems to be up to his neck in a local issue in Scotland which fits right into what we are studying in the BRIC countries.'

'Is that where you went yesterday?'

'It was. I picked up important information from Mick that Calum needed to be aware of. It is bizarre how all of this is coming together and impacting our project.'

'What do you plan for the rest of the afternoon? We are due to fly out at 10pm.'

'I suggest that I take your notes, which look excellent by the way, and further refine them to see if there any holes in the information trail. If I find any, you can do a quick follow up before we leave. Meanwhile you can just continue what you have been doing to add to the body of knowledge as all good researchers say.'

'OK.'

'Tell me, did you come across anything on SERC?'

'Dr. Musselwhite did not provide any source data for SERC but I came across references to them here and there. They seem to have their fingers in radioactive pies all over the globe. Should I look for something in particular?'

'I suspect you would not find what Mick shared with me privately. I will share it with you on the plane back.'

Nerys noted that Troy accepted that their time on the return flight would be spent more productively than on the incoming flight to London and was showing real professional enthusiasm for the project work.

The balance of their day passed without unearthing any really surprising information and, by the end, Nerys felt they had good tight information to inform their enquiries when they travelled to China and India. Mick dropped by just as they were clearing up and invited them to an early dinner before they had to head to the airport.

Meanwhile, Calum was seated in Heather Randall's office. She had returned from Glasgow but had stepped out to speak with someone at reception. On impulse, Calum decided to try to reach Maggie Wannamaker again. He had sent several texts to no avail. This time he decided to phone. There were three rings and then his phone went silent. Did that mean her phone was switched off or the battery was dead?

Heather returned and they both announced they had new information on SERC. Calum indicated she should go first.

The local MSP had called Heather two days ago to say that all parties in the Scottish Parliament were in agreement that a formal request should be made to the Cumbraes Environmental Research Station to look further into the rumour of unaccounted for flasks at Farland Power Station. Advance agreement among the five parties was a rare thing and it really rendered superfluous the vote which would take place today. As a consequence, and because she had other business in Glasgow anyway, Heather had travelled yesterday to meet with Cyrus Macadam.

She was not surprised to learn that he already knew about the proposal to get the research station involved and the all party agreement on it. Generally, he always seemed to be well informed about political discussions on the Farland project. But that did not mean to say he was in agreement. Far from it. He had adopted an outright truculent stance to her suggestion that SERC and the research station offer a united front on the matter. In effect, he had said that if the research station wanted to jump at the beck and call of politicians and to blatantly check up on what were supposed to be its colleagues, then go ahead but not to expect any cooperation from SERC.

She had tried to appeal to him on the grounds that she did not want the research station to be at the beck and call of government and that, by the two contractors collaborating, they could send a message to government of a united front. She did not want the two contractors to be played off against one another. But it was all to no avail. Macadam refused outright to have anything to do with any examination of the records and procedures at Farland. He stated that her Mr. Davies had already satisfied himself on the procedures so there was no point in any examination at all.

Heather expressed her regret that he was taking this position but announced that she would be going ahead. She would form a small team consisting of Dr. Davies, a research station administrator, and herself and would make arrangements with the power station management to pay a visit. 'Go ahead and waste your time,' was the parting comment from Macadam.

Calum doubted, in spite of Macadam's hands-off declaration that he would keep out of the visit. It was obvious from his previous encounter that Macadam held power over Tom Wilson, the power station manager. He predicted that Macadam would be in touch with Wilson before, and after, any visit by Heather's team. She agreed but doubted that anything could be done to prevent it. They could, however, try to assess in any meeting with Wilson whether he was in direct collusion with SERC. If that were the case, it might be something that could be taken up with more senior personnel at the utility company.

'I doubt very much that we going to find a smoking gun, in other words clear documentary evidence that any flasks containing the radioactive waste have gone missing. When we report such, it will vindicate SERC unfortunately. In some ways we will end being used both by government for political purposes and SERC for corroboration purposes.'

'Please don't say that.'

'I fear it will transpire that way. But I can't think of how you could have got out of the government order in the first place. To have refused would have just suggested you were in bed with SERC, so to speak, and would have been downright dangerous for your future funding from government.'

Calum went on to tell Heather about Nerys's surprise visit and the bombshell she had shared with him. During her private meeting with Dr. Michael Musselwhite when they had discussed various aspects of the global problem surrounding safe disposal of radioactive waste, he had informed her that he had come across suggestions, and little more than that, that SERC might be playing an illegal part in some transactions. There was no hard proof but the name had come up a couple of times around the world.

He went on to explain how an illicit market in the sale of radioactive waste for the purpose of building weapons of mass destruction had slowly crept into existence. Sellers normally consisted of countries that were too lazy or poor to properly deal with waste disposal or even countries with a secret desire to aid and abet global terrorism. Buyers normally consisted of the well-known rogue states in the Middle East and Asia or out and out terrorist organizations with cross border affiliations. However, what were needed to bring the buyers and sellers together were classic brokers or middlemen. There were only a very few around the world and little was known as to their identities by the developed nations' intelligence agencies. However, SERC had popped up occasionally on the radar being studied by the Brits. There was nothing definitive, merely a suggestion that amidst all the legitimate environmental work and sponsoring SERC was engaged in, they might be financing and arranging the logistics of some illicit transactions. This would require large sums of money to pay off the seller and arrange the clandestine transfer of the radioactive waste. Then in turn, the waste would be sold to a willing buyer under cover of darkness for even larger sums of money.

'My God, This is terrible. So they carry on legitimate work and even build up quite a good reputation, and all the while they are profiteering from global terrorism.'

'Succinctly put. But remember the important word is might. There is no absolute proof at this stage.'

'But how could they come up with the money to finance such transactions? The sums must be vast. SERC is just a small organization owned by a university.'

'Enter Joel Wannamaker perhaps? It does not make sense that he could make a lot of money out of interim financing research projects until they get their funding as has been reported. That is a banker's work and there is not much money in it. That is why it is difficult to get regular banks to show interest in participating in research. But interim financing of illegal deals, which no regular banks would touch, would have huge profits in them and that is maybe where Wannamaker makes the money that allows him to dabble in the not-so-profitable legitimate research and waste disposal such as Farland.'

'If indeed Farland is legitimate?'

'Quite so. That is why your team's visit is important even if I have my doubts as to any likely success.'

'This is huge, potentially. Can we not get some help? This seems totally beyond the capabilities of the research station and, if you don't mind me saying so, the recently early retired accountant on the lookout for an adventure.'

'I could not agree more. But who could we go to?'

'The police?'

'The police would probably not even bother writing our statement of suspicion down. The intelligence agencies would wonder where we got the top secret speculation from and probably arrest us for some breach of the Official Secrets Act. No, our little team is lumbered with this one all on its own I am afraid.'

'We must be very careful. If SERC is even remotely involved in these illegal activities then they will play rough. Your assault might just be the tip of the iceberg.'

'Yes. I think it is important that the next steps be done as publicly as possible. SERC will not want to do anything rash that brings attention upon them, any more than has already occurred through the Daily Record. We might want to inform the Record what we are doing in response to the government order.'

'I did not think you would have much time for the Daily Record except for perhaps the sports pages.'

'I don't, but it seems that like the so-called serious newspapers are not biting on this Farland rumour at all. The Record might be our only hope. Do you have any contacts?'

'None that I can think of but I will do some calling around.'

'OK. Let's leave it at that right now. Have you seen the Wannamakers recently?'

'No. Nicholas was saying that he had not heard much from Joel now that the trusts and house deal have been completed.'

'I will see you later. Nerys was sorry she was not able to meet you. She had to get back to London to finish some research there. Hopefully, she will back over in the summer and we can all get together.'

'Yes, Mary was all eyes agog at meeting your wife. That was the first thing she told me when I got into the office. She said she was beautiful.'

'Indeed she is, in more ways than one.'

Chapter 23

Calum had been splitting the last few days into museum work in the mornings and golf championship work in the afternoons. He was happy with the progress he was making on both fronts.

He was well advanced in preparation to mount an entirely new exhibition of museum artefacts entitled *"Education in Millport Over the Years"*. Using most of the open public space in the Garrison House, he would be able to track the history of the primary school using school records and photographs. In addition, he was going to set up an online version of the exhibit. Both the online and public versions would include a feature where past pupils or their descendants could locate personal records and photographs. It was anticipated that the exhibit would be operational in June after some important beta testing. Scotty Green was delighted with the prospect of going live. It was exactly the kind of open access to the island's history that had fuelled his enthusiasm for the museum project over the last fifty years. He had despaired of ever completing the project. Now thanks to the leadership of his transatlantic friend, it was going to happen.

On the golf front, Calum was also making good progress. He had succeeded in attracting several high-profile sponsors to help with the cost of mounting the revived Marquess of Bute Cup and to provide attractive prizes. The championship would take place on the third Saturday in July which was traditionally the busiest time of the holiday season. In addition, he had devised a novel event to take place the day before. Drawing on the professional golf practice of holding a Pro-Am on the eve of a championship which featured the top professionals playing alongside celebrities and sponsors, Calum had organized an *"Ams & Hams"* event featuring the top amateurs, who would play the following day for the cup, alongside celebrities and sponsors.

When he floated the idea with the Club President, the response he got was, 'I have never heard the like of it. But if not, why not?' The event would serve two purposes. It would enhance the championship itself and most of the Friday participants would stay over to the Saturday because they were playing again, or they were sponsors and would want to be recognized, or they just might as well make a weekend of it. That would boost hotel and boarding house occupancy rates and Scotty Green was delighted when he heard about the plan. Calum was working on attracting a particular celebrity. If he was successful, it would be bring immense publicity to the event.

The final piece to be put in place was to attract the top amateur golfers from the region. His plan was not to just open the event to applicants with the necessary handicap but to do it by invitation to the very best. He hoped this would create a sense of prestige for those receiving invitations. First, he wanted to float the idea with the West of Scotland Golf Association and hopefully enlist their help in determining who should be invited. To that end, he was travelling with Millport Golf Club member Charlie Caldwell to the Glasgow Gailes Golf Club where the Association was based.

Calum was thankful that Charlie had agreed to come along. Firstly, he knew several members of the Association including its CEO. Secondly, he had a car. Calum had assumed that once off the Largs ferry, they were on their way to Glasgow. Charlie explained that Glasgow Gailes Golf Club was founded in 1787 and was the ninth oldest club in the world. It actually had two top courses, one in Glasgow and the other at

Gailes on the Ayrshire coast to the south. It was to the latter that they were bound.

They found that the officers of the West of Scotland Golf Association were just a little taken aback with the novel plans to revive the Marquess of Bute Cup. The *"Ams & Hams"* and the invitation-only rule were definitely departures from the norm but the enthusiasm of Calum and Charlie won them over. In the end, they agreed not only to endorse the tournament and participate in a publicity campaign but to facilitate the creation of the invitation list. They also suggested connecting with their East, North, and Borders counterparts to ensure that cream of Scottish golf was involved.

As they drove back to Largs, Charlie was ecstatic. He had gone from being a somewhat reluctant volunteer driver to the number one ambassador for the new tournament over the course of a day. Calum too was very pleased with their success. Having just missed a ferry sailing, mainly because Charlie was inclined to drive slower and slower the more he talked, Calum suggested they have a celebratory drink in Largs while waiting for the next ferry.

'You have been good for Millport laddie. We needed to change the way we do things and you have brought in good ideas. I am not just talking about the Golf Club. I know Scotty Green is delighted the way things are going with his museum.'

It was a long time since Calum had been referred to as a laddie but he supposed it was appropriate. Charlie Caldwell must be twenty years older than him if he was a day. But the old character was spry and alert, no doubt sharpened up by the many hours he spent at the Golf Club and on the course. He had mentioned he could shoot his age and that was something to be proud of.

'It amazes me Charlie that I can get so much pleasure doing things here that I purposely avoided doing in California. This is a great community. It is a privilege to be even a temporary member.'

'If the Marquess of Bute Cup proves to be as much a success as I think it is going to be, your permanent residence might well be made mandatory,' was the response along with loud laughter.

As they supped their ale, Calum's thoughts drifted toward Maggie Wannamaker. It was now over a week since that day up at the Glaid Stone and there had been no contact with her at all. He hoped she was well in Glasgow, or better still back in California. The end of their unusual relationship had been a bit of a strain on him because he desired that it come to an end as much as he desired that it not come to an end. It was Charlie that broke the silence.

'Dearie me. We have just gone and missed the ferry again. I better get another couple in and we better pay attention this time or else we will be spending the night in Largs.'

They did succeed in catching the next ferry and, as they sat in the car on the short trip over to the island, their attention was summoned by Constable Jardin who was parked next to them.

'How did it go?'

Obviously their trip to golf headquarters was known to the local constabulary and they both took delight in relating the success story. Harry was pleased that the island would be involved in another positive event even if it meant an extra busy weekend for him and perhaps some additional help would have to be brought in from the mainland. As they pulled into the Cumbrae Slip, Harry asked Calum to drop by the police station on his way home.

Intrigued by what it was that the police officer could not say in front of Charlie, Calum made straight for the police station once he was dropped off by his travelling companion. There was no answer at the locked station door but Harry was next door in the house and invited Calum in. This was the first time he had been in the house.

'I just got back from a briefing in Largs. Detective Inspector McBride came down especially from Police Scotland West HQ in Glasgow. We were informed that Mr. Joel Wannamaker has reported his wife Margaret to be missing. He has had no contact with her for nine days now and has no idea where she is.'

'Do the police have any leads to go on?'

'None at all. His last contact with her was a dinner in Millport. He went back to Glasgow the following morning and she was supposed to be back in Glasgow the day after. She was to stay on to receive some furniture that was being delivered. Mr. Wannamaker checked with the company and they told him that nobody was at the Millport house to meet them.'

'What is going to happen now?'

'At this stage it is to be kept hush-hush. Being an actress, she is no stranger to publicity but her husband does not want it made public at this time. She could be anywhere in Scotland or England for that matter. There is no evidence that she has gone back to the States but that can't be totally discounted. So enquiries are to take place here and there.'

'Are you going to organize a search on the island?'

'That is correct. I also need to get a statement from you. DI McBride was informed you and she were quite good friends and you may well know of her whereabouts.'

'I assume Wannamaker did the informing. I do know Maggie but not very well. I will tell you everything I know right now unless you want to wait until you are on duty.'

'I am always on duty. But at least when I am in the house and not next door in the station there is no reason why we can't have a little dram before you tell me your story.'

Having quenched their thirst to their joint satisfaction, Calum went on to give Harry an abridged version of his relationship with Maggie from their meeting on the plane, the surprise dinner with Scotty Green and Evan Davis, the cycle around the island that culminated in the Ritz Café incident, and the meeting in Minstrels restaurant. He chose these encounters because they were verifiable by others. He omitted the visit to the Wannamaker house and the Glaid Stone meeting because he believed that those could not be verified by anyone.

He characterized the relationship as one that began by pure chance on the flight over and continued by chance because she had known Evan Davis for a long time and Calum was meeting him for the first time. Thereafter, Maggie had sought him out on the cycle ride around the island to ask financial advice because of his accountancy background. He acknowledged that she was concerned about the appropriateness of the direction that her husband wanted to take on their joint finances and wanted an independent opinion that her interests were being looked after. He stated that he had limited ability to give her a definitive answer and the best he could do was advise her to get specialist help.

Harry asked him when he last saw Maggie. Now caught in the web of deceit he had spun, he had to say that the brief encounter with her and others in Minstrels was the last time.

Harry then asked him a very direct question.

'Was there something other than financial advising going on between the two of you?'

'No, there was not.'

'Why then did she choose to give you a kiss in the Ritz? A big kiss by all accounts.'

'What can I say? She appreciated that I was trying to help her with her financial concerns. She was a very effusive lady.'

'Was?'

'Is. Is. She is a very effusive lady. She was being effusive on that occasion.'

'And you reciprocated?'

'I did not resist.'

'Why not?'

'Would you have? In any case, it just happened. Maggie is one of these people; maybe a typical Hollywood type, who openly demonstrates her feelings. I don't. But, I was just caught up in it.'

'I see.'

'I hope you do Harry. I am concerned about her disappearance. What can you tell me about it?'

'All I know is her husband reported her missing after about a week.'

'Is that not odd in itself?'

'Maybe. He says he assumed she was still down in Millport looking after the furnishing of the new house but he could not reach her.'

'And they don't normally speak for a week?'

'Hmm.'

'Have you any theories?'

'Not really. The main assumption at this stage has to be that she has chosen to make herself unavailable, at least to her husband. She could be hiding out anywhere. However, we cannot dismiss the possibility that she has met with some misfortune although there is no evidence to support that at this time.'

'Is there anything I can do to help?'

'Not really. If you want to call around anyone who might be aware of her whereabouts, I cannot stop you. Likewise, if you want to take a look around the island in the unlikely event that she is hiding out here again I can't stop you.'

'That does not sound like you are very keen to have me help out.'

'You are in a very awkward position at this stage. Best that you keep a low profile.'

'Alright.'

'But, I have to ask you a formal question to bring this statement to a conclusion. You have no idea as to the present whereabouts of Margaret Wannamaker?'

'I do not.'

'Fair enough. I will have most of our chat typed up as a formal statement and will ask you to sign it tomorrow. Thanks Calum.'

Chapter 24

Nerys had been back in California for a few days and had been busy making final arrangements for the China/India trip while at the same time agonizing over the information she had learned in London.

The additional information on the two countries had caused her to expand the scope of her research project which in turn required that she modify how she was going interact with the respective government officials. She did not want the project to be a whitewash of success or a negative condemnation of failure on the part of China and India so she had to find the right balance that explored both sides of their stories.

She had roughed out the concept of an expanded project and then left Troy Cameron to do much of the design work. She was pleased to see that all of his attention seemed to be focused now on the project and she had to acknowledge that he was displaying considerable research skills. His participation could only enhance the project and findings and she was relieved that they seemed to have been able to move beyond their embarrassing misunderstanding in London.

The other information she had garnered was quite something else. Even a suggestion that SERC might be involved in illegal dealings was a potential bombshell to her project and to the California University in general. After all, the university technically owned the corporation even though it had a very hands-off relationship with it. The problem was that the speculative information was highly confidential. She had given her word that she would not share it with anyone other than Calum. That included Dean Salisbury who had very much been in the loop thus far. Excluding her now was causing Nerys no end of angst. Her highly curtailed report to the dean when she had asked about the trip was still troubling her greatly.

Nerys seriously wondered whether she should be getting independent legal advice. However, she also worried that any consultation would be construed as a breach of the confidentiality that she had undertaken to maintain. Even Troy only knew a little about the SERC suspicions and did not seem to grasp the enormity of the possible consequences. Therefore, she was left to ponder what the next steps were all on her own.

She decided to consult with Calum because he was at least known by London to be somewhat in the loop. A long telephone conversation had taken place when it was midnight her time.

Calum confessed that with the Maggie Wannamaker disappearance coming up he had not had time to do any research on the UK record on radioactive waste disposal.

'That is not so important right now. I would just include anything you turn up from a comparative perspective when I come to write up my findings. There is no hurry right now. But why should her disappearance be affecting you?'

That was a difficult question to answer. Calum told her that in his couple of meetings with Maggie she had shared with him her concern that her husband was basically stealing their joint assets for his own purposes. And, she had expressed fears for her marriage and by extension for her own safety. Now she had either disappeared of her own volition or something else had happened to her. That obviously concerned him given what she had told him. He mentioned he had given a statement to the police but he wished he could do more. He just did not have a clue how to go about it. Nerys expressed concern that he get involved in more intrigue and suggested he leave any investigation to the authorities.

She then went to lay out in some detail the dilemma she was facing over the allegations Mick Musselwhite had shared over SERC. It was not just how they might affect her project, given her dependence on the funding to carry out the research. It was also the fact that ultimately the university was responsible for SERC. Any scandal would have a bad impact on the university's reputation and how would the president and her dean feel if they concluded she had been concealing information that they might have been able to use to mitigate any damage.

'You are definitely between a rock and a hard place. You owe an allegiance to your employer that is at least as great as the undertaking you gave Musselwhite. I think if you let the promise prevail, you would not have much to stand on if challenged by the president and dean.'

'What are you saying?'

'Here's an idea. You told me Dean Salisbury had already gone along with guaranteeing absolute confidentiality between the two of you. I suggest you go back to her and confirm that guarantee is still in place in light of more, far-reaching, information you want to share with her. If she agrees, I would tell about the SERC allegations.'

'What then?'

'That would provide some protection for you if it all blows up. I would expect in turn that she would want to share the information with the president to protect her own self. I can't see how you could do anything but go along with that request. I don't owe President Ramirez any favours at all but I think she would want to be included in the loop.'

'What would you expect them to do with the allegations?'

'They are not really even allegations at this stage, more like unfounded rumours. But I would expect them to follow up with the university attorneys and the CEO and perhaps Board of SERC. I am not sure what the corporate structure of SERC is. It looks like the university technically owns it but does not even have a seat on the board of directors. Nevertheless, there has to be some sort of formal reporting relationship, possibly just between the SERC CEO and the university president. Unless the president is in cahoots on this illicit stuff, she would want to be acting on it sooner rather than later.'

'And if she is in cahoots, what then?'

'I don't have an answer for that yet.'

'And what if the dean refuses to maintain the confidentiality she agreed to previously? Do I share the information with her?'

'I'm afraid I don't have an answer for that yet either.'

'I don't like this one little bit. Maybe I should get Mick Musselwhite to connect with them directly.'

'I very much doubt he would agree to that. He passed the bomb to you because he cared about your project and wanted you to know what you were dealing with. I do not think he intended to do anything himself or with his shadowy government pals because it is premature. The rumours are just too sketchy. I also do not think he would expect you to just sit on the bomb, so to speak, without consulting your superiors. That is why I think starting with the dean is the way to go.'

Nerys and Calum talked on and on and round and round, as they often did in situations like this, and eventually got back to what Calum had first suggested. They agreed that she should seek a meeting with the dean as soon as possible.

They ended their call quite exhausted but confirming that they needed to keep closer in touch as everything they were involved in on both continents got more and more complicated. As he hung up, Calum realized they had not even mentioned Farland.

Chapter 25

Heather Randall called Calum to confirm his availability for a visit to Farland Power Station with John McDonald, the Cumbraes Environmental Research Station Operations Manager, and her. She had connected with Tom Wilson the senior manager responsible for decommission of operations and equipment at Farland to make the arrangements. Falling a good deal short of enthusiastic, he had nevertheless agreed that the team could visit and would be able to study the procedures and the records. Heather had made a fleeting reference to the earlier abortive visit by Calum and hoped that this latest visit could be more successful given that the government had taken an interest. The inference did not draw any comment from Wilson.

Calum asked about John McDonald and was told he was a steady if unspectacular employee of the research station. He had been there for fifteen years and was responsible for all the office operations including shipping and receiving. He should have a good sense of what was required to successfully pack, load, and ship out the flasks while maintaining records. His very low key presence and manner might also serve to diffuse some of the tension that Calum had experienced first time.

'I don't know about that. Wilson seemed a bit mousy as well but I never got a chance to talk to him personally. It will be interesting to see how he interacts with us if Cyrus Macadam is not there. No word of him changing his mind?'

'I have not heard a word from him since he said he did not want to be involved.'

'We will see. Anyway, I am ready for the visit. I will come round to the station at 9:30am on Friday in plenty of time for the ten o'clock ferry.'

Calum continued to scour all forms of media as he had been doing before Heather called. He could find no reference anywhere to a reported disappearance of Margaret Wannamaker. Obviously Joel had got his way and, surprisingly, the information had remained within the police ranks. That was surprising because in Calum's experience there was always a constable who was prepared to tip a journalist off for future considerations.

He continued to give the whole disappearance a good deal of thought. He could accept that Maggie was either so spooked by events surrounding the creation of the trusts, or still so pissed as to what her marriage meant afterward, that she might have just wanted to take off someplace. It was not so easy to fly anywhere without leaving a trace but she could have hired a car and driven any place in the UK or even crossed to Europe without it being recorded. There were however two things that suggested that would not have been her chosen course of action. She was American and had no real knowledge of the UK, never mind Europe. And secondly, given that lack of knowledge, why would she choose to just take off without saying goodbye to him and at least finding out from him about where she planned to go? In fact, why had she not even tried to persuade him to go with her? The last time he had seen her she was proposing visiting him with her toothbrush. Yet, she had not even texted to say change of plans.

The disappearance seemed unlikely but any alternative seemed totally nonsensical. What could have happened to her? Could Joel have kidnapped her? Could he have done worse? If he had done either, would he have reported her missing and set in place an investigation, albeit a low-key one at this juncture? He could at least have bought some time by doing nothing but he had initiated the investigation. It was one thing coercing his wife into signing away her share of their assets; did he have what it would take to do her a mischief? Calum gave his head a shake. Things like that only happened in the movies.

He seriously contemplated trying to connect with Wannamaker ostensibly to see if there were any news but also to see if he would reveal anything the police did not know. Then he remembered Harry Jardin's reluctance for him to get involved and let it go. Instead he resolved to spend time visiting different places on the island where the two of them had been together and later just places where she might have found to hide out. The walks and searches might produce nothing but would keep him busy and healthy.

Calum had to focus on other matters because he was scheduled to have another telephone conversation with Nerys after she had met with Dean Salisbury. He had decided to make no reference to the Maggie situation.

'Hi love. How did it go with Anna Salisbury?'

'I think it went well in the end. I got the feeling as I spelled out what I had learned in London that she first was miffed that I had not told her earlier. Then she seemed to accept the dilemma I was suffering had caused the delay. She could see that I felt I had given my word to Mick but, as she said, by sticking to that promise I was putting myself out dangerously on a limb.'

'What was her reaction to the rumour?'

'She found it hard to believe. But she confessed that she really did not know a lot about the workings of SERC other than its existence and the good work it did in sponsoring research. She did not know anything about the research work that SERC apparently does on its own account therefore did not know that there could be bad work as well as good work.'

'What did she propose next?'

'Just as you predicted. God I hate when that happens.'

'How so?'

'She said that I had now put the pressure on her or passed on the bomb as you called it. She wanted to bring the president into our confidence because it was potentially such a high profile issue. And, it would serve to cover her butt!'

'That is only human nature. The president gets paid the big bucks to deal with the big issues.'

'At least I did not get any impression that Anna was involved. The look on her face confirmed that when I told her.'

'So now you wait for the meeting with the president. I take it you will both meet with her?'

'Yes. Unfortunately, she is out of state until Friday.'

Calum went on to describe his Friday which would entail his second visit to Farland. Nerys commented that it sounded a whole lot safer and likely a whole lot more productive to be going back as part of a team and not having to face the odious Mr. Macadam. Calum had to agree but predicted that Macadam would be a presence in the background even if he were not there for the visit. He hoped they would either be able to shake Wilson up or better still get him on to their side.

Nerys mentioned that she had searched the Internet for anything on the rumour that the Daily Record had picked up on. There was nothing except the original article and a couple of copycat pieces by other papers. Nobody on her side of the world had picked up on it all, not even one of the environmental groups who normally made it their practice to scour world news for things that they could use to keep the US government on its toes.

'It seems weird that the story will just not take root. The implications are so serious, especially in a country like the UK where you do not expect such things to happen. I guess you have to be prepared for finding out that it was just a paperwork error and nothing more. It won't mean the end of your detective career or anything just because you couldn't find a smoking gun.'

'Very funny. I would be quite happy, in fact more than quite happy, to prove that it was just an error. However, so far that has not happened. We will see on Friday.'

'Let's plan to talk on the weekend. That might be our last opportunity before I leave for China and India next week.'

'You don't see any chance that the university might want you to cancel your trip, or at least reschedule it?'

'Don't even think about it. I got no hint of that from my meeting with the dean.'

'OK, good luck with Friday.'

'You too.'

Chapter 26

On Thursday evening, Calum was sitting in Fraser's Bar having a pleasant drink with Jimmie Morrison from the research station. They were laughing at Jimmie's description of a young English university professor in charge of a visiting group of students who had fallen overboard from the station launch while pointing out a species of kelp to his undergrads. The door to the bar opened and a stranger came in and went up to whisper something to the bartender. Big Bob the Bartender looked around the bar then pointed to the corner where Calum and Jimmie were seated. Though he had a fifty percent chance of not being the object of the newcomer's attention, Calum had a sinking feeling about what was to come next.

The stranger wandered over and sat down on the spare chair.

'Mr. Davies?' He said looking from one to another.

'That would be me. What can I do for you?'

'I am DI Paul McBride form Police Scotland West based in Glasgow. Could I possibly intrude on your evening and have a word with you in private sir?'

'Sure.'

Jimmie made to get up to leave them to it but DI McBride indicated that it might be better to go over to the police station for more privacy.

As Calum and the officer walked around Clyde Street to the station, DI McBride asked if he was wondering how his location had been ascertained.

'I would imagine Constable Jardin predicted it. Right?'

'First time.'

'There is not an awful lot else to do on an April night in Millport and Fraser's is my favourite. This will be about Margaret Wannamaker I am assuming?'

'Right again.'

Calum had thought that Harry Jardin would be present but the interview took place only with DI McBride.

'I have read the statement you provided to Constable Jardin. I need to clear up some discrepancies between it and other things I have learned while carrying out my enquiries. I have been put in charge of the case and will be spending some time in Millport.'

'What is the status of the case?'

'The case remains one of a missing person. Whether that disappearance was voluntary or involuntary is unclear and we are keeping an open mind. Now I get to ask the questions if you don't mind.'

'Go ahead.'

'In response to an important question put to you by Jardin, you stated that the last time you say Ms. Wannamaker was in Minstrels restaurant. I am going to invite you to reconsider your answer.'

Calum had known it was coming. He had been stupid. You do not give the police half-answers. One of the things they do in any investigation is corroborate what they hear from one witness with what they hear from any other witness that has related knowledge. The taxi driver and perhaps even Tommy Duncan, the person who was tailing Maggie, could have blown his story. He squirmed for a bit before answering.

'I was not totally forthcoming with Constable Jardin. I don't think it is of material importance and I held it back because I was concerned that people would get the wrong impression if it got out. I will now tell you of two further occasions I was in the company of Maggie that were not in my statement.'

'Two is it? I thought I was only missing one. Tell me.'

Calum proceeded to tell McBride about the visit to the Wannamaker house, which the latter was not aware of, and the meeting at the Glaid Stone, of which he was familiar. Calum characterized both meetings as more of the same from the other meetings and that meant listening to Maggie's concerns about how her husband was rearranging their financial affairs and trying to offer some advice. However, the problem was always that each time he met Maggie, the story had moved on and the advice which he had provided at the previous meeting was effectively rendered useless.

At the last meeting at the Glaid Stone, she had told him that she had executed the documents and was making noises about trying to make her marriage work. However, her parting words to him at the Lady Margaret Hospital, where they had called a cab, were that she intended to visit his home that evening. She never turned up and no message was received from her. He had not heard from her again. He had tried to text and phone her after that simply because she had not turned up as promised. He believed that her mobile was switched off or the battery was dead because his mobile simply rang three times then gave up on the calls to her.

'So that is three meetings, one of which did not ultimately happen, that you chose to conceal from us. Why was that? Were you having an affair with Maggie?'

'No I was not. But that is why I kept the information back because I was afraid that people would jump to that conclusion just as you appear to have done.'

'I am not aware that I have jumped to any conclusion. I am merely asking questions because you have been less than forthright with my colleague.

If you were not having an affair, how do you account for so many meetings?'

'I made friends with her on the plane over from America. At that point, there were no financial concerns mentioned. She was just a little pissed at being dragged over to Scotland to watch some soccer. But after that, when I cycled round the island with her, she was increasingly desperate about the deterioration of her marriage and her husband's pretty obvious measures to transfer joint assets into his name alone by way of complicated trusts. Not knowing anybody else in Scotland and certainly not in Millport, I guess she turned to me for consolation and advice on both matters.'

'Seems unusual to turn to someone you have just met on a plane.'

'I agree but I think it was just a case of nobody else to turn to. I can't say I was comfortable with her, especially on the personal side of her relations with her husband. I felt my advice was always pretty weak but she seemed to appreciate it, even if she did not end up following it much.'

'What do you think has happened to her?'

'I have thought a lot about that. I just can't see her taking off anywhere in the UK or Europe. She has never been here before that I know of. If she were planning to do that, I feel for sure she would have come to my place that night to ask advice. That was the kind of relationship we had developed.'

'Mr. Wannamaker does not appear to have too high an opinion of your relationship.'

'That does not surprise me but how is he to know? I got the impression that having doubts about Maggie's fidelity helped justify his plan to get his hands on the joint assets. So casting doubts on the relationship could well be self-serving on his part.'

'Fair point.'

'He did suggest to me privately that her state of mind was suspect.'

'So you think that her disappearance was not voluntary and therefore it had to be involuntary. Any ideas?'

'I can't even say that. I know that Maggie on more than one occasion said she was fearful of Joel's intentions but I think that more related to finances and maybe even the ending the marriage. I have no sense that she feared physical harm from him. And furthermore, while I don't like the guy I have no sense of whether he would be capable of causing her physical harm.'

'So you just don't know what has happened to her?'

'I do not and I am not prepared to even guess. As I said, I have thought a lot about it and I cannot come to a clear conclusion.'

'I see. That pretty much sums up the police take on things at this stage.'

'Is there anything more I can tell you or do? I really would like to help if I could.'

'I don't think so right now. If you are sure that you have now told us everything you know, I will accept that with a stern warning never again to try to mislead or undermine our enquiries.'

'You have my assurance on that.'

'Thank you. I may need to talk to you again. Will you be remaining in these parts?'

'I expect to be here until the fall. Please keep in touch with me about any progress you make and don't hesitate to ask me to help if I can.'

'I would not sit waiting by your phone, sir. Best leave these matters to the police.'

By the time Calum emerged from the police station, it was almost closing time at Fraser's Bar so he walked toward Barclay House instead. He called Scotty Green on his mobile. Scotty was just clearing up the dining room and invited him round for a night cap. As he walked out of the West Bay toward Westview he could not help but go over what had taken place with DI McBride. He seemed to have survived his stupid withholding of information. In fact he seemed to have established a little bit of rapport with McBride, probably because he had been fully cooperative at the second time of asking. He had likely provided more information around Maggie's state of mind and concerns than anyone else save for her husband. That would allow McBride to corroborate what Joel was telling him.

However, it was safe to say that nobody seemed any clearer as to what had happened to Maggie. Calum resolved to continue to do what he could behind the scenes. Again, he thought about contacting Joel Wannamaker but by the time he arrived at Westview he had dropped that idea, at least for the time being.

'Come away in. I am expecting another late guest now. Ah, that looks like his vehicle lights coming round the bend now.'

The police van pulled into the rear parking lot and Harry Jardin got out, thankfully on his own.

'McBride has gone to the Royal George to write up his notes and then turn in. So that frees me up.'

Scotty poured hefty drams all round as they settled in the front lounge. The lights of Arran and Bute twinkled in a dark night where the new moon was barely making an impression. The rain had just started to fall adding to the twinkling effect of the lights.

Calum felt obligated to apologize to Harry for not giving him all the information the first time around. Harry shrugged and said he understood the hesitation. People would think he had spent all his waking time with Maggie. And, those same people would assume that extended to all his non-waking time as well.

'You know what this place is like.'

'That's exactly what I was afraid of. Our meetings were entirely innocent but it is difficult to get that side of the story out there.'

'Especially to those who frequent the Ritz Café,' Scotty observed dryly.

Calum started to jump in protest before realizing that Scotty was just winding him up. They all had a good laugh at his discomfort.

Each man then went on to offer his own theories as to what might have happened to Maggie. There was no real clarity of course. Scotty and Harry were prepared to entertain the notion that she had just taken off for parts unknown but they also acknowledged Calum's doubt that she had enough knowledge to do that. They each expressed a dislike for Joel Wannamaker but stopped short of agreeing that he had it in him to do her some mischief. The resulting loose consensus was that the matter was as yet a complete mystery.

Scotty opined, 'I doubt McBride will be a big fan of Wannamaker either.'

'What makes you say that?' asked Calum.

'Well his old man was Jack McBride and he played most of his days for Glasgow Erin. Jack made it his business to stick it to WCI whenever he could. He scored a hat-trick at Hampden in the Scottish Cup Final and claimed it was personal. He plain did not like WCI and what they stood for. I don't suppose the son has any different views.'

'It is amazing how so much of Scottish society beliefs are played out through the religious divide in football. I could not believe what I heard from high court judges, surgeons, and even a very senior police officer at the WCI reception I attended with Neil Christian.'

'Aye. It is not just the great unwashed that perpetuate the conflict of King Jamie and King Billy. The five estates all have a heavy investment in it.'

'And two football clubs depend on it to make them bigger than all the other clubs.'

The conversation drifted back to Maggie. Calum stated his intention to continue to poke around for information despite being discouraged by the local constabulary. Harry said that was up to him, but to be careful. There was clear indication that there was no love lost between Joel Wannamaker and Calum, and the former was becoming a powerful man in Scotland.

Scotty agreed that he would keep his ear to the ground and let the other two know anything interesting that he picked up. Harry added that he would keep Scotty informed of the police progress and if Scotty chose to share that with Calum that was just fine with him.

Upon toasting his two best friends on the island, Calum drained his glass and announced his intention to walk back home. However, the local police provided a drop-off service in addition to the many other services that seemed quite unique to Millport.

Chapter 27

On the Friday morning, Calum cycled around to the research station. He had chosen to take his bike so that he had a means of getting home because he did not know what time they would be getting back to the island.

Heather Randall and John McDonald were waiting for him. As Heather drove them to the ferry terminal, Calum got to know John a bit. Heather's description of him as unremarkable appeared to hit the mark. He demonstrated a good understanding of what should be happening at Farland to properly account for the packing, loading, and shipping of the flasks containing the radioactive waste. But he showed no excitement or enthusiasm for the nature of the visit. Perhaps his low-key outlook was a good thing.

As they were waiting for the ferry to come in, Heather dropped a bombshell.

'I got an email late last night. It was from Cyrus Macadam. Surprise. Surprise. He will be there today and so too will Graeme MacTavish. He is a very senior manager in BritPower the utility company. Tom Wilson will report to someone who will to someone who will report to Graeme MacTavish probably. What do you make of that?'

'Macadam does not surprise me. I was just waiting for it to happen. MacTavish's presence might be a good thing. It might suggest the utility company is starting to take the rumour seriously.'

'I have not met MacTavish. I think he is based in London.'

John McDonald broke into the conversation.

'Graeme MacTavish is responsible for all BritPower's nuclear power stations around the country. I have seen him quoted on their decommissioning programme. He is actually based in Cumbria.'

Heather and Calum exchanged glances at the junior man's knowledge. She started to believe that the team could work well on this visit, which would be important now that she had involved the press.

'Well Dr. Davies, I doubt you will end up being mugged today. I let the Daily Record know about our visit and promised to give them a statement afterwards. The reporter actually asked me about your mugging and if I thought it might have been linked to your first visit. I said I did not think so. It does show, however, that they would like to make a connection. SERC will have to be on its best behaviour today.'

When they pulled up outside the gate at the Farland Power Station they were welcomed by the same guard that had been on duty when Calum first visited. His demeanour was a whole lot friendlier this time. Perhaps he had been given explicit instructions.

'Good morning. If you will just park in that spot inside the gate, I will walk you over to the management offices.'

'Thank you. I assume you have our names.'

'That I do Dr. Randall. And how are you, Dr. Davies? That was a terrible business that happened to you the last time you were here. Did they ever get the buggers?'

Calum grunted, 'alas not,' and asked for the name of the guard who had assisted him along with the bus driver. He realized he had not thanked either of them.

'That will be Jackie McGregor. I will write down his phone number and give you it on your way out.'

Jenny was there to welcome the trio as they arrived at the management offices. There was a smile on her face. Tom Wilson took the lead to make introductions all round as they sat down at a large round table in his office. Graeme MacTavish said all the right things about BritPower's desire to nip this annoying rumour in the bud by demonstrating to the satisfaction of the team that it only involved a paperwork error. Macadam stated that SERC had already been satisfied but that it was important that both of the contracting consultancy organizations held similar views on the matter. Heather responded that she appreciated the cooperation and priority that was being shown. Calum smiled inwardly. It was a whole lot different from the last visit.

Tom Wilson spoke at length about the procedures, taking time at every step of the way to describe the scientific considerations particularly at the packing stage and the logistical considerations of efficiently moving the material to Beagg. John McDonald nodded his head at several stages indicating he was in agreement with the procedures and Calum could find no fault with them either.

Next, the group left the office and went to the semi-circular reactors. After donning bulky safety suits and helmets, they were taken inside one of the reactors to see how the plutonium was compressed into the ceramic pellets and in turn the pellets were inserted into hollow metal rods. Outside the reactor, the rods were inserted into sold steel flasks which were sealed then stored within a locked compound.

It just so happened that a craft was at the wharf in the process of being of being loaded so they were able to observe flasks being mounted on a gurney then carefully pulled by a small locomotive along narrow tracks from the compound right on to the jetty. From there a crane mounted on the jetty transferred each flask to the hold of the craft.

MacTavish noted that the crafts were small and very manoeuverable in the water. This had been a deliberate choice because they were ideally suited to the tight loading conditions at both the Farland end and Beagg end, they could handle rough sea conditions well, and in the event that one had to lay over in a port en route because of weather or other conditions, they could be accommodated in any one of several small ports along the way. Calum noted that the choice of small crafts and their valuable features must have been a trade off against using much larger container ships and barges at either end. With the latter strategy there would be fewer trips and the incidence of risk would be correspondingly reduced. MacTavish agreed that both had been considered and the small craft approach had been selected on safety and cost grounds. He acknowledged the good point Calum had made. Calum, however, had also witnessed the hostile glare from Macadam. That was more like it he thought.

The group then returned inside to the warmth of another office where Wilson pointed out files of records.

'These are the loading and shipping records for each trip. They show that each consignment is signed off by the person responsible for packing and loading and is verified by another observer and then by me. Then the captain of the craft signs for his load and that is verified by an observer and me again. When the consignment reaches Beagg and is unloaded the records are endorsed in a similar way at their end. Finally the craft brings back a copy of the record to be stored here.'

John McDonald nodded in agreement and asked to look at a small sample of records.

'By all means. You will also be able to see a continuous reconciliation statement of the amount of waste remaining here, on route to Beagg, and stored at Beagg in comparison to the original inventory. That too is signed by three people on site including me.'

John and Calum spent almost an hour spot checking the shipping records and studying the reconciliations while Heather chatted to the others.

They concluded that they could find nothing untoward with the procedures or the evidence presented.

Calum took Heather aside and presented her with their findings. She indicated that it would be appropriate for Calum to share the findings with the BritPower and SERC representatives.

He gave a quick synopsis of what he and John had looked at and what their findings were.

'Good show,' bellowed MacTavish. 'I am glad that we can now say we are all on the same page.'

'Yes indeed,' echoed Macadam. However, he failed to disguise the irony in his voice.

Tom Wilson smiled and wiped his brow.

They all shook hands. Heather mentioned that the Daily Record had shown an interest in the visit and she would be able to give them a clean bill of health. As they were leaving, Calum turned toward the others.

'Just one other thing I almost forgot. We did not see the records where the error was made. Did we?'

Tom Wilson was first to respond.

'Oh they were destroyed and replaced with corrected versions. If you looked at the January records, you likely saw them.'

John McDonald replied with something of an air of self-importance about him. 'We did. I picked January in my sample deliberately because I knew that was the period in question.'

Calum responded. 'That's fine then. Thanks.'

As they sat in the lounge of the ferry on the way back, Calum said that he was pretty satisfied with what they had seen. However, he did note that he would rather have seen the January documents with the original erroneous information struck out and the correct information inserted than just new replacement records. Anyone could create records after the fact to support the physical inventory. The same was true of the reconciliations. They had also obviously been adjusted to reflect the changed records. The new records were not absolute proof of paperwork error but they were probably the best they were going to get.

John McDonald made as if to speak then thought better of it. He had been quite proud of the initiative he had shown in the sampling and he did not want to prolong Davies' alternative theories.

Heather noted the faint hint of friction between the two men but chose to let it go.

'All I can say it feels like a good job done and I appreciate both of you being in on this. I will call our MSP and then I will call the Record and give them a statement from me. It will be straight forward with no technical jargon that can be queried or further investigated by them.'

By the time they got back, the research station was closed for the day. John McDonald went straight to his car and left for home. Calum and Heather chatted for a moment or two.

'Do you feel like that much promised banquet of fish and chips washed down with Irn Bru?'

'Mmm. I don't feel much like cooking tonight. Let's do that.'

'OK. Come round to my place about eight o'clock. I will have obtained the necessary ingredients.'

Calum expected Nerys to call at about 6pm her time which would make it 2am here. Therefore, he quite welcomed a distraction for the evening that would keep him awake for her call.

He timed his visit to the Deep Sea restaurant to pick up the fish suppers and Irn Bru perfectly so that he was just returning to Barclay House at 8pm precisely as Heather was pulling up in her car.

The fish suppers were delicious. Calum had often joked with Nerys about his life-long quest around the world to find a fish supper to equal that of the Deep Sea in Millport. Most had not come near.

The batter was frequently too heavy. Or, the alternative fish was not as good as fresh haddock. Some had come close, particularly one in Parksville, British Columbia and another in Oceanside, California. But none had surpassed or even equalled the Deep Sea. Though the ownership had changed a few times in Calum's lifetime, somehow the magic of the fish and chips they produced had persisted.

The Irn Bru was politely declined by Heather once she learned that there was a chilled Pinot Grigio on offer as an alternative. Calum decided to go with the wine too. "Scotland's Other Drink" would be available in the fridge for some other day when a thirst required quenching.

'I have to say that was magnificent,' enthused Heather.

'Indeed it was. You cannot beat the Deep Sea.'

'That is only about the third time in ten years that I have had fish and chips on the island.'

'You poor deprived specimen. I have pledged my life to finding a supper equal to that one. I have had a few thrills but mostly disappointments.'

'You sound a bit deprived of something too. Like perhaps a life?'

They both laughed and agreed that their simple meal had brought to a perfect end a very interesting day. Although their suspicions about what might be going on at Farland and the hand that SERC might be playing in it had not been entirely removed, they had to acknowledge that they had done all they could and no smoking gun had been unearthed. All they could do for the future was continue to watch what happened and be ready to respond if any further rumours were to come up.

They sat and chatted about all manner of things from families to world events to the inevitable return to school days. Eventually, when the new day was well established Heather reluctantly took her leave.

After all, one of them had work to do tomorrow, sorry later today.

Calum managed to keep awake for the hour or so until Nerys called. She reported that it had been a good meeting with the president and dean. Like Anna Salisbury, the president appeared totally shocked at the information Nerys passed on from London, which suggested that it was unlikely she was in cahoots with SERC. She listened intently to what she was told and did not offer any comment until Anna had been given the opportunity to add her perspectives. Then, she had allowed Nerys to offer her opinion on what the next steps should be.

Ultimately, the president stated that the possible allegation of illicit dealings by SERC was potentially extremely damaging to the university. There was not a lot of public or faculty knowledge of SERC but what existed definitely connected it to the university. If allegations were proven against SERC, they might as well be levelled at the university too. What could be done right now? The president suggested that no open charge could be made against SERC because there was not enough evidence. However, she would have to take advice from the university attorneys, who did not act for SERC, form a closer and more accountable relationship with the SERC CEO, and start to attend SERC board meetings. Although the university did not have a seat on the board, there was a standing invitation to be present at board meetings. Up to now, the president had missed far more meetings than she had ever attended. From now on, she would attend all meetings or send an alternate which would be the dean. They had debated whether the course of action suggested was too passive but had concluded that, in the absence of more definitive evidence, it was all that could be done for now.

As far as Nerys was concerned, it was decided she should continue with her planned visit to China and India and her research project. Again, there was nothing of any certainty at this stage that suggested the project should be abandoned. Furthermore, Nerys was ordered to maintain a close relationship with Michael Musselwhite, keeping him informed of the university's actions and in turn obtaining from him any further information that came into his possession. She was cleared to travel back to London whenever she felt her presence there was warranted.

Overall, Nerys felt that the president had adopted the correct response to the issue and that she could now count on both her support and that of the dean as she faced up to the potential impacts on her project. She was no longer out on a limb on her own. In addition, she was pleased that the project would continue. She had invested a great deal of time and energy thus far to even consider delay never mind abandonment.

Calum agreed that the outcomes were the best that could have been hoped for. It would be important for Nerys to keep in close contact with Mick as the SERC status had to be seen as fluid until more solid information was obtained.

He gave her a quick report on the visit to Farland Power Station, the result of which had effectively given SERC a stay of execution. Although some form of public statement would appear in the media, he suggested that Nerys pass on his information to Mick to complete the loop. In addition, she should invite Mick to connect with him so that ongoing collaboration could be maintained.

Then two tired individuals on either side of the Atlantic talked very briefly about other things and said their goodbyes. Calum was in bed and falling asleep within minutes of the end of the call.

Chapter 28

A few days later, the wind started to blow and the rain started to fall and neither looked like they might ever go away again. This was Millport marooned in the middle of a not atypical April storm. First, the ferries went off. That was not surprising. On the last run over to the island, the waves were washing over the car deck and threatening to swamp the cars. Later, the trains from Glasgow to Largs went off because the 100mph winds exceeded the safety limits for the railway line. Millport was effectively cut off from the rest of the world. There was nothing for it but to settle down in one's home and try to refrain from looking out of the windows.

Calum was surfing the Internet trying to get a start on researching the history in the UK of the development of a nuclear waste disposal strategy. He had promised it to Nerys to include as background in her final research report. There was plenty of information. It was just a case of sorting it into coherent and chronological order. The consensus among objective commentators was that the UK had done a half decent job of developing a strategy; and recent results of actual disposal seemed to be bearing that out. Farland was the most current actual disposal programme.

He was surprised when his mobile rang and an unknown number showed. The surprise related to the fact that the cellular service was even still operational in this weather and secondly that somebody he did not recognize had his mobile number. Since acquiring his new phone he had enjoyed a period of no crank calls and nobody selling anything because he had given his number to very few people.

'Hello. Can I help you?'

'Is this Dr. Calum Davies?'

'It is. How did you get my number?'

'Dr. Heather Randall gave it to me. She thought it would be OK to call you.'

'You better tell me who you are then.'

'I suppose I better. My name is Charlie Williamson and I write for the Daily Record.'

'That's bad luck. Maybe journalism was not meant for you?'

'That is too funny.'

'I try.'

'Are you prepared to answer some questions about the visit you recently made to the Farland Power Station with Dr. Randall and another person from the research station in Millport?'

'Actually Dr. Randall is the spokesperson for that particular event. I know she gave you an extensive statement after it.'

'So she did and that was published yesterday. I just wanted to get your perspective on a couple of angles and she thought you would be prepared to give me it.'

'You have me at a bit of a disadvantage. First, I have not spoken to Dr. Randall since we visited the power station so I only have your word that she is OKing me to speak. Second, I have not read her statement in yesterday's Daily Record. There was no reference to it in the newspaper I did read. So, ask your questions and I may or may not be able to answer them.'

'Fair enough. This was the second visit for you to Farland. I get the impression you were not satisfied with the answers you got first time. What was different this time?'

'Your impression is inaccurate. I was not dissatisfied with the information that was provided first time. The information was more detailed on the second visit because more people were involved.'

'Were you surprised that Graeme MacTavish was there?'

'No. Why should I be? He is in charge of decommissioning power stations for BritPower.'

'Did you feel that BritPower was finally taking seriously the rumour that the Record picked up on Beagg?'

'I have no idea how BritPower operates or reacts to rumours. I was pleased to see him there however.'

'What is your impression of SERC?'

'I have very little knowledge of them. They seem to be doing OK at Farland.'

'Your wife is also associated with them I understand?'

'That is a completely unrelated matter. SERC sponsors environmental research. My wife is a political scientist and researcher. They are providing sponsorship of her research in Asia.'

'I see. You have answered my questions but not with any great fullness. I am thinking I will just hold the information you have provided. There is not enough to do a follow-up story at this stage.'

'Your call. I have given you the best answers I could.'

'Thank you. My number is 0141-331-1048 if you think of anything else. Goodbye for now.'

Later in the day Calum was feeling the onset of cabin fever and decided he had to get out even if it meant getting soaked. Having a car would have been a good idea right about now. However, he did not have one, so instead he donned every piece of waterproof clothing he had, along with the stoutest shoes and braced himself for the ordeal.

The walk from Barclay House to the nearest pub, Fraser's Bar, was nothing ever less than a short, extremely pleasant stroll up West Bay Road and down Cardiff Street. Today it was long endurance test of nightmare proportions. When he staggered through the door of the bar, he was surprised to find it quite heavily populated. Obviously other people were beginning to suffer as he had and had decided to make a break for it.

Big Bob the Bartender extended a laconic welcome.

'Bit damp out today Doctor. Not exactly your California weather.'

'You can say that again.'

'Bit damp out today Doctor. Not exactly your California weather.'

'Stop it. You are cracking me up.'

'I suppose you will be wanting a drink?'

'No thanks. I was just out for a walk.'

'Very good. Would it be a dram or a pint or a dram and a pint?'

'Yes please.'

Calum sat up on bar stool and waited to see what he would be served. Big Bob the Bartender returned with a whisky and a beer and showed no acknowledgement of Calum's attempted humour. It was difficult to get one up on a dour giant with only a hint of arid humour that surfaced once in a while.

Calum enjoyed the malt whisky, good choice, Bob; then started to wash it down with some of the Belhaven Ale, again good choice, Bob. That was the mark of a good bartender. He knew better than you did what you fancied.

As he looked around the bar, he was surprised to see the police force at a table in the corner nursing a couple of pints. Constable Henri Jardin and Detective Inspector Paul McBride were in deep conversation. Thinking he might get some information on the search for Maggie, Calum wandered over and sat down on the spare chair.

'What is this then? Are their special dispensations for the constabulary on very wet days that allow them to take shelter in the pub?'

'Yes, but only in Millport. What do you want?'

'I was going to buy you both a pint, DI McBride, in return for your latest information on the search.'

'That would not be much of a deal for you. We have made virtually no progress because our hands are tied behind our backs. But, you may buy us a pint.'

'Sure. What do mean your hands are tied?'

'Well, Mr. Wannamaker is still refusing to allow his wife's disappearance to be made public. That means we are only able to discuss it with other police forces. We cannot appeal for public help and so it really is impairing the search.'

'That sounds just dumb. He wants her found but he is preventing you from looking properly. It makes you wonder if he really wants her found.'

'That had crossed our minds too but so far we have not been able to come up with anything that would suggest she could be a victim and he could be responsible.'

'It frustrates me so it must be frustrating you guys no end. Harry, at least I could be stepping up the search on the island if this rain ever goes off.'

'If DI McBride has no problem with it, I would appreciate the help.'

'Do I get a deputy's star to wear?'

'This is not the Wild West, Dr. Davies.'

'That is not what the people from Edinburgh think.'

'Is that where you come from originally? I knew you were annoying. Now I can see that you are doubly annoying.'

'Now. Now. Detective Inspector. Don't let your prejudices show. How come you are stuck on the island anyway? Is there no crime in Glasgow today?'

'Because that is exactly what I am, stuck in Millport. There is no ferry to get me back to Largs.'

'Does Police Scotland not have a launch?'

'We actually have several but they are grounded right now. Nobody would want to be out on that sea today.'

'Hmmm. A thought just hit me. Do either of you happen to know if the latest Farland craft took off for Beagg? I don't think it would want to be out on that sea any more than the police launch.'

'It is probably stuck at the wharf at the power station or if it did get away it is likely holed up in one of the ports along the way. This weather is hitting the entire country but it is worst down the length of the west coast. The trip from here to Beagg would be treacherous right now.'

'How could we find out where the craft is?'

'Call the power station I suppose. Tom Wilson should be there.'

Calum happened to have the main station number in his mobile having previously called to thank the guard who had assisted him. He called the number. There was no answer at all.

'Likely they have shut up shop for the day. Not much work can be done in this weather.'

'One other thing I was thinking about. I assumed you found out about my meeting Maggie at the Glaid Stone from the taxi driver and Tommy Duncan. Then I got to thinking maybe it was only the taxi driver?'

'It was Billy Glennie who runs Glennie's Taxi that told us. Where does Tommy Duncan come into it?'

'Well, Maggie was convinced that her house in the East Bay was being watched and she was being followed whenever she went out on the island. She described the person as tall, curly haired, and driving a little blue van."

'That would be Tommy right enough,' Harry put in.

'After Maggie got back in Glennie's cab at the hospital, I cycled past the farm and sort of ran into Duncan. He was being nosy and I guess I wound him up a bit. He let slip that he would be in touch with Alec Taggart and Mr. Wannamaker. Maggie could have been right. Duncan could have been tailing her and reporting back to Taggart and Wannamaker. If that was the case, Duncan may have seen her after I left her at the Lady Margaret.'

'And, you are just getting around to telling us that, are you, Dr. Davies? For fuck's sake man. That could be important information.'

'I am sorry. I was assuming you had spoken to Tommy Duncan as well as Glennie because you knew about the Glaid Stone. It was only later I realized it might have only been the taxi driver. In which case, you might know nothing about our suspicions regarding Duncan.'

'Harry, we need to follow up on this. Where would this Tommy Duncan hang out on a day like this?'

'Probably nothing doing at the farm; so he is likely at home up behind the Cathedral or drinking in the Newton Bar.'

They finished their drinks and the two police officers decided they had better have a drive around the island to make sure nobody was in trouble before going to look for Tommy Duncan. On the way, they dropped Calum off at Barclay House and he ran into the building but he still managed to get wet all over again.

Once settled in with a cup of coffee to warm him up, he could not help think again about the dilemma the police faced trying to investigate the disappearance without being able to make it public. McBride had bristled when Calum had expressed surprise that the information had not been leaked to the press by some police officer. But that is what needed to happen. After mulling it over for quite a while, Calum picked up his mobile and dialled the number Charlie Williamson from the Daily Record had given him.

'Dr. Davies. I did not expect to hear from you. Did you remember something else you wanted to tell me?'

'Nothing like that. I can't think of anything more about the Farland operation that would be of help to you. Except maybe one thing. It would be interesting to know if the latest craft for Beagg is out at sea in this weather.'

'I suppose Wilson at the station would know.'

'I tried that. Nobody is answering their main phone.'

'I think I might have his mobile number somewhere. I will try to connect with him.'

'Let me know if you do please.'

'Will do. What was it you wanted to talk about in the first place?'

'This has to be off the record.'

'Nothing is off the record when it is on the Daily Record. Surely you see that.'

'Then I won't tell you. I could get into hot water if my name were associated with what I could tell you. I would need your guarantee that my name will be kept out of it.'

'Is it a big story?'

'Big for the Daily Record.'

'OK then, I give you my word that I will not divulge my source.'

'Tell you what. Hang up the phone and text me that guarantee. When I get it I will ring you back.'

'You are one cautious fucker. This is not an American detective story you know.'

'Your choice.'

'OK. OK. Stand by for a text.'

When the text came through, Calum studied it to determine whether it would stand up in a lawsuit if it were not honoured. Satisfied that it might, he rang Williamson back.

'You will have heard of Maggie Wannamaker?'

'Of course.'

'Did you know that she has been missing for the best part of two weeks?'

Chapter 29

For three long days the storm blew, before it started to die out, leaving a trail of destruction across Scotland. On the west coast, which had been hit particularly hard, it took another day before most services could be restored. Even at that, some communities would have to wait for another five days before power was fully reinstated. Great Cumbrae and Wee Cumbrae had been hard hit with incessant wind and rain causing all forms of transportation from the mainland to be cancelled. But amazingly, power had been maintained and the islanders had simply battened down the hatches and waited out the storm, just as they had done many times before.

Calum had found it quite an experience, far worse than anything he had ever seen in previous visits. But he was beginning to understand the island mentality. When you are physically cut off from the mainland, you just have to accept it. Most islanders had supplies to last them more than three days. And those that did not were helped by those who did. The inconvenience of being cut off seemed to bring out the best in everyone. As just such an example, Calum had had several phone calls (how does that private number get around?) and even calls in person from bedraggled souls to make sure he was OK. It was quite touching.

However, the good feeling coming from the support of the islanders, and the sight of the storm beginning to abate was suddenly destroyed when a call came through on his mobile from Charlie Williamson.

'How are you doin' over there?'

'I am hanging in there. It has been quite a storm but I think it is starting to blow itself out.'

'Have you been looking at the Record website? I know you will not have seen an actual newspaper in a few days.'

'Charlie I get my news from the Telegraph and Scotsman. Does that not tell you something about my politics and reading standards?'

'Well I would suggest you slum it and take a look at the Record website today. There are two barnstormer stories under my by-line which we were first to break, thanks to you.'

'Do you mean......?'

'Just read them then call me back.'

Calum opened up the Daily Record website and two headlines jumped out at him. He opened the first.

"Hollywood Star Missing

Margaret Wannamaker the Hollywood actress who was just pipped for an Oscar last year by Meryl Streep has gone missing on Millport. Yes, the tiny holiday island on the Clyde was the last known place that the star was seen over two weeks ago. Her husband Joel Wannamaker, the new owner of WCI Football Club, has spoken exclusively to the Daily Record and confessed that he has not heard a word from his wife since she went down to Millport to oversee the delivery of furniture to the mansion they have just purchased there.

For the first week, he kept the disappearance secret out of respect for Margaret's Hollywood studio in case the publicity harmed a new movie about to be announced which will star the New York-born actress. However after a week, the police were informed and they have been carrying out discrete enquiries on both sides of the Atlantic.

Mr. Wannamaker now feels that the disappearance must be made public in order to broaden input and assist the police. He chose the

Daily Record as the vehicle to move to the next step having being impressed in his short stay in Scotland with our depth of readership and our professional handling of both football and financial stories concerning WCI. We are pleased to offer our help in his time of need.........."

Calum skimmed the rest of the story to determine there was no real news about Maggie's whereabouts. He was relieved to see that Williamson had kept his word about keeping his name out of the story. He was also amused to read that Joel had chosen the Daily Record. It was more likely that the Record had given him the ultimatum of cooperating with the newspaper or the story would be printed regardless. He found the whole article distasteful but if it served to quicken finding a solution to the mystery, it was probably the right thing that he had done.

He now turned to the other story which was given equal prominence as one of the two lead stories of the day.

"Craft with Radioactive Waste Reported Missing

The dreadful storm that has battered our coastline over the last three days may have sunk a craft that was moving radioactive waste from the decommissioned Farland Power Station to its last resting place in a special storage tunnel on the remote island of Beagg. The project has been cloaked in controversy as previously reported in the Record and this latest news may be the worst case scenario feared by environmental groups since the beginning.

The craft lost radio contact with both the BritPower Project HQ at Farland and HM Coastguard Service in the early hours of Monday. Later its GPS tracking was lost somewhere in the Sound of Jura as Special Project Craft Three (SPC3) was approximately 100 miles into its slow, careful, 300 mile, five day voyage from the Clyde to Beagg which is a totally isolated island 75 miles due west of South Uist in the North Atlantic.

Efforts by the coastguard and the Royal Navy to locate the craft have thus far been severely impaired by the storm. As the weather begins to improve, it is expected that search efforts will be stepped up.

A spokesman for BritPower, Graeme MacTavish, who has responsibility for overseeing the decommissioning of several nuclear power stations around the country, said that it is much too early to speculate that SPC3 has foundered. The craft was specially designed to carry highly dangerous cargos in difficult sea conditions and is crewed by experts in the field that were recently working in the Persian Gulf before the Farland project began. He noted that BritPower would be working with the Cumbraes Environmental Research Station and the SoCal Environmental Research Corporation of Long Beach, California to manage communication of this potentially catastrophic emergency...................."

Oh boy, thought Calum. Our worst fears might be realized. These crafts are supposed to be amazingly durable and adaptable and there are any number of ports and bays in addition to the official stopping ports where they could have sought safety. But there are also two fairly long stretches of open sea on the journey and crossing the Sound of Jura was one of them. If it had got into difficulty during the storm in the open sea, who knows what the outcome might have been. Calum would attempt to get in touch with Heather Randall now that the research station was implicated in the story but first he called Charlie Williamson back.

'Wow. You were not kidding about the barnstormers. Either one would have been big. But you have two to carry.'

'Thanks to you. I owe you a drink if you are ever getting off that island.'

'I wish neither of them were happening. I am glad that I slipped you the tip on Maggie Wannamaker. I just can't see the police making any progress on it without it being out there in the public. Maybe now they will get a lead from somebody somewhere. She could be anywhere but at least being a movie actress she is readily recognizable. The Farland thing I am just sick about. I don't know why but I just had a bad feeling when the storm arrived. Surely they were able to consult weather forecasts and would have been better keeping SPC3 in dock at Farland until it passed over.'

'That is one of the things I will be taking up with Graeme MacTavish when I can connect with him again. The local guy Tom Wilson is staying mum on the whole disaster. His office refers everything to MacTavish and MacTavish is difficult to track down.'

'He is usually based in Cumbria apparently if he is not at Farland.'

'I can't find him either place. Word is he might be in London. Although I also heard a rumour that he might have set out for Islay. There is no ferry running yet but with his money he might be able to commission a helicopter.'

'Have you spoken to Heather Randall yet?'

'Yes. She is pretty upset. Her station will be working with BritPower and those Yanks. I am supposed to be liaising with her and Cyrus Macadam. I know him from the earlier rumour about flasks going missing. Not a particularly nice guy and a fabricator of the facts when he needs to be. It will be interesting to see how he handles this latest problem.'

'I know him too and have the same opinion of him. Listen Charlie, I will probably get brought into the equation by Heather Randall so it is important that you maintain your undertaking to keep my name out of both this story and the Wannamaker story.'

'OK. What did you make of the Wannamaker piece?'

'Tacky to say the least. But I suppose you would argue that you have to sell newspapers.'

'That is a bit harsh.'

'Look if it helps find her then I will call it the best piece of investigative journalism since Woodward and Bernstein.'

'That's better.'

'How did Joel Wannamaker really take to your approach?'

'He was pissed. Threatened to sue us if we published. Said it would threaten her safety. But over three hours I talked him around. He was very keen to know who had leaked the story to us. I told him I did not know but assumed it was from within the police force. That was his greatest fear that the police would not keep it under wraps for long.'

'Surely he sees that there is more chance of locating his wife now that her disappearance is public? I never understood his logic and the movie studio excuse is lame. Those guys crave any kind of publicity—good, bad, or indifferent. They would have been able to work in an angle that served the purpose.

They agreed to keep in touch on both stories but Calum suspected he would have to do the chasing. He was not as much use to the journalist now that his tips had been acted on.

He sent the Record articles by email to Nerys just to keep her informed. She would be on the verge of setting out for China so would have other things on her mind.

Chapter 30

Calum and Scotty Green had been sitting in the Tavern having a quiet lunchtime beer when they had been joined by Alec Taggart and Charlie Caldwell, fresh off the golf course and thirsty after a demanding round. The fine old course had not yet fully recovered from the major storm and patches of surface water on greens had made putting a bit of a challenge.

Taggart grumbled that he had shot Charlie's age which was considerably higher than his own age and his normal score. Charlie commented that he was just lucky to make it round the course in one piece.

Then Calum's mobile rang. It was Heather Randall returning his call and looking for someone kind enough to buy her a drink first and food second. She was invited to join the group, which suited her because the Tavern was the closest bar to the research station as it sat in direct line with the Crocodile Rock on the promenade.

Calum thought this was a motley crew as Heather sat down, especially as it included Alec Taggart with whom he had crossed swords at the Cumbraes Council. It might be interesting but he would have to watch what he said in front of him, given his suspected connection to Joel Wannamaker. However, all eyes were on Heather as she supped a welcome chardonnay and not just because she was by far the prettiest thing in the bar. The fact that she was one of only three women in the bar helped but in truth she was rather pretty.

'Well Dr. Randall, what news do you have from the power station?' asked Scotty before anyone else could ask the same question.

'Heather please, Scotty. I am afraid I don't have any news one way or the other. Now that the sea has calmed down, there are major searches being carried out by the Royal Navy, HM Coastguard Service, and by a private group hired by BritPower. Right now they are concentrating on the Sound of Jura approximately between the end of the Mull of Kintyre and Port Ellen on Islay. Right in the middle of the Sound is where the craft's GPS last registered the craft's location. The most difficult thing at this stage is coordinating the efforts of the three groups and making sure they do not get in each other's way. They are searching both the open sea, in case in SPC3 has sunk, and the two coastlines in case she has landed somewhere. There is a lot of territory to cover. So far there is no trace of anything.'

'That might be good thing. If she had sunk there would be debris and perhaps an oil slick not to mention the radioactive waste if the flasks had been breached. So perhaps no news is good news?' offered Taggart.

'In the short-term you are probably correct. But it cannot have vanished off the face of the planet. The longer we go without finding it grounded or even anchored in a bay somewhere, the more likely it is that she sunk. Then the fun starts. If she sunk in deep water and the flasks have not been breached, there might be a case to be made for leaving her where she rests. Those flasks can last for an awful long time even in salt water. However, if they are breached then we are looking at massive environmental damage and a very complicated clean up.'

Charlie asked, 'I assume if there is leakage that will put paid to fishing in a very good fishing area?'

'Without a doubt all of the marine population could be adversely affected depending on the scope of the leakage. That's what makes it very complicated. Until we find her we can only hypothesize the possible responses and solutions.'

'Do you think this is going to cause the Beagg project to be put on hold or even cancelled?'

'That is a very direct question Alec. It is impossible to say at this stage. Certainly this disaster, if that's what it is, will very much feed into the concerns and arguments that the various environmental groups have been putting forward from day one. They have said that a 300 mile voyage to take the waste away from the mainland and on to an isolated uninhabited island is just too risky. Of course, they are usually unable to come up with a viable alternative.'

'I heard that blowhard from, what do they call themselves, the Green Crusaders say on BBC TV this morning that it just goes to prove that nuclear power stations should never have been built. Then he sits back smugly as if he has solved the problem,' Scotty complained. 'The truth of the matter is nuclear power stations are here and waste has to be disposed of. We can't just leave it at Farland.'

'I understand that is exactly where the Americans are at right now—fighting over disposal sites and storing the waste in the power stations meantime. There is one very close to my home in California.'

'And you might have one very close to your home here if the "Greenies" have their way,' Taggart predicted.

Calum got up to refresh drinks and get Heather a sandwich. The men had declined anything to eat. He would grab something later. As he came back to the table with a tray and off-loaded the various requests, he noticed the radioactive waste disaster conversation had played itself out and talk had turned to summer events on the island.

Charlie said with obvious pride that the revived Marquess of Bute Cup golf tournament was going to be the highlight of the season followed closely by the new museum exhibition and both was thanks to the great efforts of the person buying the drinks. Calum made all the right noises about both projects being team efforts and how pleased he was to be able play a part along with the islanders. He could not help but give Taggart a dig with his next comment.

'Progress has been made but there is an awful lot more to do if we are going to rejuvenate Millport as a holiday destination. The development plan is crucial to finding lasting solutions and we need everyone pulling together in the same direction.'

Scotty smiled. Heather smiled and nodded. Charlie nodded vigorously. Taggart reddened notably and made a series of noises through his teeth that were impossible to decipher, his head nodded however indicating support or at least submission.

Scotty decided to rescue him by changing the subject, after all Taggart had all the petrol on the island so he was not somebody you wanted to totally beat up.

'And now Calum that you have been recognized for all your great exploits, is that lovely wife of yours going to be able to come over to share in your successes during the summer?'

'I am not sure. I just got an email from her this morning. She is in China on the first leg of her big research project. It looks like the project will now take a couple of years to complete. It just keeps getting bigger and bigger. It seems that it is not just Scotland that has waste disposal problems. She is off to see what China, India, Brazil, and Russia are doing.'

'They are all big countries. They will just dump it in the country next door and threaten to invade them if they complain about it.'

'Charlie, I trust you are joking but there might be some truth in what you are hinting. That is why Dr. Jones-Davies' research is so important. We need to create openness about how waste disposal is carried out so there is no cheating.'

'Well said, Heather. Nerys would be proud of you. Certainly, she is very keen on this project. It will probably be the highlight of her academic career. And, that makes me worry that she might just be too busy to make it over to Millport this year. I know she would love to come. We have talked about exploring Wee Cumbrae and that is dear to her heart.'

'It would be a waste of time going to Wee Cumbrae. There is nothing there.'

'I don't know about that Alec. There are lots of interesting seabirds that you never see on our island. Then there are the new and old lighthouses, the castle and the mansion house. Maybe we should bring up at Council about placing more of an emphasis on Wee Cumbrae in the development plan. If only we could get the owners of the island to get involved.'

'Scotty, the two lighthouses and the castle are damned near derelict and the mansion house is headed that way too. The owners don't give a hoot about Wee Cumbrae. They must have bought it for a tax write-off or something. Wee Cumbrae cannae help Great Cumbrae and we are best to ignore it.'

'You might be right Alec, but it would be a pity,' lamented Charlie, and in doing so brought the conversation to a close. Further drinks were declined and the disparate group arose to go their separate ways.

Heather said to Calum as she got into her car, 'I might need your help on this SPC3 thing depending on how the search turns out.'

'Just say the word. And in future, leave five minutes earlier and walk round to the pub from the station. You need the exercise.'

The unsightly vision of the station director and respected scientist sticking her tongue out was witnessed by no one except Calum.

Chapter 31

After an uneventful thirteen hour flight from LAX, Nerys and Troy Cameron jockeyed their way through the teeming Beijing Capital International Airport. With their luggage to hand and not needing to be claimed, they made their way out of the arrivals doors and looked around for indication of ground transportation. Instead, they were surprised to see a large sign being held up heralding the arrival of Dr. Jones-Davies.

The sign was brandished by a diminutive young lady attired in western designer clothes who introduced herself as Fang Chongmei. She represented the Ministry of the Environment and was at the service of the illustrious academician and her assistant for the duration of their stay. Nerys gave Troy a bewildered look and after each had shrugged their shoulders she indicated to Ms. Fang to lead ahead.

Instead of heading for the taxi rank where an enormous line of new arrivals waited, they stepped up to an imposing black limousine and entered at the behest of a liveried driver.

'Wow. This is a ZIL,' whispered Troy.

'It is?' replied Nerys.

'Yeah. Famous Russian limo. Probably has a steel-plated body. It's a favourite among politicians and gangsters.' Troy exclaimed in probably too loud a voice.

'No politicians or gangsters. Just humble civil servants.' Ms. Fang said with a smile.

My God, she is such a cutie thought Nerys and Troy independent of one another.

'We will go to your hotel now. We have taken the liberty of changing your accommodation. You will now stay in the new Jumeirah Hotel. It is a very nice hotel with unique architecture. It is on the same street, Jianguomen Road, as the hotel you selected but is much nicer. The Scitech Hotel gets too full of Russians if you know what I mean,' she said with another engaging smile.

Nerys thought to herself—how did they even know we were booked into the Scitech, we didn't tell them? I guess that means welcome to China.

The Jumeirah Hotel was indeed impressive with a mixture of western opulence and eastern mystique. Nerys was given a large two bedroom suite on the top 15th floor and Troy was located in a slightly more modest room on the 13th floor. There was no 14th floor. Superstition extended to the Orient, or perhaps it originated there, even if the number in question differed.

They were left to relax and unwind after the long trip. Ms. Fang would call for them later to take them for a quiet introductory dinner. It would be a simple affair in contrast to the banquets scheduled in their honour on the two succeeding nights.

Later after enjoying a quick power nap, something Calum had introduced her to; Nerys's room phone rang with Troy on the other end.

'Chongmei is here. We are in the lobby. She got here early so we have been having a drink. Are you ready to go to dinner?'

Several things sprang through Nerys's mind before she answered—Ms. Fang had become Chongmei, she had arrived early, and she had contacted Troy.

'I will be right down,' she replied with the firm intention not to hurry.

The next morning Nerys was still feeling overfed as they were ferried in the ZIL to Tiananmen Square. If that had been a quiet simple meal, what did a banquet constitute? The comparison between the Chinese food she and Calum enjoyed at the Silver

Moon in Irvine and the food they had eaten last night did not extend beyond the name.

The Ministry of Environment offices looked out over the massively imposing Tiananmen Square where a squadron of soldiers was doing an elaborate procedure which looked like a changing of the guard. All highly orchestrated, arms swinging and goose-stepping like a scene out of 1930s Germany.

The meeting would be with Zhang Pan, carrying the westernesque title of senior executive director. He was a young looking man to hold what obviously was a senior position. After handshakes and smiles initiated by Ms. Fang, Dr. Zhang professed to speak no English and indicated that their charming colleague would serve as translator.

Over the course of the day, Nerys met a series of eminent scientists attached to the Ministry of Environment, who, together with Dr. Zhang, had worked on development of the public policy statement on nuclear waste disposal. Very few of the scientists, who were wheeled in and out with almost clockwork precision, spoke much English beyond "honoured to meet you Dr. Jones-Davies" and so Ms. Fang was hard pressed to keep up the translation hour after hour. But she managed it with aplomb and a suitably studious face throughout. Her engaging smile had been rested for the occasion.

It was obvious to Nerys that the Chinese had advanced a lot more on their policy development than the Internet had been able keep up with. They showed her a highly sophisticated statement that called for the highest ethical and scientific standards for waste disposal and seemed to include a far greater system of checks and balances to ensure policy adherence than she had seen anywhere in her research to date. She enjoyed the conversations with Dr.Zhang and in spite of their stilted nature due to the need for translation she felt that they were both being open and honest in their examination of the Chinese model and its comparison to western equivalents. Every question she asked received an answer eventually after translation and careful thought by the senior civil servant.

All the while, Troy was made to play a very subservient but ultimately useful role of note taker.

The meeting eventually ended with the Americans quite exhausted from the intensity and length of the proceedings. They had not even stopped for a light fruit-based lunch which had been served at the meeting table as talks and presentations continued uninterrupted or for the endless ceremonial servings of tea. Now Dr. Zhang and Ms. Fang escorted them on a tour of the incredible buildings that framed the famous square. The tour was quick because the early evening had become intensely cold. Nerys was relieved when they were ushered into an imposing building that turned out to be a banquet hall. And there, already seated, were all the scientists they had met over the course of the day. As one, they rose to applaud the arrival of the star guest.

Course after course of the most amazing food arrived at the table the minute Nerys hesitated in consumption of the previous dish. And with each course came a toast, delivered with freshly charged glasses, by one of the scientists in Nerys's honour. She secretly said a prayer of thanks to her husband for increasing her stamina in the consumption of alcohol. Otherwise she was sure she would now be under the table.

As the banquet ended, Dr. Zhang turned to Nerys and expressed his delight over the very successful meeting and his hope that they could continue to collaborate on this very important work. He explained that the next day would be spent with Brigadier General Doctor Xing Dun at the Central Military Commission, which housed the Ministry of Defence. That ministry was responsible for activation of the public policy on nuclear waste disposal. Nerys returned the compliments and thanked Dr. Zhang for a most productive day. She also expressed admiration for his now perfect English!

Back at the hotel, Nerys felt more than satisfied with the first day as she stood at the bay window, looking out on Jianguomen Road. Goodness, even at 11pm it was still a thriving thoroughfare filled with everything from ZILs and Lamborghinis to rickshaws and bicycles. She glanced downward and was intrigued to see the clear profile of Troy. Because her room was in a recessed section of the unusually shaped building, she could see into his bay window and the reflection from a dressing table mirror gave her a full view into his room. She felt she was intruding and stepped back quickly.

Before turning in for the night, she decided to email Calum with a short report of her interesting day. She mixed the technical content which had greatly contributed to her project with the cultural wonders like the banquet and the cultural quirks like the pretence not to speak English. It all made for quite an experience.

She sent the email and then put her iPad on charge overnight. After a quick shower, she decided to take one last look at the amazing Beijing vista before getting into bed. Almost involuntarily, she glanced down at the next floor. She could not believe what she saw in the reflection in the mirror. Troy was stretched out naked on the bed as if waiting expectedly for something. Then another figure came into vision. The diminutive and very naked Fang Chongmei moved with grace of a ballet dancer and the stealth of a cat. Soon she had buried her head in his groin and all that could be seen was her shapely little butt and arched back.

Nerys almost exploded with anger and quickly pulled the drapes closed. Sleep escaped her for a long time. She could not make up her mind whether her anger was caused by a sense of Troy's betrayal of the professionalism of her project, or caused by simple jealousy. Either way, she was going to have it out with Mr. Troy Cameron in the morning.

The ride to the Central Military Mission in the morning was unusual for several reasons. On this occasion the ZIL was flanked by motorcycle outriders, two in front and two bringing up the rear. Their flashing lights caused the congested traffic to part like the Red Sea under Moses' command and allowed the limousine to make good speed in a city otherwise condemned to gridlock. Inside the vehicle, Ms. Fang sat with a serene look on her face beside the driver. However in the back Troy could feel the icy atmosphere. If he had a knife, he could have cut it in half. She must have found out. There had been no other issues to cause Nerys's open hostility. She must have found out. But how?

The Central Military Mission, China's equivalent of the US Pentagon, was a huge imposing building inside a series of building and gate circles that served as security precautions. It was probably impossible to get into the heart of the complex without being stopped at half a dozen security checks. Yet the ZIL sped through gates that opened as if by magic upon its approach. The threesome was met by a military person with rows of medals on his newly pressed uniform that glinted in the morning sun. They were ushered into an elevator that went to sixteen floors (there was a fourteenth floor here, no room for superstition in the People's Army) and an extra floor above that could only be accessed once a special key was inserted. The car went all the way to the special floor.

Xing Dun was an unremarkable man. Short and squat with a creased face as if he were perpetually frowning and his eyes squinting. It was almost impossible to see into his eyes. As Ms. Fang made introductions, he took a cigarette out of his mouth and that hand pointed to seats at a small table set up to view a large screen that looked like it had been specially assembled.

'Sit down please.'

'I speak English. Do you speak Chinese?'

'Alas not.'

'Then I will speak Chinese, and you will speak English, and comrade Fang Chongmei will translate for us.'

'That will be fine. I want to thank you for taking the time to meet with me and for arranging the visits to the nuclear decommissioning sites. We had a marvellous day yesterday with Zhang Pan and saw the fine work that has been done here to develop public policy on the disposal of nuclear waste. The policy statement is probably the finest I have seen in existence. And the opportunity to see it in action by witnessing actual disposal projects is a tremendous opportunity for me as a political scientist.'

'There will be a slight change in plan. It is impractical to visit any sites. It is still winter in China and the locations are either too cold or too wet. Instead we have prepared for you a series of films that explain exactly what is being done in each case in carrying out the intentions of the Peoples' Decree on Disposal of Nuclear Waste.'

Nerys found it difficult to hide her disappointment. When word had come through over two months ago that the Government was prepared to grant access for her to actual sites where decommissioning was taking place, her research project took an exponential leap in academic credibility. Now she was going to have to make do with viewing films. But what choice did she have?

'I look forward to seeing what you have prepared for us. Will it be possible for us to obtain copies?'

'Waste disposal is a matter of national security. I am sure you will understand that such material cannot be released generally. You may however take notes.'

Over the rest of the day, they sat watching a series of films with English soundtracks that purported to show the Peoples' Decree in action. Radioactive waste from decommissioned power stations and nuclear weapons from military installations was shown to be thoughtfully transported across land to tunnels in wilderness areas.

Every so often Xing Dun would add his own commentary to augment what had been said on the film. In addition, he chain-smoked incessantly to the point where the air conditioning, if there really were any, had surrendered and the room was fogged in smoke.

'You will note that we are wise enough to transport the waste only over land, not over water like the British. I understand you were in Scotland recently. My latest news is that they have not yet managed to locate their missing cargo of waste. Perhaps they are looking in the wrong place?'

'I am sorry to hear that,' was all that Nerys could offer in response to his surprising scope of information.

In the afternoon, several scientists who also held military titles like Xing Dun were brought in to comment on their areas of expertise and to answer questions. Nerys tried her hardest to ask probing, yet not provocative, questions but each one seem to be answered confidently with much the same message and outcome. The overriding message was that the Peoples' Decree was the best public policy in the world and was being followed to a T; ergo, the Chinese must have solved a problem that hitherto had troubled the rest of the world.

Nerys's eyes were now smarting painfully from their exposure to forty or more cheap Chinese cigarettes and she was almost relieved when Xing Dun abruptly brought the meeting to an end.

'I know that you are heading to India tomorrow so I will not cause you to have a late night at a large banquet. That will also suit me because I am very busy with military matters. You see my chosen field of study in environmental science is only part of my job. I am also a serving soldier who is charged with finding solutions to uncooperative neighbours of the People's Republic of China. I bid you goodbye.'

By the time Ms. Fang had translated, he was already out of the room.

'I guess that's it,' Troy said uttering his first words of the meeting.

'The Brigadier General is an extremely busy man. It is a clear indication of the respect we have for Dr. Jones-Davies' project that he has graciously given you his time today,' Ms. Fang replied in rebuttal which seemed to take Troy by surprise.

'Quite so. I appreciate the effort. I will try to incorporate as much of the information that has been imparted today into my report as is possible.'

'Thank you Dr. Jones-Davies. There will be a great deal of interest in it when it is published. Now it will be my pleasure to take you to dinner. We will be joined by Captain Doctor Dah Ni whom you met earlier today.'

After a more subdued meal than either of the earlier nights, Nerys and Troy said good night to Ms. Fang at the hotel then retired to the bar at her suggestion.

'An interesting day Troy, don't you think? It was about as diametrically opposite from the previous day as was possible. We learned very little today that was not out and out propaganda. It makes you wonder if what we learned the first day was true or just propaganda too.'

'So you see the trip as a bust?'

'No. No. We cannot control the information we are given. We can only place it in a comparative context along with the already established body of knowledge on the subject. The million dollar question is whether China really is ahead or has created a smokescreen to suggest it.'

'Certainly Old Dun did his best to create a smokescreen all on his own. My eyes felt like I was crying out loud and then I looked at you and you were worse.'

'Yes, there were a number of messages that could suggest he was just treating us with contempt including the language thing, subjecting us to co-smoking more than two packs, cancellation of the site visits, and taking away our supper. On the other hand as sweet Ms. Fang said he is an extremely busy man with border conflicts to look after as well.'

Troy laughed. He enjoyed the banter that he and Nerys engaged in. He had been waiting with trepidation when they stepped into the bar for last night to be raised. It looked like he had dodged the bullet.

'Another drink Doc?'

'I don't think so. I wanted to give you a message about your little soiree with dear little Chongmei, or Candy as I heard you calling her today when you thought I wasn't listening. As tempting as those lips must have been, you showed poor judgment for the second time in our association. There will be no association after a third one. Do I make myself clear?'

'Oh come on. It was just a little bit of fun. It did not need to bother you.'

'Troy, it was one of two things. At best it was unprofessional when I am trying to present this project as leading-edge research in a controversial subject area. At worst, think about it. This is still a communist country. Did you not hear all the things that she and our hosts said about us that they had no right to know in the first place? Information is power for them and the more the better. Your little assignation last night probably contributed more to information gathering than you realize, much as you might like to think it was love at first sight.'

He sat and stared at her without comment.

'You are proving very naive in the ways of international research. It is just an extension of international politics and needs to be played out very carefully. I want you to give that some thought and bear in mind my warning—three and out!'

'I am sorry I seem to have screwed up.'

'Learn from it. Now let's go upstairs and get some sleep. I wonder what the sub-continent will bring us tomorrow.'

Chapter 32

Calum had decided that he needed some sea shells to finish off a display he was mounting in the Garrison House to publicize the upcoming educational exhibit. He knew there tended to be an abundance of very attractive shells on the west side of the island, in particular around Fintry Bay, but he only needed a few and felt sure he could find them on the beach at Cosy Corner not one hundred yards from his home in Barclay House.

He was stooping on the beach, sifting through sand and turning over shells looking for suitable candidates when a voice addressed him from over the low wall in front of the police station.

'You should know that all contents of public beaches belong to Her Majesty the Queen and by removing same, as you appear to be doing, you may be charged with common theft and may be held in my cell until the next hearing of the Sherriff Court in Rothesay. Would you care to join me for a cup of coffee so that we can discuss your eligibility for bail?'

Calum laughed up at Constable Henri Jardin and replied in his best American accent.

'Why Officer, I was totally unaware of the law in these here parts. I can only throw myself on the mercy of the court and hope that it can see its way to be charitable toward a humble colonist and sinner. I will be up for that coffee just as soon as I have collected some shells that I need.'

This was Calum's second visit to the adjoining house having escaped the threat of the accommodation next door and he settled down to a half-decent cup of coffee, not something you tended to find in abundance in Scotland.

'Anything new to report on the missing person case?'

'Nothing really solid I'm afraid. The publicity through the Daily Record has certainly opened things up. I wonder how that rag got hold of the story? Anyway, for every piece of potentially useful information that comes in there are half a dozen useless and crank pieces. We are sifting through it all right now. There have been reported sightings in Hollywood, New York, London, Edinburgh, and even Stornoway in the company of someone looking suspiciously like Brad Pitt. Angelina Jolie has been informed and has threatened to belt his lug.'

'Ha ha. Stornoway would be a good place to hang out for a dirty weekend.'

'We should not joke about a serious case but the crank stuff has to make you laugh. I think as we sort out the serious information over the next week we might begin to get a lead or two. It is frustrating at this stage still not knowing whether it was a voluntary or involuntary disappearance.'

'How did you and McBride fare with Tommy Duncan?'

'We caught up with him eventually. We did not really have much to go on other than to ask him outright. Needless to say, he denied having anything to do Mr. Wannamaker and he denied being anywhere near Mrs. Wannamaker. I said there had been a report of his van been parked close to their house but he explained that away by saying he had looked in on his old pal Murray McCabe two doors down from the Wannamakers. McCabe confirmed that Tommy had visited him but could not remember exactly when.'

'So it is a bit of a dead end by the sound of it?'

'It is for now. I will keep an eye on him but I seriously doubt he is holding her in custody somewhere on the island. For one thing, he does not have the brains and, secondly, he is pretty visible to be getting up to any mischief. He splits his time between the farm where he works, the Newton Bar, and his cottage and that is about all he does.'

'Well, thanks for the coffee. I need to get back to my house to pick up some gear. I am going fishing with Jimmie Morrison this afternoon.'

'Do you have a license sir?'

'Bugger off!'

Jimmie Morrison was scheduled to take a group of students from Newcastle University over to the shore at Skelmorlie, north of Largs, to collect specimens for a class project they were doing as part of a short-term certificate programme. They would need about two hours on the beach which would allow Jimmie time to call in on Gavin Mackenzie in contiguous Wemyss Bay. Mackenzie was the local Zodiac dealer and Jimmie needed some parts for the research station's inflatable boat. The window of time should also allow for an hour or so of fishing off Skelmorlie which is why he had invited Calum along. He reckoned an hour would be enough for an occasional amateur like the Yank before he got cold and wet. It was not quite the peak fishing season yet.

Six giggling long haired students jumped into the station launch with Jimmie and Calum. They were dressed for the occasion in oilskins trousers and jackets with large sou'westers to cap it off, making determination of genders difficult. They were obviously enjoying their time in Millport and were pumped up for their field trip. Over the roar of the launch's engines, Calum explained to them what a Californian was doing along for the ride.

The students were safely deposited on the beach with orders not to disappear to the pub and to be ready for pick up in two hours, or two and half at the most if the Zodiac dealership was busy. Jimmie knew the dealership would not be busy, it never was. That just allowed a little more slippage of time for fishing.

'We should go to Mackenzie's right now and get it over with. That way we will know how long we have for the fishing. OK with you?'

'Sure thing. You are the skipper.'

'That I am. A couple o' thae Newcastle lassies are no half bad. Did you see them?'

'I had difficulty sorting out the lassies from the laddies in all their wet weather gear. Were they expecting another storm?'

'You never know. We like to build up the excitement for them by having them dress for the part.'

They pulled into the commercial quay at Wemyss Bay, tied up the launch and went into the small shed bearing the name of Mackenzie that served as his shop. They were surprised to find Gavin helping two police officers with their enquiries.

'If you gentlemen would kindly wait outside. We are almost finished here,' said the burlier of two burly officers.

'I wonder what Gavin has done to attract the boys in blue.'

Eventually after a good thirty minutes had passed, the officers emerged and got into their patrol car. Jimmie and Calum swooped into the shop.

'Well, did you confess?'

'Like hell I did. Some bastard has stolen one of my Zodiacs that I hire out.'

'When did this happen?'

'I don't rightly know. I have been away for a few days visiting my sister in Paisley. The inflatables are locked up in that compound. When I got back it was empty. I knew one was out on hire but the other had vanished and the funny thing is the compound was still locked.'

'What did the polis reckon?'

'You know them. Couldnae find stolen goods even if they tripped over them. They took the details and will put them in the log of stolen goods. Other than that they will wait for the thief to come forward and gie hissel' up.'

Calum sensed that his fishing was in jeopardy as the other two continued their diatribe toward the local constabulary without ever getting close to the acquisition of the parts which was the reason for the visit. He wandered outside on the quay and was having a look around when a big powerful Zodiac appeared around the head of the quay and headed toward the shop .Calum poked his head through the door.

'Hey this might be your missing Zodiac coming in right now.'

The other two came out of the shop.

'Naw. Naw. That's the ither wan. That's the SERC boys bringin' it back. They will be bringin' it into the compound.'

Two strangers to Calum tied up the Zodiac, came up on to the quay, threw the keys to Gavin and one said, 'That's it for this time. We will probably need it again later in the week. Just leave the keys where you usually do in case you are not here. Remember and send your bill to Mr. Macadam. See you later.'

'Wait a minute; you might be able to solve my mystery. When you picked up your Zodiac, how many were here?'

'Just the one. I assumed you had rented out the other. You had agreed to always have one at our disposal. Why?'

'The ither wan has been nicked, that's what's happened. OK lads it will eventually be an insurance job I suppose. See you the next time.'

A dark car pulled up where the police car had been parked and picked up the two men. Calum was interested in knowing more about the SERC contract.

'Aye, yon Mr. Macadam arranged it a while back. They are working on shipping the nuclear waste out o' Farland. So they want wan o' my boats available at all times for them. They pay me a retainer and they pay for all the time they use it.'

'How do they pick up the boat if you are not here?'

'I leave the key under the mat outside the back door o' the shop. They know where to look.'

'How often do they use it?'

'Oh at least wan time a week. Sometimes more.'

'What do you think they need a Zodiac for?'

'I dinnae rightly ken. I never asked. Nane o' ma business.'

'Did they have the Zodiac out on rental during the big storm?'

'Aye they did. But I doot it would have been goin' anywhere. Disnae bother me. They will still hae to pay for the time.'

Jimmie had been listening to the conversation with interest. He was wondering why Calum was so intent on knowing about the SERC use of the inflatable.

'I have seen them when I have been out and about in the launch. It looks like they escort the dangerous cargo crafts for a bit when they pull away from Farland.'

'Have you seen how far they escort them?'

'No really. The furthest oot I have seen them is just off Arran.'

'They must go a fair distance ye ken because they go through a shitload of petrol. Still I am no complainin' mind, cos' it goes on their bill.'

'Interesting.'

'Ach Calum, have you seen the time? We have spent our fishing time jabbering with this character. We only have time to get my parts then we will have to go back to pick up the students. Bugger it. It will have to be the next time for you.'

Calum was mulling over what he had already caught.

Chapter 33

Calum had sent a long email to Nerys with the latest on Maggie's disappearance and the Farland craft disappearance. He only had the Daily Record initial story and follow-ups and Harry Jardin's comments on the former. He did not think the story was making a very big splash around the world judging by the Internet. The erratic behaviour of the Hollywood population had been over-reported in the past and now carried little cache unless it was extreme and provable.

He also told her about his discovery at the Zodiac dealership. He characterized the information as being perhaps important but without knowing just where it fitted in at this stage. Public news on locating the craft had not really advanced since the story first broke. No trace of SPC3 had been found in and around the Sound of Jura. If the final reporting from its GPS was to be disregarded, the scope of search would have to be increased substantially at enormous additional cost. Already the Royal Navy involvement was being scaled back.

Commentary and debate was centreing on what to do if it was found, and what to do if it was not found. The latter was being contemplated and it was posited that if no discernible trace of contamination emerged anywhere then perhaps it was better to leave well alone. Even if it were found and the cargo were intact, a strong lobby was being put forward that it would be best to leave it where it was if it posed no risk of contamination. Naturally, the environmental groups took different views that called for the rescue of the cargo and its relatively safe disposal someplace else. However, they put most of their energy into reiterating that the nuclear power stations should never have been built in the first place, and if they must be built, a safer method must be found of dealing with the spent waste.

Almost every political show on British television and even the chat shows that usually focused on visiting movie actors and musicians were consumed with the radioactive waste debate. Farland, which had been one of the lesser known nuclear power stations in the UK, was now the best known, having been thwarted in its attempt to slip into obsolescence.

Nerys read the email with interest over and over again until the flight attendant got impatient and ordered her to turn her iPad off or she would be removed from the plane. She eventually complied and settled down for the five hour flight to Indira Gandhi International Airport in Delhi. Thanks to the vagaries of JetAirways' seating procedures, she was separated from Troy Cameron today and perhaps that was a good thing.

She spent part of the flight thinking about how the so-called developed countries' approaches to disposal of radioactive waste, impacted by the very latest UK situation in Scotland, would interface with her BRIC findings and how she would present the comparison in her report. Who was ahead? Was anybody ahead? What did being ahead look like? Was it a race to get ahead? Seventy five years ago it was not even a research topic.

She spent the rest of the flight dozing.

Nerys and Troy sat down over afternoon tea to discuss the two days ahead once they were safely ensconced in the Taj Mahal Hotel, one of the most prestigious in Delhi but still relatively reasonably priced. The splendid tradition from days of the Empire seemed to mellow them and an unspoken truce had broken out.

They were to be hosted by the Department of Atomic Energy whose headquarters seemed to be widely scattered throughout the capital. They had been assigned to Dr. Anwil Praha, who was normally located at the Bhabha Atomic Research Centre in Mumbai, but he had suggested meeting in Dehli because he would be there on business. Dr Prahat had a nationwide remit on waste disposal policy and seemed likely to be a good source of information. However, given their experience in China, Nerys was not surprised that their visit was to be confined to corporate offices and there would be no site visits, despite their request.

That evening they enjoyed the delights of Indian cuisine. Although neither was vegetarian, they ended up visiting both the lavish meat eater and equally lavish vegetarian buffets in the hotel restaurant. They both agreed that vegetarians were better treated in India than they were in the US.

Next morning, there was no Ms. Fang to cater to their every need, but with the assistance of a jolly taxi driver they were able to find their way to Bikaner House. The majestic edifice was a testimony to the grand days of the British Raj and now technically came within the purview of Rajasthan, the largest of the states of India. However, it was also hosting a visit from Dr. Prahat and so the meeting had been located there.

Dr. Prahat was a charming, Cambridge and MIT educated, scientist and bureaucrat. He made Nerys and Troy instantly welcome and addressed them for over two hours without a break. He explained that India had a nuclear history in both energy production and weapons, the former in the quest for an affordable, efficient supply of electricity to a vast country and the latter in response to the volatile relationship it had with its near neighbours, initially China and later Pakistan. Development of the technology had not been a problem. India had a well-developed education system and a natural propensity toward engineering and the sciences. No, the problem, as with a number of other countries, was the disposal of the spent waste in power stations and stockpiles of obsolete weaponry.

His country's strategy had borrowed somewhat from its former mother country Britain and consisted of trying to maximize spent fuel processing, then short-term storage for up to 30 years, with the long-term solution being a deep repository in the crystalline rock of Kalpakham. The strategy was technically sound but the activation was something else. India had a history of natural climatic disasters that has been exacerbated by human incompetence, corruption, and a tendency for federal policies and procedures to be diluted at the state level and outright ignored at the municipal level.

Dr. Prahat and Nerys engaged in intense discussion about the admitted dilemma facing India of having reasonable public policy but highly uneven implementation across such a large physical mass.

'But at least we have not lost any waste like the poor Brits.'

'Can you be sure of that? How good are your records, particularly at the local level?'

'Touché.'

'My sense is that most countries are struggling with exactly the same problem as India.'

'Perhaps, but without some of the same spectacular disasters we have had to endure. Still with a population of 1.3 billion, we can always afford to lose a few thousand at a time. Please do not quote me on that!'

For the second day of the visit, a symposium had been arranged for fifty leading scientists and civil servants. Nerys and Troy were given the surprise news they would be expected to make a formal presentation on their research project including some prediction of what results might emerge from it. Their middle night was not spent further exploring the sumptuous delights of the buffet table but rather in her hotel room hastily preparing the presentation.

At the conclusion of the symposium, Nerys felt they had done a good job to represent their academic work-in-progress. It had been well received, vigorously debated, and fitted easily within the context of the rest of the subject matter. Dr. Prahat, too, was delighted with the outcome and quietly congratulated himself on turning a chore in entertaining the Americans into a learning experience for a good portion of the Indian scientific community.

After a celebratory dinner, Nerys felt it appropriate to note Troy's significant contribution to the symposium. All thoughts of their personal difficulties in Beijing were forgotten and she was convinced they could partner effectively for the rest of the research project. And, she felt that, while in China she had been not treated with respect by academic colleagues, the opposite had been true in India. They now left the country with excellent material for the report and a good feeling that they had been welcome and acknowledged researchers.

They were half-way toward completion of the project, at least as far as the information gathering was concerned. Maybe she could afford to take some days off over the summer to visit the Cumbraes.

Chapter 34

Today was the day! Calum had been working hard on the organization of the revitalized Marquess of Bute Cup golf championship. Just about everything was in place to relaunch the famous old tournament in July. He was about to see if he could provide the icing for the cake. It would begin with a call to Evan Davis in Nashville. Armed with his personal number that had been provided by Scotty Green, he dived into the task.

'Evan. This is Calum Davies calling. Do you remember...?'

'Calum old buddy. Are you still in Millport?'

'I am.'

'You better watch out. It is like the Hotel California. You can check out any time you like but you can never leave.'

'Would that be such a bad thing?'

'Ha ha. No, I quite envy you.'

'Evan. I either have a big favour to ask of you or I have a great opportunity to put to you. You get to judge which as long as you agree to do it.'

'Sounds intriguing. Let me hear it.'

'Since you went back to Nashville, I have been doing various things. The saddest one has been trying to make sense of Maggie's disappearance. You haven't heard from her, have you? The happiest one has been organizing the Marquess of Bute Cup golf tournament. It has not been played for a few years but on the third Saturday in July it is going to be back, bigger and better than ever. I want you to come to Millport to play golf and music.'

'Whoa. Whoa. Wait a minute. Did I get all that right? First of all, the police have already been on to me. I have not heard a dicky bird from Maggie. It is really weird. And yet maybe it is not. She was always a bit of free spirit, especially when I knew her well in the early '70s. She would often drop out of the scene and then just re-appear. She liked to take off to Joshua Tree National Park in the desert to commune with nature and smoke some dope. I told the police to look there. If she is going through a bumpy patch with her husband as she hinted at and Scotty filled me in on, it would not surprise me for her to just opt out for a spell. Joshua Tree is a bit far though, maybe Wee Cumbrae?'

'What you say makes some kind of sense. But the longer it goes on, the more I worry that it is going to end in sad news.'

'You can only leave it to the police. Something will come up. She has lots of friends in the US, not so many in the UK I don't think, but if she plays to par, she will contact one of them when she is ready.'

'I guess.'

'You got the hots there, man?'

'No. I just got to like her a lot, as a friend you know.'

'I know.'

'Now you were talking about playing to par. Let's get back to the golf.'

'Yeah. Tell me more.'

'We have, what I think will be, a cracking tournament on the Saturday with almost all the top amateurs in the country committed to play. On the Friday we are going to have an *"Ams & Hams"* tournament. That is where you start to come in. We will pair you and a sponsor with a top amateur for an exciting round. Then on the Saturday after the big tournament, we are going to have a concert in a big marquee pitched on the grounds of the Garrison House. That is where you come in again. I would really like you to headline it.'

'I don't know man. I have not really been performing much at all lately. It is got to be well over a year. I don't have my shit together. I have been concentrating on producing and a little writing again but no performing. I have forgotten how.'

'A guy like you never forgets how. You probably just have to be in the mood.'

'True.'

'How often do you play golf?'

'Well that I have been getting back into. I am enjoying it a lot.'

'OK. That part is settled. What would it take to get you back on to our intimate little stage in front of an adoring audience of about two hundred and fifty, some of whom were there for you back in 1969?'

'Ha. Ha. You make it sound nice. What I would probably need is help. Big help.'

'That I can provide I think. What would you say if I told you Francesca Carlotti is prepared to come over all the way from West Kilbride to play too? But she will only play if you will play.'

'You are shitting me right?'

'I am not.'

'Francesca Carlotti the classical piano player?'

'The same.'

'And sometimes singer?'

'That too.'

'She wants to play on the same bill as me?'

'She wants to play on the same bill as you and she wants to close the show with you.'

'What could we play? I am a little rusty on my Chopin and Mendelssohn.'

'Maybe, but she is not averse to rocking it up a bit with some Beatles and R.E.M. I suspect she would be game for a bit of Dubus too.'

'Man Oh Man. You have got me thinking. Are you sure she would do it?'

'Yes, but only if you do it too.'

'Count me in. I may be nuts but you have got those old Millport juices pumping through my veins.

Me and the hottest classical chick on the planet! It has got to be. Count me in. Count me in.'

'Consider it done. I will email you all the details and you can see what the Marquess of Bute Cup is all about so far on www.marquessofbutegolf.co.uk. I will make the changes to the website to now include the all-star concert with your permission.'

'Sure go ahead. Francesca Carlotti. Wow.'

'You are a good man, Evan. Of course I can't pay you. All the proceeds of the concert will go to help the primary school catch up with technology.'

'Great cause. I don't want paid. You just did, by bringing Millport and Francesca Carlotti to me.'

'Thanks Evan. See you soon.'

Calum wiped the perspiration from his brow and removed his soaking shirt. One down and one to go. He knew very well that he did not have Francesca Carlotti in the bag. Far from it. He had had one brief conversation with her when she had done more giggling than committing to the concept of playing with Evan Davis. But she was intrigued. He knew she was intrigued. Plus, it was heavily reported that she had just taken up golf!

Francesca Carlotti was the wunderkind of British, no global, classical music. After winning the BBC Young Musician of the Year Award, her career had taken off big time. Her refreshingly strident piano playing had breathed new life into everything from Beethoven to Wagner. Heck, she had even put the Chopin Polonaise on the rock charts. And she had a voice to die for to fall back on when her fingers got tired. And she reportedly loved rock music but had never been seen doing any in public. And she came from West Kilbride just south of Farland Power Station, funny enough. Mum and Dad were still there. And she played golf, did I already say that? Go for it!

'Good morning Ms. Carlotti. It is Calum Davies calling you again about the Marquess of Bute Cup and concert taking place in Millport on the third weekend in July.'

'Oh yes. Are you still as enthusiastic as you were when we talked before?'

'Even more so Francesca. I'll tell you why. I have just got off the phone with Evan Davis. He has signed up to play the *"Ams & Hams"* tournament on the Friday and the closing concert on the Saturday night. But here is the catch. The latter is conditional on you agreeing to headline the concert with him. He would do his thing. You would do yours. We will lay on your favourite Bechstein, don't you worry. And then he hopes the two of you can close the show together. You will get a chance to rock like you never have rocked before. You know he is a legend in his field just like you are in yours.'

'I love his music. I got to know "I Know You Rider" when Dubus had that surprise comeback hit in the early 90s. I was just seven years old. But I went back to discover all their old songs and his songs with Sam Whiskey, the DRB Band, and the Country Rhodes band. I just love him.'

'I can see that. And I can tell you he is a lovely fella with profound feelings for Millport. Will you do it?'

'I don't know. I am kind of scared. It's all very well singing Beatles in the shower. Could I keep up with him?'

'He asked the same question, could he keep up with you? You will feed off each other. If we could bottle the adrenalin that will fall out of that duo, we would and then sell it for a good cause.'

'I was planning to be home that weekend anyway.'

'Bring your Mom and Dad. They will love it. Do they golf?'

'My Dad does, avidly.'

'Then he is in the *"Ams & Hams"* along with you. OK?'

'Yes OK. I am so looking forward to it.'

'Fantastic.'

'How will I work things out with Evan?'

'His number is 615-738-0202. Call him now while you are pumped.'

'I am going to.'

'We are going to have a ball. I can't pay you but all the proceeds will be going to the island primary school.'

'That's just fine. Getting to play with Evan Davis is payment enough!'

Calum put the phone down and leapt for the bottle of whisky sitting on the table just out of his reach. A hefty dram to celebrate, or else to calm him down? Whichever, it did not matter. Now he had to get on to the BBC. They could not miss this opportunity to film the concert of a lifetime and sell it on to PBS in the States.

Chapter 35

On this, the first day of May, Calum was on his way to have dinner with Heather Randall and Nicholas Gorman. He had set off a little early, walked a little too fast, and now found himself with a little time to kill. A pit stop at the Newton Bar was appropriate and there he stood at the bar supping a McEwan's Export instead of his favourite Belhaven just for a little change. He hoped that Jimmie Morrison might drop in, this being his joint favourite bar with Fraser's Bar along at the south end of the promenade. He had not seen him since the ill-fated fishing trip. Alas, he did not appear. He must be patronizing the other favourite watering hole. Calum did, however, notice Tommy Duncan sitting on his own through in the room that contained the pool table. He looked a little worse for wear and was downing what was obviously not his first pint of the evening.

'Hello Tommy. All on your own tonight?'

'Aye. Nae doot others will be in later tho'. Fancy a game o' pool Yank?'

'I am not really a Yank and that maybe explains why I don't play pool. But I will sit with you awhile if you don't mind.'

'Suit yersel'. I was just getting up to buy another pint.'

'Let me get you one.'

'Suit yersel'.'

Returning with two fresh pints, Calum sat down to do a little digging. Tommy's slurred speech hinted that his guard might be down compared to when they had last talked up at the farm.

'You know we did not get off to the best of starts, one way or another. How about we start again? Tommy, I am Calum.'

'Aye right. Cheers.'

'How do you like working on the farm?'

'It's OK. It's the only work I am likely to get oan the island.'

'Have you lived here long?'

'Aw ma life.'

'You are a lucky man. I love this place.'

'Aye well I dinnae feel aw that lucky.'

'What is like to be on the Cumbraes Council? That must be pretty interesting for you. It seems to be doing good work.'

'Aye well. Well, I am soarry about voting agin you. Half the time I dinnae understand what is goin' on but Alec Taggart tells me ahead o' time what tae vote for and that's how I ended up agin you. Actually I thought you said some good stuff when I could follow you.'

'Thanks. I only have the betterment of Millport at heart.'

'Whit was that?'

'I only care about Millport just like you.'

'Aye.'

'I heard that the police were asking you about Maggie Wannamaker.'

'Aye, that they were.'

'I don't care if anybody was asking you to watch her; I only want to find out what happened to her. After you and I met at the farm that day, did you by any chance see her again?'

'I'm no supposed to say.'

'Please tell me. I am not the police. I just want to help her.'

'Fancy her d'you?'

'That is not the reason. I only just met her. I just hate the thought of her coming to harm.'

'Alec says that her husband thinks you fancy her.'

'Well he is wrong. I just care. There is a difference. I suspect you could say you care about her and it does not mean you fancy her.'

'Naw. I would prefer that I fancy her.'

'Right. I can understand that. Is there anything you can tell me?'

'I never seen her again after you and me at the farm. But, I know Alec had to pick up Mr. Wannamaker off the last ferry and take him tae the hoose.'

'So Wannamaker came back that night having only left earlier in the morning?'

'You better not tell anyone I telt you.'

'I won't you can rest assured.'

Tommy belched and Calum feared he was beginning to get a bit resistant to all the questions.

'Do you know anything of what happened later that night or the next day?'

'Naw. Alec just telt me to stop watching her.'

'Hmm. Tommy, I have enjoyed our little drink and chat. I have to run because I am late for a dinner appointment. Let's do this again sometime. I will drop by the Newton some other night.'

'Aye OK. Cheers the noo.'

Dinner with Heather and Nicholas Gorman was again a pleasure. Heather could assuredly cook with the best of them, Nicholas had outstanding wine knowledge, and the conversation that flowed was stimulating and often hilarious for as long as the topics of Maggie and Farland were left off the script. And for most of the evening they were. It was only when three delicious courses had been consumed and brandy and cigars were being proposed for the sitting room with that southern view that things changed.

As Heather got up to clear the dessert plates, Calum offered to give a hand.

'No, let Heather do that, if you will, my dear. I need to have a quick word with Calum on the business side.'

Calum sensed her irritation but she said nothing as she went through to the kitchen and the men retired to the sitting room.

'I am sure you are following this sad affair of Maggie Wannamaker's disappearance.'

'Unfortunately that is about all I have been doing—following it. I sure wish I could be doing something to track her down.'

'Well that might be possible in the future. I have been asked by Joel to set up a meeting with you. You two have not exactly hit it off since day one but he wants to call a truce and see if two heads are better than one in solving the mystery. He does not have a lot of faith in DI McBride and is thinking about bringing in some private help.'

'Wannamaker wants to meet with me?'

'That is what I am saying. A meeting on the QT mind you. Just the two of you. I would not be there.'

'Whereabouts?'

'Down here. He is proposing to come down from Glasgow tomorrow. He is suggesting that you meet at his house at 6pm.'

'I guess I could do that. I don't like the man and I can't quite shake the notion that he might be tied up in Maggie's disappearance. But I will meet with him. Maybe it will persuade me one way or the other about him. Yes. OK you can tell him I will be there.'

'That's good. He is pretty desperate I think.'

'He must be. Off the record, what do you make of him as a person and not necessarily a client?'

'Deep. Complex. Ambitious. Maybe even ruthless. He is close to me when he needs to be and keeps me at a distance when he doesn't. I wouldn't say he is a terribly likeable man. But he pays his bills on time.'

'I see.'

'I much preferred Maggie. Who wouldn't? If you can help him find her that would be good.'

'I notice you refer to her in the past tense. A lot of people seem to do that. Are we finished? I feel bad about excluding Heather.'

'Sure, go and call her in.'

Calum moved quickly through to the kitchen to find that Heather had cleared up all traces of the meal.

'I am sorry about that. Nicholas states that you may join the gentlemen now.'

Heather swung around and her eyes flared until she realized that he was joking.

The men smoked fine Havana cigars. All three enjoyed generous Napoleon Brandies. Nicholas was moved to praise Heather for finally developing a liking for brandy.

'You would never touch it before.'

'It just so happens that I have developed a liking for it in these cold winter nights on this island. But don't ask me to smoke one of those foul smelling things.'

They sat contentedly gazing out at the view of Wee Cumbrae and Arran. The days were getting longer now and the two islands were still clearly visible in the gathering dusk.

'You know I have a feeling that Joel Wannamaker will not want to keep the house here. I think he bought it mainly for Maggie and regardless of what ends up there, I think he might want to get rid of it. If he puts it back on the market, you should be ready to grab it Calum. I could not act for you but I could recommend a good solicitor.'

'I don't think so. It is a beautiful home but a bit too rich for my blood as a second home. I don't see Nerys and me making this our first home.'

'It sounds like you have been inside it to know it is beautiful. Have you?'

'No. I am just talking about the appearance from outside. Though I am sure the inside is just as nice.'

Heather spoke with the intention of interrupting what might become an interrogation by Nicholas. He had a habit of doing that as if he had someone on the stand in court.

'You don't think the two of you will come here. That is a pity. The island needs some more professionals and characters.'

'I didn't say we would not come. I just don't see as being here, even semi-permanently. Certainly not while Nerys is still working. And we just could not afford a big house here as well as one in California.'

'I see.'

'Now that little place I have in Barclay House is a different matter. I would scoop that up in a second. But that is unlikely to happen. The owner is not motivated to sell. In fact, he has just given me notice that he will not renew my lease at the end of June.'

'How dreadful. What do you have in mind?'

'It might work out for the best. Once the golf tournament is over in July I will have no pressing reason to stay any longer so I may just move in to somewhere like the Westview for July and then head back to California.'

Heather's 'Aw,' was covered up by Nicholas's loud exclamation.

'Hell yes. I was meaning to compliment you on that golf thing. I heard the BBC Scotland talking about the concert and the tournament. Quite a coup to get Francesca Carlotti. Never heard of the other chap but I suppose he will appeal to some. I say old man, any chance of getting me into the ham thing? I don't play golf as much as I used to but I don't suppose the course here is too challenging.'

'I think that right now the *"Ams & Hams"* is full but if a space comes up I will try to get you in.'

'I play golf too you know, can I get in?'

'Really Heather. I think there will be a certain standard.'

'Oh I'm sure the standard would not be diminished. I am interested in ensuring gender balance and local involvement so I will bear Heather in mind too.'

Nicholas made a huffing noise and did not see the wink pass between the co-conspirators. Calum was almost relieved when the conversation switched to the Farland story.

'Damned strange that there has been no trace of the boat. I have advised Heather to keep as low a profile as possible. There is nothing to be gained from being in the news while the thing is still missing. The story will blow over when something else comes along.'

'That something else might well have come along. I heard on the radio when I was confined to the kitchen that there has been a bad train wreck in Somerset. Lots of deaths and injuries. In any case, it is not my job to keep a low profile. I have to be there to advise BritPower and the two governments before and after SPC3 is located.'

'I say leave it to that SERC. They seem to be doing a fine job. You would be better sticking to education my dear. Education and politics never seem to mix that well in my estimation.'

'If by that you mean that politicians are seldom well educated I would agree.'

'Well said, Calum.'

'That was not what I meant at all. This whole radioactive thing is a mess and it will end up bringing down the government if they don't watch out. The best approach is to let the story die. This train crash might just be what is needed.'

'When my dear husband fears for his government, he is of course referring to the only real government, the one in London. Aren't you dear?'

'Let's not get started on that. I am sure Calum needs to be heading out. It is getting quite late.'

Chapter 36

Calum had decided that it would be right to inform DI McBride that he would be meeting with Joel Wannamaker at the latter's request. He had already run afoul of McBride on withholding information so he figured that giving him all information was the way to go even if the police officer did not need it. It also gave him the opportunity to get the latest information from the police side if McBride was willing to share.

McBride was not in his office in Glasgow but Calum was able to track him down on his mobile number which he had been given.

'Yes Dr. Davies, what can I do for you?'

'DI McBride, I wanted to tell you that I have been invited to meet with Joel Wannamaker tonight. I don't know what he intends but I thought you should know. Have you any thoughts on it?'

'I have no thoughts at all. You are free to meet with him if that is what you mean.'

'No, not really. Assuming the misgivings about him and perhaps some involvement in Maggie's disappearance, I wondered if there was anything I should know or anything you wanted me to try to find out.'

'Look Dr. Davies, you may have misgivings about Mr. Wannamaker but as far as I am concerned I have no reason to doubt him at this stage. He has cooperated fully with our enquiries.'

Calum silently cussed McBride. Getting him to cooperate was like getting blood from a stone. He had hoped, once the issue of withholding information had been cleared up, that McBride would see him as being on the same side and would act in a more collegial manner. That did not seem to be happening.

Why did he always think of colleges when the term collegial came up? The words must be related in some way. Yet in his experience, people in colleges never acted in a collegial manner. Seems it was the same in the police force.

'Well then, can I ask you if there has been any change as a result of your enquiries?'

'The enquiries continue without Ms. Wannamaker being located. We have received a lot of information from the public around the world. Most of it is quite useless but it all has to be checked out.'

'So at this stage you are still not able to say if the disappearance was voluntary or involuntary?'

'Quite so. And the longer we go without finding any evidence of an involuntary disappearance, the more likely it may be that she has voluntarily gone to ground. We may just have to wait it out until she feels like resurfacing.'

'That does not mean you are closing the case?'

'That does not mean we are closing the case but there will come a time perhaps when we are not in the position to deploy as much in the way of resources as we are at present.'

'So nothing has emerged to indicate where she might be. How about her credit card or debit card?'

'We have checked with her bank. Neither has been used in quite some time. We understand she was in the habit of carrying a fair bit of cash on her which would keep her going for a while.'

'I see. While I have you, can I ask about my other favourite topic? What is the police involvement in the missing Farland craft SPC3?'

"The police role is one of staying in the background on that one. We are not able to put resources into the search at sea. That is being handled by the coastguard and on a very limited basis by the navy. The private outfit which was also looking seems to have been stood down now. I have the dubious honour of heading the case but as I say our role is background at this stage. Why?'

'I might as well tell you that I have doubts about the involvement of SERC in the whole Farland thing and you might know that SERC and Joel Wannamaker are connected in some way.'

'I know nothing about your theories. And, quite frankly I don't want to know. I have to go now. If your meeting with Mr. Wannamaker should throw up a new fact, by all means contact me. Goodbye for now.'

Well, that was a waste of time thought Calum. He could understand the police being wary of well-intentioned amateurs with their own theories. He would just have to soldier on himself until he turned up some new facts.

At 6pm, Calum showed up at Chez Wannamaker and was immediately presented with a welcome drink. Wannamaker made a lot about the two of them getting off on the wrong foot over Maggie's distractions and Calum's involvement in questioning SERC's actions at Farland.

'I understand that you did what you thought you had to do at Farland. I can tell you that it riled up Cyrus Macadam. From what I have seen it does not take much to rile him up. Me, I am prepared to let it go. You did not find anything wrong which, at the end of the day, is a good thing in trying to maintain public confidence. God knows SERC needs everybody on the same side with this missing craft now.'

'I was acting for the local research station here. They have legal obligations too.'

'Yes but I don't understand why an educational institution is even involved in a business transaction in the first place. Academics should stay on their campuses.'

'I am no longer an academic and I have been a professional all my working life.'

'OK. OK. I am trying offer a truce here for the sake of Maggie.'

'What do you have in mind?'

'Maggie has been acting very strangely now for some months. I thought bringing her over here away from the Hollywood madness would help. But I think it has made things worse. I was sure that you two were having a fling. Jesus, you would not be the first. But now I think she was just desperate for some company. WCI is keeping me pretty busy'

'Actually, she was keen to get some professional advice concerning the financial proposals you were throwing at her. I did not feel I had the local knowledge to advise her appropriately and that was how it kind of morphed into a friendship of sorts. I was not having a fling with her although it seems like everybody I speak to would like to think I was. But I got to know her well enough to care about her welfare when she suddenly vanished off the face of the earth.'

'OK. I get it.'

'You were made aware no doubt that I last met her at the Glaid Stone on the Thursday afternoon. I never saw her or heard from her again.'

'What did she say to you that day?'

'That she had signed the trust documents. That you were treating her better. That she planned to work on her marriage.'

'Really?'

'Yes. I felt that was a positive sign. I did not get any hint that she planned to take off.'

'That's what makes it weird. Neither did I."

'When did you last hear from her?'

'I went back to Glasgow on that Thursday morning because there was a press conference about the derby match with Glasgow Erin. Then I planned to surprise her by coming back down here that night. When I got in there was no sign of her.'

'I was not aware you had come back that night.'

'Why would you be?'

Calum thought to himself that the police did not seem to know he had come back that night after having talked to Joel. Joel had now confirmed what Tommy Duncan had said. He wondered why the police version was different. He did not answer the question, rhetorical or otherwise.

'And she has not been in touch since?'

'Not a word. There is no evidence in the house here or at our place in Glasgow that she intended to take off. All her clothes and things are in their normal places.'

'Nicholas Gorman mentioned you were going to get some private help.'

'I am thinking about it. I don't see the police making much progress. DI McBride is positively unhelpful. What do you think about the idea?'

'It might be worth it to augment the police effort. There is only so much they can do and sustain after the first few weeks. But I would imagine that private help would not come cheap.'

'What's money? If it would bring her back alive, I would pay anything.'

'Have you any reason to believe she is not alive?'

'None at all. Have you?'

'No. It is just that the longer things go on, fatalism creeps in to one's thinking.'

'Have you any theories?'

'The police asked me that. I had doubts about her just taking off from here because I am not sure that she knows many people and places. But I have no evidence whatsoever that something tragic has befallen her.'

'So where does that leave your thinking?'

'I was talking to Evan Davis about Maggie. Do you know him?'

'The washed-up rock star?'

'I would not describe him as that. Anyway, he knew Maggie years ago and he said she had a tendency back then to just take off when she felt the urge to do so. His money would be on her doing that again this time. I guess in the absence of anything else I would be inclined to agree with that.'

'I suppose that is the hope for the best outcome but it still does not sit very well with me. She has never taken off before in our time together.'

'Is there anything I can do to help? If we are through throwing barbs at each other and there is a modicum of trust between us, I am willing to help.'

'Thanks. The only thing I can think of is contacting her friends to test Evan Davis' theory.'

'Do you have a list?'

'I had my housekeeper in LA locate and send over Maggie's address book. I had never seen the contents before. It is vast. There must be a few hundred names in it. Mostly in the US, some in Canada, and some in the UK. Very few in Europe outside of the UK. Could I ask you to start making phone calls?'

'I have some jobs I am doing here on the island but I could fit in some calls each day. But I would need access to a phone. All I have is a throw-away mobile since I was beaten up at Farland.'

'Yes I heard about that. Bad luck. Tell you what I could do. I will give you a key for this place. I am going to be mostly in Glasgow as the soccer season hots up. You could make your calls from here. Would that work?'

'I could make it work. Am I just asking the obvious questions—have they heard from Maggie, any ideas where she might be?'

'I guess so. The police may have contacted some of them but I doubt they have done much digging into her friends.'

'Alright, I can start tomorrow.'

Wannamaker passed over the address book. Calum shivered as he flicked through a couple of pages and recognized big Hollywood names. It would be odd just making a cold call to people like that.

'Anybody off-limits? I see some big names here.'

'Heck no. If they are on the list she must have been able to phone them. You are just phoning on her behalf. And mine as well of course.'

'OK will do.'

'Thanks Calum.'

Calum spent a little more time having a couple of drinks. Talk strayed to football. Wannamaker was just as smug as he had been previously about being instrumental in making WCI great again. He noted with relish that they were drawn against Edinburgh Waverley in the quarter final round of the Scottish Cup. It was good to get an easy draw. Calum could not help taking the bait.

'But the game is in Edinburgh. That might make a difference from the last time we played.'

'Believe me it will not make one little bit of difference. Waverley was very lucky to keep the score down the last time. Their form if anything has gotten worse than it was back then. It will be a blow-out. Do you want tickets?'

'No thank you. If I were to go to the game I would want to be with the right supporters.'

'OK but let's keep in touch on your calls. I will give you my private mobile number. If you find out anything worthwhile you tell me first. Then I go to the police if it warrants it. OK?'

'Good enough.'

Chapter 37

The rest of the month of May passed with only minimal movement on either of the stories that were now consuming a large part of Calum's attention.

No progress was being made on locating SPC3. The search of the Sound of Jura had been wound up with no sonar or visual location having been obtained. There was ample opportunity for the craft to still be out there but the authorities were unable to continue to commit the resources to maintain the search. On a positive note there was no trace of contamination reported in the area which suggested that if the craft were on the seabed, its cargo was still intact and could remain so for an indeterminate future.

There was also an alternative theory that the last GPS recording was somehow false and that the craft was situated or had foundered elsewhere. However, there was no real evidence to support this theory and no resources available to broaden the search to test out the theory.

The decision had been made by BritPower in consultation with the governments of Scotland and UK, SERC and the Cumbraes Environmental Research Station to put the search on hold until some physical evidence emerged that would guide it. In addition, it was decided to resume shipping the radioactive waste between Farland and Beagg. The schedule had begun again and each voyage was being monitored with increased intensity. Fortunately, the weather in May was cooperating and the prospect of calmer summer seas was ahead before next winter had to be faced.

The investigation into the disappearance of Maggie Wannamaker continued but with ever diminishing resources being deployed by the police. In the absence of any evidence that she had flown or sailed back to America, the police there quickly put the case into their not closed but inactive category. The Scottish and English police continued to follow up on tips from the public but those that were deemed promising invariably led to a dead-end ultimately.

The media, having posited all the possible explanations, seemed to have landed on the notion that Maggie had just taken off somewhere. Evan Davis was now being quoted indirectly as recalling that to have been one of her habits back in 1970s. With free travel around the UK and over to the Continent of Europe in the absence of the same kind of record keeping that there would be with transatlantic travel, the potential for her to eventually end up a long way from Millport was taken for granted. The story had gone quiet and would remain so until she popped up on a Croatian beach or in a Bavarian mountain resort.

Calum could not let either mystery go, although his ability to influence them was very limited. He scanned all media daily for news of the Farland situation. In addition, he continued to research the UK radioactive waste disposal history for Nerys and the background to SERC in pursuit of his growing obsession.

He was surprised to find that SERC UK was only tangentially connected to the mother company based in Long Beach, California that was in turn nominally owned by the California University. The UK subsidiary had a registered office in London and seemed to have a good deal of financial and operational independence. He noted that it was current in its financial and tax reporting and its auditors were Brookes & Co. That firm took Calum back. He had articled with them back at the beginning of his career. It was a small company that had resisted the amalgamation mania that had led ultimately to there being the big four companies which audited 99% of the companies in the FTSE 100. Brookes had relatively few clients but they were usually small, high profile companies with whom they had long relationships. SERC did not exactly fit the profile of a Brookes' firm. Calum wondered if Archie Young was still working with them.

Calum and Archie Young had joined the training programme at Brookes, Edinburgh office on the same day. Both were straight out of high school, the former from a state senior secondary school and the latter from a prestigious private school that numbered prime ministers, field marshals, company executives by the score, and three of the last four captains of the Scotland rugby teams among its alumni. Calum and Archie had grown close over their five year apprenticeship and both headed the graduating group of newly minted accountants in 1974. Thereafter, they went in diametrically opposite directions. Calum did not buy into the "loyalty for life with a partnership to follow by the time his hair had greyed" maxim and immediately left the firm for pastures new which ultimately led around the south of Scotland, to Canada, and the USA; and along the way crossed from the professional office to the university campus. Archie was a Brookes' man through and through and slowly edged his way up the hierarchy as had been promised on graduation.

The two kept in touch sporadically. That amounted to a letter at one time, now an email about every 18 months and a get together about every five to ten years. Calum had not seen Archie in at least five years but recalled his last email in which he was finally contemplating retirement having made it all the way to managing partner of the Edinburgh office. If anybody could provide some inside information on SERC UK it would be Archie, and Calum decided that he would have to contact his old friend.

As promised to Joel Wannamaker, Calum had spent part of each day working through Maggie's address book. He had spoken to the rich and famous, and to the anonymous, but pretty much with consistent results. Nobody had heard from her, many had some vague idea where she might hide out if that was on her mind, and all wished him good luck in his search. He even had a comical chat with Rod Stewart who seemed more interested in finding out the score of the Glasgow Erin game going on at the same time as his call. Calum could not help chuckling as he confirmed that Rod's favourite team was currently losing to Aberdeen.

It was obvious that virtually all the people in Maggie's book held her in high esteem but nobody could shed any light on the mystery. It was particularly disappointing that UK residents were no more helpful than others. Calum faithfully passed the information on to Wannamaker but did not see him again in person.

May had also been a month of catch up for Nerys. The trip to China and India had realized a large amount of information that had to be analyzed and written up for her final report. In addition, the month was generally busy on campus with classes coming to an end and semester examinations and final examinations taking place. Although she had been able to use SERC funds to buy herself release from teaching responsibilities for most of the semester, she felt a duty to help her students and was now busily engaged in giving tutorials to ensure they were best prepared for their exams.

Troy Cameron was able to contribute effectively to moving the research project along. He was quite adept at sorting their findings and had even assisted with some of the writing. However, he had dropped a bombshell that he would have to drop out of Nerys's project after the summer in order to dedicate all of his attention to his PhD dissertation which had taken rather a back seat since the start of the year. That was a blow for Nerys but she set goals for the two of them to achieve by the end of August including the planning of the second leg of travel to Russia and Brazil. She flirted with the idea of asking Calum to accompany her and take on the duties that Troy had carried out. He was certainly qualified. It only remained to determine if he was motivated. Six months ago it would have been futile to even ask but he was now visibly energized. Perhaps she could tap into it and she would broach the subject during a quick visit to Millport in July to share his glory around the golf competition he had organized.

Nothing more had come from Nerys's discovery via Michael Musselwhite that SERC might be involved in suspect environmental activities. The president of the California University had begun to take a more hands-on approach to the governance of SERC and had shared all that she had picked up with Dean Salisbury who had in turn kept Nerys informed. Thus far, nothing untoward had been revealed which was good news for Nerys given the large financial commitments she faced to complete her project and her dependence on SERC to fund them.

Toward the end of the month, Calum eventually tracked down Archie Young after the latter returned from a vacation in California where he had been trying to look up him and Nerys and had failed to connect with either. Archie was delighted to hear from his old sparring partner. He did not know a lot about SERC off hand but promised to look into them and proposed that they get together to discuss the results rather than put them on record. He had two tickets for the cup tie between Edinburgh Waverley and WCI so why didn't they get together there? Many's a game they had attended together in the old days but the club's gradual demise had tested Archie's long standing loyalty and first he given up his season ticket and then he had stopped attending games altogether. Perhaps the return of the two friends to their old stomping ground would bring Waverley some luck. For sure they needed some. Calum was delighted to make the date for the upcoming Sunday even though the game would be shown live on television.

The prospect of seeing Archie got even more appealing when Calum told Heather Randall that he would be going to the east of the country for the game and she revealed she intended to visit her brother in Edinburgh on that day and would be able to give him a ride. She mentioned that she would welcome the company. Nicholas was leaving for Los Angeles to testify in a court case that had begun when he was based there over ten years ago and had dragged on to this day. An example of the fast-track American legal system he had grumbled but at least his passage was being paid for by the appellant party.

It was on the morning of the game and Calum was skimming the local newspaper over breakfast when he came across a short story that immediately caught his attention.

"Stolen Boat Located

Local Zodiac dealer Gavin Mackenzie was surprised to be informed by police that his inflatable that he recently reported stolen had been located. Alas there was not much of it left when it was found washed up on a skerry on the west side of the Isle of Ghiga. It was possible, however, to make out the registration number that tied it to the Wemyss Bay resident.

Neither the police nor Mackenzie has any idea how the Zodiac ended up on Ghiga which is on the west side of the Mull of Kintyre. Mackenzie stated that it was an insurance matter."

Chapter 38

Calum and Heather Randall made good time along the M8 Motorway up to Glasgow and then across to the capital. Between them, they tried to interpret what the discovery of the stolen Zodiac on Gigha might mean to the Farland situation. By the time they arrived at the turn off for the Edinburgh bypass, they agreed it could mean only one thing. The Zodiac had been taken by SERC on one of the occasions they were picking up the other one from Mackenzie's and it had been used in some way when the SPC3 had disappeared in the Sound of Jura. But how did they pursue their suspicions? Would McBride bite on them?

Heather dropped Calum at the new Edinburgh Waverley ground next to the new Royal Infirmary. The sale of their iconic stadium in the Murrayfield area of Edinburgh for housing had been meant to secure their financial future with the money raised being used to build a state-of-the-art stadium with a larger capacity. Instead their Russian owner had cut corners on the construction of the new stadium and, two years after opening, it still remained unfinished. That had allowed him to pocket the balance of the proceeds which disappeared with him when the going got hot. On top of that, the new stadium on the very outskirts of the city was not popular with the fans who were staying away in droves from all but the most important games. Edinburgh Waverley was meant to be in the heart of the city as it had always been.

Calum had arranged to meet Archie Young at C Entrance on the half-way line on the north side of the stadium. This was the completed side that looked across to the uncompleted side.

There he was. Archie Young. Probably the only person at the game including the WCI directors and the Edinburgh Waverley liquidators who was wearing a three-piece, pin-stripe suit, white shirt, and club tie.

'Archie you old rogue. I could have picked you out if there had been 100,000 in attendance. Don't you own a pair of blue jeans?'

'The best we can hope for today is 20,000 and as a matter of fact I do not own a pair of blue jeans, or any other colour for that matter.'

'Well you are looking well for an old auditor.'

'May I remind you that I am the same age as you? It is just that I don't have that California sun to keep me looking young.'

'You will always be "Forever Young",' Calum crooned.

'Hardy har. Let's go in and get seated. I do hope we are not among Glasgow hooligans.'

'Quite. I much prefer Edinburgh hooligans every time.'

There were thirty minutes to go before the kick-off so Archie filled in Calum on what he had been able to unearth.

Brookes & Co. had only taken on the SERC portfolio two years ago. They had been brought on by the managing partner of the London office and the new audit had been quite controversial among the senior partners nationwide. It had been characterized as a new direction for the grand old firm, one they must take if they were to survive in these days of the Big Four audit firms. That was not a compelling reason for several of the old guard. Archie who stuck pretty much to his northern circuit when it came to company politics had been ambivalent.

SERC's parent company of the same name was based in California but the London subsidiary enjoyed considerable autonomy. It was self–sufficient as far as financing was concerned and most of its income was obtained from overseeing sticky environmental operations similar to its present assignment at Farland. It did not do much of the philanthropic sponsorship of research that its parent was known for.

'So the London side does the dirty work and the Long Beach side gets the glory of funding environmental research?'

'Something like that. But most of the money made in Europe by the London side actually stays here. It is quite wealthy. Their goal has always been to minimize their tax obligation to the Exchequer and that is what attracted them to our managing partner in London. Giles Freeman fancies himself as a bit of a tax Svengali.'

'Since Enron, aren't auditors prohibited from being management consultants and vice versa?'

'In theory, dear boy.'

'Don't tell me good old Brookes is doing something shady after 105 years.'

'I wouldn't say that. The audit is legit. What Freeman is doing on the side for backhanders, I would not like to speculate on. Not when I am so close to collecting my pension.'

'When are you finally going to retire?'

'Would you believe at the end of next month? Truly the end of an era.'

'That will be 45 years. My God! Such loyalty.'

'Speaks to a bit of a lack of ambition I am afraid, dear boy.'

'Get away with you. Tell me more about SERC.'

'I looked into your suspicions. I can't say they are not correct but I could not find any evidence to give you at such short notice. A lot of money flows through their coffers but for the kind of work they do, they are handsomely paid. When an oil slick needs cleared up or a nuclear leak sealed off, the owners just open their cheque books and ask how much?'

'Did you find anything juicy on Cyrus Macadam?'

'He is the Chief Operations Officer of the parent company but he seems to be the absolute top dog in the London subsidiary. Slippery and ruthless were two descriptors I picked up. He had a bit of a personal run-in with the Exchequer here a few years back but bounced back after reaching some compromise on taxes owing.'

'Does he spend much time in America at all?'

'It does not look like it. He is essentially based here and only goes back to Long Beach for board meetings a couple of times a year.'

'What about Joel Wannamaker? Did you pick up anything on his association with SERC?'

'He is definitely a bit of a fish. Everybody in the City seems to agree there is a bit of a smell there.'

'Which city?'

'London, Glasgow, Edinburgh. Take your pick. Although I would not shout it aloud, today of all days, the conventional thinking is that WCI and he are well matched.'

'What about any connection to SERC?'

'He is a major interim lender. In fact, he is probably their biggest lender. But the details of their transactions are kept well under wraps. In theory, he is providing SERC's working capital on a project until their funding comes through. That doesn't sound too exciting but apparently he charges exorbitant interest rates and SERC is content to pay them. That makes me wonder why some of the less well established merchant banks and risk capitalists would not want a piece of the action. But SERC seem to go back to Wannamaker consistently.'

'Is it legal?'

'I doubt there is anything illegal about the financing transactions unless the money is being knowingly used for illegal purposes. That is where your suspicions come in. There have been mutterings about a couple of projects being suspect. There was one in Spain and another in Serbia of all places. In both cases it involved clean up of a government mess and was work that nobody else was interested in taking on. But they were and they were well paid for it. You know the old saying about "where there is muck there is money".'

'And did you pick up anything stinky on this Farland fiasco?'

'Not really. I am sorry dear boy.'

'Don't be. You have done a great job. If you did not owe me countless beers from the old days, I would offer to meet your fee.'

'I do not recall any beers owing. In any case, my delicate innards cannot handle beer these days so I confine myself to champagne and Glenmorangie malt. Depending on the result of today's game, you can buy me one or the other after it.'

They settled down to watch what they hoped would be an evenly matched game. It was not. It was men against boys. It was eleven highly priced foreign imports, each with numerous international caps for their respective country, against eleven Scots lads, few out of their teens and for whom a cap was a thing worn on the head when it rained. It was 3-0 at half-time and 6-0 at full-time. It was agony for the Edinburgh Waverley fans who were not outnumbered this time by the WCI hordes at the start of the game but were by the end of it. The two auditors of yore stayed almost to the bitter end. However the lure of a drink at the Steading Bar where Heather had arranged to pick Calum up was too much with five minutes to go and the very real prospect of a seventh goal still looming large.

A taxi ferried them to the Steading with haste, the driver barely hiding his disgust at so short a trip.

'You need not frown, dear driver. At least you did not have to watch the match.'

'Yeah. At least my team cuffed that useless Waverley bunch.'

Calum thought back to Neil Christian's article about what was wrong with Scottish football as they entered the bar which smacked of the lull before the storm. In five minutes it would be a seething mass of punters celebrating or seeking to drown their sorrows, both with same choice of poison.

'Did you ever read that article Neil Christian put out on the Internet?'

'Internet?'

'I forgot Ned Ludd. You don't recognize the Internet as anything more than a passing fad. Neil cited the example of there being more folks in Edinburgh supporting WCI and Glasgow Erin for religious reasons than Edinburgh Waverley and Leith Albion. I guess our cabbie was a prime example.'

'Yes, tribal warfare is alive and well in dear Scotia. I must admit that I take my hat off to Neil Christian. He was a rough uncompromising bugger when we watched him play but he has turned into Edinburgh Waverley's last hope before they go out of existence. If he really can rally the supporters and touch some of the wealthy mandarins in this fair city, perhaps he can raise the funds to stave off bankruptcy. As long as he does not talk to a Russian of any kind.'

Heather slipped into their booth and asked cheerfully, 'Well, did you win?'

'Do not ask.'

'Bad as that?'

'Worse.'

'Well then I better buy you boys a drink to commiserate.'

Archie would have been more than happy for Calum and his enchanting school friend to stay until closing time. However, mindful of the last ferry to the island at nine o'clock, they said their goodbyes, wished him well in retirement, encouraged him to keep in touch on Farland matters if he should unearth any more information and took their leave just before 6 pm.

The journey back was uneventful until Calum's phone announced an incoming text from Joel Wannamaker. He read it with undiminished disgust.

"Bad luck. I really thought the fifth goal might have been a tad offside!"

As they breathed a collective sigh of relief at catching the last ferry and settling down in the lounge for the ten minute voyage, Heather summed up their now extensive discussion on the discovery of the stolen Zodiac.

'It is just too much of a coincidence that the Zodiac should end up washed ashore in the general area where SPC3's last GPS reading was recorded.'

'Yes. Surely even McBride would concede that.'

'We ought to contact him tomorrow. You never know, he might already be following up on what we have been conjecturing on.'

'Somehow I doubt it. I don't get a sense of strong commitment to the case. If the craft were found, and especially if its cargo were leaking, the case would in all probability be taken away from him and assigned to a national police organisation. He probably feels it is not worth putting a lot of effort in to it.'

'If there were some skulduggery attachable to SERC through the Zodiac that might change things. If a crime had been committed on his patch, surely he would have responsibility to pursue it?'

'You would think so. I will come round to your office in the morning and we can try to contact him. I have his mobile number if he is not in his office.'

Chapter 39

On the following morning, Calum appeared at Heather's office bearing coffees and croissants from the Dancing Midge Café for them both, as well as Mary, the administrative assistant. His standing with the latter, already on the high side after his alleged dalliance with the Hollywood starlet, was climbing steadily.

Somewhat to their collective surprise, they managed to reach DI McBride in his office in Pitt Street, Glasgow. His voice revealed a mixture of politeness on first hearing Heather's voice and resignation when Calum intoned his good morning as well.

They went on to make reference to the report in the local paper that Gavin Mackenzie's stolen Zodiac had been found washed ashore on the Isle of Gigha in the Sound of Jura. They further suggested the possibility of its involvement somehow in the disappearance of SPC3 in the same approximate area. And finally, they conjectured a connection to SERC given that the company was in the habit of hiring the other Zodiac and collecting it with the hidden key when the premises were closed, thereby giving them ample opportunity to purloin the second Zodiac. The more the two of them laid out their theories, enriched with opportunity and perhaps motive, the more they felt they were on their way to solving the puzzle. Alas, the logic of the thinking and the obvious conclusions were lost on McBride.

'I don't know anything about a stolen Zodiac or a found Zodiac.'

'Don't you read your own theft reports?'

'Do you have any idea, Dr. Davies, how many theft reports cross my desk in a single week?'

'OK, forgive me. When I learned of the theft, I immediately saw the possibility of a connection to things that SERC might be getting up to with the other Zodiac that they were openly hiring. No proof of anything of course. But when the stolen one turned up in the rough proximity of the GPS signal, well that just strengthened my suspicions.'

'You have got to get into that mind of yours that you will see connections when you want to see connections. I have to be objective. I may not see what you think you see. Tell me once more all that you know about the Zodiacs.'

'You make them sound like a band. OK, here goes. Gavin Mackenzie in Wemyss Bay keeps two Zodiac inflatables for hire......'

After a very slow and deliberate description of all the facts known to them and a repeat suggestion as to what the conclusions might be, ergo SERC had used the stolen Zodiac in the disappearance of SPC3, Calum and Heather waited with baited breath while McBride appeared to be thinking about what he had heard. Either that or the silence was due to him having slipped out of his office at some stage. Eventually the silence was broken.

'Are you still there, DI McBride?'

'Yes, Dr. Randall, I am still here. I am carefully considering what I have heard. I am slightly more inclined to put more weight on your theories than those of your colleague. If you are saying the same, I will take them seriously.'

'Should I be offended by what you have just said, McBride?'

Heather kicked Calum on the shin and said, 'Nobody is offended. We are just trying to get to the solution.'

McBride went on to commit to follow up with the local police on the Mackenzie Zodiac story and to test their theories. He said he would have to be extremely circumspect about any discussion with

SERC folks, particularly Cyrus Macadam. He was already aware that Macadam believed Calum to be dangerously close to slandering the company with his suspicions. He did not want to get Police Scotland involved in anything that might lead to a slander case.

On the first day of June, a large crowd assembled in and around the Garrison House to celebrate the opening of the very first exhibit put on by the Cumbrae Museum utilizing not only the museum space but all the common area of the ground floor of the restored historical building that dominated the promenade in Millport. *"Education in Millport over the Years"* was an intriguing documentary and digital record of the primary school that had been on the island since the 19th century. It included detailed pupil registers from 1880 onwards along with graduation records, report cards, sports and recreation reports with photographs, and articles about notable alumni.

After speeches by local dignitaries, Calum was introduced as the organizer and asked to say a few words.

'Today is a great day because it is the realization of a dream. It was not my dream. I just got a heaven-sent opportunity to put the finishing touches to it. The dream goes back fifty years to when Scotty Green was just a young man. No, the rumours that he attended the opening of the primary school back in eighteen fruitcake are exaggerated. (Great cheers emanated from the audience.) But for fifty years he has had a dream of celebrating this little school that has so ably served this island and its children. There were stories to be told, there was no shortage of material but it was all carefully, and not so carefully, stored away where nobody could access it. However, Scotty knew where it was and he had a rough idea what it contained. Now thanks to some very welcome funding from various branches of government which are represented here today, Scotty has been able to put his dream into reality. I suppose my coming along with time on my hands has helped too. Many a morning we have spent in the storage room together with me unearthing some more records that would be pertinent to this exhibit but not knowing exactly how they would fit and Scotty looking over my shoulder and saying things like—*"oh aye that is the 1922 field trip to Rothesay and you will probably find Donald Templar in the photograph. He was in his last year before moving to the big school in Rothesay. His family remains on the island to this day"*. Those were the kind of trips through history that I enjoyed almost every single day and the historian with the amazing memory was Scotty Green. I think it very appropriate that we now hear a few words from the man himself.'

The audience erupted in applause and cheers.

'No. No. I have nothing prepared.'

'You have had fifty years to prepare something. That report card which said you were a bit slow in your work must have been correct.'

More applause and cheers rang through the building and among the crowd outside listening in on a loud speaker system. Both BBC and STV had been persuaded to make the voyage to the island to capture the occasion for the six o'clock news.

Eventually, Scotty made his way to the podium, after much shaking of the head and mutterings about never being able to rely on Yanks. Thereafter, Scotty proceeded to delight the audience for thirty minutes with his recollections on the little school on Bute Terrace and the part it had played in the lives of Millport people. And, he did it without a script or even a note. That would have to be edited for the six o'clock news but was received with loud acclaim by all who heard it.

Later during a special reception, Calum wandered among the dignitaries, locals, and visitors and could not help but feel he had found a new home even though he had been visiting here almost all his life. A good number of people shook his hand and patted him on the back. One remarked, 'You are not such a bad lad for a Yank. You did Scotty proud.'

The BBC asked him on camera what it meant, as an American, to be leading this venture.

'As a Scot who happens to live in America, it feels very good to be able to give something back. A few months back my wife said that now I had retired I should be looking for an opportunity to give something back in return for the good life I have enjoyed. I did not go looking for this opportunity. I think it went looking for me and I am so glad that I have met Scotty and all the other islanders and been able to help them finish their project. If it helps put this little jewel of a place into the crown of Scotland, so much the better.'

Eventually, Calum came face to face with Scotty as the crowd began to thin out a bit.

'You bugger. You knew I did not want to speak. It was your show. You must be the only modest Yank in existence.'

'I am a Scottish-Canadian living in the US. I am seldom accused of being modest. And it was not my show, it was yours. I just helped with the finishing touches.'

There were tears in both their eyes as they hugged one another to the delight of the hawk-eyed photographer from the local paper, who captured it for posterity, and the next edition.

Much, much later that day after many of the worthies had retired to Fraser's Bar for an extended celebration; Calum was about to make his way home by the familiar route up Cardiff Street when he was met by Henri Jardin walking the streets of the town to make sure that all the inhabitants made it to their homes safely.

'Dr. Davies. Quite a day for us all. You must feel good.'

'I felt good the day I stepped again on this island. Today has just been a special day.'

'I will walk with you as far as the police station. I need to check in. I also want to tell you about a conversation I had with DI McBride this evening. He said I could tell you that he has spoken with the Wemyss Bay officers, Gavin Mackenzie, and the SERC folks, after you and Dr. Randall called him. He is by no means satisfied with the responses he got from the four SERC guys. Three of them would not answer any of his questions willingly, while Cyrus Macadam was downright truculent, and basically told McBride to mind his own business unless he had something specific to charge them with. McBride wants you to know that Macadam quickly brought your name into the discussion and said he was fed up with your muckraking and slander and would be pursuing it by whatever means were open to him. When asked what that meant, he had replied that Davies would find out soon enough. McBride says to be careful. Macadam is a loose cannon and his sidekicks look to have more brawn about them than brains.'

'That does not sound so good. Was Heather Randall implicated too?'

'Not by the sound of it. You were the focus of his ire.'

'What is McBride going to do now?'

'You will not like this but he said enquiries would continue. That is the standard answer we have to give.'

'Well at least he now appears to be taking our suspicions seriously.'

'That he is.'

'We will just have to watch out for the SERC mob. I have often wondered if the three guys who jumped me outside Farland were Macadam's sidekicks.'

'Not a bad guess but very difficult to prove. Perhaps if we can pin something else on them, we can get them for your assault too. But on its own, I doubt it.'

'I hope I can count on your protection?'

'Aye, you can on the island. As far as I know none of them has been over here. If I do spot them, I will be watching their every move. If you go to the mainland, that is different matter and you will just have to watch out for your own back. The mainland bobbies will not protect you unless there is a direct threat issued. They will of course respond if there is an incident.'

'That is reassuring, I don't think.'

'Good night then, I assume you do not carry a gun in the American style?'

'You assume correctly. But don't forget Macadam is American too and I can't speak for him.'

'Take care of yourself.'

Chapter 40

The following Saturday brought another well-established community event. In fact, two of them would be going on at the same time. A great many of the locals, augmented by some interested individuals from the mainland, got involved in either the great beaches clean-up or the annual restoration of the old stone pier project. The former was an obvious response to the high and wild tides of the winter and involved gathering and shipping out seaweed and other debris. Most of the work was done by hand with a front-end loader used at the end to fill several skip loads which would be deposited in the land fill site on the west side of the island. The latter involved yearly repair and replacement of the old stone pier which sat at a point on Great Cumbrae where the distance to Wee Cumbrae is shortest. The replacement stone was obtained from the quarry located near the reservoirs. The quarry was no longer a working proposition, having provided much of the stone for building the town of Millport and surrounding farms with the exception of the buildings constructed in the distinctive red sandstone, but could be relied upon to provide enough material for the pier project.

Calum had volunteered for the pier project and armed with Scotty's ancient pickup truck was a member of the convoy that continuously made its way between the quarry and the pier. There were volunteers to load each vehicle in the fleet which ranged from tractors and trailers through pickups to big old cars with extra large boots. At the pier end, there were more volunteers to unload the vehicles and place the stones strategically on the pier. No cement was used. It was all a case of finding the right fit for each stone. The entire operation was supervised by Adrian Weatherhead, a retired Welsh master stonemason who lived in a small cottage behind Westview. Adrian described the project as a labour of love which would never be completed in his lifetime but by the time he passed on, there would be enough islanders who understood the methodology to carry the project on. At 79 years of age, Adrian showed no signs of an imminent passing as he hauled large stones about until he found the right spot to locate them. As if to complete the uniqueness of the picture, he also spent much of the day flying between the two sites on an ancient Douglas motorcycle to make sure the volunteers were doing what was required of them. Nobody understood why the "Duggie" was still running almost eighty years after it left the factory, but Adrian appeared to know.

The work was tiring, even for a nominal driver like Calum because he invariably left his cab at either end of the journey to help with loading and unloading. He marvelled at the banter that went on among the volunteers. Who would have thought that community labour could be so much fun? The beach clean-up squads seemed to be having fun too. As Calum came down West Bay Road with another load he met a squad from the research station just arriving at Cosy Corner to begin their work. A loud blast on the pickup horn, which Calum had not expected to work, was met by big cheers from group decked out in special tee-shirts identifying their workplace. He noted the group included everyone from the director, to her administrative assistant, to scientists he had never seen in anything but white lab coats. And all were having a great time.

At seven o'clock, having put in almost twelve hours of work save for a couple of short meal breaks, Adrian pronounced himself satisfied that they had done enough work to ensure that the old pier would last another year. Amid cheers of relief, most volunteers quickly made off before he changed his mind, some to their homes, most to one of the pubs.

Calum had enjoyed getting to know Adrian and marvelled at both his expert knowledge and his energy level for one so senior. He hung around chatting about the history of the pier which had its heyday when there was much more activity on Wee Cumbrae, such as farming, lighthouse operations, and permanent residents in the mansion house. A boat could sail from the old stone pier; to either the new lighthouse on the west side, or the quay beside the mansion house and ruined castle on the east side, and either journey would be the shortest possible, and roughly equal. Most supplies and provisions were transported through Millport to Wee Cumbrae rather than directly from the mainland, so the pier was well used.

Stephen McDonald, the owner of the nearby boat house and repair business joined the two of them. Technically, one had to pass through his land to reach the pier, so his cooperation was essential to the annual project.

'Well Adrian, another one in. Well done. The old pier is looking as good as it has done for a long time.'

'Hello Stephen. Yes, I had a good squad this year. We made a lot of progress. She should hold up fine over the winter till next year. Have you met Calum Davies?'

'No I have not. But I have heard a lot about you. Scotty Green was waxing lyrically about you and the museum exhibit in the Garrison. I am sorry I missed the opening. I had to be on the mainland picking up spare parts.'

'I am pleased to meet you. I have heard lot of good things about you doing your bit to boost the economy of the island.'

'I have a lot of different wee businesses in addition to the boatyard and I suppose they all add up to help the economy. The only problem is they keep me bloody busy and off the island way too much for my liking. I am supposed to be cutting back on work but it never seems to go that way.'

'I came here expecting not to do very much but I have ended up busier than I was when I was working full time in a university. You better watch if you do cut back on your business ventures, the days will just fill up with other projects.'

'Especially with folks like Adrian around. He only works for one day of the year but it probably feels like a week's worth of work at least.'

'Oh I don't know. I think I just lead them through a gentle day's labour.'

'That's not what my back is telling me. Stephen, we were just talking about the history of the pier and how important it was to Millport and especially to Wee Cumbrae. If we can continue to refurbish it, maybe even put in more than one day a year, do you think the pier could become useful again even if the needs on Wee Cumbrae may never return?'

'Do you mean on a commercial or recreational basis?'

'Either or both. Do you see any tie-in to the boat yard?'

'Possibly, if it could be extended to provide a safe haven.'

'Jesus Thomas! That would be a big project.'

'Now, now Adrian, you would not have to do it all on your own. Calum has got me thinking.'

'Aye well, I am not getting any younger.'

'You have plenty of life left in you. No, if we could build a section at right angles to the existing pier it would provide commercial opportunities and recreational ones as well, although I would not want to discourage visiting boats from anchoring in the main bay, seeing that I own the moorage rights there. We are starting to see a few more boat tours and fishing parties again. They almost died out in the

1980s. They could operate out of an extended harbour over here.'

'Perhaps I should bring the topic up at the Cumbraes Council. I am supposed to be helping them with their development plan. This would come under the "thinking outside of the box" category.'

'I think I had better come along to the meeting in case I get appointed to oversee a giant project.'

'They would not do that to you, I can assure you. But they would welcome your input. Yours too, Stephen.'

'I am not one for committees of talkers. I am a doer.'

'I hear you. We need both.'

'Well, I'd better be getting along. You have certainly got me thinking about the pier's potential. It is a funny thing, but back in March when we had that real wet day, a Thursday I think it was, I saw one of Gavin Mackenzie's Zodiacs from up at Wemyss Bay tied up at the pier for a bit. Buggered if I know what it was doing there on a night like that. I would not have seen any potential for the pier that night. But on a nice calm day like today you never know.'

'Are you sure it was Mackenzie's?'

'I am. Do you know him?'

'I have met him. He lost one his Zodiacs but it just got washed up on Gigha so I guess this must have been his other one. Did you see who was in it?'

'Looked like a couple guys. Probably tourists in panic mode. However, the next time I went out of the boatyard it was gone. I think a car had been through to visit with them because I saw it leaving but I don't know what was going on.'

Calum walked the short way to Barclay House intending to have a night in for once. However, his mind was racing with the new information so instead he kept walking and thinking, the two always went together. By the time he realised it, he had almost walked to the East Bay so he stopped off at the Tavern for a nightcap or two.

By the time he finally made it home he had abandoned plans to email Nerys with tales of the Garrison House shindig and the new Zodiac information. He would do it in the morning.

He never got the chance. His mobile rang at 5am.

'Nerys, is there something wrong?'

'Sorry I could not wait any longer to call you. Something terrible has happened.'

'Slow down and tell me.'

'This week, I have just been wrapping up my project business plan for the next phase in Russia and Brazil. When I emailed SERC a courtesy draft copy all I got back was a curt notice that funding on the project had been terminated forthwith.'

'How can they do that? Did they give you a reason?'

'All it said was the conditions of the grant had not been met. What do they mean by that? I have done exactly what I said I would do up to this stage and the next phase is exactly as was originally proposed.'

'Oh shit. I think I know exactly what has happened?'

'What for chrissakes?'

'I hadn't got round to telling you this but the police have been questioning Cyrus Macadam and his cronies in connection with the missing Farland craft. Apparently, he was royally pissed off and seemed to think that the police were hounding them at my behest. Macadam said he would get back at me. The police warned me to look out for myself. I never thought they would get back at me by getting at you.'

'Damn it all, Calum. What have you done?'

"I haven't really done anything. I have just been joining up the dots a little quicker than the police and passing my observations on to them. It was up to them whether they chose to pursue things. They did obviously and Macadam is getting nervous. But look, he does not run SERC in Long Beach. There must be others in SERC you can appeal to.'

'How?'

'I would start with Anna Salisbury and the president. They have been supportive of you. I am sure they would not stand for your funding being stopped because of what is happening over here. The two are totally unconnected. SERC Long Beach is owned by the California University.'

'What do you think I should do next?'

'I would call Anna in the morning. Don't do it tonight; you are too steamed up. See if you can get a meeting organized with the president. If it helps I can come in on the speaker phone to explain what has been happening at this end. I am sure Macadam must have fed the grants committee and/or the board misinformation. But he is only one person. They need to know the full story and both sides of it.'

'I think I will call tonight.'

'I would leave it until the morning when you are calmer.'

'It's not your project going down the chute.'

'I know but we have to be professional and subtle about this. We are dealing with a powerful and I suspect evil man.'

'OK maybe I will wait.'

'Good. I have lots of other things to tell you but they can keep until tomorrow. Call me tomorrow, preferably at a more decent hour. And Love, don't lose heart. We will find a solution to all these problems. Your project will succeed.'

Chapter 41

Calum was preparing for a special trip with Jimmie Morrison to Wee Cumbrae. The Cumbraes Environmental Research Station maintained several weather recording devices around the area and each had to be reset from time to time. That was one of Jimmie's jobs to do the resets, log the readings, and record when the next resets were due. It was an intricate task on each device but generally did not take more than fifteen minutes. All the time was spent in getting to each device from the station. Wee Cumbrae was actually the closest but would still take over half an hour each way. However, the morning schedule would be able to accommodate an hour's fishing as well.

Calum was well aware that he and Nerys had planned to explore the island together but he felt the opportunity to join Jimmie was just too good to pass up. In addition, perhaps this was the day when he was going to break his duck and catch a fish.

As Jimmie was gathering his fishing tackle from his office, Calum was chatting to Heather Randall about Nerys's funding woes with SERC. What was a clear case of retaliation by Cyrus Macadam had been reviewed by the SERC board in Long Beach at the California University President Ramirez' explicit request. It had transpired the board had originally been persuaded by Macadam that Calum's interference in SERC's activities in Scotland had been enough to constitute failure on the part of Nerys to live up to the conditions of her funding. Both President Ramirez and Dean Salisbury, who had also been in attendance, upon hearing the rationale for the decision had attacked it with vigour. As soon as the point was made that the decision would never stand up in a court of law, there had been visible shifting on the part of board members and, without the presence of Macadam to offer any objection, the original decision had been overturned and the funding reinstated. Nerys had been relieved and grateful to her two feisty supporters who had been more than a match for a board of male suits. However, that was not to say that Macadam would simply go away.

On the voyage to Wee Cumbrae, the sky transformed from a relatively clear blue to heavily clouded in a matter of minutes in a manner typical of the area. Soon that light misty rain that generally followed was coming down in sheets. They tied the station launch up at the quay in front of the mansion house and crossed to the small islet of Allinturrail that was accessible by a narrow causeway only at low tide. That islet contained the ruins of the castle dating from the 16th century although there may have been an earlier building from the 14th century constructed by the daughter of King Robert the Bruce and her husband on the same site. Also located on the islet was a cylindrical box somewhat like a traditional British post-box that contained the weather recording equipment.

The equipment was by no stretch of the imagination state-of-the-art, hence the need to manually reset it on site. More up-to-date versions could be controlled remotely with a laptop. The equipment was also very sensitive and needed to be handled carefully. Jimmie went through a ritual of blowing on his hands to warm them up before gingerly placing them into the box.

'Finicky little buggers these instruments. One false move and you knock it completely out of balance. I did that once to the box on Arran and the contents had to be removed and sent to Portsmouth of all places for rebalancing.'

On this occasion the specially warmed hands did the trick and the resetting was completed and would be good for another year.

'Now how about a bit of fishing?'

'In this rain? That is not very appealing. If you don't mind I would like to spend a little time on the island instead. At least it is not as cold on land as it is on the water.'

'Good fishing weather. But suit yourself.'

'OK. How long do you plan to fish?'

'Just an hour. I will only go out about a hundred yards and anchor. I will come back in at eleven o'clock so be back on the quay by then.'

'Sounds like a plan.'

As the launch took off, Calum turned to wander up to the mansion house and outbuildings. The main building was a fine example of Victorian architecture consisting of twelve bedrooms, five reception rooms, and three bathrooms. Alas, it was all too obvious even from the outside that the house was not in the best state of repair. One could only wonder about the interior condition. The house had changed hands several times and the present owners were of the absent variety which did not bode well for refurbishment any time soon.

Calum did not want to peer in the windows or try the doors so he bypassed the house and started to walk up a steep path to a ridge that ran behind the buildings and would offer a magnificent view eastwards to the mainland, Farland Power Station notwithstanding. It was half way up the path that Calum started to notice one, then two, then three dead seabirds strewn around his feet. By the time he reached the ridge, he had already lost count. On the ridge itself, there was absolute carnage with bodies of birds everywhere together with carcasses of several small animals.

Calum's sense of distaste turned to one of alarm. Something had wiped out the wildlife population. It had to be something that was unnatural. And, if it could kill the wildlife, what might it do to a human?

He suddenly decided he did not want to be on Wee Cumbrae anymore and turned to look out to sea. There was Jimmie anchored as he said he would be. Calum made his way back down the path a whole lot quicker than it had taken him to climb it. When he arrived at the quay he realized that it was still a good forty-five minutes until their arranged meeting time. He decided he did not want to remain on the island a minute more than necessary and started to try to attract Jimmie's attention to abandon his fishing and come in to collect him. However, five minutes of shouting and waiving of arms brought no response from the launch. How could Jimmie not see him if not hear him? He must be fishing off the boat to the east side.

Panic was now setting in. Calum was trying not to breathe in the air which might contain who knows what. That made shouting impossible. There was nothing left for it but to swim out the launch. It was within his range but only just and he was already wet in any case. He took off his shoes and cast them aside. They could be picked up later. He got into the water which felt icy. So much for the theory that the sea felt warmer when it was raining. One hundred yards it might be but his initially powerful strokes seemed to make no headway and he suddenly panicked further at the thought that perhaps the launch was moving away from him.

He stopped swimming, treaded water anxiously, and tried shouting again. There was no response. He had no choice but to carry on. He knew his strokes were getting weaker now. He looked around and saw he had probably covered about fifty yards from the quay and the distance to the launch now definitely appeared less than it had originally but his pace was slowing by the minute. He stopped and tried shouting again. There was no response.

He was getting colder now and his strokes were getting more and more laboured. The launch was clearly in sight and he could even see the back of Jimmie's head. He was huddled over, probably baiting his line and all the while concentrating his focus eastward and away from Wee Cumbrae.

The last twenty yards was almost Calum's last swim of all time. His arms and legs now felt like lead. He was barely making progress. Incessant shouting was also weakening him but he did not want to stop. Just as he finally made it to within two strokes of the launch, one more shout attracted Jimmie's attention and he swung around with a bewildered look on his face.

'What the hell?'

'Get me in you useless fucker. I am dying here.'

Jimmie stooped to grab Calum's collar and pull him upside the launch. Getting him in was another matter because Calum was now bereft of any strength to assist. Eventually, Jimmie managed to pull him onboard, laid him out flat on the deck, and covered him with an emergency blanket before firing up the launch to return to Great Cumbrae. He had thought about taking the launch into Wee Cumbrae again but Calum had shouted, 'No. No. Fucking home.' And, he had then passed out for a while.

As they had all but reached the Old Pier at Millport, it being closer than the research station, Calum came around and growled at Jimmie.

'How the fuck did you not hear me or see me trying to attract your attention? There is something seriously wrong on that island.'

'Well now. It seems like you have lost that funny Yank accent all of a sudden. You are swearing like a native Scotsman. What do you mean there is something wrong there?'

'All the birds and animals are dead. They are stretched out like there has been a war. Like a goddam nuclear war. What am I saying?'

Jimmie helped Calum out of the launch and up on to the pier. He was now able to walk with effort but was still cold and wet so they went to the nearest business which was the Royal George Hotel. The owner willingly made a room available and after a long hot shower Calum retired to the bed for a very welcome sleep.

The doctor had been called and arrived from the Garrison House just as Calum was dropping off. He examined him and pronounced no lasting damage. No evidence of hypothermia was noted and a good sleep was the recommended recovery plan.

When Calum came to, a few hours later, Heather Randall and Jimmie were in the hotel waiting for him. His clothes had been washed and dried and awaited him. The owner kindly proffered a pair of replacement shoes. Dressed and feeling only a little weary, he met the others in the lounge. Heather suggested that a medicinal brandy might be in order and could be met from the station budget because the incident had occurred while on duty. Jimmie opted for a pint but Calum gratefully sipped a brandy and began to tell his story.

He described how all he had seen was carnage with no sign of any living wildlife.

'That is odd. Usually when somebody sets foot on the island, the seabird population goes crazy. There are hundreds if not thousands of them resident there. Surely they can't all be dead?'

'And it was not just seabirds. I saw other kinds of birds like ravens and I saw dead rabbits and little mouse type things too.'

'That is very unusual. Once in a while a virus might hit the birds but that would not affect other wildlife. If this is a natural phenomenon, it is very unusual.'

'And if it is not a natural phenomenon?'

'What are you thinking?'

'There is a nuclear power station in the middle of dismantlement not a couple of miles away.'

'How could that be?'

'We need to find out.'

'Yes, we need some carcasses for analysis. We might be able to do a preliminary post mortem at the research station but more than likely it will have to be done at Glasgow University.'

'You will have to be very careful even going back to Wee Cumbrae when you don't know what caused the slaughter.'

'We have the necessary suits and masks. I will send a scientist with Jimmie. No volunteers this time.'

'Thank you for that.'

'In the meantime, I will have to inform the necessary authorities including the police. But I suggest that we keep the news from the media until we know what we are dealing with.'

'Yes. That makes sense. Can I suggest something else?'

'What?'

'Don't inform SERC either.'

'You think they are tied up in this?'

'I have no idea but I don't view them as collaborators or colleagues in the least. There is nothing to be gained from telling them and nothing to be lost either.'

'OK. I can live with that. Again, until we know what we are dealing with there is no obvious connection to Farland and, therefore, no obligation to include SERC.'

'Good. Now I think I need to get out into the fresh air on terra firma.'

'Are you feeling well enough?'

'Yes, I think so. I will need to settle up with the hotel for the use of their room.

'I already tried, and they say it is on the house. They don't want to lose a visitor. It is bad for tourism.'

'About twenty yards from that boat of yours, I really thought my adventures were over.'

'Oh I suspect you have a few more left in you. Maybe long distance swimming is not the sport for you however.'

Calum made his own way home to Barclay House while Heather returned to the research station and started to make telephone calls. Each authority she spoke to concurred with her suggested approach and desired to be kept informed. The media would be left out of it at this stage. The head scientist at Glasgow University agreed that preliminary testing could take place at the station and only if no prognosis could be determined should the remains be sent up to Glasgow. If necessary, he would send a scientist down to the island to assist the local staff.

Thereafter, she arranged with one of her own scientists to go with Jimmie, suitably attired and equipped, back to Wee Cumbrae to pick up some carcasses.

Sometimes, it felt like life on Millport was pretty routine and nothing of any real scientific note ever took place. This was a welcome departure from the norm which would help maintain the interest of her staff.

Chapter 42

Nerys had been horrified to hear from Calum about his dice with death and the slaughter of the wildlife on Wee Cumbrae. While there might be some viral reason for the carnage, her thoughts immediately turned to some of the stories she had picked up from China and India about leaks and mishandled disposal of radioactive waste that had entered the food chain and cause direct human deaths. Surely the work being done at Farland had not contributed to the Wee Cumbrae situation; there was no physical connection between the two places. Yet it seemed too much of a coincidence, given the relative proximity. She and Calum had agreed that Dr. Michael Musselwhite in London should be informed. He was not on the original list of agencies that Heather Randall had drawn up and contacted, but Calum made sure that she added him. There was still nothing to connect the situation to any criminal activity so it would be up to Mick as to whether he informed his intelligence colleagues at this stage.

The initial post mortem was carried out at the Cumbraes Environmental Research Station in Millport. It revealed that the carcasses all showed signs of burns and stomach contents suggested some form of poisoning although the exact nature could not be pinpointed. The following day the scientists were joined by a leading scientist who had been sent down by Glasgow University.

More extensive tests were carried out during an intensive twelve hour session in the laboratory. At the end of it, Heather was summoned to hear shocking news from the expert.

'Your staff did a good preliminary job which led me to try some very unusual testing. The results are startling. I would say I am 80 per cent certain of my conclusion but I would like to take all the evidence back to the university on the first ferry tomorrow to replicate my testing in a more controlled environment. At this stage, I have to tell you that I think the birds and animals have died due to intensive plutonium intoxication.'

'Plutonium? It must be something to do with Farland.'

'That would be my guess. The level of toxicity that must be evident could not have occurred through any natural phenomenon. However, I just cannot imagine airborne transmission from the mainland either without other similar results having been noted at and around the power station. This likely level would directly affect humans and there are a number of workers still based at the power station.'

'I should make a preliminary report to all the appropriate agencies, don't you think?'

'I would recommend that yes. However, it is going to be difficult to keep this information under wraps. The media and the environmental groups will have a field day with it.'

'I will need to take advice on the information flow. The two governments will want to control it as much as they can.'

Once left on her own, Heather sat stunned for a few minutes trying to take in the ramifications of what she had just heard. If the wildlife on Wee Cumbrae had perished due to plutonium poisoning, the toxicity level might be relatively high and of immediate risk to humans on the island and on the neighbouring islands. That could pose an emergency the like of which those islanders had never ever faced. And beyond that lay larger populations on the mainland including Glasgow to the north. The safety of as many as one and a half million people might be dependent on the prevailing winds.

Stop it, stop it she told herself. You have got to get this doomsday scenario out of your head. You have got to remain calm. You have got to do what you were trained to do to. You have got to lead the containment of what might be a major environmental disaster.

After calling all the agencies that had an interest, and the list was getting longer, she called Calum to give him the news.

'Oh no. It is our worst fear come true. But I had a hunch ever since I saw those birds that it was connected to Farland.'

'We don't know yet that there is a positive connection to Farland. But we do know the birds died from plutonium poisoning and the chances of such contamination coming from something other than the power station seem highly remote.'

'Exactly.'

'I think we will hear for sure from the University of Glasgow scientists tomorrow confirming the plutonium.'

'OK. What are the agencies going to do?'

'Some bigwig in London is proposing the immediate formation of a special task force that incorporates the interests of all the affected agencies and avoids different agencies doing different things and not sharing the information with each other.'

'You mean the American way?'

'The Brits are normally quite good at that too, so the proposal makes sense.'

'Will you be on the task force?'

'Yes.'

'Good.'

'I imagine the next step after confirmation from Glasgow will be a visit to Wee Cumbrae to take readings. Those readings will at least allow us to scope the magnitude of the risk to other islands and the mainland and to take appropriate actions. I don't see at this stage how it will reveal how the contamination occurred in the first place but that maybe comes later.'

'How about the media?'

'They are to be kept out of the loop at least until after the confirmation from Glasgow. After that I imagine the task force will develop a communication plan. The information cannot be kept from the public for long.'

'How about SERC?'

'I have not told them anything so far. The task force will have to take up that issue.'

'Is SERC on the task force?'

'As the matter is now one of national security, I gather they are not to be included even though they are based in London.'

'I am glad of that. Mark my words; I am convinced that they will come into the story in some way at some stage.'

'All will be revealed. As for you, you should go to the doctor for a further check-up now that we know what we might be dealing with.'

'Will he have the ability to check me out?'

'The local doctors can certainly do a preliminary check. If the prognosis were positive, you would have to go the mainland, likely to Glasgow. Let's hope it is negative. You did not hang around on the island and you did not touch anything so that is a good thing.'

Chapter 43

Late the following day, Heather Randall had been joined by Dr. Michael Musselwhite from the University of London and Marcus Brown from a special department within the UK government dealing with environmental security who had been selected to co-chair the task force. A helicopter was at their constant disposal so it had been decided that they would base themselves in Millport and would stay at the Westview, which incidentally was among the closest buildings to Wee Cumbrae. Their presence would be quickly noticed by the locals and a first priority would be to engage the media.

Just as they were completing an interim communication plan, the call came through from the University of Glasgow. Death by plutonium poisoning was confirmed. The level of toxicity among the sample of birds and animals that had been gathered from essentially the same place on the island was quite strong.

Brown was the first to respond.

'OK. The plan goes operational. Tomorrow morning we meet with the media. In the afternoon we test Wee Cumbrae.'

Heather was surprised by the confidence of the statement. 'Can you be organized as quickly as that?'

'We are well prepared. In many ways, we have been expecting something like this to happen since the decommissioning of nuclear power stations commenced so we have done a fair bit of advanced planning.'

'You tie it to Farland?'

'Have you another suggestion? I am not sure the Syrians are even aware of Wee Cumbrae?'

Musselwhite added his comments that showed much had been planned in advance. 'It must be tied to Farland but how we don't know at this stage. That is why the testing must happen fast. That will surely cast some light on how it has happened.'

Brown added, 'If the contamination proves to be airborne from the power station we at least know the how but then have an immediate task of shutting it down and assessing the damage on the mainland.'

Heather dropped Brown and Musselwhite off at the hotel and just as they were entering the lobby Calum and Scotty Green were exiting the bar. Heather made introductions.

'These are two people you will want to know. They are probably the most influential among the locals and will be able to offer you any help required.'

Musselwhite gripped Calum's hand. 'We meet at last. I know your wife well and she 'as kept me apprised of the several different angles concerning this case. We will want to involve you and get your foughts.'

'Anything you want.'

'Good. And you Scotty will be crucial in keeping the islanders of Great Cumbrae informed and reassured as to their safety. Can I ask that the Cumbraes Council take on that role under your chairmanship?'

'Of course. You seem well informed as to local matters.'

'In the last twenty-four hours we 'ave made it our business to get informed. Prior to that, the Cumbraes were a sleepy little holiday island destination and a sleepier little private island for an uninterested Glasgow businessman. All that might 'ave changed.'

'We will do whatever we have to do.'

'Ow easy would it be for the Council to call an open meeting?'

'Quite easy. Word can get around the island fast. Just let me know when you need to have a meeting.'

'Stand by for tomorrow. Now let's get some sleep. Tomorrow is going to be a busy day.'

Early the next morning, the two co-chairs left Millport by helicopter for Glasgow to oversee a press conference at Glasgow University. Every branch of the media had turned out amid rumours of a big-breaking story on the Clyde somewhere. The presentation of the facts was handled with consummate ease by the two professionals with Musselwhite being able to comment on the scientific content and Brown on the procedures that had been set up in the last twenty-four hours. Questions in abundance followed.

'Do you suspect terrorists?'

'At this stage we have no indication of terrorism.'

'Are humans at risk?'

'In a toxic environment such as this, humans will always be at risk. We do not know if the contamination is confined to Wee Cumbrae at this stage but we believe that there are no people living on the island so that may well minimize the risk. So far casualties are confined to wildlife.'

'Is the contamination from Farland?'

'We would 'ave to assume so given its proximity. But 'ow the contamination crossed the water when the island plays no part in the decommissioning project we 'ave yet to ascertain. This afternoon's visit to the island by a team of experts will give us some of the answers you, and we, are looking for.'

'Does this have anything to do with the missing craft?'

'Sorry I have to say again that at this stage we don't know. Nothing will be ruled out until it is deemed safe to do so.'

'Is the power station and the surrounding area contaminated?'

'I can comment on that one. In the last twenty-four hours, tests have been done on the power station facilities and personnel and sample areas within a five mile radius on the mainland. No trace of contamination has been discovered.'

'Who discovered what had happened on Wee Cumbrae?'

'That was a representative of the Cumbraes Environmental Research Station who was visiting the island to do routine maintenance on a weather information gathering station.'

'Is that person sick as a result?'

'No, 'e 'as undergone medical examination and will undergo more today. Thus far 'e 'as a clean bill of 'ealth.'

'You folks are obviously English. What is the Scottish government doing about this?'

'As I mentioned at the beginning, a task force that includes all interested parties, being BritPower, representatives of both governments, and scientific experts is leading the response. The Scottish government is fully involved and fully committed to help resolve this matter.'

What about those Yanks, is it SERC they call themselves?'

'The work now being undertaken is beyond the scope of the contract with SERC. However, we expect that their representatives will be called upon to assist the task force where necessary.'

'If that is all the questions for now we will call this press conference to an end. My colleague and I need to get back to Millport to oversee the afternoon's activities. I will end by asking that members of the media do not travel anywhere near Farland Power Station or Wee Cumbrae or Great Cumbrae for that matter. We need to give the experts room to do their work. The two of us will take responsibility for keeping the media informed at all times, either through electronic releases or further face-to-face conferences here at the university. Thank you for coming.'

The Millport research station was a hub of activity. A temporary command centre had been set up utilising every spare space. Classes had been cancelled and the small number of students that had been present had been sent back to the mainland and home to their schools. Most of the station staff had been told to stay home unless called in for particular duties. The station was now manned by a large team of strangers who had travelled from all corners of the UK. An impressive communication centre had already been established that would allow the team going to Wee Cumbrae to be in full contact. In addition, all the branches of the armed forces that had now been put on full alert, as well as the coastguard, were in direct communication with the station.

Heather had cleared Calum and Jimmie Morrison as essential personnel and the three had watched the press conference on STV.

'Very competent. They said all they had to say and answered all the questions put to them.' Heather noted the professionalism of the co-chairs.

'Yes. I think that will keep the media at bay for now. They will be desperate for more news from the team visiting the island. I just hope some clear information comes out of that.'

'Will I be taking the team over?'

'No Jimmie. The team is assembling two Zodiacs for all the experts as we speak. If you look out the window there, you can see them scurrying around on the Keppel Pier. You will be held in reserve in case the station needs to do anything for the team.'

'When will the team set out?'

'I understand they will leave just as soon as Musselwhite and Brown get back to give them a last briefing. Their helicopter is on the way.'

'Heather, I suggest Jimmie and I go out in our Zodiac after they leave. We will keep well away from the action but will be available by radio should a call come in here that we are needed. That way we can respond quicker.'

'Alright, that makes sense. But keep your distance. You have already been too close to the action without knowing about it.'

'Understood.'

'What did the doctor say when he looked you over this morning?'

"All three doctors were there. Probably don't get a case like this in Millport very often. There was no trace of any poisoning. They want to monitor me on a daily basis for the next week. Sounds like I won't have to go to Glasgow.'

'That's good.'

At that moment the peace and tranquillity of Millport was shattered by the return of the helicopter. Musselwhite and Brown emerged to be met by Heather and proceeded to the nearby Keppel Pier. Musselwhite announced he would be leading the expedition. 'This is science. Science is wot I do.'

While Musselwhite gathered his protective clothing, Brown addressed the other team members and established objectives for gathering readings, protocols for assembling the information and communicating it back to the command centre. All members were warned to wear their full suits and helmets at all times even if some of the readings suggested little or no risk. 'Assume full contamination of the island until you can confirm or refute it. We will not change that assumption, if we do, until you are back off the island so be on full alert for the entire time you are there. Good luck.'

The two Zodiacs took off on what might have appeared to be a highly unlikely expedition on the River Clyde. But the expedition was being treated with total seriousness.

After Calum and Jimmie had chatted to Brown about their intentions, they left about fifteen minutes after the main party. They could see the two Zodiacs ahead about half way toward the east side of Wee Cumbrae. Instead of simply following, Calum suggested they skirt by the power station first. As they neared the wharf at Farland they could clearly see SPC1 tied up. It had obviously been in the midst of loading when the emergency unfolded. It now looked like loading had been suspended. Calum radioed back to the station to find out what the status was of operations at the power station. He was told all operations had been suspended and all personnel had been stood down today and told to stay home today and probably tomorrow as well. All had received clear medical reports.

As the station Zodiac crossed to Wee Cumbrae it could be seen that the two Zodiacs had arrived at the quay in front of the mansion house and the task force occupants were dividing into two-person teams to spread out over the island. The helicopter had arrived from Millport and was ferrying a team at a time to the more inaccessible areas of the island and a couple of all-terrain vehicles belonging to the island's owners had been found in one of outbuildings and were being put into use.

Calum and Jimmie decided to circumnavigate the island while observing the teams fanning out across the difficult terrain. They headed around the north of the island and came upon the so-called new, but now abandoned, lighthouse. They could see that the helicopter had put down a team there. As they reached the southern part of the island, Calum noticed a series of caves some of which were heavily concealed by rocks and vegetation. It was only because they were able to travel close to the cliff edge in the fast moving inflatable boat that the caves were even visible at all.

'I have never seen those caves before or heard them mentioned, Jimmie.'

'Most are totally inaccessible, even in a boat like this, but there are a couple of big ones that you can get into. One around the south-east side has a name—Ewart's Cave—and is totally hidden from land and sea. But if you know what you are doing you can squeeze in behind a big rock and suddenly it opens out into a fairly big cavern. You can land once you are inside the cave. Mind you, you can only do it high tide and you can't stay long if you want to get out again on that tide.'

As they reached the east side, Jimmie pointed toward the cliffs and said, 'Ewart's Cave is somewhere in there but you would never know it even though we are less than fifty yards away.' The old castle on Allinturrail came into view and eventually they could see the mansion house. By the look of it, teams were making their way back to the mustering point at the quay.

Calum again radioed back to the command centre and Heather came on. The Wee Cumbrae teams had mostly gathered their data and were returning to the Zodiacs. Results, which could be ascertained immediately with the high-tech equipment in use, were interesting. The contamination levels were varied and ranged from fairly toxic to almost negligible readings. The initial prognosis was that the differentiated readings were consistent with a minor leakage which had got into the island water supply, a stream from a natural reservoir on the high ground that ran down to the mansion house area, and the wildlife had done the rest by spreading the contamination. But how there could be a leakage was not immediately obvious.

Calum and Jimmie arrived back at Keppel Pier just before the expedition team. Brown asked Calum to arrange with Scotty Green for an open meeting of the Cumbraes Council that evening. It was important that the islanders got direct information no later than it was presented to the media in Glasgow.

The expedition teams and the station personnel met in a meeting room to debrief on what had been discovered. After much discussion of the differentiated readings and their locations, the scientists reached consensus that confirmed the earlier prognosis. The amount of contamination and the high variability of toxicity levels throughout the island were consistent with a relatively minor leak around the proximity of the mansion house. Thereafter, the contamination had found its way into the water system probably thanks to birds or animals and the rest of the wildlife had been affected by either being in the hot area or having drunk from the stream. The reservoir itself was essentially clear with only a level minimally above natural levels being noted. Contamination must have occurred also at several locations downstream to account for the higher reading where the stream flowed out near the mansion house.

The most important thing now was to locate the source of the leaking and eliminate it. Preliminary views were that if that could be done, contamination could probably be confined to the island and may not be particularly long-lasting through natural mitigation.

Next steps were discussed and the contents of the media communiqué were carefully drafted. Then Brown and Musselwhite set off again in the helicopter to Glasgow for a late press conference. Heather was nominated to address the Cumbraes Council because she had sufficient scientific knowledge to interpret the findings for laypersons and she was local, so her credibility was stronger than outsiders.

The hastily convened meeting of the Cumbraes Council that normally would have taken place in the Garrison House boardroom was first moved to the largest room in the complex and then to the recently erected marquee on the complex grounds as the number of islanders in attendance swelled rapidly. News did indeed get around fast.

Eventually almost an hour later than advertised, the meeting was called to order by Chairman Green. He immediately introduced Heather and Calum and handed over to them. Heather did a good job of relating the story from the very beginning with Calum and Jimmie's visit to do minor maintenance to the latest findings of the task force and how they could be interpreted. The overflowing audience listened patiently and then launched into questions once Scotty called for them. Most people seemed to express satisfaction with the information and felt reassured that there was no immediate risk to the occupants of Great Cumbrae. There were a few questions that fell into either the cynical, or hysterical, categories but Heather handled them with aplomb and patiently diffused the alternative views that were being espoused.

Calum had intended to play visible support for Heather and back-up on information should it be required. As it happened, he was not required to say a word due to her comprehensive knowledge and easy delivery style. He was thinking that the meeting had gone particularly well and was now on the point of winding down when a voice came from the rear of the tent. It might have been Charlie Caldwell or someone else of his vintage.

'What does that SERC have to say about the contamination? Are they not in charge of this thing?'

It had to happen. Calum and Heather looked at each other. After a brief hesitation, he nodded to her. She turned to the audience.

'I am going to let my colleague answer that one.'

'That is a good question. As Dr. Randall has told you, the experts are not sure yet how Wee Cumbrae came to be contaminated. Thus far, it seems like the island is the only location among the islands and on the mainland. Obviously Wee Cumbrae played no part in the shipping of the radioactive waste from the power station to Beagg. Therefore how there could be a leakage on Wee Cumbrae is for the moment a mystery. SERC will provide information on the various voyages again as they have previously done. There was no connection with Wee Cumbrae reported before but we will check again.'

As Calum squirmed somewhat with his answer, two further questions came from different voices near the back.

'Will the trips to Beagg be ended?'

'Is this anything to do with the missing boat?'

Calum continued. 'Both matters will have to be taken up by the task force. Again, I can say there is no reported connection between SPC3 and Wee Cumbrae. All indications are that it went missing in the Sound of Jura a long way from Wee Cumbrae. The whole decommissioning project is controlled at the highest levels of government and whether it continues is up to them, no doubt based on advice from the task force. At this stage I can say that nothing has been said to suggest that the project would be abandoned. Isn't that correct Dr. Randall?'

'That is correct.'

Scotty banged his gavel and asked if there were any further questions. If not, he would end the meeting. He assured everyone that the task force and the Cumbraes Council were committed to keeping islanders fully informed. Thus far, the news was not as bad as it might have been.

As people exited the marquee, Calum bent over to speak in Heather's ear.

'Great job. You were open and honest and came over as totally believable. I think you will have allayed most of the fears.'

'Thanks. But I did get kind of caught out on SERC. Thanks for bailing me out. I suddenly did not know what to say.'

'Yes, but I ended up covering SERC's butts and that is the last thing I wanted to do. We simply must get the task force to address the SERC situation one way or another. Right now they seem to have vanished into thin air.'

'I agree. See you in the morning. We will take it up with Mick and Marcus.'

'I wonder how the press conference went.'

'Well, I would imagine. These guys seem to be on top of their game.'

Chapter 44

Calum had stopped off at Westview to pick up some material for the exhibition currently going on at the Garrison House. Scotty Green had stored the material in his largely unused room at the top of the house. The room was a perfect square with windows on all sides offering incredible views on three sides ranging from the mainland to the east to beyond Rothesay and on to the Cowal peninsula to the north-west. The two stood staring out toward Wee Cumbrae. There was a storm brewing. The rain had not arrived but the wind was up and the sea was rough.

'Another storm, even in June, Scotty. Bad show.'

'Aye we can get them in the middle of summer just as easily as we can in the middle of winter. The only difference is they don't tend to last as lo....'

'Sorry for interrupting. Do you see that thing coming into sight every time the swell drops? Just out there from the lighthouse.

'No. I didn't see it. Wait a minute. I have binoculars up here somewhere.'

'Quick. I see it again. It looks like it is headed into the lighthouse inlet.'

'Here, try these.'

'Yes. Yes. There it is. Looks like a Zodiac. Maybe three people on board. Here you look.'

'My eyes are not as good as yours but I would agree.'

'Now who would be landing on that side of the island in a Zodiac? Not Jimmie Morrison I would wager. Could it be our friends from SERC?'

'That is not an easy landing at the lighthouse on a good day. Today is not a good day. They must really want to be there.'

'Hmmm. Look Scotty, I need to get going. I need to be over at the command centre and I will drop off these materials at the Garrison House on the way.'

'Take the truck. It will be quicker. I never use it these days in any case. You might as well hold on to it.'

'Thanks. It goes against my new philosophy but that was formed in different times. Speed may well be of the essence in these crazy times.'

Ten minutes later, Calum was in the command centre at the station. The first thing he did was call Gavin Mackenzie hoping he was there. It seemed that more often than not he was off somewhere. The phone was answered, to his relief.

'Gavin. This is Calum Davies. We met a few weeks ago.'

'Aye. The Yank. I remember you.'

'Yeah. Yeah. Everybody seems to remember the Yank. I have a question for you.'

'Oh aye. And what wid that be?'

'Do the SERC folks have your Zodiac out right now?'

'Yup, they sure do. They took it again a couple o' days ago and said they would be huddin' on tae it for the foreseeable future. Those was the exact words. Gid news fur me. Aboot the only business I am daein' these days and this weather today is no goin' tae help.'

'That is exactly what I wanted to know Gavin. Thanks a lot.'

Calum joined Heather Randall, Marcus Brown, and Mick Musselwhite in her office. He learned that additional equipment was going to be brought to Millport by the coastguard helicopter based in Belfast, Northern Ireland which happened to be placed presently at RAF Campbeltown, on the south of the Mull of Kintyre, after an earlier callout. The equipment which was stored at the former RAF base in Macrihanish on the west side of Kintyre was sophisticated enough to pinpoint the source of the leak on Wee Cumbrae, if indeed something was leaking and the contamination was not airborne from the mainland.

'That is a good example of cooperation,' said Calum.

'Yes. We cannot complain. All the services are getting behind us on this one. Nobody likes the fought of radioactive contamination,' Mick stated. 'As soon as the equipment arrives, we will send a small team back to Wee Cumbrae, weather permitting. If somefing is leaking there, this equipment should help us find it.'

'Heather and I would like to talk to you about SERC.'

Marcus immediately told them that SERC appeared to have disappeared.

'We are working with Police Scotland.'

'DI McBride?'

'Yes. Seems a decent guy, if a bit slow.'

'You read him correctly.'

'Anyway, he has been to their offices in Glasgow and there is no sign of life. The folks in the business next door say there has been nobody home in the last couple of weeks. They can't be at Farland Power Station because that is still closed as of today.'

'I heard it was going to reopen today.'

'It was, but a decision was made last night to stay closed until next Monday.'

'How about the London office?'

'We thought about that. The Met boys checked it out. It was all closed up with no sign of life. Again the business next door said there had been very few comings and goings in the last few weeks. There was a receptionist coming in but she stopped last week and nobody has been near the place ever since.'

'I just came from your hotel and as we were looking out toward Wee Cumbrae I saw a Zodiac trying to put in at the lighthouse. The weather is pretty grim and they were having a struggle. Nobody would have any business there, especially on a day like this. I just phoned the dealer in Wemyss Bay who rents out a Zodiac to the SERC people on an as-needed basis. They have the Zodiac and have had it for the last few days. And they intend to hold on to it for the foreseeable future. That may be where they are holed up.'

'You could be right. It is going to be difficult to get on to the west side of the island. If anything, that weather is getting worse. Look the rain has come on.'

'Can you get the coastguard helicopter to have a look as it flies over Wee Cumbrae? If the Zodiac is there, then we know they are most likely there.'

'That is a good idea Calum. You are getting right into this cloak and dagger stuff. Ain't he Marcus? Maybe you 'ave a space for 'im in that shady department of spooks that you 'ead up.'

'Well done Mick. Now I not only have to kill Calum and Heather but you as well.'

Calum and Heather looked at each in concern as Mick uttered, 'Oops.'

'I am only joking. At least for now I am only joking. But I do need you both to not even speculate amongst the pair of you where I come from never mind talk about it to anyone else."

Heather beat Calum to a response. 'Our lips are sealed.'

'Good. But Mick is right. That is a good idea to have the coastguard take a look. I will go to the command centre and get them on the radio right now.'

Early in the afternoon, the coastguard helicopter put down with some difficulty on the improvised landing pad by the side of the Keppel Pier. The pilot staggered out, pointed out a package behind his seat to a task force member who had ventured out to meet him, and set out to battle the sheets of rain as he made his way into the research station.

Once inside, and out of his already soaked outer clothing, the pilot stated firmly to the welcome party.

'That pad is too damned near the water. One little slip in this weather and I am in the drink.'

Heather took responsibility. 'I am sorry about that. We do not have a helicopter pad at the station and we just commandeered that little bit of spare ground during this emergency. If the weather keeps up, and we have more landings, we better look at making them on a bigger space elsewhere.'

'There are soccer fields in West Bay and behind the houses in East Bay. They would do the trick. We could arrange for any helicopter to be met there.'

'I assume my transatlantic colleague is referring to football fields. They will do nicely. I am Marcus Brown. This is Mick Musselwhite and you have heard from Heather Randall and Calum Davies. All are doctors of one kind or another but you should not hold that against them. Now let's hear what you saw over Wee Cumbrae.'

'The wind and rain was just a bugger. It was difficult to see down at ground level and I did not want to drop down too much over the lighthouse but I can confirm that there is a Zodiac tied up at the jetty. It seemed to be getting a fair old buffeting so I don't know how long it will be tied up. It might be in Northern Ireland before this storm is over.'

'Looks like we may have located the SERC folks. Good job. That may be important to this mission.'

Mick asked about the equipment which had now been deposited in the command centre. The pilot replied.

'That part went fine. The weather is not so bad over the other side of the Mull of Kintyre and somebody was there to meet me even though the base is closed. I suppose he was a local and part of the group that have bought the base. The equipment was already packed and clearly marked.'

Marcus replied. 'Again good show. This equipment is vitally important to this mission. I don't think we are going to be able to put a team on Wee Cumbrae until the weather improves. As for you, I suspect you will want to stop over here for a while until we get a break. We can offer you some hospitality.'

'Suits me. I will just have to radio my HQ in Belfast.'

'And I will put in a call to McBride about the SERC guys at the lighthouse,' added Calum. 'They can be ready to move once the storm abates.'

Chapter 45

The storm did not die down until well into the evening thereby grounding all proposed operations for that day. The coastguard pilot stayed over at the Westview and joined a boisterous group for drinks and dinner there. Calum had taken time out to send a long email to Nerys bringing her up to date with the unfolding drama but had now joined the happy ensemble. He shook his head as he thought about all the different walks of life they came from, how they had been thrown together, and now how, in this lull after the storm, they were partying like a well-established group of friends.

Scotty Green considered this to be a pivotal event for Millport and was determined to treat the guests to the best the Westview had to offer. Several elaborately prepared drinks were served before a special three-course dinner that any London restaurant would have been proud of. As people clearly unwound after the tensions of the last few days, it became obvious that warm feelings were developing for the Cumbraes. Scotty and Constable Jardin, who happened to drop in as part of his putting-the-island-to-bed round trip, joined the group for a nightcap.

Harry Jardin was brought up to date on the situation including the likely sighting of the SERC folks. In a strange motion, all parties turned to look out the restaurant window toward the lighthouse which was presently invisible in the black inky darkness of night. So near and yet so far. Harry had already been contacted by DI McBride about the planned helicopter ride to Wee Cumbrae in the morning to intercept them at the lighthouse. He was to be picked up at West Bay Park and included in the police group as the activity was occurring on his patch. Clearly he was quite proud to be part of the action.

Eventually all agreed that good sleeps and clear heads would be needed for the next day and the party broke up with most making their way upstairs to their rooms and Constable Jardin providing the customary ride home, in this case for Heather Randall to East Bay.

Early next morning with bright blue skies attempting a denial that there had ever been a storm, the mission moved into full systems go. From Keppel Pier, a Zodiac under the guidance of Jimmie Morrison and including a special team headed by Mick Musselwhite armed to the teeth with high-tech equipment set off for Wee Cumbrae. The coastguard helicopter set off for Campbeltown and then back to HQ in Belfast. Heather Randall, Marcus Brown, and Calum positioned themselves in the command centre by radios, phones, and computers to oversee the action unfold.

The police helicopter was first to report as it landed briefly at West Bay Park to pick up Harry Jardin. DI McBride's voice came through loud and clear and sounded almost enthusiastic at the prospect of one of his cases coming to fruition. Not ten minutes later, he was back on the radio.

'The Zodiac is gone! We managed to land quite easily and there is definite proof that somebody has been living in the abandoned lighthouse personnel homes but there is nobody here now. We are going to take a look around and put out an appeal to all police stations to look out for the Zodiac and its occupants.'

'Shit. They must have got out at the crack of dawn or really risked things yesterday during the storm.' Calum slapped his hand on the desk at the news.

Marcus responded to McBride. 'Understood, keep us posted and let us know if you need any help.

The scientific team should be landing on the east side of Wee Cumbrae any minute now.'

'OK. Over and out.'

Heather was just saying 'That was not a good start,' when the radio crackled into life again. It was the coastguard pilot.

'I heard what the police said. I will keep an eye out for a Zodiac on my way back. I am just south of Arran. I can't see any Zodiac but I can see the Farland craft down there heading for Beagg.'

'OK. They must have got an early start this morning.'

The radio room went quiet for a moment, and then Calum yelled out.

'That is not SPC1 from Farland. The last time I saw her she was less than half loaded and the power station has been closed ever since. You know what this means? It must be the missing SPC3 making a break for it. What do you think?'

Over the next minute or two, three voices in the command centre and one on the radio desperately competed for airtime as each reflected on the possibility of what Calum had conjectured. Eventually Marcus yelled over everybody else.

'Stop! I think he could be right. Take your chopper down as low as you can and tell us what you see.'

As they waited on tenterhooks for the pilot's report, Mick Musselwhite's voice came on.

'We 'ave landed. I'm 'earing the other conversations so will keep off the radio just now. Good luck.'

The endless radio silence ran on until finally the coastguard helicopter came through again.

'I think you are right. I can clearly see the SPC3 name. The craft is loaded to the gunnels with shiny cylindrical flasks. She must be way overloaded because she is very low in the water and is barely doing five knots. She is about a mile off Ailsa Craig heading for open water. You need to scramble the services and see who is able to intercept her.'

Marcus replied. 'Leave that to me. Well done again Captain Johnson, you have given us invaluable help.'

Soon, he was using both radio and phone and speaking to London and various naval bases around the west of Scotland and England.

'It will be dodgy if she makes it out of the Clyde. And because of the cargo it has to be the Royal Navy that does the job. The RAF or the Royal Marines would gladly blow her out of the water but we need a clean capture. Somebody will get back to us soon with the best option for deployment.' Marcus had very much taken on the role of commander and Heather and Calum could only admire his coolness under fire, so to speak.

'That was quick thinking on your part Calum, coming up with SPC3 angle.'

'While I am on a roll let me fly this by you. It seems possible that SPC3 has been hidden around Wee Cumbrae all this time. The only place I have heard of that might have provided that cover is a place called Ewart's Cave on the south-east side. I gather it is only accessible by water and only at high tide. I wonder if it is possible there is a way out of the cave by land. It might be worth getting Mick to focus his work on that area.'

'How the heck do you pick up this stuff Calum?'

'It was your staff member, Jimmie Morrison, who told me about it, Heather. And he is with the team on the island right now.'

Marcus had heard enough and turned back to the radio.

'Mick, come in.'

'Mick 'ere.'

'Mick. We think SPC3 might have been hidden in a sea cave called Ewart's Cave on Wee Cumbrae. Jimmie Morrison is with you. He knows where the cave is from the water and could probably lead you close to it overland. What do you think about heading straight there? If you can get close and the leak emanates from there, the equipment should take over at some stage.'

'Anyfing to limit the possibilities. Right now, it is a bit like looking for a bleedin' needle in an 'aystack even with the technology. Let me talk wif Morrison and I will get right back to you.'

Heather noted that there had been nothing from the police in a while. 'Could it be that the SERC folks are on SPC3?'

'Possible. Somehow I just can't see Cyrus Macadam as a buccaneer but we will find out soon enough.'

'OK we are going overland toward the general area of Ewart's Cave. Jimmie thinks there is a track of sorts to the old cemetery so we'll take ATVs we found 'ere. The area of the cave must be a mile or so beyond the cemetery.'

Marcus responded. 'OK Mick. Good luck. Over and out.'

'This is quite exciting for Heather and me but I guess it must be old hat for you Marcus. I am not asking you to comment in case you have to kill us.'

'Never done anything like it in my career. But that is a state secret. I wish the navy would get back to us.'

Just then the phone rang. Marcus answered and responded to what he was hearing with several "understood" and hung up.

'Well?' asked Heather when no explanation seemed forthcoming.

'A ship has been deployed. That is all I am allowed to say.'

'Oh come on. We are all on the same side surely.'

'Sorry. Can't.'

The awkward withholding of information was disturbed by DI McBride coming on the radio.

'Just got word of a possible sighting from Whiting Bay. Taking off now. Taking Jardin with us even though it is beyond his jurisdiction. Over and out.'

'Whiting Bay?' Marcus asked.

'Little sea-side village on Arran. Not far from the lighthouse. An obvious place to whip over to in a Zodiac wouldn't you think Heather?'

'I would agree. We have a weather reporting facility there.'

For the next two and half hours, the threesome sat listening to silence and could only wonder what was happening on all three fronts. Eventually one of the staff came in to say that the media was going nuts. There was a strong sense that things were happening and they were desperate to know. Marcus told the staff member to say that several things were happening but that we were not in a position to comment at this delicate stage. 'Tentatively schedule a press conference in Glasgow for 11pm. That should whet their appetites.'

'Will you go up for that?' asked Calum.

'I will have to. I imagine old Mick will be pretty tired and up to his armpits in whatever by then. But I might take you two along for local interest.'

'I come from Southern California.'

'Better than being English like me, in many local eyes.'

Just as they were making arrangements to have some dinner brought in, news broke at the command centre. In fact several pieces of news broke.

Firstly, DI McBride radioed in to report that they had taken three individuals into custody in Whiting Bay where they had rented a cottage and jetty. None of them had resisted arrest; however they had been hesitant to give their names at first. Names had now been established and verified. Cyrus Macadam was not one of the three. They would be proceeding to Glasgow where the men would be held and interviewed in the morning. An all airport and sea-terminal alert had been put out for Macadam.

'Excellent work,' Marcus enthused in response and then when the radio connection had been broken, 'The boys in blue get their man for once. It will be interesting to see what the interviews produce. Of course, we don't know that they have done anything wrong. We just have your hunches to go on Calum. But they seemed to want to disappear in a big way so that probably suggests they were up to no good.'

Secondly, Mick's ecstatic voice came over the airwaves.

'We have found it! By God we 'ave bin and gone and found it. The mad bastards were skimming flasks off certain voyages and storing them in the cave. Then they tried moving 'em out of the cave by way of a very overgrown path that Jimmie Morrison never even knew existed and on to an ATV. They had cut a track beyond the cemetery so they could then ferry 'em, one at a time, all the way to one of the outbuildings at the mansion house. Then they got greedy and hijacked SPC3. We saw evidence of it being moored wifin the cave. Then the old ball burst. They 'ad only started moving flasks to the outbuilding when they dropped one on the narrow path and its seal was broken. That is where the leak has been coming from. I need you to send a welder over here 'toot sweet' and we can reseal the bloody thing. What do you fink of all that?'

'Amazing, Mick. Well done.'

"It was well done, Calum."

'I would never have known if Jimmie had not told me about Ewart's Cave.'

'Blimey. We must have the only modest American on the planet. You are pretty good at joining up the dots, at least allow yourself that.'

'This is great news Mick. I will get that welder to you tonight before we lose the light. Do you have enough kit for him?'

'We have one extra suit. I assume he will come over in our helicopter. I will send back some of our team by helicopter. No need to detain 'em here now that we seem to have cracked it. 'Ave you fought about the media?'

'It is in hand for 11pm tonight. I will do it. Let you get some rest. I am going take my two assistants here.'

'Excellent idea.'

We will stay in Glasgow and see you down here in the morning.'

Over and out.'

The threesome shook hands, clapped each other on the back, and then went into some form of group hug that probably not one of them had participated in before.

'Two down, one to go. God, this is exhilarating,' whooped Calum.

'You better watch you do not overdose on adventures Calum.'

'What do you mean Heather?'

'It is a long story Marcus and one for the bar of the Westview when this is all over. But suffice it say that Superman here is not all he seems. In another life, he is actually a mild mannered accountant.'

Marcus' bemused look at the two old school friends giggling like they were still in school was broken by the piercing ring of the telephone. He took the call and as before did a whole lot of listening punctuated with the occasional "understood" and even a rare "good show". At the end of call as he put the phone down, Marcus' face was priceless. He tried ever so hard to remain serious in keeping with the expectations of a good command centre commander but in the end his face broke into a smile, then he started to laugh, and then his booming laugh caused the other two to start to laugh even though they had not a clue what they were laughing at.

Eventually, the shadowy civil servant was able to compose himself and reveal the third piece of good news.

'That was the Admiralty in London. You are never going to believe this.'

'We will. We will. Tell us,' implored Heather.

'I am actually allowed to tell you because it has been decided at the highest levels that the story will be made public.'

'You would never have killed us anyway. But do tell.' Calum pleaded.

'Don't bank on it, old boy. But here is the news. I can confirm that a submarine surfaced in front of SPC3 somewhere off the south-west coast of Scotland as it was making for the west of Ireland by the look of it. The crew surrendered the craft after a shot was fired across her bow. That was a good thing. When you think about it they could have chosen to scuttle the craft and then who knows what kind of environmental mess we would have had. On board were the entire original crewmembers of SPC3 who were obviously doing some freelance radioactive waste exporting. The submarine will tow SPC3 into Stranraer and put its crew ashore there for immediate arrest by the authorities. That should happen by midnight.'

'What a magnificent show of cooperation,' said Heather.

'Oh you don't know the half of it,' replied Marcus and started to laugh again.

'What is it man? Contain yourself. Spooks are not supposed to laugh.' Calum admonished him.

'I'm sorry. The submarine in question, to which we owe a big thanks, was the Ohio Class Submarine USS Alaska. Yes, an American submarine. All that delay in London and at the naval bases was while they determined which ship was in best position to execute the interception. In the end, it was determined the closest was the Alaska which is currently visiting the British Submarine Base at Faslane on the Gare Loch and was out on manoeuvers with a couple of British subs. The "Top Brass" had to swallow their collective prides when it was found Alaska was by far the closest and ask the US Navy for help. They had to ask their masters back in the former colony. That's what took the time but I suppose by military bureaucratic standards the decision was made in uncommonly rapid time. Thus the good ship Alaska saved the day.'

'I love it. The US Cavalry was not available to ride in so we sent for the US Navy.'

'That is a good line. Save it for your press conference but don't come over all American on us'

'I am a Scottish-Canadian I will have you know.'

Chapter 46

The goings-on in Scotland had been noted with keen interest by academics in the California University. President Ramirez had now firmly established a working relationship with the CEO of SERC in Long Beach. They were in clear agreement that the corporation had to be in damage control mode for its own sake and that of its parent university. Cyrus Macadam was at large and had been officially deemed to be no longer representing the corporation, in other words he had been fired. All operations of the London subsidiary of SERC had been suspended pending clarity from the police investigations. It was not abundantly clear that the Long Beach corporation could make an arbitrary decision on its London subsidiary given the complicated relationship between the two but the decision had been made; and made publicly. The attorneys could sort out the legalities of the action later on.

Nerys had been reassured that the SERC funding for her research project would be continued irrespective of what the outcome of the UK investigations was and, as dryly noted by the CEO, irrespective of the role her husband had in bringing down the London operation. The whole London operation was characterized as rogue and nothing to do with the Long Beach headquarters.

Nerys had been in long telephone conversations with Calum to get his perspective on the whole story thus far so that she could compare it with the widespread media coverage on both sides of the Atlantic. They talked about how this completely unanticipated series of incidents, with its world-wide interest, could be worked into her final report without straying too far from the objectives of her study. In many ways it was a dream come true for a researcher trying to combine dry academic facts and findings with current events.

Back in Scotland, things were moving more slowly on the day after the day in which the whole Farland story exploded.

The leaking flask had been successfully sealed thereby stopping the contamination on Wee Cumbrae. Work had begun on carefully returning the flasks to the power station. It was interesting to note that the skimming of flasks was suspected to have occurred every time SPC3 made a voyage and the number secreted on the island far exceeded the shortfall noted at the Beagg end. That number, together with the last SPC3 voyage cargo, augmented by as many more that could be loaded, represented a tidy amount of plutonium for an illegal transaction somewhere. To date that information had not been ascertained.

Shipping of the waste by SPC1 and other crafts had been suspended indefinitely pending police investigations. The flasks returning from Wee Cumbrae and the repatriated SPC3 were being stored in the compound and security had been considerably beefed up. The local manager of the power station, Tom Wilson, had been suspended with pay by BritPower and was now helping the police with their enquiries.

The scientific team had continued to examine the situation on Wee Cumbrae. The highest level of contamination lay around the ground entry to Ewart's Cave. That area would have to be sealed off for the foreseeable future. There was higher than acceptable contamination readings in other pockets of the island including around the mansion house and outbuildings and on some parts of the stream down to where it flowed out into the ocean. The ocean did not show any evidence of contamination above acceptable levels. Mitigation would have to be gradual with much of the contamination simply dissipating into the atmosphere in time. Where soil and parts of buildings were contaminated, they would have to be removed and actively mitigated in a designated area probably close to the cave area. Regrettably, a controlled virus would have to be introduced to the island to eliminate the remainder of the wildlife who might be carrying the poison. This would mean Wee Cumbrae would for a period of time be devoid of wildlife. At a later stage, natural migration of seabirds and the introduction of other species would address the absence.

Police Scotland West under the leadership of DI McBride had responsibility for questioning the crew of the craft SPC3, Tom Wilson, and the three employees of SERC. Initially, very little progress was made with neither group of individuals being prepared to talk about anything and Wilson stonewalling, with legal help.

It was established all the crew members were Lebanese and each professed to have no English including the one assumed to be the captain. When a translator was brought in, the interrogation remained painfully slow with no explanation for their actions being offered and all references directed to Tom Wilson.

The SERC men tried to maintain total silence at first, referring all questions to their boss Cyrus Macadam, and later insisted their activities centred solely around the loading of the crafts at Farland and escorting them out into open water at Ailsa Craig. They denied any knowledge of anything to do with Wee Cumbrae including the cave, mansion house, and lighthouse and anything to do with SPC3. It was clear to McBride that the men were lying but all efforts of interrogation within the regulations of Scots Law proved unsuccessful in the first forty eight hours.

Tom Wilson, who had been responsible for overseeing the loading and shipping of the crafts with the radioactive waste, proved to be a difficult customer as well. He had got himself a sharp Glasgow lawyer who was well known for defending the criminal fraternity and assisted Wilson in resisting all efforts by McBride to get him to talk. The lawyer's constant response was "Charge him or release him." McBride did not feel he had enough evidence to proceed with charges at this stage.

Fortunately, the authorities caught a couple of breaks on the third day.

Marcus Brown had waited patiently while the police followed the regulations they were bound by without succeeding in breaking through the resistance of the suspects. He requested access to the SERC men. The request was denied. A call came from London to the Chief Constable of Police Scotland. McBride reluctantly permitted Brown to join him while he conducted further interviews of each of suspects. One was determined by Brown to be the weakest. Brown then interviewed the suspect on his own. One hour later, McBride was invited to join the interview where a badly shaken suspect indicated his willingness to provide a full statement. McBride had difficulty understanding the suspect's speech as he seemed to have suddenly developed a need for dental treatment but he had no doubt that talking was about to begin. The plan was to obtain as full a statement as possible then use it as leverage against the other two men.

Later in the day, Cyrus Macadam was apprehended at Schipol Airport in Amsterdam as he attempted to board a plane for Seoul, South Korea. He had succeeded in getting out of Britain on a cross-channel ferry but had been spotted by a sharp-eyed airline employee who had just read the latest Interpol bulletin. He was to be escorted on a direct flight to

Edinburgh where he would be met by Police Scotland and transferred through to Glasgow.

Sensing that Macadam had a strong influence on all the suspects under investigation, McBride made sure they were all informed about his apprehension. The effect was immediate. Tom Wilson immediately indicated his willingness to give a full statement and his shady lawyer handed off to a junior partner of the law firm. Instead of having to play one SERC man off against the other two, all three now indicated their willingness to cooperate. Even the captain of SPC3 recovered his lost knowledge of English and started to talk.

By the end of the day, Constable Jardin was regaling Calum and Scotty Green with the latest intelligence over drinks in the latter's lounge.

'Oh aye, it took a while for them to find their voices but I hear now they are all beginning to sing like they were in a choir.'

Scotty clapped his hands. 'Getting a hold of Macadam was the key obviously.'

'You are so right. They think everyone was downright afraid of him and while he was loose they were going to clam up. Now that he is in custody they will all want to try to cover their own arses.'

'What have they revealed so far?'

"It is early days but the SERC guys are saying they were hired by Macadam solely as muscle. They gave you the doin' Calum, on Macadam's orders. They are denying much to do with Wee Cumbrae. They say the crew of SPC3 handled all the skimming of flasks and the disappearance of the craft during the storm. They deny being involved in the moving of the flasks from the cave. The crew was hidden on the island all the time the craft was missing. The three have admitted setting up the bogus GPS signal in the Sound of Jura and ditching Gavin Mackenzie's Zodiac.'

'That is a lot of information to have been acquired in one day.'

'The word is that the spook from London had his way of loosening tongues and the arrest in Holland did the rest.'

'How is McBride feeling?'

'Typical. He is pissed off about being ordered by the Chief Constable to give access to the spook.'

'But he surely must be pleased with the progress and the likelihood of clearing the whole case up. That will reflect well on him.'

'Aye. But you know what he is like. The glass is always half-empty.'

'What about Tom Wilson? I just knew he was implicated.'

'Well Calum, he had a real notorious criminal lawyer protecting him all the way until Macadam was nicked. Now he can't say enough. He was basically bought off by Macadam to turn a blind eye into what was going on and to doctor the books. It looks like the crew of SPC3 did all the physical unloading of flasks on Wee Cumbrae at the beginning of each voyage. They always left late in the day and were able to slip into Ewart's Cave unseen. The SERC guys in their Zodiac were able to keep a lookout for them.'

'So Wilson was just in it for the money?'

'Appears he has a gambling problem. SERC's money kept away the loan sharks who were threatening cut his head off.'

'Jesus. This is the Wild West.'

'I think Wilson will be needed by the Crown to nail Macadam. He will not be an easy nut to crack. By cooperating, Wilson might get off lightly. He might even be able to mount a defence that he was coerced into what he did.'

'What about the crew?'

'They are Lebanese. Only the captain can speak English so questioning will take a lot longer.

However, it seems like once they knew Macadam was in custody, they started to change their tune. Heaven knows what charges they will come up against. Could be theft; could be piracy, could be wildlife genocide on Wee Cumbrae.'

Scotty refilled the glasses. 'You know it is amazing how this has all unfolded. It was happening under our noses and yet nobody saw it.'

'Your buddy there was the one who started to question things. Maybe because you were from the outside Calum you were not prepared to just accept things at face value?'

'I don't know why I got so sceptical. I have a tendency to doubt things but not do anything about sorting out the wrong from the right. This time I just had a bad feeling about Macadam from the first time I encountered him which was not even here at all. It was in the States when he was bullying my wife over her research funding. After that I was a bit like a dog with a bone. I would just not let it go.'

'What will happen next, Harry?'

'I suspect they will just hold on to Macadam for a while and see what they can get out of everyone else first. He will know they are singing but hopefully will not be able shut them down. There are no indications he has criminal backup, at least here in the west. He can be remanded in custody. There will be no bail. He has already shown he would be a flight risk.'

'I hope the American Embassy does not poke its nose in on behalf of one of its own.'

'Somehow I doubt it. This case could well lead to international terrorism and you know how the US of A is the self-appointed Global-Cop when it comes to terrorism. They will want to be involved in the interrogations but will not block them. I would imagine Mr. Marcus Brown will pop up someplace to collaborate with his fellow spooks.'

'And Mick Musselwhite. When Nerys first talked about him I thought he was a dry old scientist.'

'That he might be but there was also a bit of Indiana Jones about him too when he was leading those expeditions to Wee Cumbrae. That was a lot of risk there of the unknown concerning the plutonium contamination but he just charged in and dealt with it and he isn't any spring chicken.'

'Well it certainly was an adventure. Now if we could just track down Maggie Wannamaker I would be happy and I suspect you would be too Calum.'

'Hearing that name again, Harry, has any connection been made between Joel and Macadam?'

'Nothing dramatic so far. These cases are bit like peeling an onion. As more and more is revealed, sometimes surprising people get drawn in late on that you had no evidence on earlier. Maybe Mr. Wannamaker will prove to have more than just a simple business relationship with SERC.'

Chapter 47

DI Paul McBride and Marcus Brown of unknown rank in an unknown department of UK intelligence services were seated in a quiet corner of the Bunker Bar just around the corner from the police station on Pitt Street in Glasgow. They were about to sup their third beer. The first two had been consumed with little conversation but now they were warming to the notion of actually chatting to one another.

'You know Paul; this Scottish beer is not bad. I am a bitter man, by drink and, some would say, by nature. But I could mellow under a half dozen more of these McEwan's Scotch Ales.'

'We have had a hard week. We need to unwind. This is usually where I do my unwinding. I am glad to get to know you a bit socially. It can't be all work and no play.'

'It has been a tough week. But, I think we have made good progress.'

'Yeah. It is interesting to see how this one is rolling out. Macadam is the real villain but he will be difficult to bring to justice. The more we can get out of his minions the better chance of nailing him.'

'How do you see it playing out?'

'A lot will depend on how long we can keep him on remand. That will give us more time to build the case against him from what the others have told us.'

'I don't have a lot of experience of Scottish Law but I imagine it is not too different from our law. My area of operations is generally outside of the law if you get my meaning. What is your read on the CPS? Do they think we have enough to bring these guys down?'

'You will be surprised at the differences between the two laws. For a kick off, there is no Crown

Prosecution Service. In Scotland, it is the Office of the Procurator Fiscal. The PF in Glasgow is a feisty lady who tends to take no prisoners. The word I have is she is encouraged by our work to date and anticipates several prosecutions.'

'That's good. As you know I have flitted in and out of the interviews. They are not really my domain. Once the UK Government was satisfied that its interests would be looked after in the Scottish legal system, it was only right that you and your PF should take the lead.'

'Is that why I got the call from the Chief Constable to let you loose on the SERC guys?'

'Not really. That was just a feeling on my part that there are things I could do that you are not allowed to do. Just kind of speeds up the process.'

'And Marconi's dentist thanks you for the business.'

'I don't know what you are talking about. I thought he always spoke funny like that.'

'You are lucky he has not filed a complaint. I guess he is hoping to strike a deal and does not want to rock the boat.'

'Whatever. Summarise for me what you think the findings are to date and who did what.'

'While I am composing myself you better get in another couple of pints. This will be dry work.'

McBride looked about to see that nobody was within earshot. The few punters at this time of day were all congregated at the bar itself. That is why he liked this pub; you could carry on business without the fear of the content finding its way onto the front page of the Herald.

'There you go Paul.'

'Thanks. In a nutshell here is what I think we have found out so far. Macadam is operating outside of the American company SERC although he occasionally goes over there for board meetings. He is in the business of being the middle man in the supply and demand for radioactive waste to build dirty weapons. You passed on the information from Dr. Musselwhite that Macadam had come up on his radar for the same offence. From what his associates are saying, we appear to be able to prove that. We don't know who he is selling to, but his attempted flight to South Korea might be an indicator.'

'The wacko to the North methinks?'

'Possibly. Macadam hired three heavies from Glasgow to oversee the Farland operation. There don't appear to be any other employees of SERC. There was a receptionist in the London office but she was paid off a couple of weeks ago. Macadam is essentially a one man show as SERC UK.'

'Go on.'

'He bought Tom Wilson. Wilson is a disaster. He had gambling debts up to his armpits. Some Glasgow cowboys acting for loan sharks were threatening him. He was to just turn a blind eye to anything that did not seem right and doctor the shipping logs when told to by the skipper of SPC3. And also to act daft when anybody come nosing around as Calum Davies did. For all of that, he was paid handsomely which would have allowed him to settle all his debts. As I understand it, he has paid off half the debts and has placed a bunch of crazy bets with the rest of the money. There can't be too many bets being taken on Scotland winning the 2018 World Cup but he has a big one on. He is a real sad case. I would wager he won't be safe from the cowboys out of prison and I doubt he will be safe inside prison. That would be a safer bet than the ones he puts on.'

'Oh boy. Just prime material for Macadam as you said.'

'I'm afraid so. We have found that Macadam also paid the owners of Wee Cumbrae also to just turn a blind eye and not visit their vacation place. I don't think they were much inclined to do so in any case since they found out the cost of renovating the mansion house. I doubt we will be able to nail them with anything. They will argue it was a vacation rental and they had no knowledge what was going on there.'

'What about the SPC3 crew?'

'All four crafts and their crews were supplied by a Greek shipping agency. They do similar work to Farland all around the world. The crew of SPC3 is Lebanese and they were on their first contract. I suspect Macadam just sounded them out and found them criminally inclined and prepared to do his bidding for the right price. We have not been able to establish what they got paid yet but I think it would been a sizeable sum, at least for the skipper who is the only one with any English and any trace of a brain.'

'They did everything on Wee Cumbrae?'

'It looks like it. Every time they left Farland, they nipped into Ewart's Cave and dropped off some flasks, and then they were on their way again to Beagg. The skipper says Macadam gave him the plan about hiding SPC3 in the cave and said it was because his buyer was getting impatient that the skimming approach was not moving quickly enough. The crew members were to stay on the island until the transfer of all the flasks could be made. He does not know how that transfer was to be made. Probably a large cargo ship under cover of darkness. The cave was too small to store all the flasks so the decision was taken by Macadam to transfer some to the outbuildings by the mansion house. Needless to say the hapless crew managed to move some but they dropped one and it started to leak. They did not know it was leaking and are now scared shitless of the consequences. None of them are particularly sick but they all have significant traces of poisoning. The effects may not show until later. They are now definitely motivated to testify because they want hospital treatment.'

'The other guys did the GPS decoy?'

'Yes. While that god-awful storm was raging, they rented a truck, slung the Zodiac on it and drove all the way down one side of the Mull of Kintyre and half way up the other. Then when the weather let up for a while they put the Zodiac to sea, ditched the GPS, wrecked the Zodiac on Gigha, and caught the ferry back to Kintyre once it came back on.'

'What about the earlier GPS readings that the coastguard noted before they lost contact in the Sound of Jura?'

'They admit now that there were discrepancies between the two earlier GPS readings and the radio calls. The GPS readings were actually from land but the radio calls came from the sea so they just assumed the GPS was playing up and the craft was where it said it was, on its way to Beagg. The calls were of course faked from Wee Cumbrae.'

'It is all too easy when you want to create a deception.'

'It is, when you are in middle of storm like that one.'

'How do the SERC guys explain going to the lighthouse on Wee Cumbrae and the village on Arran?'

'Whiting Bay you mean? They say they were told by Macadam to lay low for a while and started off at the lighthouse on Wee Cumbrae. When they heard helicopters overhead they panicked and headed off to Whiting Bay where they had previously rented a place. They did not know why they had been told to do that, but I suspect it might have had something to do with the planned transfer of the flasks which of course never came off.'

'What prompted the sudden burst for freedom by SPC3?'

'In spite of efforts to keep the information from Macadam, he learned about Davies' discovery of all the dead wildlife and the plan to investigate. He had to get the bulk of his booty off the island and so SPC3 was ordered to sea. It was headed for the west coast of Ireland to put into somewhere small and isolated there. The skipper never got further orders as the shit had by now hit the fan. We have heard a name Alec Taggart from Millport come up a couple of times and suspect that he got wind of the Wee Cumbrae emergency and passed the word to Macadam. He was apparently in the hotel when Davies was brought in exhausted after the Wee Cumbrae trip and after that he kept his ear to the ground on what was going on.'

'Hmm. Seems like you have a lot to throw at Macadam.'

'I think so. We plan to start his interrogation in about three weeks. The remand order allows for that.'

'Could I sit in on the interrogation?'

'I don't see why not, but there will be no smacking him around even if you are sorely tempted.'

'Understood. But you also have to understand that as we get beyond all the details of how this went down and get into the intention of it all, that is the sale of plutonium to a hostile power or organization, it becomes a government matter and I may have to get more actively involved depending on my orders. I say government. I really should say governments because I am sure the Americans will want to get involved.'

'You know I don't like the sound of that.'

'Well you better get used to it. We play different games, you and I, and we have different chiefs. We just have to do what we are told.'

'I suppose so. It is just that I have trouble sorting who my friends are from my enemies.'

'If I were to buy you another pint, would that help?'

'No it would not. In any case it is my round.'

Chapter 48

It was now June 22 and normality was gradually returning to Millport. Through a heavy infomercial campaign paid for by the Scottish government, the safety of visiting Great Cumbrae had been emphasised, and with the assistance of better than average weather, the number of visitors had held steady and was even up slightly on the previous year when winter did not seem to recede until well into July. Tourism was the lifeblood of the island and any boycott based on the stories of contamination and wildlife genocide on its neighbouring island could have been catastrophic to the economy. Scotty Green and the Cumbraes Council were mightily relieved that the media campaign seemed to have allayed fears. In fact, the notoriety of Wee Cumbrae might actually have succeeded in putting Great Cumbrae more prominently on the map.

The usual summer season activities were under way to entertain the tourists and much focus was being placed on the revived Marquess of Bute Cup golf championship which was now just one month away. The event had enjoyed considerable publicity thanks to Calum's efforts and the novel nature of the competition, combined with the concert featuring the youthful classical pianist/vocalist and the seasoned rock star, was capturing a lot of imagination among all musical interests. Hotels, bed and breakfasts, and self-catering establishments were all reporting no vacancies in the days before and after the highlight weekend. It was many a moon since Millport had put up a "house full" sign.

The media was full of reports of the "Farland Affair" as it was dubbed and each day brought new revelations from those assisting the police with their enquiries. It appeared that most of the details of the skimming of flasks, the disappearance of SPC3, the plutonium leak on Wee Cumbrae, the dramatic capture of the fleeing SPC3, and the apprehension of all the suspects had been revealed. Now the media and the public alike eagerly awaited the interrogation of the suspected ring-leader Cyrus Macadam to see just how much of the plot could be laid at his door. The two governments and, to a lesser extent, the utility company at the heart of the drama had decided that public faith was most likely to be restored if there were full disclosure of the legal proceedings now underway. In addition, the UK government had promoted a much more open and transparent process of dealing with the breakdown of its nuclear waste-disposal protocols in order to regain its standing with other countries, particularly America. This was an approach that Marcus Brown found highly unusual but even he had to buy into the declaration that this was not a time for sweeping things under the carpet. As a consequence, he had become about as well-known as DI Paul McBride to media consumers who sought their daily reports and quotes. He was probably the only one wondering what this new fame would do to his future career as an undercover agent.

Calum was now spending almost all his time on his pet projects, the exhibition in the Garrison House entitled *"Education in Millport Over the Years"* and the upcoming Marquess of Bute Cup. However, he had accepted an invitation from Heather Randall to join another expedition to Wee Cumbrae, this time to obtain the results and reset the recording equipment on the other device which was located almost on the highest point of the island near the old lighthouse. The work was not due to be done until later in the year but she had decided, with the introduction of a controlled virus to get rid of the remainder of the wildlife population scheduled for August, it was probably wise to get in now and not run any possible risk from the viral environment later.

Calum was only able to keep up with the insatiable desire from California for updates on what had been going on in Millport by emailing or calling Nerys every day. With his disposable mobile exhausted and replaced twice, he had now taken to making his calls to her from Joel Wannamaker's phone on the days that he continued his task of trying to track down Maggie Wannamaker through her extensive list friends and acquaintances.

'Hi Calum. What is new today on the adventure scene?'

'Hello. Today looks like it is actually going to be quite quiet and very welcome. I have just spent an hour on the Maggie trail with the usual results. Nobody has heard from her. Most of the showbiz types are not too bothered. I keep hearing she probably just wants to duck out of the spotlight for a while. She will come back when she feels like it. They are a strange bunch.'

'I cannot imagine that a person whose very existence is dependent upon being in the spotlight would want to be out of it for too long.'

'That is my thought exactly but those who are consistently successful in movies seem to believe that they cannot fail and the whole industry revolves around them rather than the other way around. I did not get the sense that Maggie was that self-absorbed but perhaps she is.'

'Do you hear much from her husband?'

'I check in every week. At times I think he just views my report as a formality and does not seem too upset with my lack of success. Then other times he seems really intense and gets quite upset when I report in.'

'Anything new on the police investigations?'

'Nothing new today that I can see. The media seems to think that almost the entire story has now been revealed. Everybody that is being interviewed seems to be pointing the finger at Macadam. You know the usual—*"I was only obeying orders"*. I think the police plan to interrogate him in a couple of weeks. That will be very interesting. He is hardly likely to plead guilty so a long court case is on the cards.'

'Will you have to testify?'

'I never thought about that. I have told the police everything I know several times over but I suppose they will have to verify facts in the actual court. That could bring me back over here earlier than planned depending on when a trial begins.'

'That would be a pity. I had plans for you, come the fall.'

'What kind of plans? The kitchen does not need painted again does it?'

'Nothing like that. With Troy Cameron bowing out of my project, I was hoping to persuade you to take his place on the trips to Russia and Brazil. I was even going to let you do a bit of writing. I would offer you 5% of the book royalties.'

'That is very interesting but I could not do it for less than 7.5%. I might have further adventures to finance.'

'You are unproven as a writer, no more than 6%.'

'No seriously, hold that thought. I might well be very interested in doing that if the trials here do not get in the way. Let's talk more when you come over. You are still coming over?'

'Yeeesss. My entire academic calendar, never mind my personal life, revolves around my plan to be there for ten days over your golf thing. As long as you do not ask me to play.'

'I could not fit you in even if you wanted to. The demand for the *"Ams & Hams"* is enormous. But that is great that you will be here.'

'I am looking forward to it.'

'I'd better go now. It is not my dime again. Love you and talk to you soon.'

'Love you too but make it tomorrow.'

As Calum was leaving the Wannamaker house, Heather Randall called on his mobile.

'Where are you? I was hoping to entice you to the research station for lunch in the cafeteria. I need to talk to you about the trip to Wee Cumbrae.'

'I can do lunch if you are paying.'

'I suppose so. When can you be here?'

'In about five minutes flat. I am just leaving the Wannamaker house.'

'OK. Walk slowly. I need to make some calls. See you in fifteen.'

Over a pleasant seafood salad which seemed to Calum to be the best thing on offer in the cafeteria constantly, he learned what Heather was proposing for the trip on the following day.

'I figure the quicker we get it done the better. The island is already closed to the public and will be closed to even us pretty soon I hear. Can you make it?'

'I will need to consult my busy diary but I am sure that if I move some things around I will be able to fit you in.'

'Good.'

'Who is going?'

'Ian McArdle, Jimmie Morrison, and you?'

'What's Ian's claim to fame?'

'He is a nice guy, one of my scientists. He was on the original station party that picked up the samples after you discovered the carnage and did the first round of testing.'

'Is this not a bit of a waste of his time and talents? Jimmie seemed to know exactly what to do if it is the same as we did to the castle device.'

'I suppose it is, but I want him to take some more contamination readings between the new lighthouse up to the old lighthouse. The readings Dr.

Musselwhite took said the contamination level was reasonably well within permitted limits. I just want to confirm that there has been no worsening of the situation.'

'Will we have to wear suits?'

'Best to do so initially. If the early readings closer to the ocean come out OK you can take them off. I think it is quite a climb up to our recording device and on to the old lighthouse so you will be hoping that you can discard the suits early on.'

'Alright. Sounds good. What time do you want me?'

'I think Jimmie said he would use the launch and take off from here at 10 am. He said he can pick you up at the Old Pier at 10:15. It will save you walking all the way around to here.'

'10:15 it is.'

Chapter 49

As Calum stood on the deserted Old Pier the next morning, he shivered in the cold wind and looked up at the now threatening sky. The day had started calm and sunny but he knew only too well how the weather could change very quickly, even now that summer was officially here. He admitted defeat and donned his heavy waterproof jacket that had previously been wrapped round his waist just in case. Just in case had arrived.

Right on time the research station launch came into view and pulled up at the pier. Calum climbed down the ladder and stepped aboard. He was getting better at embarking and disembarking boats with all the practice he had had in the last six months. No longer did he have the fear of disappearing through the gap between the boat and the pier.

He introduced himself to Ian McArdle. He had seen him around but they had never spoken. Ian was a pixie-like character of no more than five feet with a cherubic face that looked it had weathered more than a few voyages in the bracing wind and spray of the sea. Doctoral titles were quickly dropped as they got to know one another.

'Good to meet you Calum. You have acquired quite a reputation according to the director. I hope we are not in one of your adventures today.'

'I have to be honest and say I have no control over what I seem to get into these days. You never know what might come up but let's hope it is just a straightforward trip to Wee Cumbrae and back.'

'How are you today, Calum?'

'I am just fine Jimmie. What is the agenda for us?'

'Well I thought we might sneak in a little fishing. Ian is quite an enthusiast. But, we are both agreed the weather is suspect so we will be better to just head straight over to the new lighthouse, while the tide is still right, then head up to the top of the island. If it clears up, we might be able to fit in some fishing afterwards. You know we will have to wear the protective suits, at least at first?'

'Yes. That will be an experience for me.'

'We will be just like three Michelin Men,' guffawed Ian as the launch headed out from the pier.

The sail over was not too unpleasant although the wind had whipped the sea up into quite a frenzy. Berthing at the new lighthouse was another matter. The waves were by now lashing the rocks and flowing over the jetty which was not in the best state of repair.

Jimmie yelled instructions. 'Stand by to get your feet wet I'm afraid. When I get the boat alongside the jetty, the two of you jump on to it while each carrying a line. Try to secure them through the rings as quickly as possible and pull them as tight as you can. Don't bother with a knot, just hold them tight until I get ashore and I will do the tying up.'

As Ian and Calum leapt ashore, a larger than average wave washed over the jetty causing both of them to stumble and sway. However, they managed to keep their footing and did as instructed with the lines. Jimmie quickly followed and secured the launch at bow and stern and then added additional lines just in case.

The threesome then scrambled up the overgrown path to the lighthouse and residence buildings that were now all out of commission and abandoned. Ian had a rucksack on his back, that threatened to make him fall back over, containing his scientific instruments while Jimmie carried a large tote bag containing the safety suits and masks.

Once arrived at the buildings, Ian said, 'Best put the suits on first just in case. Then we will see what the readings are like.'

Calum would like to have poked around the old buildings but the others were all about getting the business done.

Calum had trouble getting his suit on top of his waterproof jacket and at one point stood immobilized because everything was so tight. Eventually he discarded the jacket and more easily donned the suit along with the less than comfortable mask. Once all three were satisfied with their apparel, Ian knelt down, rummaged in his rucksack and pulled out several pieces of apparatus. Soon he had assembled the pieces and set to work. After a few minutes, he pronounced, 'So far so good. The reading is actually marginally lower than the one taken by the Musselwhite team for this location. That is a good thing. The drop may just be within the margin of error or it may indicate the level of contamination is already dissipating.'

Calum pointed hopefully at his mask asking if that it could be removed.

'Not quite yet. I suggest we make our way up to the start of that steep path that leads up to the plateau. That is a rise of about 100 feet. If the next reading is OK, we can jettison the gear.'

The rise to the bottom of the steep path may not have even been 100 feet but it felt like 1000 feet to Calum as he stumbled along in his suit. Three Michelin Men they were indeed, especially Ian who now looked as broad as he was tall and if he fell over he might roll all the way down to the frothy sea.

The next reading was about the same as the first one so Ian had to ask for one more reading some way up the steep path before he was satisfied. The ascent was now very slow and laborious. As they turned a curve, they came upon a small cave by the side of the path which Ian suggested would be ideal for stowing the clothing if the reading permitted. Thankfully it did. This reading, at about 200 feet above the lighthouse level, was significantly lower than other two.

'That is a very good sign. The contamination shouldn't increase the higher we go, given the leak's original source. This reading now shows below acceptable thresholds and is probably no more contaminated than downtown Los Angeles on a good day, Calum. We can take our suits off.'

The threesome made much better progress thereafter although the path was steep and heavy going. Eventually it levelled out onto a plateau at about 350 feet. The plateau contained the weather recording device. However its location was not immediately obvious because the entire area was so overgrown with tall and strong grasses and reeds. It was impossible to actually stand on the ground and progress was only made by stamping down the foliage one step at a time. While Ian took more readings, Jimmie, who had a rough idea of the location, tramped over to find the equipment followed by Calum.

'It is about here someplace but this stuff has grown like weeds since the last time I was here.'

'That might be because most of it is weeds.'

'Thank you Professor. Ah there it is.'

They proceeded to cut back the growth around the device to reveal a similar post-box-like contraption to the one down by the ruined castle. Jimmie carefully went through his procedures again, taking care not to upset the delicate balancing of the instruments. Just as he was completing his work and placing the data records in the tote bag, Ian stumbled through the grasses to join them.

'Looking very good. The level is down again. Normally this island would have a very low reading; it is a quite pristine, unspoiled area. Not even the power station operating at full belt could affect over here. Now the levels up here are quite acceptable by any standards given what has happened down below.'

'Good stuff Ian.' Jimmie said. 'Once the island gets back to normal we really need to get some clearing equipment over here to restore the pathways. Otherwise we are going to lose this device someday.'

'We could do with that. In theory, it should be much easier to get here on an all-terrain-vehicle from the mansion house if only the paths were kept clear. I for one am getting too old for that clamber up the west side.'

'What now chaps?' said Calum. 'We forgot to pack a picnic.'

Ian replied. 'I have one final request. I would like to take a reading from up there at the old lighthouse. Then we will have all elevations of the island on record.'

Almost straight up from the plateau for another 50 or 60 feet stood a mound with a circular stone tower on the top. The open fire lighthouse was built in 1757 by James Ewing and was the second of its kind in Scotland. It was known as the old lighthouse once it was replaced in 1793 by the new lighthouse where their trip today had begun. The climb was not much in distance but was extremely taxing because there was no path.

Both Ian and Jimmie had remarked previously on the absence of birds. Normally when they had visited the island, their arrival had prompted a tremendous cacophony of sound from hundreds of birds who flew above them and covered every inch of the incursion into their domain. This time, they had seen very few birds all the way up their climb and had assumed the genocide to be even worse than had first been reported. However as they looked up they could see a large number of birds circling and diving into the top of lighthouse.

To make the final ascent, they were required to stamp down the grasses one step at a time but now on a steep incline rather than on the level of the plateau. Calum likened it to an extreme high stepping aerobic exercise and the others did not disagree.

They finally reached the small summit that held the tower and very little else. Ian flopped down to do his last reading. Jimmie just flopped down because he was exhausted. Calum took several more of the comical steps to reach the doorway to the tower. He was not going to struggle this far without examining the inside of the lighthouse. From the outside, it looked like a simple cylindrical tower built in roughly hewn stone and was in pretty good shape for its age. It operated just like a large chimney with the fire laid out on a ledge near the top, which had eroded over the years, and the flames and smoke that emerged at the top providing guidance to mariners of the day.

As Calum stepped inside, he was almost overcome by the smell and mess and noise of the birds flying over the top and diving into the circle within the tower. There was nothing much to see at ground level so his eyes moved skyward. There was a small circular hole at the top of the tower through which the sky was barely visible due to the presence of the birds. As his eyes grew accustomed to the gloom, he noticed the remains of the ledge running around the interior, about twelve feet off the ground. It seemed to be the magnet for all the birds that ventured within. His head swivelled around as he followed the line of the ledge until it suddenly stopped and his eyes gradually focused on an outline.

'Oh fucking hell.' He let out a pained and echoing yell and staggered out through doorway and let out another pained yell. 'There is a body in there. I think we've found Maggie Wannamaker. Or at least what is left of her.' Then he fell on his knees and threw up mightily.

The other two rushed up and peered inside. After their eyes got accustomed to the gloom they could make out the shape of a body up on the ledge with a ravaged arm hanging over like that of a rag doll.

As Calum staggered back to the doorway, Jimmie asked. 'How can you be sure it is her?'

'Look at the rings on those fingers. That is no ordinary woman. It must be Maggie.'

None of them could stand the stench so they all quickly exited and Jimmie called emergency services on his mobile. He gave them the location and the suspected victim. It would take a while for a helicopter to be mustered and flown to the island. It could land on the plateau but there was not enough room up by the lighthouse. The services were informed that speed was not of the essence on this occasion.

The three men simply sat stunned outside the lighthouse until the noise of the helicopter shook them from their state of shock. The air ambulance personnel scrambled up the incline but quickly found that only very deliberate high stepping strides permitted any progress. Eventually, they reached the top.'

'Where is the body?'

None of the three men seemed yet capable of talking. Calum finally managed to summon up the strength to point behind him through the doorway.

'You are going to need a ladder I'm afraid.'

Chapter 50

Later, all branches of the emergency services had gathered at the old lighthouse to remove the body by helicopter to Glasgow and to examine the scene of the suspicious death.

Calum, Ian McArdle, and Jimmie Morrison had been allowed to leave once they had given preliminary statements to the police and had recovered some of their composure. Once Calum had been dropped off at the Old Pier he went straight home to Barclay House. This would be his home for only one more week then his lease would expire and he had made arrangements to move into Westview.

Not knowing what the police procedures would be, he decided to phone Joel Wannamaker himself. After all, he had been tasked with finding Maggie and that he had done although not in the way that anyone imagined. He knew that Wannamaker was in Malaga with the WCI squad undergoing a bit of rest and relaxation after a hard season as well as starting preparations for the new season. Football these days was a year round operation.

Calum got through to Wannamaker's mobile straight away. He could tell from the voice that Wannamaker was already anxious to be receiving a call from him.

'They have found a dead body on Wee Cumbrae.'

'Is it Maggie?'

'The authorities are not saying but I noticed a lot of expensive looking rings on one hand, probably the left hand.'

'Maggie always wore a fistful of rings.'

'I am sorry but you better prepare yourself for the likelihood that it is her.'

'How the fuck did she get to be on Wee Cumbrae?'

'That will not be known until later but it is not an impossible task to get there. Perhaps she really did want to just drop out for a while as her friends have all been telling me.'

'But how did she die?'

'It is way too early to know. She might have died a natural death. She might have died as a result of the plutonium. She might even have been murdered.'

'Oh come on. How can you say that?'

'You are right. I have no way of knowing. I was just listing the possibilities.'

'When will we know?'

'Well first of all they will have to establish that it is Maggie. I have got to warn you that the body looked in bad shape. It has been out in the open air and the birds.......you know.'

'Christ!'

'As I was saying, they first have to identify it and then they will determine the cause of death. They will do the autopsy in Glasgow because it is technically a suspicious death.'

'What the hell does that mean? Are you saying she was murdered?'

'No. No. Suspicious only means not immediately explainable I guess. I don't know. I am not a cop.'

'What am I going to do?'

'I think you should head back to Glasgow. And I think you should contact the police before you leave. They are probably trying to contact you. The officer in charge on the island was a guy called McAnespie but I don't have a number for him. You know DI McBride don't you? I would call him. He will probably be involved too because he was heading up the search and because it happened on Wee Cumbrae. Do you have his number? I have it.'

'I have it. I didn't think he was doing much to search for her.'

'That is neither here nor there now. I would call him.'

'I will.'

'And Joel, I am sorry it had to end this way.'

'Yeah. Thanks for letting me know. And thanks for trying to help all along. Jesus Christ!'

The line went dead. Calum sat for a while. He really did not like the guy. But, at this point in time he felt deeply sorry for him. Maybe he was trying to repair things with Maggie. That had been among her last words. Why was she on Wee Cumbrae? How did she get there? How did she die?

It was midnight in California but he dialled Nerys and gave her the news. She had been asleep and was nursing a twenty-four hour flu but slowly she started to take in what he was saying. She was as much concerned for the fact that it was he who had found the body as she was for Maggie's death. He assured her he was OK. In fact, it had not really sunk in that it was he who had found the body. He was just dealing with the shock of Maggie being dead.

Next, he tried to reach DI McBride in Glasgow. His mobile went straight to messages and he asked the policeman to call him when he had a chance. Then he called the landline and was informed McBride was in interviews and would be for the rest of the day. Another message was left. He found out from whomever he was speaking to how to contact McAnespie and tried that number. Again a message was left.

He sat back and thought maybe he was doing the wrong thing. The police would want to speak to him again. They would contact him in their good time. He should just wait for that to happen. But he could not help himself and he stood up to walk over to the local police station.

Constable Henri Jardin was in the office for once. He had heard the news from McAnespie. McBride was going to try to call him in the evening.

There was nothing that he had to discuss with Calum right now so he suggested to him that he simply remain available to the investigating officers when they wanted to follow up with him.

Feeling at a loss now as to what to do next, Calum wandered on to Fraser's Bar. Big Bob the Bartender had shaken off his usual lethargy and was leading an animated discussion with the few drinkers at this time of day about the discovery on Wee Cumbrae. Calum could not face engaging in the topic and immediately turned around and left the bar. He walked over to the Old Pier and stood looking into the water. This was where it had all started.

He did not want to be alone and decided he had two choices—to walk toward East Bay and try to meet Heather Randall or to walk back toward West Bay and look up Scotty Green at Westview. For no particular reason, he chose the latter. He and Scotty spent the rest of the day drinking and speculating on what had happened and drinking and trying to talk about anything other than Maggie's death. Long after the hotel bar had closed, Harry Jardin came by and gave Calum a ride home.

By next morning, the media world-wide had got hold of the story and were reporting it extensively including a wide-range of speculative reasons for Maggie's death. There was a strong temptation to link it to the contamination on Wee Cumbrae that had also enjoyed a degree of coverage globally. It was the slight favourite among journalists closely followed by murder. Outside of Scotland, this theory tied nicely into a perception, if not a reality, that the country had a high crime-rate and Maggie had been in the wrong place at the wrong time. There did not seem to be any consideration that the crime-rate on Wee Cumbrae was probably amongst the lowest of all where records were kept. A fairly popular theory in America was death by drug overdose, simply aligned to the fact that Maggie was an actress and actresses did drugs. In fact, there had been no record of Maggie ever being associated with drugs since the heady days of the 60s and 70s if those journalists had bothered to do a bit of research before pumping out their theory. Death by natural causes was another theory and there may have been some credibility in attributing it to her wild days, in effect she had chased the dragon for long enough and now it had chased her back.

Calum was disappointed but not particularly surprised to read some of these wild speculations. It brought thoughts of Joel Wannamaker back and how hard it must be for him if he were reading all this stuff. Maybe he was ignoring it as best he could. He must, however, be getting hounded by the media for comments because Calum was beginning to notice that he, as only a small player in this saga, was also being called every few minutes by the UK media at least. He answered the first few calls and simply declined comment, even to the Daily Record which had broken the story of the disappearance at his prompting, and quickly decided just not to answer his phone at all after that.

In the early afternoon, Harry Jardin knocked on his door to tell him that DI McBride wanted him to come up to Glasgow to talk about the Farland Affair and the Wannamaker Case because in McBride's words, "he seems to be up to his neck in both". Arrangements were made for Calum to catch the first ferry of the following morning in order to be at the Pitt Street police station for 9am.

Chapter 51

Calum was to spend a long and intense day that lasted the best part of twelve hours engaged in talking with police about the two cases. He had a feeling that McBride was getting his own back for Calum's alleged meddling all along. There was almost continuous questioning with very few short breaks. McBride was joined by McAnespie for the Wannamaker part and another sergeant Calum had not met before for the Farland part. That meant each police officer could spot off for the other without delaying the proceedings while Calum had no such luxury. He was answering questions for the entire time.

McBride was intrigued to know how Calum had come to be the one who discovered the body after earlier having being involved in the case and having offered his own theories on the disappearance. Calum professed that it was just a coincidence, knowing immediately from the many crime stories he had read and watched that the police tend not to believe in coincidences.

'If it had not been for Ian McArdle's desire to take a reading at the very top of the island, we would not have climbed up to the lighthouse. Quite frankly we were exhausted and would have been happy to give it a miss if not for Ian. He will confirm that.'

'And why were you on the trip in the first place?'

'I was just helping out with the gathering of data and resetting of the weather recording equipment. Not that I was really required to be there. Jimmie Morrison had it well in hand. I think the research station director just thought it would be good for me to return to Wee Cumbrae for a drama-free visit after my experience the previous time.'

'Did she indeed?'

'Look, there was nothing sinister in my being there and were it not for McArdle's thoroughness, the body might not have been discovered for many more months, particularly if access to the island is to be shut down.'

'You told the others and later the emergency services that you thought the body to be that of Maggie Wannamaker, yet it was perched up on a ledge twelve feet above you. How did you reach that conclusion?'

'It was not a conclusion. It was a suggestion based on the fact that I could see the heavily ringed hand on the arm that was hanging down from the ledge. I had noticed that Maggie wore lots of rings on both hands but particularly on her left hand when I met her. That plus the obvious fact that she was missing led me to suggest the body was hers.'

'I see.'

'Has the body been confirmed as Maggie's?'

'Her husband formally identified it this morning.'

'I wish it were otherwise, but I suppose then it would just be some other poor soul.'

'A post mortem will be conducted starting this afternoon to determine the cause of death. As somebody who has not been slow to offer his theories in the past, what do you predict will be the outcome?'

'I have no idea.'

'How about why she was on the island in the first place?'

'No. I don't know. As you yourself have said in the past, there is the dichotomy of voluntary and involuntary disappearance all over this case. You will have to establish if her travel to Wee Cumbrae was voluntary or involuntary.'

'I doubt I made any reference to a dichotomy, whatever that is.'

'You know what I mean.'

'Do you still have a theory that her husband could have been involved in an involuntary disappearance?'

'I have got to know him better. I volunteered to work through Maggie's book of telephone numbers to see if any of her friends and acquaintances could shed any light on the disappearance so I guess I was helping him out. I even was the first to reach him with the news because he told me he would be in Malaga and I had his mobile number. But would I disregard him as a suspect? No. I still have a funny feeling about him. And it is no more than a feeling. I have no proof.'

'That did not help us earlier and it does not really help us now.'

'You asked and I told you.'

'Dr. Davies, you remain the last known person to have seen Ms. Wannamaker alive. That makes you a person of interest to us.....'

'Wait a minute. I have told you exactly what I did after seeing her in the afternoon. The last thing she said was she was going to drop by my place in the evening; she never did. My wife arrived on the last ferry. She can vouch for me from that time. I was never out of the house after arriving home in the afternoon. It was bucketing down rain.'

'You have told me all that before. It does not confirm your movements between about 3pm and 9pm.'

'Why are you picking on me? I had no desire to do any harm to Maggie and I certainly did not help to spirit her away.'

'OK. Stick to your story.'

'It is the only one I have. I am not sure when her husband got back to the island but he could not find her. That might narrow the gap of unexplained time.'

'No. You are wrong. Mr. Wannamaker was down on the Wednesday, stayed over and left the next morning. You were seen with her on the Thursday afternoon. He does not help you.'

'No, it is you that's wrong. He went back to Glasgow for a press conference or something but he then came back later. He could not find her. He told me so himself.'

'That is not what he told us.'

'Well, he told me and someone else told me the same thing—Tommy Duncan.'

'That might be important. I will follow up on it.'

As the police are apt to do, when McBride stopped asking questions and took a backseat, his sidekick Sgt. McAnespie suggested starting at the very beginning and having Calum tell everything he knew from the plane ride from Los Angeles to finding the body. Calum threw his hands up in horror at the prospect of going over everything yet again. But he knew that to not cooperate would just bring trouble on him and he seemed to be in enough trouble as it was with McBride's "person of interest" jibe. The interview finally ended in mid-afternoon.

During a short break Calum was given a soggy sandwich and a cup of lukewarm coffee and left alone for fifteen minutes. Then McBride returned with a Sgt. Norman and the gruelling ordeal switched to the Farland Affair.

'Dr. Davies, we are making quite good progress in our interviews with all the suspects. There is some corroboration of their statements and we are starting to get a pretty clear picture of what was going on. All that will be put to Cyrus Macadam who we suspect to have been the ringleader. We do not expect cooperation from him. However, the Procurator Fiscal has indicated she thinks we have enough to lay formal charges against Macadam. The plethora of charges against the others will be refined as some deals may be done to ensure that we get the right testimonies to nail Macadam.'

'Just like Law & Order. You do deals with the small fish in order to hook the big fish.'

'If you say so but the resemblance between TV crime shows and real criminal prosecution is at best fleeting. You have played an important if unwitting role in this whole case. Your actions and the actions of others that were prompted by your uncanny hunches are all over this case. You will have to testify at some stage or stages. It is not clear yet whether there will be one big trial or we will hit Macadam first and do the little fish, as you call them, separately; or even do the little fish first to get everything possible on record then do Macadam later. That will be up to the PF. But rest assured you will be needed and it may be for quite a while.'

'I was planning to return home at some stage soon.'

'If you do, we will want to bring you back when we are ready to roll.'

'That might be from Russia or Brazil. I was planning to help my wife with her research.'

'We will pay for you to return from wherever you are. But it will be important for us to know exactly where you are any time so you will have to keep in touch. Are you OK with that? How do you feel about that?'

Calum took a minute or two to think things out. In the end, he decided that it would be quite something to be the star witness who was now at last being treated seriously.

'Of course. I am happy to do anything to help the case.'

'That is good news sir. Now you can start to provide that help right now. I want you to go right back to when you first heard about the decommissioning of Farland Power Station and tell us absolutely everything you know right up to the present day.............................'

The interview dragged on. Calum could see the last ferry to Cumbrae from Largs leaving. Then he could even see the last train from Glasgow to Largs gone. When they finally finished and Norman had left, Calum enquired as to what would happen to him now. McBride replied that since he had missed all his connections home, he was prepared to offer him a cell for the night. Calum, as was his wont, was already rising to the bait with a protest when he noticed McBride smirk. The man was not capable of a smile but there was a definite smirk.

'You are booked into the Regency Hotel not five minutes from here. A nice room and breakfast at the taxpayers' expense. You have been most helpful to us. Thank you.'

Chapter 52

Over the next couple of days, the media was awash with stories, some opinion pieces and some fact based, of the Farland Affair and the Wannamaker Death. The facts sometimes came from the daily press conferences held by the police and sometimes from the time-honoured unofficial source which meant that somebody close to the cases was earning a favour from a particular reporter or newspaper. Gradually the two cases started to merge into one when the cause of death was released.

Maggie's ravaged body took a long time to give up the cause of her death. In the end, it was concluded that she had died from substantial plutonium poisoning. This was confirmed from close examination of her organs although her exterior was almost totally unrecognizable due to burns and the damage inflicted by the birds. Consequently, there was no obvious connection between the plutonium poisoning and the location where her body was found. To have sustained such contamination, she would have had to be very close to the source of the leak or to one of the hot spots elsewhere which the wildlife would have created before they perished. The top of the island had never been thought to have been badly contaminated from the earlier and later recordings. How then could her body have met its end in the lighthouse? Or, did it meet its end someplace else and was moved to the lighthouse? If so, by whom?

The voluntary and involuntary dichotomy in explanations remained as strong as ever. If the former path were followed with her choosing to go to Wee Cumbrae, being exposed to the radio-active contamination by accident, and dying through her own misadventure, how did she end up at the top of the island? If the latter path were followed and say she were kidnapped and held on the island, did she die by accident or through a deliberate act. And if deliberate, on the part of whom?

These threads of the mystery were unravelled on a daily basis in the media without any clear conclusion. Calum spent many hours examining the same possibilities without solving the problem either. The constant thinking was driving him to despair and he was almost relieved to be distracted by his move to Westview. The owner of the quarter unit of Barclay House had come down to see Calum move out. At first he had hoped the owner had had a change of heart and would agree to extend his lease. But no such luck. Ironically, the owner said he was much attracted to the golf championship that was going to take place and had decided to move his family down to Millport for the month of July rather than go to their place in Spain which was their normal practice.

The six months had been an unforgettable experience for Calum in many ways-most good, some not so good. Certainly, the opportunity to stay in the house he had visited annually as a child was top of the positives. That location had contributed greatly to his feeling of coming home to Millport, a feeling that was now so very strong and had little to do with all his previous short visits for vacations.

The move to Westview was achieved with little effort. He had not brought much with him in the first place and even in six months he had not acquired much. His lean and mean existence was in direct contrast to his California lifestyle which was based on having everything-clothes, gadgets, technologies, wine cellar, multiple cars etc. Although not quite a monk-like existence, he was enjoying the minimalist experience. He knew that life with Scotty would be good. Of all the relationships he had forged, the one with Scotty was the first and the strongest.

It was while sitting together having a beer, once Calum had settled into the room next to the one always reserved for Evan Davis, that they reviewed the latest media reports.

'It is interesting to see how most of the stories are bringing Maggie's death into the Farland plutonium story.'

'Yes Scotty, it is. There seems to be a stronger feeling now that aspects of Maggie's death, if not the actual death itself, were criminal just like the whole plutonium story.'

'The police need some more evidence now.'

'They need one or more of the suspects they are holding to start to connect up the death to what they were doing on Wee Cumbrae.'

'If that is the case, it will likely lead more toward Cyrus Macadam rather than Joel Wannamaker who was your tip.'

'One of my theories Scotty. I would not go as far as calling it a tip. I also fingered Macadam for the Farland thing so if it is connected to Maggie's death then tying him to both might make sense. But you are correct; they need a confession or two.'

'Harry was telling me that Marcus Brown, the spook from London, has floated in and out of McBride's interrogations. Apparently he has techniques that are not exactly according to the Queensberry Rules. He can do things that McBride can't. It has loosened some tongues. Maybe he needs to get another shot at them. Tom Wilson seems the most likely to spill his guts. He has got nothing going for him now. His only hope in avoiding a long jail sentence is to cooperate like mad with the boys in blue.'

'Even that may not save him. I hear he has Glasgow heavies after him for his gambling debts so if he avoids jail he still has that to face.'

'Stupid bugger. I met him a few times when the decommissioning of the power station was first announced and he seemed like a decent enough guy. He even talked about buying something in Millport if the job was to last a few years. He obviously didn't know that we no longer have a bookie on the island.'

Chapter 53

Over the first two weeks of July, Millport settled into its peak tourist season. The weather was generally holding up and most people agreed it was slightly better than average and infinitely better than last year. Discussion of the weather always figured prominently among the locals and was often tinged with a pessimistic hue, such as "it's nice today but I dinnae doot it winnae last". In spite of that, tourist numbers were healthy. Calum welcomed seeing people on the promenade, cycling around the island, and even sitting on the beach. A few brave youngsters ventured into the water which was never anything but extremely cold even during the days of Farland Power Station and now in its demise.

Nerys had reported that the American media was beginning to get its teeth into the Farland/Maggie story. Both aspects of the story appealed to the average American consumer of light news; the former because there was a tendency on the part of the media to say that the incident could easily have happened at home because the US was not as organized as the government would like to have everybody believe and the latter, well just because it was Hollywood related and now a real story, not just an unexplained disappearance. She also said there might be an unanticipated personal benefit from the SERC problem in the UK. It seemed the parent company in Long Beach was trying to go out of its way to not only distance itself but was also bent on increasing its positive profile in California. Nerys was now becoming something of its poster child and there had been several articles about her research project, the coming trips to Russia and Brazil, and of course the generous and visionary actions of SERC in sponsoring it all.

Interrogations in Glasgow were now switching toward Cyrus Macadam as DI McBride tried to lay much of the responsibility for actions admitted by the other suspects on him as the ultimate leader. Probably because this phase of building the case would be much more difficult, news releases became much less frequent and much more guarded in what was said.

Calum was getting frustrated that the information flow was slowing down. Harry Jardin would always tell him anything new that he had heard but it seemed like he was out of the loop now as well. It was while chatting to the policeman one morning that Calum decided that he would talk again to Tommy Duncan. It had been obvious all along that Duncan knew a bit about what was going on between Maggie and Joel Wannamaker and how Alec Taggart was involved. Duncan was not the swiftest and Calum felt that if he tried again to befriend him, some more information might be revealed.

He started at the Newton Bar but was told that Duncan had not been in at all in recent days, which was unusual for him. Not knowing exactly where he lived, Calum's only other recourse was to visit the farm up by the hospital where Duncan was employed. However, he was informed that Duncan had been off sick for a week; at least that was the message that had been left on the farm phone. He learned the name of the cottage behind the Cathedral where Duncan lived.

Calum next sought out the cottage and knocked on the door. Nobody answered and he wrote a short note saying he would like to meet Duncan at whichever place Duncan wanted and included his mobile number.

Calum was surprised to get a text from Duncan later in the day suggesting a meeting in the Cathedral at six o'clock. He was surprised that Duncan knew how to text and he was surprised at the melodrama of the meeting place.

The Cathedral of the Isles was built in 1851 and was recognized as the smallest Cathedral in Europe. At that time of day, it was not unsurprisingly deserted. In fact, Calum thought Tommy Duncan had not showed up until he spotted him sitting in the shadows at the rear of northern transept. He quietly sat down beside him and squeezed his arm.

'How are you keeping Tommy? I hear you have been poorly.'

'Aye, I have no been weel at all but that is no all that is botherin' me.'

'What do you mean?'

'I'm richt glad you came lookin' fir me. I was thinkin' I would try to speak to you after the last time in the pub.'

'What did you want to talk about?'

'I'm scared Mr. Davies since that poor actress wis found deid.'

'Why would you be scared Tommy?'

'I know mair than I telt ye last time.'

'Well why not tell me it. If you are in danger maybe we can get Constable Jardin to look after you.'

'Ach Jardin. He is just as bad as his faither. Aye pokin' their noses in where they are no welcome.'

'OK. I will try to make sure you are protected. How about that?'

'Mind I telt ye that Alec Taggart picked up Mr. Wannamaker frae the last ferry oan the night his wife disappeared? The day you and me talked up at the farm.'

'I remember.'

'Well, Alec drove her tae the old stone pier and she went awa' in a Zodiac tae Wee Cumbrae. Even though it was pissing rain.'

'How do you know about that?"

'Alec telt me hissel'. Mind you he telt me to keep it tae masel'. I wid hae tae but the police are gonna get oan tae it sooner or later and I dinnae want to be the wan keeping it frae them.'

'This is important Tommy. Do you know if Alec Taggart took Maggie Wannamaker to the old stone pier before or after he picked up Joel Wannamaker from the ferry?'

'I dinnae ken that. It wid hae been the 8.30 ferry. He wid hae got hame just after nine.'

'Yes. But do you know when Taggart took the wife to meet the Zodiac?'

'He never rightly telt me that.'

'OK Tommy. This could be important. I am going to tell DI McBride. He is heading up the investigation. He will probably want to talk to you.'

'Cin you no look after that?'

'Only up to a point Tommy. I am sure he will want to hear from you everything you know.'

'I'm no keen tae dae that.'

"You must be prepared to talk. You are important to the case. In the meantime, I think you should go back to work. You don't want to lose your job and I think the farmer is getting suspicious. You should also start going back to the Newton. You don't want to appear be to hiding. That will just draw attention to yourself. Act normally. But, don't talk to anyone else about the case. Except maybe Alec Taggart if he wants to talk to you some more. But, do not tell him you have spoken to me. Same goes for Joel Wannamaker. I don't think he will want to talk to you but you never know. Are you OK with this Tommy?'

'I telt ye I'm no keen.'

'I know that but I don't think you have any choice. You have to help the police and the best way to do that is just to act normal.'

'I suppose so.'

'I didn't know you had a mobile. Just text me again if you need to contact me.'

'It wis ma lassie's. She did it for me.'

'I did not even know you had a daughter. Does she live in the cottage with you?'

'Aye. Just the pair o' us.'

'I would like to meet her sometime.'

'She's no that keen on folks. She wis in when you stopped by the cottage earlier but she widnae answer the door.'

'OK. Well at least thank her from me for helping you keep in touch. I will text her number if I have anything to tell you.'

As soon as Calum had left the Cathedral, he phoned DI McBride on his landline. He had no expectation of getting straight through to him on either phone but by calling the landline he would speak to someone, if it were picked up. It was picked up and he learned that McBride would be in interviews all day. The person could not say when McBride would be able to return the call but promised to give him the message.

Calum next called Heather Randall. They had not spoken for a few days. She told him that now the Farland Affair was a matter of criminal investigation, at least it meant that she was not so preoccupied with it and could turn her attention to other matters concerning the research station. Student numbers, just like tourists, seemed to have been given a strange boost by Millport's new found notoriety and the summer would be busy with numerous classes. She had also been told that she would have to testify when the cases came to court but she had no idea when that might be. She thought it might be as long as twelve months before they were required as witnesses.

That evening, Calum was having a drink with Jimmie Morrison in the Newton Bar when Alec Taggart came in and spoke to the barmaid.

'Has Tommy Duncan been in tonight?'

'No. You are second person that's been asking for him.'

'Who else?'

Calum ducked his head down behind Jimmie in the hope that she had forgotten.

'I can't remember. It will come back to me.'

Taggart about turned and walked out the door and Calum straightened up and continued his conversation with Jimmie.

'Hey it was you Mr. Davies, wasn't it?'

'What was?'

'It was you asking about Tommy.'

'Not me. Must have been somebody else.'

'Suppose so. My memory is getting worse.'

Calum said a silent thanks for that. Jimmie was rattling on about the cricket test match at Trent Bridge which was at a crucial stage in the final day and the highlights of which were due to be shown on Sky TV in ten minutes. He stated if the bar did not show the correct programme he was going home to watch it. Calum was looking out the window and could see that Alec Taggart had sat down on one of the public benches in front of Newton Sands from which presumably the bar had acquired its name.

'Tell you what Jimmie. I am going outside to talk to Alec Taggart. That way you can watch the cricket here if it comes on, or at home. I will catch you later.'

'Aye OK.'

Calum wandered out of the bar and sat down beside Taggart.

'A grand night for contemplating, is it not?'

'What do you want?'

'Actually I wondered if I could have a little word with you.'

'What about?'

'I am still trying to help find out what happened to Maggie Wannamaker. I was talking to Stephen

McDonald at the boatyard and he said that he thought he saw her and you heading toward the old stone pier the night she disappeared. Would that be right?'

'No it wouldn't. What would I be doing with her? Who do you think you are? The polis?'

'No. I am obviously not the police. But I am trying to help them. They will be speaking to you soon again I would guess. Are you saying you did not drive her to the old stone pier to meet the Zodiac?'

'Fuck off! Think you are a detective? I don't need to answer your crazy questions.'

'No that is true. I just wonder why Stephen would think it was you if it wasn't. You drive the only Lexus RX 450 that I know of on the island.'

'I am out of here. I don't need to tell you anything,' Taggart said with such emphasis that spittle sprayed all over Calum.

'Oh, but I think you might just have already done so. I will away back into the Newton to dry off now.' Calum said as he strode back in that direction leaving Taggart to fume then head off toward his notable motor parked in front of the Garrison House.

That was easy; thought Calum, to make up the story about Stephen McDonald, and Taggart had fallen for the bait. But, it was imperative that he connected with McBride to give him the information in order to protect Tommy Duncan and possibly himself.

On his way home, Calum dropped in to the police station to tell Harry Jardin all about his conversations with Tommy Duncan and Alec Taggart. Harry was alarmed that Calum was getting in too deeply and getting ahead of McBride which would not please him.

'I know Harry. That is why I need to speak to McBride. Can you put in a call as well? He might be more inclined to call you back. You can tell him what I was going to tell him and maybe set up a conference call.'

'I'll try. You have a bit of a brass neck using Stephen McDonald like that.'

'Agreed. But I think Taggart revealed enough to suggest that he won't be going to Stephen to check out what Stephen said. We know that Taggart did the driving from Tommy. We just don't know the circumstances and when it happened.'

Chapter 54

The following morning Calum was at the Police Station by 7:30am having been informed late the previous evening that was the only time DI McBride had for a conference call. Harry Jardin had laid on some of his more than acceptable coffee (it really must have borrowed from his French side as opposed to his Scots').

McBride was not a morning person it appeared.

'Are you both there?'

'Aye. Yes.'

'Dr. Davies, what the hell are you up to this time? Have you nothing better to do than interfere in police matters? Did you ever want to be a policeman?"

'My brother was a cop. I never wanted to be. I am more of a concerned citizen and sometimes interferer.'

'You are driving me batchy.'

'God. I have not heard that word since I was a kid.'

'You drove people batchy then as well I imagine. PC Jardin has told me all you have been up to with Tommy Duncan and Alec Taggart. You should not be talking to these people about the case. But now that you have, give me your thoughts please.'

'Certainly. Firstly, I tend to believe what Tommy Duncan is saying. He is scared of somebody, probably Alec Taggart but it could be Wannamaker or Macadam or all three of them. He volunteered the information to me. I was going to ask him but I did not need to really. He just wanted to get it off his chest. He seems to trust me.'

'What exactly did you learn from him?'

'Taggart picked up Wannamaker from the last ferry on the Thursday night. Taggart also drove Maggie to the old stone pier to be picked up by a Zodiac, the one Gavin Mackenzie rented out to SERC I would wager. She went to Wee Cumbrae.'

'Go on.'

'I don't know the exact time she was driven. That could be crucial. I will follow up with Stephen McDonald if you like?'

'What did I tell y......?'

'If Taggart took her before picking up Wannamaker that might absolve Wannamaker. If it was after, that might implicate Wannamaker. Don't you think?'

'It is only important if Maggie's departure was involuntary.'

'Yes. But, I am kind of working on that assumption.'

'You have proof?'

'Not at this time. Either Taggart will tell us or what she ended up doing on Wee Cumbrae might tell us.'

'Yes. I suppose that makes sense.'

'Calum, tell DI McBride what you made of Taggart.'

'Well, he was royally pissed to even be asked questions. He was on the lookout for Tommy Duncan and that might not bode well. Taggart is no heavy but there are other ways of controlling the likes of Tommy and I think he has quite a hold over him. He is probably worried that Tommy has been laying low and he has not been able to see him recently.'

'You misrepresented what Stephen McDonald had said. That is probably some sort of entrapment. Taggart might have a claim against you.'

'I don't think so DI McBride. I was just borrowing from the Marcus Brown playbook. When I intimated that Stephen had recognized Taggart's car at the old stone pier, he visibly panicked. He did not admit it but he might as well have done so. Stephen McDonald did not say he recognized the car when he told me about the Zodiac but that needs to be put to him now, without putting words in his mouth.'

'Thank you Officer Davies. I don't know where we would be without you.'

'Have any of your interviewees admitted anything about Maggie on Wee Cumbrae?'

'I am coming to that. First, I want to tell you that I am sending down Detective Constable Anna Greaves this morning. She is new but very bright and as yet untarnished by lethargy. She will conduct formal interviews with Tommy Duncan and Alec Taggart. Based on her discretion and input from you, PC Jardin, either one or both may be taken into custody and held in your cell until they can be transferred back here. DS McAnespie will be the officer-in-charge but I can't spare him from here. He will be available to Greaves by mobile. Do you get all that?'

Harry replied, 'Yes sir.'

'Now back to what Maggie got up to on Wee Cumbrae. We have questioned the Lebanese guys and Wilson but they don't seem to know anything about her. The SERC guys are hiding something. This morning, Marcus Brown is going to have a go at one of them—Tony Marconi. He is the tamest of the three and he is shit scared of Brown for good reasons that only he and dentist know about it. We should get something out of him if this old stone pier thing is for real.'

'This sounds promising. By tonight, we might know a lot more.'

'Yes Dr. Davies. I will keep you informed but I don't want you leading my team. Understood?'

'Absolutely. I will keep in the shadows.'

'I would prefer you stay home and read another detective novel.'

'Anything else sir?'

'No Jardin. Good luck.'

Calum and Harry looked at each for a while. After refilling the coffee cups Harry commented that maybe they were on the verge of a break in the case.

'You piss McBride off most of the time but it is thanks to you talking to Duncan and Taggart that we might be able to crack this. At least, we are close to placing Maggie on Wee Cumbrae via the SERC Zodiac and that connects her now to other things going on at the island.'

'I think he secretly likes me. It is just his hard upbringing that prevents him showing it.'

'That would be right and no mistake.'

'Have you met DC Greaves?'

'Never heard of her. She must be real rookie.'

'Well, we are here to help her. McBride sort of implied that, didn't he?'

'He mentioned my input. He did not mention yours. He told you to go home and read a book.'

'I am sure that was just an oversight. He also did not mention who should speak to Stephen McDonald. I will try to reach him before she arrives. If he is going to be useful, we can then pass him on to her for a formal statement. That would be helpful would it not?'

'I did not hear what you said.'

'OK. Get in touch with me when DC Greaves arrives and I will come over.'

Calum fished McDonald's calling card out of his wallet. It contained several numbers on the island and mainland but no mobile for some reason. He sat on the wall overlooking the bay at Cosy Corner and started dialling numbers. After several calls that ended with no answer or no idea where McDonald was, he was told that he should be at the boathouse and given another number not on the card. When Stephen McDonald answered on the first ring, Calum was able to invite himself over, being only ten minutes away on the other side of the West Bay.

'How are you Dr. Davies?'

'Just fine but it is Calum. I wanted to ask you some more about the night you saw the Zodiac at the old stone pier over there.'

'Oh aye. You sound like the police.'

'I am not. But you should be aware that it might be connected to the Maggie Wannamaker disappearance and the police may well want to follow up with you.'

'I see.'

'That night you mentioned Gavin Mackenzie's Zodiac being tied up at the old stone pier. Can you remember the time you saw it and then the time when you noticed it was gone?'

'I came over here to the boathouse about 8:30. I was bored in the house. I saw the Zodiac when I arrived. It looked like there were a couple of guys hanging around on the pier. I stepped out to see if the rain had gone off at about 10 and noticed it was gone. Damn strange. The rain was still chucking it down and Zodiacs, good as they are, should have not been out that night except in an emergency.'

'You did not see it out on the water, did you?'

'I could barely see the pier in that weather. Just could see that she was gone.'

'OK. Now this is important. During the time you were at the boathouse, did you see or hear any vehicle pass on its way to the pier? The only way there is through your property and the gate has to be opened and shut.'

'Right you are. It was such a lousy night and the rain makes a racket on this tin roof that I must have missed it going in but I did hear a car going out just before ten o'clock. That was what partly made me get up a few minutes later and go outside when I noticed the Zodiac gone. When I heard the car I walked over to the window and just caught sight of the back of it as it went out on to West Bay Road.'

'Did you recognize the car?'

'Not really.'

'Colour?'

'It was light. Probably light gray or silver. I don't think it was white.'

'Any idea what kind of car?'

'It looked pretty big. Had a broad back. Probably a SUV.'

'Good. A silver or gray SUV. Can you think of any on the island?'

'There are not many SUVs here permanently. Nobody can afford the petrol. Everybody has these wee hatchbacks and Smart cars.'

'Please try to go through in your mind which islanders own SUVs.'

'Well I have a Jeep and a Range Rover. One black, one green. But I guess I would know my own car. I had the Jeep here and my wife Morag was at home all night. Let's see. The farmer up at Mill Farm has a black Jeep too. McIntryre has a yellow Porsche Cayenne. Making too much money clearly. Old Bill over at Ballikillit Farm has an ancient Toyota but it is a mix of brown and rust. Most of the farmers have Land Rovers but it was not as high as a Land Rover. The Catholic priest has a Toyota RAV but it is dark again. I can't think of anyone else.'

'Have one more think.'

'Oh Alec Taggart. The one guy who can afford the petrol as he controls it all. He has a Lexus. A silver Lexus.'

'Anybody else?'

'No. It must have been Taggart. Yes it must have been. The back looked just like a Lexus. I never liked that guy. What do you think he has done?'

'That is for the police to establish. But you should be prepared to tell them everything you have told me. They might even come over here this afternoon. Are you going to be here all day?'

'Yes. I will be here this afternoon and home this evening. Then I was planning to go down to Kilmarnock tomorrow morning.'

'That is great Stephen. You have been extremely helpful. Least I think you have. Let's hope they agree.'

'It is just about lunch time. Do you fancy a pint?'

'Definitely.'

'Let's whip along to the Royal George then. We can have a quick bite to eat too.'

Chapter 55

DC Anna Greaves had arrived on the noon ferry and was sitting with PC Jardin in the Ritz Café having a quick lunch. They were joined by Calum who had received a text from Harry just as he was leaving the Royal George Hotel.

'Here he is. Calum, this is Detective Constable Anna Greaves on her first visit to Millport. Anna, this is our American branch of investigations, Calum Davies.'

'Hello Calum. I am pleased to meet you. DI McBride has filled me in a lot about you and warned me to pay attention to you.'

'Hello Anna. That is an ambiguous message from the good DI if there ever were one. I am here to help you in any way you deem appropriate. And, I hope we will get on just fine.'

'I am sure we will.'

'Where is your accent from? Not Glasgow for sure. I am guessing somewhere around Yorkshire.'

'Very good. I was born in Leeds. I just transferred to Glasgow from Bradford. My boyfriend got an appointment at Strathclyde University.'

'Well, it is good to have you on board, particularly down here in Millport. A lot of this case centres around Millport but McBride and McAnespie seem to be always tied up in Glasgow and not able to come down here.'

'Harry has told me about the chats you have had with Duncan and Taggart and suggests we should start with a follow-up on them?'

'Yes. I would now add Stephen McDonald to that list. I spoke with him this morning. He will able to corroborate some of Duncan's story which puts Taggart firmly in the frame.'

'You certainly have all the lingo.'

'I watch a lot of Law & Order and Morse. McBride will have warned you about that. It seems to me, at least, that we can prove Taggart took Maggie Wannamaker to the old stone pier where she was taken by a Zodiac to Wee Cumbrae. The SERC guys had a Zodiac on hire. The only unknown is whether Joel Wannamaker was on the island and involved in Maggie's movement or it happened before he arrived. McDonald's story is inconclusive on the timing so you will have to get that out of Taggart.'

'OK, we add McDonald to the list. How do we find these guys?'

'I texted Duncan's daughter when I knew you were coming. That seems to be the only way to contact him these days. I got a text back that he will meet you in the Cathedral at four o'clock.'

'The Cathedral? There is a Cathedral on this small island?'

'There is. The smallest in Europe,' Harry put in with pride.

'Tommy and I met there the last time. It is all a bit melodramatic but that's what he wants. I have Stephen McDonald available after that, probably at his home. That just leaves Taggart. I would imagine we will find him at his garage, don't you think Harry? I would suggest we try to do him first.'

Anna thought about what had been said while she finished her now stone cold espresso.

'That looks a bit tired. Can I get you another?'

'No, that was fine. I think we should interview them in a different order. Let's do McDonald then Duncan and then Taggart late in the day once we have all the information we can get from the first two. Thoughts?'

Harry was first to respond. 'Makes sense to me. Can we move up McDonald, Calum?'

Calum suppressed a smile. He liked Anna Greaves already. She was cooperative but wanted to stamp her authority on the day. 'That will work. Stephen will be at the boathouse in the afternoon. How do we ensure we get Taggart after Tommy Duncan?'

'He is pretty much a one man show after his mechanic knocks off at four o'clock. The petrol operation is open until six and he mans the pumps. You will get him at the garage up till six. After that, I'm not so sure. I know where he lives. Or he might go to the pub. We can check them out if we have to.'

Anna nodded and then stated firmly. 'We meet Duncan at four. Let's make sure we get to Taggart before six.'

'OK. Let's get going. Are you coming along Calum?'

'If that is OK with Anna.'

'It would not be with McBride. But you have done most of the legwork so it will be helpful to have you there to identify if they change their stories. I would prefer you not to speak however. OK with you?'

'Yes Ma'am.'

During the ninety minutes spent with Stephen McDonald, he basically repeated everything he had told Calum in the morning. He was firm in his belief that he had seen a squat silver SUV leaving his property just before 10pm. He repeated that the only SUV he knew on the island that met that description was that of Alec Taggart. Once he had finished his story, Anna had asked him some more questions.

'Was it possible to tell how many people were in the car?'

'No. I only caught sight of the back of the car as it moved out on to the main road?'

'Is Alec Taggart someone you have seen at the old stone pier before or otherwise on your property?'

'I have never seen him at the pier. He has parked at the boathouse a couple of times. He has a cabin cruiser and I have done work on it.'

'Is it in dock right now?'

'No.'

'He would be familiar with the track that goes beyond the boathouse, through the gate, and ends up at the pier?'

'Most likely. It is pretty well known by locals. I don't think I have seen him participate in the once a year restoration project but he would likely know all about the pier.'

'I want to turn to the Zodiac. You said you thought you could make out two people when you saw it tied up at the pier?'

'It was dark and misty but I think I saw two. They were not in the boat. They were standing on the pier. They had hoods up so I had no way of identifying them.'

'Are there lots of Zodiacs around Millport?'

'There are a few but I doubt any would have been out on a night like that. In any case, I could identify the boat. I could see Gavin Mackenzie's letters and numbers on the bow. He has two Zodiacs for rent and it was definitely one of them.'

Harry noted, 'This was before Gavin reported one stolen. He confirms at that time the SERC guys had one out on rent and the other was at his place.'

'OK Mr. McDonald, I want to thank you for your help. Would it be possible for you to drop by the police station and give PC Jardin a formal statement of what you told us? How about tomorrow?'

'How about the day after? I am planning to go to the mainland tomorrow. I will be back the next day.'

'That will be fine.'

At exactly four o'clock, the three investigators stepped into the semi darkness of the Cathedral. The door had been unlocked as was usual. There were no other cars in the parking lot. At the back of the transept they met up with Tommy Duncan. He appeared nervous in the company of the two police officers, particularly the newcomer, but Calum did his best to reassure him.

'Just tell what you know Tommy, exactly as you told me. You should probably start with the fact that you were asked by Alec Taggart to keep a watch on Maggie Wannamaker.'

'Don't lead the witness Dr. Davies.'

'Whit? Whit d'ye mean?'

'Don't worry Tommy. Just tell us everything you know.'

Tommy rambled a bit and needed to be brought back to the purpose of his testimony a couple of times by Calum while Anna frowned visibly. When he finished, he had succeeded in essentially repeating everything he had had told Calum over a couple of meetings. Anna followed up.

'Tommy. You said that Taggart asked you to follow Maggie everywhere she went, to report back to him. Is that correct?'

'Aye.'

'What do you think Taggart did with your information?'

'He passed it oan to hir hubbie.'

'How do you know that?'

'He telt me. He also said I didnae need to follow her when her hubby wis on the island.'

'I see. And you were paid for this service?'

There was a long silence. Tommy showed no inclination to reveal the answer.

'It's OK Tommy. You are not in any trouble. You just need to tell DC Greaves that you were paid,' Harry tried to reassure him.

'Alec paid me fifty quid.'

'How much Tommy?' Calum asked quietly but with some scepticism.

'A hundred quid.'

'Now Tommy, let's move on.'

'OK.'

'You are absolutely sure Alec Taggart told you he picked up Mr. Wannamaker off the last ferry and he took Mrs. Wannamaker to the old stone pier?'

'I am.'

'Why would he have told you that?'

'Dinnae ken. We wis haein' a wee drinkie and he telt me. He wis a wee bit pissed.'

'Do you know which he did first—pick up him or take her to the pier?'

'Naw. He never said.'

'And he told you she went to Wee Cumbrae in a Zodiac?'

'Aye.'

'Did he say anything about the Zodiac?'

'Said he wis glad he wisnae in it. It wis a richt terrible nicht that nicht. He said them SERC guys seemed to be able to handle it......'

'Wait a minute Tommy. You never mention anything about the SERC guys to me.'

'Must hae forgot Calum. But I mind fine now. SERC they wis. Daein' something at Farland they wis.'

Anna took over again. 'This is very important information Tommy. Is there anything else you might have forgotten to tell Calum that comes back to you now? It is OK to remember other things.'

'Nah. I think that's all.'

The meeting with Tommy had taken almost two hours because of the frequent pauses and need to reassure him that he was not in trouble. Harry made arrangements to pick him up the next day and bring him to the police station for a formal statement.

They rushed along Bute Terrace and reached the garage at exactly six o'clock. Alec Taggart was standing in the forecourt and glared at the arrivals. As Harry lowered his window, he stooped and said with some menace. 'You are too late Harry. I have shut off the pumps and I am not turning them on again. You will just have to come back in the morning.'

'I am not here for petrol Alec. It's you we want a word with. Just complete locking up the garage and then we want you to come with us to the station.'

'Who's we?'

'I will do introductions once you get in the van.'

'Is that the Yank in the back? I am not speaking to him.'

'Dr. Davies is only an observer. You will be speaking to the police. Now get away and lock the place up and get into this van as quick as you like.'

A very taciturn Alec Taggart sat in the interview room glaring across at the two police officers. Then he switched his attention to Calum and his glare turned to a threatening scowl.

'First off, I want to thank you for helping us in our enquiries Mr. Taggart.'

'Like I had any choice. How come I have to speak to an English lassie?'

'I am based in Glasgow and I am part of the team investigating the death of Maggie Wannamaker. I have some questions to ask you. I want to impress on you that you are just helping us with our enquiries. You don't have to answer any question that you don't want to. If you choose, you can request the presence of your solicitor.'

'Maybe I need my solicitor to be here?'

'You have that right but otherwise you are just voluntarily answering some questions.'

'My solicitor is in Glasgow.'

'If you want him to be present, I will make arrangements for you to be detained here overnight then transferred to Glasgow where questioning will take place.'

'I feel like I am being hung out to dry here. I don't want to spend the night in the cells but I want my solicitor. Why do I have to be kept in the cells?'

'I have reasonable belief that you might flee if free to do so. I can offer you the alternative that you spend overnight here and your solicitor comes here tomorrow. You can call him now if you like.'

'Just ask your questions. I don't know why you need to talk to me; I have done nothing wrong.'

'At this stage we have not said you have done anything wrong. It is just that your name keeps coming up when we speak to other people.'

'What people?'

'Let's start with your relationship with Joel Wannamaker. How would you describe it?'

'We are business associates and friends.'

'What kind of business?'

'Nothing solid as yet. We are just discussing mutual opportunities. I don't want to be stuck in Millport all my life.'

'Do you do any work for him here in Millport?'

'I sell him petrol and service his car.'

'Do you drive for him?'

'I do on occasion.'

'I want to ask you about Thursday the 20th of March. Did you drive Mr. Wannamaker on that day?'

'I took him to the ferry in the morning.'

'Is that all?'

'Yes.'

'Did you pick him back up again off the last ferry?'

'On the Thursday? I don't remember that.'

'You realize Mr. Taggart that the ferry terminal has Closed Circuit Television cameras. We can check the footage. Do you want to reconsider your answer?'

'No need.'

'On the evening of that Thursday, did you drive Mrs. Wannamaker?'

'She called me and wanted a lift to the old stone pier. She was moving out and going to spend some time on Wee Cumbrae.'

'What do you mean moving out?'

'That is what she told me. I assume she was leaving her husband.'

'And you did not think it strange to be helping her when she was leaving your so-called business associate?'

'I don't think he would be too sad to see her go. I don't really want to talk anymore about that. I just gave her a lift.'

'She was met by some men with a Zodiac?'

'Two of them. I didn't know them. Presumably she had made arrangements for a trip over to Wee Cumbrae. I never saw her or them again.'

'You did not think it odd for her to be travelling on such a bad night?'

'Her choice.'

'Did she talk to you on the way to the pier?'

'Never said a word.'

'How did she know you to call you for a ride?'

'I met her up in Glasgow with Joel and Cyrus.....'

'Would that be Cyrus Macadam?'

'I didn't know him. If you say so.'

'No, it is if you say so. You met Mrs. Wannamaker with her husband in Glasgow when Cyrus Macadam was present?'

'If that's his name.'

'Where was this?'

'At a WCI game. Joel always gives me tickets.'

'Was Cyrus Macadam involved in Mrs. Wannamaker's relocation to Wee Cumbrae?'

'I don't know. I am not prepared to answer any more questions.'

'Did the two men work for Macadam?'

'No more questions.'

'You are refusing to answer my questions?'

'I want my solicitor.'

'Alright, you can call him now. I intend to question you at 10am tomorrow. I expect him to be here on time. If he cannot make it, you will be provided with a duty solicitor. I assume one can be made available PC Jardin?'

'From Largs yes.'

'Give me a phone. I will make sure he is here.'

Chapter 56

Another teleconference had been arranged for 7:30am the following morning. As the Millport contingent gathered at the police station, Calum turned to Anna Greaves.

'I suggest you do not acknowledge I am present. It just might set McBride off. I will sit quietly in the background and not say a word. OK?'

'That is fine with me.'

McBride came on the line and barked good morning.

'Lots to discuss at this end and maybe yours. McAnespie is with me. Who is on at your end?'

'Greaves and Jardin sir.'

'No Supersleuth?'

'Not today.'

'Good. Keep it that way.'

'Yes sir.'

'We had a big breakthrough yesterday I must say. As a result of some unconventional questioning from colleague Brown and some highly cooperative blind-eye turning from a list solicitor who wants more work, we have been able to turn Tony Marconi. He is agreeable to testify against Wilson, the Lebanese, and all his SERC cronies including the big fish Macadam. In return of course, he gets to save his own skin. But that price is worth it to get the others.'

'Great news sir. Is he going to be a credible witness?'

'McAnespie and I both think so. He has a bit of a criminal record but nothing too big. He was just out of his depth on this one. Got into it because he thought it was bit of thieving but panicked when piracy and dead bodies started showing up.'

'Can I ask what he said about the Wannamaker death? That will have a bearing on what we do later today with Taggart.'

'In a nutshell, here it is. Marconi was not in the Zodiac that picked her up. She came of her own accord. Wanted to get away from her husband. Macadam arranged it with her. She was staying at the new lighthouse. They had tidied up one of the houses and laid on Campingaz lights and stove, food, booze etc and some weed. He saw her a couple of times when he took stuff over to her on an ATV from the other side of the island. He didn't know how long she planned to stay there. She seemed to be pretty spaced out. Later she was found dead in the mansion house. Must have crossed the island and been exposed to the plutonium. Macadam ordered the three SERC guys including Marconi to take the body up to the old lighthouse to leave it to the birds. Simple as that.'

'Did he mention Taggart?'

'Marconi knew nothing about the Millport end and had never heard of him.'

Calum was hastily scratching out a message on the back of an envelope and passed it silently to Anna.

'Sir. Did you establish any connection between Maggie going to Wee Cumbrae and her husband?'

'Nah. That is Davies' half-baked theory. Marconi was asked specifically and denied any connection.'

'What will be the outcome of the death then and will there be any charges?'

'The coroner will likely rule death by misadventure. The SERC guys could be charged with tampering with a dead body but I don't see that happening. There are bigger charges to come from the SPC3 and Farland shenanigans.'

'Can I tell you about what happened last night here? Taggart came in voluntarily and answered some questions but then baulked and asked for his solicitor to come down this morning.'

'What did you learn?'

'He admitted giving her a lift to the old stone pier at her request. He also said he did not know the guys who were with the Zodiac but Tommy Duncan told us Taggart knew they were from SERC. He sort of admitted that Macadam had been present when he had met the Wannamakers in Glasgow at a game. He did not admit knowing that Macadam had arranged the trip. He positively denied picking up Mr. Wannamaker that night which is at direct odds with what Duncan says. Duncan seems to have no reason to lie.'

'That is just going down the Dr. Davies theory street again. Don't bother. It is a dead-end street.'

'Then the feeling from your end is that Taggart did nothing wrong other than give Maggie a ride to the pier as she requested?'

'That is about the size of it. Get a statement from Taggart this morning in front of his solicitor then let him go.'

'And Joel Wannamaker?'

'Leave him out of everything. Do you hear me? There is no connection to his wife going to Wee Cumbrae and there is no connection to the SERC operation. Mr. Wannamaker has made some powerful friends in his short stay in Scotland. The old WCI "proddie" connection is still alive and well. He is not a person of interest to us. Finito. Capiche?'

'Got it.' Anna and Harry both looked at Calum and shrugged their shoulders. Calum shook his head and mouthed, 'that's bullshit'.

'Sir. What is going to happen next on the Farland matter?'

'The Procurator Fiscal has been consulting with both the Lord Advocate for Scotland and the UK Attorney General over the charges. That charges will be brought is not in doubt, it is just a case of determining which statutes fit best. I don't suppose the Piracy Act of 1837 gets cited too often but it is under consideration.'

'Who is going to be charged?'

'Everybody except for Tony Marconi although the charges will differ. We expect the book to be thrown at Macadam. He has almost totally refused to cooperate or answer any questions. That is his right I suppose. When he heard that Tony was talking he sounded us out on a potential deal but we said, "No fear". He will have to take his chances in court.'

'When will it be made public?'

'When I spoke to her late last night, the PF was hoping to schedule a press conference before the end of the week. They just need to settle on the charges and who gets the glory—Glasgow, Scotland, or the UK, or all three.'

'No glory for you sir?'

'We do the grunt work. The bigwigs get the glory. You will learn DC Greaves that is always the case. Call me tonight and let me know how it goes with Taggart. Good work done there by the way. I am glad Davies was not too much of a pest.'

Anna thought to say, 'I didn't say that,' but decided against it.

Calum joined the two police officers for breakfast before the second interview with Taggart. They were seated in the Royal George among early day-visitors to the island. At Calum's request they reviewed all the testimonies from Millport and Glasgow concerning Maggie's disappearance and ultimate death.

'The only loose end is Macadam. He has not yet admitted to his role as outlined by Tony Marconi. It seems that Marconi would have nothing to gain from lying on that point but it is still uncorroborated.'

'Exactly Anna. And we still have the discrepancy over when Joel got back to the island. Duncan says Taggart told him that night. I am pretty sure Joel told me that night. Joel tells the police the next day and Taggart is not saying. It is weird.'

'I don't think you are going to make that stick Calum. You heard McBride. We are to back off. I suppose we could quietly look at the ferry terminal CCTV. Could you do that Harry?'

'I guess you're right. I went one hunch too far. We should all feel good that the mystery of the disappearance has been solved. And the cause of death seems plausible. There is no evidence of any foul play coming out of the post mortem.'

'You're right Calum. A weird matter. It will be the talk of Millport for a long time when it comes out.' Harry reached for more toast.

'Let's enjoy this breakfast. It has been good meeting you guys on my first case in Scotland.'

'You will have to ask McBride if you can be deployed to Millport next weekend for the big golf tournament and concert. Harry could do with a hand.'

'I heard you have Evan Davis playing. My boyfriend and I love him.'

'That is good to hear. You probably were not born when he was at his peak but he is still good today and will put on a good show. So too will Francesca Carlotti even if you don't like classical music. And together, it will be a blast.'

'I think I might come down with Andy if I am not on duty. I am beginning to really like Millport.'

'That is how it starts,' said Calum and smiled at Harry.

Alec Taggart was now accompanied by a sharp looking lawyer from the same firm that had represented Tom Wilson in Glasgow. He was in a foul mood as a result of having spent the night in the cells. The two police officers were not accompanied by Calum who had continued off to the Westview when they returned to the police station.

'My name is Bryce McCurdy and I represent Mr. Taggart. I want you to know that I take a dim view of your treatment of my client yesterday. And as for dragging me down here today, I want you to know that I have other far more pressing matters that I should be dealing with. This is a routine matter of simply obtaining certain information from my client and he has indicated his willingness to provide it. Now let's get on with it, if you please.'

'I am DC Greaves and this is PC Jardin. Your client showed changeable willingness in helping us with our enquiries and that is why we are back here today. He refused to answer a number of important questions.'

'And that is his right young lady. Which he will continue to exercise. As I understand it, you have not formally cautioned him?'

'That is correct?'

'Then you are seeking his voluntary help. Ask your questions.'

The questions and answers thereafter followed almost exactly the pattern of the previous evening. Taggart stuck to his story that Maggie had called him to request a lift to the old stone pier. The call had come in late afternoon. He offered for the first time that he had picked her up at around 9:30pm and taken her straight to the pier. He was back home by 10:15.

When asked if he wanted to reconsider his answer to the question as to whether he had picked up Joel from the last ferry which would have got in just before 8.45, he huddled with his lawyer and then the latter simply said, 'No.'

When asked about his association with Cyrus Macadam, another huddle ensued then McCurdy nodded to Taggart who stated, 'I met him once at a WCI game.'

'And you were in the company of Joel and Maggie Wannamaker?'

'Joel gave me a ticket for the directors' box.'

'Were you all together?'

'No, I was seated in the second row. They were in the first. Joel turned to introduce us.'

'Are you aware of Mr. Macadam's involvement in taking Ms. Wannamaker to Wee Cumbrae?'

After another prolonged huddle, McCurdy answered, 'He is not.'

'Have you had any dealings with Mr. Macadam other than meeting him at a football match?'

'None'. It was McCurdy who again answered.

Sensing that they were not getting anywhere and could not risk delving anymore into the role of Joel Wannamaker, Anna brought the interview to an end. She thanked Taggart for his assistance and he left immediately while his solicitor hastily followed behind while stuffing papers into his brief case.

'A bit of a waste of time once Wannamaker was off limits.'

'Anna, do you believe his story?'

'I think I have to. It is mainly consistent with what Duncan told us. We cannot pursue the alternative which would be an involuntary trip to Wee Cumbrae for Maggie because there is no evidence. And there will be no evidence without being able to link to it Joel somehow. And that we can't do.'

'I suppose you are right.'

'I will call McBride and tell him what he wants to hear. Then I guess I better get back to the big city'

'Do you think Taggart will make anything of being held overnight?'

'He could do, but I doubt it. You saw how quickly he got out of here. I suspect he will just let it go.'

Anna Greaves had hoped to see Calum again if only to say goodbye but she and Harry found that when they dropped by the Westview on the longer way to the ferry terminal he was out. He was believed to have gone round to the research station.

Indeed, that was exactly where he had gone and he spent a good hour with Heather Randall replaying the events of the last twenty-four hours. As he valiantly tried to hang on to his theory of Joel's involvement, Heather did her best to persuade him to let it go and eventually he agreed that it would probably be for the best. At least there was some closure on the mystery and now Calum had to turn his mind to Nerys's impending arrival and the big weekend.

Chapter 57

Calum had stepped out of Scotty Green's borrowed pick-up truck and was sitting in the warm afternoon sunshine at the ferry terminal. It was the day before the big golf weekend but he had much more imminent things on his mind. Nerys was due to arrive on the 2:15 pm ferry. He already knew she had arrived in Glasgow and had caught the train to Largs. However, in spite of the precision of her travel itinerary, he had contrived to arrive at the final stage of her journey from California with twenty minutes to spare. There was nothing better to do than sit on the bench, one of dozens on the island, and soak up the sun.

His thoughts drifted back to the dramatic first twenty-four days of July when investigations into the Farland Affair and mysterious death of Maggie Wannamaker had been concluded and a litany of charges had been bought against Cyrus Macadam, Tom Wilson, the Lebanese crew of SPC3, and two of the three SERC employees. All had been revealed in a lavish press conference held in a Glasgow hotel ballroom to accommodate the large number of members of the media from over ten countries. The senior law officers of the UK, Scotland, and Glasgow had stood together and basked in the reflected glory of apparently solving two of the highest profile cases in Scottish history and bringing those responsible to justice. The court cases were not expected to open until January of the following year at the earliest, but there seemed to be no doubt that the culprits had been caught and would feel the full force of British and Scottish justice. During the question period, due acknowledgement had been made to the efforts of the police under the capable leadership of Detective

Inspector Paul McBride and his team and to the cooperation of all the national services. A potential black eye for the country had been averted and a bad news story had been turned into a good news story with remarkable haste. Calum smiled as he thought about his totally unscripted, often decried, very occasionally welcomed and ultimately anonymous role in both cases. He would not have missed it for the world. Who would have thought that back in December he was joking about coming to Millport in search of an adventure on the sleepiest of holiday islands?

As he saw the ferry make its way out of the Largs terminal at exactly 2.15 pm, his mobile buzzed to signal the arrival of a email message.

"Hey Calum. Good news. As of last night, I can confirm that our financial rescue of Edinburgh Waverley has been successful. The funds and commitments we have obtained from the fans and some of Edinburgh's Old Wealth are sufficient to buy out the bloody Russian and pay off some of the debts. The creditors have been great. Except for the tax people, they have voted to accept a fraction of what was owed to them. That means we will have enough money left over to run the club, buy some new players, and try to win promotion back to the Elite League next season. Relegation was a blow to the club's ego but it may be a good thing to be playing in the second tier so that we can build the club back up again.

Thanks for your contribution. You are now a part-owner of our famous old club along with almost ten thousand others. I hope we will see you at some games in the future.

I am going to be spending more time now in Edinburgh but I am not going to give up my home in British Columbia. Hope to catch up with you somewhere soon, be it Scotland or Canada or

California. Or maybe Millport. You still owe me a wild weekend in your adventure paradise.

Cheers for now. Neil"

Neil Christian had saved their favourite club from extinction. That was more good news. They would not play the big two Glasgow teams or their Edinburgh rivals next season unless they were drawn together in one of the two cup competitions. But their time would come again. He wondered if Joel Wannamaker would still be around when they next played against WCI.

Calum's pondering was interrupted by a yell from Nerys as she walked off the ferry along with the other foot passengers before the cars disembarked. As usual she was travelling light with just one small suitcase. But the smile on her face indicated she that she intended to enjoy the next week at his spiritual home.

Hugs and kisses were extended to make up for lost time. Then finally, they stepped apart and just beamed at one another.

'I am so glad to be here.'

'I had serious doubts you would actually make it with all that was going on at your end and I had some serious doubts that I would be here to meet you if did make it. You would not believe what the last six months or so have thrown up.'

'I have been reading all the press reports this month but I did not see you mentioned.'

'You know what it is like. All great crime fighters like to retire to the background once the baddies have been apprehended.'

'I want to hear everything.'

'You will my love, you will.'

'Where to first?'

'I am using Scotty's truck for the last time. I thought you might have a lot of luggage so I was avoiding the bus. I might have known better. You look like you have packed a toothbrush and perhaps a change of underwear.'

'What else will I need?'

'We will return the truck to Westview, get you settled in, and then we will walk or cycle everywhere as it was meant to be on this glorious island.'

'I thought you were in charge of all the proceedings over the weekend. You will need transportation for that surely.'

'I am going to try not to. This island is going to be crazy if all the people who say they are coming show up.'

'So today we unwind and relax and get to know each other again?'

'That sounds exactly like what the doctor ordered.'

Chapter 58

Next day brought early rain and worries about the *"Ams & Hams"* tournament which was due to begin at eleven o'clock. As Calum and Nerys breakfasted, they looked out of the bay window in the Westview restaurant at a not unfamiliar sight of Wee Cumbrae shrouded in mist and rain and the Isle of Arran completely obliterated as if a demented artist had seized a brush and painted it out of the canvas forever.

'Don't worry,' said Scotty Green bringing more toast. 'The forecast is good. Clearing from the west. I see a little blue sky over Kintyre already.'

Whether it was long experience or blind faith, Scotty's prediction proved to be correct and by ten o'clock summer had broken out and blue skies framed the entire area. Arran had mysteriously reappeared. All boded well.

The golf club was already busy. It was not equipped to handle large crowds and, in particular, their vehicles so most parking had been restricted to West Bay Park and a shuttle was ferrying competitors and visitors alike up the hill. Club Captain Alastair Beddowes was in his element and he strode around welcoming all and rejoicing in the rejuvenation of the club and its flagship tournament weekend.

Calum was able to catch a few words with Francesca Carlotti and her father, the former acting with the calm serenity associated with a classical music superstar and the latter almost overwhelmed with all the fuss. His normal Friday golf game was not like this.

'Well sir, you are in a threesome with Francesca and tomorrow's favourite Ronnie Walker. Do you fancy your chances of winning today?'

'I don't know about that. I have never seen such crowds. It is as if the Open Championship has come to little Millport. I gather this was all your idea and a damned fine idea it is. I will be interested to see if Francesca has improved since she started taking lessons. She was not doing quite so well under my tutelage.'

'Dad, you were too impatient with me. You will see I am improving.'

'There you are Calum. Just as well I did not try to teach her to play the piano either.'

'Good luck to you. I hope you are comfortable in the Royal George tonight. You will be staying for the concert I hope sir?'

'Wouldn't miss it. My wife and I will be there.'

Calum caught up with Nerys who was being charmed by Evan Davis having now met the rock legend in person for the first time.

'Ah Calum. Your big day. And the weather is on its best behaviour. Nerys is way too nice for you. I have been suggesting she look at moving to Vanderbilt University in Nashville.'

'I don't think I would be very happy with that. But it is good to see you. How is the concert shaping up?'

'Great. Francesca and I got together yesterday in a little studio in Largs and worked up our setlist. It will be a lot of fun.'

'Excellent. Good luck with the golf. Come, Nerys, away from this reprobate. I have just seen someone I want you to meet.'

They squeezed their way through the thronging masses and arrived at Dr. Heather Randall and her husband Nicholas Gorman.

'Nerys, I would like you to meet a very old friend and a new friend. Heather and Nicholas meet Nerys.'

The two women looked at each other, laughed, then hugged. Nicholas bent forward to Calum and whispered.

'Thanks for getting me into this, old man. Lot of potential clients here!'

Heather said to Nerys, 'I feel like I already know you. Calum is so generous with his praise of you.'

Nerys replied, 'I could say exactly the same thing.'

Just as Calum was making up his mind whether or not to try to dodge Joel Wannamaker and the newly signed star French goalkeeper of WCI, Claude Barthe, he was rescued for the moment by Club Captain Beddowes with a speech of welcome and explanation of the rules over the specially installed public address system. As he listened intently, Calum felt a squeeze of his arm. He turned to see Charlie Caldwell, the club's senior member and the person who had helped him most to make arrangements with the golfing fraternity across the country.

'Well laddie. You did it! Congratulations.'

'Charlie, you are the only person on the island who could ever get away with calling me laddie. But I want to thank you for all your help. I would never have got to the right people without your introductions. We can be proud that the Marquess of Bute Cup is now back on the calendar.'

'Considering all that has been going on recently what with the power station and that poor Hollywood lassie, it is a miracle that we are still able to roll. But roll we will if ever old Beddowes gets to the end of his speech. He has been living for this day. I hope he has expressed his appreciation to you.'

'He has slipped me a couple of G & Ts every time I have been up here.'

'Then he has expressed his appreciation in the way he knows how.'

Eventually the *"Ams & Hams"* got underway. With each of the eighteen threesomes starting at a different hole, suddenly play was in full swing. Each group had attracted a number of spectators who would follow it around the course and a large number spectators had opted for the temporary seating around the 18th hole to witness the closing chips and putts. Millport Golf Club had never seen anything like it. And this was just the warm-up act!

Calum and Nerys started off walking with a group that included the Moderator of the Church of Scotland and the owner of the largest club/restaurant in Edinburgh. Strange bedfellows indeed, united by a love of golf and probably little else. After a few holes, they decided to hold back and meet the next group. Fate would have it that Joel Wannamaker and Claude Barthe strutted up in the company of Joan McDermott the current Scottish Ladies Champion, whose inclusion along with tomorrow's male competitors had delighted most, and startled a few, of the golfing hierarchy.

'Calum. Come and watch us. Joan is giving us a lesson in how the game should be played. Meet Claude Barthe our new goalie. Pity he will not be able to shut out Edinburgh Waverley this coming season.'

'Hello Joel. Pleased to meet you Claude. Joan, I hope you are not having any trouble with this pair. We have stewards standing by so just let me know if you do.'

'They are trying their best that is all I can say.'

Claude shrugged his shoulders. 'I have suggested Joel just go back to the clubhouse and I could go for a walk with Joan to see the wonderful views from the 9th hole but neither agreed. C'est la vie.'

Calum and Nerys walked with them for a few holes and then sat down at the 7th green to wait the next threesome.

'Well what did you think of Joel Wannamaker?'

'Seemed quite affable and friendly towards you. You would never guess he had just lost his wife.'

'Mmm.'

'Has there been a funeral over here yet?'

'There was a private service and cremation in Glasgow just a few days ago. I was invited but I did not go.'

'Still doubtful?'

'Mmm. I was kind of surprised that the coroner released the body so quickly. Joel certainly did not waste any time in having it cremated. I thought they could do further testing but apparently they were satisfied it was an accidental death and that was that.'

'I saw on the news before I left that there is to be a big Hollywood tribute service at the beginning of next month.'

'I know. We are invited to that too. I have not declined yet. Did you want to go?'

'To mix with the Hollywood rich and famous? I don't think so.'

'Not for that reason. Just to say goodbye I guess.'

'She was your friend. If you want to, I will go. Does that mean we will be both back in California next month?'

'Yes, I will be using my open ticket to go home the same time as you. I need to call the airline to see if I can get on the same flight as you.'

'But you are in first class. I am not sure I can handle that.'

'Let's try to get you an upgrade or I will get a downgrade. I want to sit together.'

They started to work backwards toward the clubhouse, meeting different groups of players on the way. As they reached the 1st tee a roar went up from the crowd. Francesca Carlotti had just holed a quite long put. She hugged her father then winked at Calum over his shoulder. Calum just looked at Nerys, shrugged his shoulders, and smiled.

By 4:30 pm, just as planned, the final threesome came in. Alastair Beddowes took to the microphone again to thank everyone involved in what had been an outstanding addition to the golfing calendar. The many volunteers seemed to be recognized individually and finally he called for Calum to come forward. Kind words were said about the fellow from the New World who had come home to Millport and had devised his wonderful event. After sponsors and celebrities had been thanked, special thanks were given to the eighteen top amateurs who had each led a threesome and had entered into the spirit of fun play on the eve of the serious stuff tomorrow. The winning threesome was identified as two executives of a Scotch whisky company, which happened to be the largest of the many sponsors, led by the captain of the British Walker Cup team scheduled to take on the Americans next year. All in all, it meant good business and good sport had been achieved.

In the evening, a grand banquet for one hundred invited guests was held in the marquee pitched on the grounds of the Garrison House. Every restaurant on the island had come together to cater the event in a tremendous act of community spirit. The high quality meal was served with consummate professionalism to the delight of the guests. Calum and Nerys were seated at the top table beside the Carlotti family on one side and Evan Davis on the other. The conversation ranged erratically from recent events to rock music to golf to classical music to the joys of the island, which seemed to be something everyone could ascribe to.

The BBC had agreed to film the concert on Saturday and the crew had turned up early to capture some of this evening. When dessert was completed and coffee was awaited, they moved among the top table asking for impressions. Everyone enthused about the weekend so far and Mr. Carlotti took it upon himself to wax lyrical about the entire event but especially the efforts of Calum.

'I think we all have tended to forget the little jewel we have in this island. He has almost single-handedly reminded us all of what we have and we are grateful.'

Nerys looked at Calum and mouthed, 'Aw shucks.'

Francesca whispered in his other ear, 'He loves you. Anybody who calls him sir cannot fail!'

The dinner wound up at almost 11pm and some guests drove or were driven back to their hotels or other accommodation. However, most walked home, just as Calum would have wished it to be. The Westview contingent had the longest walk but also the opportunity to laugh most as they exchanged stories and quips while wending their way along West Bay Road. Evan Davis said it best.

'I have been lucky enough to visit many places in the world. This remains the best. I would call it my spiritual home but this guy beside me has captured it for himself. Pity. I could have composed a song about it.'

'I would lend you it,' came the response as the twinkling lights of the villages on Arran came into view.

Chapter 59

The big day had arrived, as if yesterday weren't big enough. First tee-offs commenced at 8:30am and Calum and Nerys were at the club well in advance. Already it looked like the crowds of yesterday would be matched if not exceeded. Yet, it was not exactly the same crowd. Some had come yesterday just to see the celebrities and now were enjoying other things on the island or had already headed for home. Some were out and out golf enthusiasts and were back for a second helping. And, some were headed for the concert in the evening and had just decided to make a day of it.

Calum had met Harry Jardin on his way to the course. Harry for the first time looked like he was rattled.

'Where are they all coming from I ask you?'

'Do you not have enough help Harry? Call McBride and get him down here. He owes us a favour or two.'

'They sent me two plods from Largs. Just out of Tulliallan College. They could not organize a piss-up in a brewery.'

'What about the volunteers? I saw Adrian Weatherhead directing traffic yesterday like he was born to it.'

'The volunteers will start at eight o'clock. Maybe things will settle down then.'

'Well you will have earned a dram or two by the end of the day. The island is lucky to have you.'

Harry smiled as he waved Calum off. That was the sort of thing that only Scotty Green tended to say. Now Calum had become the unofficial Number Two on the island. Six or seven months had flown by since the arrival of the Yank and he had made quite an impression.

The local MSP was droning on in welcoming the cream of Scottish amateur golf and wishing that the best man or woman came good at the end of the day. Then Alastair Beddowes briefly explained how the competition would proceed and wished everyone good luck. His verbosity of yesterday was not in evidence today, perhaps someone had had a quiet word at dinner last night. Then play began over rapidly blueing skies after an overcast start to the morning.

Calum and Nerys were not really that excited by the prospect of following the golfers all day so they decided to spend more time around the clubhouse. There was plenty going on there. The bar opened at 9 am sharp under some obscure special license that Beddowes claimed was perfectly legal.

'PC Jardin assured me.'

'There you are then. There can be no doubt,' replied Calum.

'I can vouch for that,' said Scotty Green for once forgoing his breakfast clientele at Westview to follow what was happening at the golf club. 'I signed it myself yesterday.'

'You have that authority Scotty?'

'Apparently so. It was granted by the Vikings before they were defeated at the Battle of Largs in 1263 and never rescinded.'

Nerys giggled and was rewarded with a glare from Scotty; then a wink.

As the tournament progressed through the day it appeared that whole town of Millport was engaged. With vehicles mostly kept way from the club, there was a constant stream of people walking down the hill to enjoy a meal or a drink or just to take a look at the promenade if they were new to the island while other people were walking the other way to catch up with the scores and literally rub shoulders in the clubhouse. The clubhouse was constantly busy with continuous food and drink being dispensed by a staff that had never worked so hard in their lives.

Calum and Nerys encountered Heather Randall and Nicholas Gorman and tried to get better acquainted in spite of the throng. Heather made sure that a dinner date was made during the short time the Davies' would still be on the island.

'No doubt Calum has told you all about his adventures around here Nerys. I will give you another perspective on them. From the perspective of the person, who was nominally responsible for him.'

'Good luck! I will enjoy hearing those stories. And, I will tell you all about a guy who was languishing in California, yet reluctant to even come to his island in the first place. Now he is rivalling Action Man.'

'Yes. I heard that Palitoy is considering bringing out a new doll in honour of him.'

'Enough. I know when I am being made a fool of.'

'Nerys, I was telling Calum that you two ought to keep your eye on Wannamaker. I think he might be liable to sell his house in East Bay. You should jump on it. Then we could be neighbours.'

'Oh Nicholas, Calum never mentioned that. I would love to have a look at it. I must look out for Joel if he is still here.'

'He is. I saw him chatting up the Chief Constable of Police Scotland just a few minutes ago.'

As the afternoon wore on, it was evident that the Marquess of Bute Cup had attracted the top amateur golfers who were hell bent on lifting the trophy. Assisted by a bright windless day, scores were low and getting lower as the climax was reached. The old course, first laid out as a nine-hole in 1888 had seen some top-class competition in its lifetime but nothing compared to this for sheer spectacle. Finally, the pre-event favourite Ronnie Walker had come through to win. However he had to shoot a three-under par 65 in order to do so.

A member of the Crichton-Stuart family was on hand to present the old trophy, first competed for almost one hundred years ago and now brought out of the cabinet, dusted off, and gleaming in celebration of its revival. Mr. Walker, a winner of numerous championships including the Scottish Amateur, seemed genuinely moved to take possession of the fine old silverware. In his speech he paid tribute to his fellow competitors who had made him work so hard to come out on top. His closing statement brought a roar from the crowd.

'Just tell me where to sign up for next year. This trophy is going to look good in my new house in Forfar and I aim to hold on to it.'

'Do you hear that Calum. He is already talking about next year. Are you up for it? I am thinking I might play next year in your *"Ams & Hams"*,' chortled Charlie Caldwell.

'It remains to be seen whether I will be back Charlie. But the Marquess of Bute Cup will be and the *"Ams & Hams"* as well. I fully expect to see you in the line-up. Maybe you can get hooked up in a threesome with Francesca Carlotti; she will be back she says.'

'That would be nice.'

No one had managed a hole in one so the Mediterranean cruise prize was not awarded but by the time all the sponsors' gifts had been presented for lowest net score, lowest gross score, longest drive, nearest chip to the pin, and longest putt etc., it was after six o'clock and the concert beckoned in less than two hours. The crowds started to disperse from the golf club in search of a meal or just a drink to keep them going.

Calum said to Nerys, 'you know, I can't be bothered trying to find a table somewhere for dinner. We would only have to rush dinner. We have not left enough time between the end of the championship and the concert. We will have to remember that for next year.'

'Will we? So there is going to be a next year?'

'You heard Ronnie Walker start it. Now everybody seems full of it. There will be a next year but whether we are involved remains to be seen.'

'I would not put any money against it. Now, what are we going to do about eating something? I am famished.'

'What do you do when you are hungry in Millport? You go to the Deep Sea for fish suppers.'

'Let's do it.'

As they walked down Golf Road to the town they noticed that a few others had grabbed the same idea. The line-up was out of the shop and all the way around Quayhead Square. Nevertheless, they joined the line and started to enter into the banter with the waiting masses only to be interrupted by a loud call from Jimmie Morrison who was about to enter the shop for service.

'Come right up and join me at the front o' the queue. These are our illustrious Yanks everyone. They deserve a wee vote of thanks.'

The line–up cheered and the couple sheepishly made their way up to the front.

'I am so embarrassed,' said Calum.

'I'm not.' replied Nerys. 'I could handle being a Millport celebrity more than a Hollywood one.'

They sat on the edge of the Old Pier eating their complimentary fish and chips; the owner of the Deep Sea had insisted in that strange Scottish/Italian dialect common of such purveyors, 'These ara ona da house. You broughta all da visitors. Good times are a backa.'. They thought maybe the good times are back.

By eight o'clock, the marquee was packed to overflowing. In a different location, the police chief or the fire chief might have come by to close down the event on safety grounds. At this event, the island police constable and head of the volunteer fire brigade were seated together in the audience and just as enthusiastic as everyone else. Those who did not have tickets were camped outside around the marquee.

Shades of '69 thought Evan Davis as he looked out from the Garrison House where the temporary dressing rooms had been located. Calum was buzzing around making sure both the stars were comfortable and in need of nothing. He had been given the honour of emceeing the event and was maybe more nervous than either of the professionals.

When eventually Calum appeared on the small stage, the audience hushed and broke into applause.

'Thank you for coming. We have had two great days of sport and now we are going to witness a musical concert the like of which has never been seen before. We are all in for a treat. First up I would like to introduce someone who has had this island close to his heart for fifty years. He lived and worked here for a while. He brought the cream of rock music here. And when his career eventually took him away to the United States, he never forgot this place. Tonight he says he is here to give something back for all the joy Millport has brought him. Ladies and gentlemen please welcome home.......Evan Davis.'

A tall, not as slim as once, figure dressed in blue jeans and checked shirt came out to wild applause. He waved. He bowed. He waved again. Then he sat down on a stool and armed only with a twelve-string Rickenbacker acoustic guitar and two microphones he proceeded to lift songs from his lifetime songbook.

Drawing works from all stages of his career and different groups that had been effectively stripped down to be performed solo, he enchanted the audience with each song. Each was instantly recognizable and was applauded after the first couple of notes and again at the end.

After his allotted thirty minutes, he said his goodbyes for now but the audience would have none of it and two encores were demanded. The first was *"Illusions"*, one of Dubus' biggest hits and recorded right here at Westview and the second was a song nobody had heard except Scotty Green and his then chef now long departed from the island. *"Thinking About An Island"* brought the house down because the audience could relate to the heartfelt lyrics about how you could leave Millport but Millport would never leave you. Evan almost abruptly stood up on the final chord and walked off. He had nothing more to give. Once the applause finally subsided, there was a short delay while the Bechstein concert piano was moved to the front of the stage.

As Calum waited by the side of the stage, Henri Jardin sidled up and whispered in his ear, 'No joy on the ferry terminal CCTV. They don't keep the tapes that long. We can't prove Wannamaker came back that night.'

'We can't win them all.'

'We nearly did.'

Calum stepped back on to the stage to get the concert going again. Just as warm a welcome was accorded Francesca Carlotti when the willowy, raven haired young woman, dressed in a stunning long black and silver dress, slowly walked on to the stage. Though worlds apart in musical terms, she shared the same initial reaction as Evan Davis of slight hesitation, almost bemusement at the audience's reaction, then warmth and enthusiasm for what she had to give.

Francesca played a stunning programme of Rachmaninoff, Schumann, Brahms, Chopin, and Bach. The choice of material and the playing were of the absolutely highest calibre to satisfy the most discerning classical ear, of which there were many in the audience, and yet both were easily accessible to those in audience not familiar with the genre of which there were also many. Each piece was concluded to rapturous applause. After almost forty minutes, Francesca declined an encore with an intriguing statement to the audience.

'Sorry I can't play anymore. I have got to get ready for something else.'

Although the planned collaboration between the two artists had been leaked in the press, there were many in the audience who were not quite sure what was coming next.

After ten minutes, the two walked back on to the stage after what had obviously been a rapid costume change for Ms. Carlotti. Now she was dressed in the tightest jeans and a glitter top straight out of Vegas. Evan was dressed in white tails, white shirt, and white bow tie. The audience was just getting used to the vision after applauding for fully five minutes when the marquee was shattered by the opening riff on the piano by Francesca of Bob Seger's *"Old Time Rock and Roll"*. The two hammered their instruments and sang their hearts out. The audience sat in stunned silence for a few lines then started to clap in time and then started to join in on the chorus.

Thereafter, each classic raucous rock and roll song they introduced was treated in the same way. The energy was electric. The audience outside the marquee was making just as much noise as the audience within. Francesca and Evan were on a high but had to find a way of bringing the concert to a close with something slower. They first chose a reprise of *"Thinking about an Island"*, this time arranged for keyboards in which Francesca's exquisite playing made it sound like an entire orchestra was up there with them. Then each artist said how much they had enjoyed playing together and announced that they had thought long and hard when choosing a final song for this unique occasion.

They went out with the Beatles' *"Hey Jude"* with the famous closing refrain lasting even longer than Paul McCartney intended and seeming to include every voice on the island. That was that. There was no way to follow that and the audience knew it. However as the marquee emptied, the familiar refrain could still be heard on the promenade as concert goers relived the experience of a lifetime.

Calum felt he was floating as he made his way back to the Garrison House for an after concert reception for a few very select guests. He was stopped at the entrance by Joel Wannamaker who had scored an invitation somehow.

'Great concert Calum. You did a fine job putting it together.'

'Thanks. It felt like it went like a dream.'

'Can I ask a favour of you? I want to catch the ten o'clock ferry tomorrow but I want to leave my car down here. Can you come by and drive me to the terminal then return the car to the driveway in front of the house?'

Calum was tempted to ask if Joel was above taking the bus to the terminal like most other folks but something stopped him. Perhaps some time with him would be worthwhile.

Chapter 60

'Are you off already? You were mad to agree to drive him to the ferry,' said a very sleepy and somewhat hung-over Nerys the next morning.

'Ach I did not feel I could say no. I will cycle round to East Bay and will be back for lunch. Just you have a sleep in.'

'Last night was incredible, wasn't it? Did you know they were going to perform like that?'

'No. They hatched it up together. Talk about putting the island on the map. The Beeb has sold the rights to PBS. We will be able to see it in California some time. We should have a Millport party at home and invite your dean and president.'

Joel Wannamaker was still packing when Calum arrived and looked like he had enjoyed a wild night as well. Once they got going, Calum realized they were not likely going to make the ten o'clock ferry but made no effort to speed up. As the terminal came into view after passing the Scottish National Watersports Centre, the ferry could be seen already pulling away from the dock.

'Jeez Calum, You ought to have gone a bit faster. I suppose I can get the 10:15.'

'No. This is a Sunday. Ferries are every half hour before noon.'

They parked in parking lot away from the line of cars already assembling for the next ferry and looked out over the water toward Largs.

'I am enjoying Millport but it gets harder and harder to make the time to get down here. And, it is not the same without Maggie.'

'Mmm. She seemed to really like it after having never heard of it before.'

'Me too. You know I never really thanked you properly Calum for all you did to try to find her. Nobody would ever have thought of looking on Wee Cumbrae.'

'I thought about it but unfortunately I did not follow up until it was too late.'

'I am just going to have to throw myself completely into my business interests now that I am on my own.'

'You won't have Cyrus Macadam as a partner for a good long time.'

'He was never my partner. We just did the odd piece of business together.'

'You are going to have to do a lot more than the odd piece of business with Alec Taggart to keep him quiet. He is your Achilles heel.'

'What do you mean?'

'I have this theory Joel. It is only a theory for now but you never know. You see I think you came back that night, probably drugged Maggie and that was how she was taken to Wee Cumbrae. Once there, she was locked up by Macadam and eventually murdered. The plutonium leak was a convenient cover. I think the post-mortem might have proved that she had been injected with the stuff if it had been done more diligently or she had been found earlier. You are probably safe with Cyrus sticking to your story but Alec Taggart might not.'

There followed an eerie silence. Both men looked straight out the window at the ferry now starting to emerge from the Largs terminal.

'You could never prove it.' The face was tense and then was punctuated with a nervous laugh.

'Maybe. Maybe not.' Calum's expression never changed.

'I think I will just get out of the car and wait outside for the ferry. Make sure you put the keys through the letterbox when you park the car, along with my door key. No need for you to have that now.'

The Author

Edwin Deas is a recently retired accountant, who never encountered any adventures in his lifetime. Therefore, he had to make them up in this his first work of fiction. Along the way, he had to borrow some places and people, heavily disguise the latter so as to be unrecognisable, and would like to thank them for their important participation.

Edwin Deas was born in Edinburgh, Scotland over sixty years ago and has split his life between Scotland and North America, the latter involving British Columbia, Canada and the USA. He is unsure which nationality to own up to and tends to use whichever suits the circumstance. He does, however, have a deep and lasting love for a certain island back in Scotland.

Edwin Deas is a Chartered Certified Accountant from the UK; a Chartered Professional Accountant from Canada and holds a Doctorate in Educational Leadership from the University of San Diego, California. He strenuously denies that writing financial statements prepared him for writing works of fiction and he enjoys the necessary learning experience to do the latter.

Edwin Deas lives in Oceanside, California with his wife, Bronwyn Jenkins-Deas, who puts up with a lot but is never anything other than loyal and supportive. Jasper the dog completes the household.

Made in the USA
Charleston, SC
07 June 2016